# DRIFTING WEST

## *A Stone Cold Adventure  Book 3*

## Robert Knox

**Revphule Publishing**

*To my amazing wife who supports and encourages me everyday.*

*Thanks to everyone who keeps reading this series and my other books. I hope they are getting better and that my editing is improving. Thanks for reading through it all.*

# CONTENTS

Title Page

Copyright

Dedication

Prologue   1

Chapter 1   6

Chapter 2   14

Chapter 3   22

Chapter 4   30

Chapter 5   37

Chapter 6   49

Chapter 7   58

Chapter 8   69

Chapter 9   83

Chapter 10   99

Chapter 11   107

Chapter 12   116

Chapter 13   128

Chapter 14   136

Chapter 15   147

Chapter 16   160

Chapter 17                                  172

Chapter 18                                  183

Chapter 19                                  195

Chapter 20                                  206

Chapter 21                                  218

Chapter 22                                  229

Chapter 23                                  244

Chapter 24                                  254

Chapter 25                                  266

Chapter 26                                  278

Chapter 27                                  287

Chapter 28                                  299

Chapter 29                                  310

Chapter 30                                  323

Chapter 31                                  335

Chapter 32                                  345

Chapter 33                                  355

Chapter 34                                  364

The End.                                    375

# PROLOGUE

That first drive was a rough learning experience. I'd expected it to be hard, but it met and exceeded those expectations. You can't really understand what it takes to drive half wild long horns two thousand miles until you do it. The older hands warned me Max even talked to everyone who hadn't made the drive before we left. He'd been honest, reminding us how many drovers never saw the end of the trail. The only thing he could promise anyone was a decent burial and even that had caveats.

I'd learned and done it fast. There was no room for anyone who couldn't pull their weight. Max was better than most, but every hand on the trail cut into profits. More than one drive never made it to the railhead because too many punchers died. That first year left its mark on me.

A midnight stampede put a nice scar on my thigh from a fear crazed steer. Two drovers died on that night of madness, all because one steer got spooked by god knows what. It was like a tide of horns rampaging out of the darkness, crushing anything that was in its path. You only had two choices if you wanted to live. Out run them or get out of the way, neither was easy in the dark of night. Turning them hadn't been possible until they tired out.

Another puncher died from a rattlesnake bite. The damn thing was curled under his saddle. He'd bent down to pick it up after chow and forgot to kick it first. The viper managed to sink both fangs into his cheek before he could jump back. He'd put a .44 through his head before the pain really started.

Heat washed over us from dark to dark. There was no escaping it, if trailing a herd across Texas was a taste of hell, I needed to change my ways. The sun mercilessly roasted you from above, and the body heat from the animals took care of the rest. Riding nighthawk was no better. The cool breeze that swept across the open land turned oppressive. The heat from two thousand head turning it into a hot wind. Cutting through the herd was like standing to close to the campfire. On cool nights steam rose off them like mist in a mountain valley. It made watching the sleeping herd near impossible some nights.

The dust and smell added to the misery. Everything smelled like beefs and sweat. River crossings helped, but then the smell of wet animal overpowered everything. Minutes later the dust that covered beast and man turned to mud on your skin. For the rest of the day, it washed down your body in rivulets of sweat. The grit itched and caused chaffing on animal and man.

From the Bar C to Dodge City everything we ate was seasoned with dust. Coffee had a gritty finish that wasn't from the grounds. The food was better, if only because Smythe knew his craft. Even then, more often the not, you ended up spitting out sand between bites. Jose and I had it better than most of the crew. Staying ahead of the herd kept us out of the worst. That good luck ended at Waco, another thing Jose had predicted.

We rode into the dust of another herd a few miles ahead of us. After that, it was a dance trying to keep the two separated by at least a day. Drovers didn't dictate the pace of a herd. You guided it in a direction other than that it was either stopped or moving. Those were your choices. The mossy horned lead steer set the pace, slow and steady. No one wanted to bring thin beefs to market, not after all it took to get there. All the drovers did was to keep them in one group. By luck, good or bad, their lead steer was a bit faster than Lucky. That old beast had led drives for Max before. Unlike most that particualr long horn he was fairly calm.

The second year finished any lingering doubt I had about the how hard the trail could be. We lost three hands to stampedes, two in a fight with a war party, and one more to Kansas rustlers. We lost near four hundred head along the trail that year with the men. Some died from the heat and lack of water because of a spring drought that left more than one river bed dry. Some more went to rustlers wearing 'Kansas livestock inspector' badges. The rest were trampled under a thousand hooves in stampedes.

Dodge City's rowdy nights claimed another two hands before we left for home. The returning crew was barely enough to get the remuda to the fort. Of the men I left with that first year, there was just Jose, Chet, Max, Smythe and myself. The rest were buried in unmarked graves along the trail. That was the last year we used the Chisholm Trail. I wasn't sure if the Western was any better, supposedly it skipped part of Kansas. Max was done dealing with the Kansas rustlers who hid behind a made up badge. Two ranchers he knew lost their herds to them. Adding insult to injury, they'd had to pay a bond to get their hands out of jail.

Max decided he was done with the drive to Dodge City after that last trip. Cattle prices had stabilized well enough. He could get a fair price in Fort Worth at the new railhead and never leave Texas. Next year he planned on picking up a few drovers in Uvalde for the shorter drive. It wouldn't be as profitable, but he was tired of burying hands for a few dollars extra at the end. I had to tip my hat to his foresight. The man recognized change was coming and adapted faster than some.

We didn't need any hands for the winter. Trent met us in San Antonio with a wagon as usual. After picking up the supplies, a tired group of punchers rode south to the ranch. Jose and I were at the cabin not long after, preparing for another winter. It passed just like the last one, cold and in good company.

Riding the line tightened the bond we shared. We both knew things were about to change for both of us. This would be our last year at the cabin, after this we'd part ways. He'd met a beautiful señorita in Uvalde last year. When he could, they'd attended church together hoping to get the padre's approval for their marriage. It was something he hadn't really thought would ever happen. He wouldn't be leaving with me after the drive and I didn't blame him. She was the perfect woman for him, the bright light to push back the darkness that haunted him. Staying behind was weighing on his mind, but I didn't want to bring it up until he was ready to talk.

The snow was melting and spring was fast approaching when he finally brought it up. We'd both been out riding the line that day since the weather finally broke. I'd even taken an early spring buck just after noon. Now the cabin smelled like smoke and cooking meat, something we'd been out of for a while. The venison steaks were the first fresh meat we'd had in weeks. The rest was already in the smoker. It should last the rest of the winter with some to spare.

"Amigo, you know about me and Cassandra?" He was sitting at the table looking any where but at me.

"Figure you're about to get married an settle down." I could just see the stunned look on his face over my shoulder. The last of my New York accent was gradually changing to the south Texas drawl.

"You are not mad, amigo?"

"Amigo, do you think I'm going to hold a grudge 'bout you getting hitched? Hell no! I'm happy for you." I turned with the cooked heart and liver steaming on a plate. The steaks would be done in another minute. "Sides three years an you still can't cook."

"Amigo, neither of us has learned to cook." He laughed, spearing a piece of heart from where I'd set it. "Will you come back from Fort Worth?"

"No, I'm still going to see the ocean. I'll head west at the end of the drive. Maybe head for Los Angeles."

"I should be going with you, amigo."

"No, you should be marrying that amazing woman before she comes to her senses." I smiled at the man who'd shared some rough trails with me. "You love her an I want to come back here to see the scary man I've ridden into hell with bouncing a baby on his knee."

"Amigo, when you get that hacienda we will come. I will be your Segundo."

"No, you will come as mi amigo."

"Only if you hire a cook." He laughed, breaking the tension.

# CHAPTER 1

Smythe showed up at the campsite the next day. We met him there and helped set up the camp. The man wasn't any more pleasant, but I'd earned his respect and that was enough. For more important to us, his arrival meant we didn't have to eat our own cooking anymore. Just that was worth the sweat we worked up gathering and chopping wood for him.

TJ showed up the next day with the rest of the hands. That signaled the end of our simple days. The actual work started the next day while the sun was still chasing the shadows across the flats. The next month was spent doing the same dangerous work that happened every year. Chasing wild longhorns out of the brush into temporary pens to start herd breaking them. The air was filled with the smell of burning hair and rawhide. Branding irons only cooling when the sun set and it was too dark to work. Young bulls became steers and were turned back out. Older steers were molded into a herd.

Two weeks before the drive, Max and TJ went to Uvalde to pick up four more drovers. Jose rode with them as security, leaving me to protect the rest. I pitched in willingly, branding, riding nighthawk, helping where I could. Max would be back in time to work in the new drovers. Then we'd be moving down an unfamiliar trail. The Chisholm would take us near to Fort Worth, but Max wanted to use the old Shawnee Trail. It had less traffic and would have better graze to fatten the herd. For me, it meant seeing another part of Texas before leaving.

The men they brought back were an interesting group. Two vaqueros, Cortez and Jesus, were easy to work in with the other hands. They knew their job and did it without complaint or debate. Like most vaqueros I'd met, they were good with the cattle but excelled with the horses. Cousins from another fallen hacienda. This would be their third drive as drovers. I think both were hoping the Bar C would keep them on after the drive. More than once I caught Max watching the two, TJ had already made up his mind. It wouldn't surprise me if they got their wish. There was no backup in them and the other hands got along with them.

The others were a strange pair. An old gruff man who knew the job well enough, but the way he did it felt off. Like he was used to watching men do the work more than he was doing it. My guess was he'd been a ramrod or ranch owner for a lot of years somewhere. He didn't argue when told to do something, if you watched his eyes though you could see it. It'd been some years since he had to take orders from another man, it rankled the man. It wasn't anger, not exactly, it almost felt like sadness and frustration.

His partner was young, without much experience. I spotted that just by the way they sat a horse. They knew the rhythm, but the seat seemed off in some way. He had to be the most feminine man I'd ever seen, which made me more uncomfortable than it should have. Something about his presence just seemed off. For the life of me, I couldn't figure it out. He worked hard every day, never questioned anyone about the jobs they gave him. I had to let the mystery go, a drive wasn't the place to be sidetracked. That was Elias and Jesse, the strangest drovers I'd seen in a while. They would do for what we needed and the rest didn't matter.

A week later, the herd was as ready as it was going to get. Jose and I rode night hawk the last night, letting the rest sleep.

Tomorrow would be the hardest day. All the men needed to be fresh and ready in the morning. The first few days with a fresh herd were always rough. Half wild steers wanted to run back into the brush at every opportunity. Most of the herd wasn't used to men on horses pushing them behind the lead steer. More than one youngster would challenge that mossy horned beast, but he'd do the job and put them all in their place. It was all one big recipe for disaster, but it was one most of us knew.

That night we wove through the sleeping herd, carefully doing our best not to disturb them. The song of the night filled me as I rode. It was a familiar song by now. One I knew like an old favorite that spoke of safety and home. The yips and bawling changed, but the basic rhythm of the land stayed constant. Nothing felt out of place, no shadows moved against the wind. Just before false dawn, a shadow darted from the camp into the bushes. By its size it was the new guy, Jesse. He must've woke up with a strong need to find a bush.

Not long after, the sparks floating into the darkness when Smythe stirred the embers back to life told me the day was starting. The scent of coffee drifted across the herd like a call to the sun. It answered soon after when the horizon lit up in golden hues, shifting away from violet as night faded. The song changed with it as the lowing beefs started their day. It was like a wake-up call to the rest of the men. Shadows started moving around the fire. The strange dance of men waking up always made me smile.

Pug and Tink came out to relieve us not long after the smell of bacon blended in with the rest. They'd become old hands with the poppers and wouldn't be going on the drive. Tipping out hats to one another, Jose and I turned our horses toward camp. As we rode closer, camp talked filled the air competing with the cattle. Max talking about the day, laying out his plan and where he wanted who. Letting the new hands know what he expected. It wasn't anything we needed to hear, but we still listened out of respect.

A quick breakfast, then we'd be riding out scouting for the next camp site. Riding ahead of the herd was more dangerous in some ways. The tradeoff was not having to deal with the half-wild herd. It would be easier than normal for the next while. We knew every twist or turn between Uvalde and the ranch, including good campsites for the herd. That didn't mean we could relax. The Nueces Strip was never truly safe. The biggest thing in our favor was most knew the Bar C reputation and left us well enough alone.

For Jose, this whole trip was going to be over familiar ground. That didn't mean it'd be perfectly safe. There were still Apache, rustlers and the natural dangers. River crossings, snakes, even other wild cattle could cause us problems. There were a few thousand different things that could spook a herd into a stampede. None of this was new, that was just the way it worked trailing a herd to market. Everything wanted to make it harder, kill you or the cattle. We'd do what could be done, but most of it was out of our control. There was more than one story told around the fires about herds just deciding to run. No one ever found out why. They just collected the beefs, buried the dead and moved on down the trail. It was all part of what made having a good bunch of hands important. Men who knew the land, and the animals were important. Men who knew those things and trusted the other hands could be the difference between life and death.

The last of those thoughts left my head when I stepped onto Shade's back. Now my mind needed to pay attention to the job. With a nod to Max, we set out, slowly weaving through the herd. It didn't take long for the familiar landscape to open before us. The first rays of dawn were still painting the trail in dancing shadows. My mind wandered as we rode, not without keeping my awareness on the land around me. My eyes by now scanned every shadow and bunch of scrub almost automatically. It made thinking about the future easier. Having part of myself studying the terrain kept some of the fears at bay. It helped remind me of how much I'd changed in the last three years. I sorted through the noise to find what was needling me.

What had me off balance was doing it alone. Until Jose met Cassandra, I'd always planned on him being with me. The first night they met I knew that wasn't going to happen. Even before he knew it, the smile on his face told me all I needed to know. Not that I faulted him for being smart enough to pick a truly good woman over wandering across the country with me. He'd proposed before we left and they'd be married in the fall. My only regret was missing the wedding. I'd thought about delaying for another year just to be there for him.

He didn't know it yet, but I'd left an account book for them with Max. There was two thousand dollars in it for them to start their life. They would need it since he wasn't staying with the Bar C. There was no housing for married men on the ranch. Max preferred it that way. He had strong opinions about married hands. Mostly, he felt strongly that it created a divide between the men. That's what he said, anyway. The truth was he'd told one too many wives that they'd become widows. He couldn't do it anymore. It was that simple.

I hoped Jose would finally buy the ranch he was dreaming of. Land wasn't too expensive yet. They could get a decent spread and have enough left to start building it. He'd said something more than once about them going to Arizona Territory. There was some good land still available for cheap from the railroad. They had been selling off their grants to pay for new tracks. If he was lucky, he might find a place near a proposed railhead.

10

My eyes caught movement in a shallow arroyo to my left, interrupting my thoughts. My focus came back to the present, instantly recognizing something that didn't belong. It had been a flash of light with a bit of color. I'd only seen it for a split second, but there was no denying it. Nothing out here should reflect light like that, least wise, nothing that was supposed to be out here. My Winchester was always across my thighs, loaded with my thumb on the hammer. Slight pressure from my knee made Shade shift toward the spot. Almost casually I changed the angle of my barrel, preparing to aim and fire if need be. Stopping fifty yards in front of the arroyo, my eyes scanned it one more time before I spoke.

"Ya been spotted. If ya don't mean trouble, ride outta there real peaceable like." We were still on Bar C land and calling out a warning was expected by Max.

"Lemme get my britches back up an I'll ride out proper like." The voice was a bit off. It sounded like someone caught in a bad way, which matched his words.

Chuckling to myself, I sat my saddle waiting for the poor soul to finish his business. My Winchester was facing his direction, but I kept it pointed down. My thumb did lock the trigger back out of habit. Everything seemed fine, but that slight difference might save my life if the man was looking for a problem. No one would be out here on a pleasure ride, but that didn't mean much. There were many reasons someone might be crossing the strip: outlaw, lawman or just someone drifting for their own reasons. None of it was my business if they didn't mean to interfere with us.

A lone man rode out of the scrub on a decent-looking paint pony, showing me both his hands. He looked a bit older than me, dressed in fairly new trail clothes but still sporting a fair amount of dust. Either a puncher on the drift or one of the other types that crossed Bar C range.

"Sorry 'bout that wasn't try'n to cause no trouble." He looked a bit embarrassed, but I could understand that. What I couldn't was the small puff of dust that sprung up from the arroyo. The barrel of my rifle shifted up as I spoke.

"Won't be no trouble if whoever's with you comes out." Now the cold was easing over me and my voice changed with it.

"We don't want no trouble, mister." The one in front of me said, but I cut him off.

"Y'all are on Bar C range, heard of it?"

"Yup, heard y'all don't give folks any trouble' bout crossin it."

"We don't, but the herds back a bit heading this way. Makes us be a bit more particular 'bout who's in the area."

"Shit! Johnnie come up outta there. Hiding with a herd com'n 'ill get ya stomped ta death." He turned back to me when a kid no older than fifteen rode into sight. "Sorry mister, didn't know no herd was on the trail. We'll light a shuck."

"That's fine, just light out west for 'bout five miles. It'll put you far enough to not be a concern."

"That'll put us on the trail ta Laredo?" The older one was the talker. The kid hadn't spoken yet.

"Nope, if that's where you're heading, cut east. About the same distance, then dead south after a few miles. Ya should find the road from there pretty easy."

"We ain't outlaws we're lookin.." I cut him off again.

"None of my concern. Don't mean to be rude but it's part of

the boss's rules. We don't ask an don't want to know." Jose was sitting about a hundred feet on their flank now. I was pretty sure they hadn't noticed him.

"Fair enough, mister. 'precciate the advice, we'll cut trail an be gone."

He tipped his hat before they both turned east. Normally I'd worry about them, but something told me they wouldn't be back. I nodded slightly to Jose, and we both turned back to scouting. He waited for me to catch up and I knew what he was going to ask before the words left his mouth. When he pulled in beside me, I laid out the story for him.

# CHAPTER 2

"Heading to Laredo, had no clue a herd was coming up. No reason they could know, probably never see them again."

"If you say so, amigo. The one looked young for that place."

"Lucky if he's fifteen. Can't figure why they're headed to Laredo, course I told 'em we didn't want to know."

"That is true, but it does not stop the mind from wondering?"

"No, it doesn't amigo." I laughed.

He started drifting off to the west, scouting his side of the trail. I slowly rode up mine, constantly scanning the landscape. It was another hour before reaching the first campsite. It wasn't more than a deep hollow, just big enough to make night hawking easy with decent graze and water. We worked around it, checking for anything that might cause problems. Sign from predators, two-legged and four-legged ones. The granddaddy rattler Jose shot was all we found. Damn thing was easily six feet long, with fifteen rattles.

We gathered some wood for Smythe while we checked the place out. It would save time and got us a bit of extra chow. I was just dropping an arm load around the fire pit when movement out against the horizon got my attention. Using my field glass to scan the horizon, searching for whatever it was that had caught my eye. A lone rider heading this way, still a good ways out but on track to ride into our herd. After checking in a wide arc, I dropped them back into my saddlebag before climbing into my saddle. I rode out to meet him slowly, scanning the land as I went. My rifle was resting across my thigh, thumb hanging on the hammer. Stopping about forty yards away, my voice broke the silence.

"Got a herd coming up. I'm gonna need ya to drift east or west."

"Ya think you can order a body 'round?" The sneer he wore was nothing I didn't expect.

"On Bar C range, absolutely certain 'bout it." Now he would either know what that meant or he'd learn. I'd let the cold loose because of his aggressive tone. The audible click of my hammer locking back punctuated my words.

"Ya ain't real friendly 'bout ask'n." He sneered at me. It was an obvious attempt to keep my attention but I still noticed his hand flip the thong off his pistol.

"Didn't ask. Ain't real concerned how ya feel about it either. Make your choice move off or draw."

"Ya seem mighty brazen. Bet ya wouldn't be if ya know'd who I am?"

"Don't care. You ain't a Bar C hand, anything else don't matter. Quit jabbering an make your choice."

"What if I'm not alone?" That got me to give him a wolfish smile before I responded.

"Your pard's hav'n the same conversation."

"How did..." His words cut off when the sharp crack of a rifle echoed around us.

My eyes never left the man, watching as realization slowly spread across his face. Either his pard or mine was dead. The potential to avoid a fight had died with that shot. I waited, letting his mind think about it all the way down the path in front of him. It didn't take him long to puzzle it out. His right shoulder suddenly dipped when his hand shot for the pistol butt. The man was used to getting caught out like this. He was probably used to picking his own tune for the dance.

My right hand shifted the barrel of my Winchester to point past Shade's head. My left hand moved from the saddle horn to wrap over the worn wood under the barrel. Before my grip closed around it, my finger was easing back on the trigger.

Shade danced at the noise but didn't move enough for me to notice. The screaming ball of lead rolled him backward out of the saddle when it impacted the bridge of his nose. The force sent his pistol spinning out of his grip, finally falling to the ground behind him. I had to admire the mare he was riding. She barely flicked an ear when he hit the ground with a loud whoop. She hadn't twitched in the slightest from start to finish.

Unlike him, I had no concerns about whose shot that was. It had been Jose's rifle. There was no question in my mind about it. That proved true a few minutes later when he rode up, leading a new horse. I was levering the dead man across his saddle but hadn't bothered to search him yet. We needed to get them away from the area before the herd arrived. Longhorns had powerful reactions to the scent of blood they didn't spill. If they gored someone, it was fine. If it came from another source, they almost acted offended by not being involved.

"There is a deep overhang to the east. His amigo is waiting there already. They can be buried without much work."

"Beats digging a hole. Funny how you always get the ones close to a burial site." I smiled up at my friend.

"He was rude as well?" Jose grinned back at me after turning to the east. "That is experience, amigo. Not something I would leave to chance."

"Didn't seem to know the rules or be interested in learning them. He did seem to think I ought to know his name. Got right funny about it when I didn't."

"Seems an odd thing to be bothered by." He laughed, leading us to the spot he'd seen earlier.

It wasn't the first time this had happened. New outlaws and lawmen had crossed our paths before. Most of them didn't challenge us like these fools, but there had been more than a few who thought about it. Most grumbled when we turned them away from the ranch, either toward Eagle Pass or Laredo. Usually, that wasn't the badges. They tended to be easy to educate, the bounty hunters were always the ones who wanted to debate it. Outlaws never argued with us. It struck me as funny at first, but Jose had explained it.

"The outlaws do not need more problems. They only want to escape." He'd been proven right often enough that I took his words on faith.

"Not badges." I said as we rode. "Chasing a bounty, I figure. No other reason to be so stubborn about staying the path."

"Si, that is my guess."

We dropped down into a shallow gulch carefully. I could see the overhang he was talking about. It was washed out enough that dropping it on the bodies should be easy work. Might even be enough dirt to hide them from the scavengers for a few days. Burying men like this was quick and dirty. We both knew it wouldn't keep the critters away for long. For folks who weren't worth the time to dig a hole, this was as good as they got. We found seventy-two dollars between the two, each had colt new army and loaded gun belts. They'd go to the wagon with the Yellow Boy and Model '73. Their saddle bags had the normal dirty clothes and extra ammo for each weapon. I found a wanted poster in the vest of mine and it made me laugh.

"Two hundred and fifty dollars for that kid we ran into earlier." I showed Jose the poster.

"I am not surprised."

"Shame they couldn't have just been polite." I hefted the man on my shoulder, staggering over to dump him under the overhang.

"It is the way of men who think they are always right." Jose pulled his man closer to mine, insuring both were tucked back into the space.

It took a few stomps to break the overhang, and it did the job. When we walked back down, I took a minute to examine the horses. Shade was still my only horse, and this mare had my interest. She was mostly Morgan, but there was something a bit taller mixed in her blood. Whatever it was had stretched the normal Morgans' height up to a bit over fifteen hands. The impressive part was it hadn't sacrificed what made a Morgan such a good horse.

She looked fast and agile. Her chest was deep enough to let her run all day. Swapping saddles before stepping up to get a feel for her gait. Part of me wanted to keep this mare. When I stepped into the stirrups, she looked at me for a second, seeming judging if I was worthy of her or not. Stepping back down to walk around in front of her. If she had questions, we'd find the answer. She studied me for a minute and it felt like she was deciding my value. Shade and Danu both had done the same thing in their own way. What surprised me was when she stepped forward, bumping her head into my chest.

This time when my back side settled into the unfamiliar saddle I was braced. Half expecting her to buck in a whirl wind of kicks trying to throw me. Instead, she shifted slightly under me, adjusting to the weight of a new rider. She was five, maybe a bit less, but someone had trained her well. Moving off, I was impressed with how smooth her gait was. It wasn't the shuffle that Shade had, but she moved smoothly and covered ground with ease. Max was likely to want her for breeding stock. He was always looking for good mares, slowly building Banes herd into something serious. If he did, I'd let him take her. It would be years before my wandering stopped. Shade wouldn't willingly stay away from her once she went into season. Maybe we could trade for a mare in the future, one from her and Bane. For me, that would be not only easier but better in the long run.

Smythe was just coming thru a shallow arroyo heading our way when we got back. A smile crept across my face, watching him count the horses. A laugh escaped my lips when he glared at us. The man didn't mind how we got them. What bothered him was when one of us got hurt. That might cost him a poultice or interrupt his dinner preparations to put in some stitches.

"Neither of us got any holes to plug." I chuckled when he got closer.

"Good! Too damn early to be using my supplies up, 'specially on you two." He growled.

"Got ya some firewood stacked an waiting, ya grumpy cuss." I handed my reins to Jose so he could start a picket line. Without waiting for his retort, I started helping unhitch his mules.

"I ain't grumpy. Ya'll just always seem ta need patch'n up more than most."

"I'll have you know my long handles are almost a year old and only have one hole in them." I shot back, leading the team to the stream. "An it's from a steer, didn't even catch skin."

"Ya know, I liked it better when ya was a polite greenhorn."

"You're not the first to mention that." We both chuckled at the memory. Picking up the leads, I took the mules to the stream before putting feed bags on them.

My ears could hear the herd coming our way. They'd probably smelled the water a ways back and picked up the pace a bit. They hadn't been without water long enough to run, so it wasn't anything to worry about. Last year, with the drought, we'd almost had a stampede coming up to a river after one stretch. Four days without water had pushed the herd's patience to the breaking point. It didn't look like that would be a problem this drive. Today, the hands had probably spent all day chasing strays back into the herd. It would take a few more days before they were broke to the trail. Should be pretty settled by the time we crossed the Nueces.

I was right. Max wanted the mare for Bane's growing herd. Agreeing to giving me a two-year-old of my choice, after my ranch was up and going. He could have just taken her, but the man was too respectful for that. He stuck to his agreement of found. I'd killed the man that made his gear mine. Maybe some hands would have dug in their heels about it, but Max knew I'd never do that. Truthfully, Max would make sure her bloodline continued in his herd. With Bane as the stallion, he would probably improve on it. Max decided to send her back with the ranch hands at the Leone River.

Bull's crew was sticking with the herd until we left our

home range. It was normally the way it worked. Giving us a few extra hands to help keep the herd together for the first leg. Usually, after we crossed the river, the herd had settled and there were fewer strays to chase. There was plenty of water and graze between here and Waco. The steers being away from their range helped keep them together too. The second part was a bit more subtle. We pushed them as fast as possible to keep them tired. It was tricky balance because you didn't want to run the weight off them, but you wanted a herd that bedded down and stayed down for the night. I still remembered asking about that change in my first drive. I'd caught hell for that from Chet until Jose reminded him about the time he got lost crossing the Red.

That memory hit me like a rock. Soon I'd be leaving these men behind. Some, like Chet, had been with me since Dodge City. That was only three years, but it was my entire life out here. These men, the ones still above ground, were my family. The knowledge and lessons I'd learned from them would serve me for the rest of my life. Too many of them were dead now, lost along the trail in one way or another. A quiet melancholy fell around me when I thought back on those losses. Juan was the first one that had left his mark on me. He'd been a little older than me when we buried him in the nations. Killed by ambushers who wanted nothing more than money or horses. Those bastards had been left for the buzzards after Jose and I tracked them down. It hadn't eased Juan's loss, justice never made the loss right. It only hoped to prevent others from being hurt.

"Remember the man, not the ghost." Jose said, easing down to sit beside me. My brother had long ago learned to recognize my dark moments.

"You know me too well." I laughed, shaking off the dark thoughts.

"No amigo. This will be your last ride with us. Same for me, I think. It is natural to remember those we lost."

"You know, when I first started down this road, that was

something I didn't consider. I've lost more friends in three years than in the sixteen before."

"It is the way of things out here. Someday maybe not, but today is when we live." Jose's philosophical side was peeking out again.

"Amigo, you're wiser than you know." I smiled and just then Smythe called for chow. If we were lucky, we might grab a nap before riding nighthawk.

# CHAPTER 3

A boot scraped to my left, waking me up. I didn't know who it was, but waved them off after sitting up in my bedroll. They let out a gasp of surprise that got my attention. For a minute, I thought that was a female, but knew that wasn't possible. It hadn't been the vaquero who woke me. He looked as put off as I felt. My surprise faded when a flicker of flame revealed Jesse. He should still be in his bedroll? Call of nature maybe, none of my concern. Still, that noise had sounded damn odd.

That man was just strange all the way around. Did his job well enough from what I heard, both of them did. There was just something off about that pair to me, nothing nefarious but something dishonest. They made the back of my neck itch but couldn't explain why. It felt like sitting at a poker table playing against a bluff. I could feel it but couldn't be sure how much of a lie it all was. They were temporary hires, not something I needed to worry about for long. Their business was their own as long as the job got done and they didn't affect the drive.

Checking my boots before stomping into them. I slung on my gun belt and tied it down after standing. Picking up my tack, I walked toward the picket line to tack up. Shade stepped toward me in the dark and stood while I saddled him. He'd calmed down with some age, becoming as dependable as sunrise over the last few years. Doing whatever I asked of him and doing it right the first time. I still thought about Danu, but the truth was Shade had been my pard over far more ground. Slipping him an apple after cinching the saddle tight, I patted his neck before stepping into the saddle.

Drawing my Winchester, I checked to make sure there was a round in the chamber, then eased the hammer down. Shade didn't need any help to pick his way through the sleeping longhorns. By now he knew exactly what I expected of him on nighthawk. On the far side, we started pacing the outside edge of the herd, slowly working in a circle. Like a few other punchers did, I recited books after being told my singing would start a stampede. I don't know why it worked, but it did seem to quiet the herd. Tonight, I was going to finish the last act of King Leer.

Other than my voice, the night was quiet except for the familiar song. Its comforting hum filled me, telling me everything I needed to know. Shadows danced around the edges in the breeze. Nothing moved that didn't belong to the world around me. When I heard Jose start a song in Spanish, I stopped reciting the play. His rich baritone harmonized with the land. It almost felt like the two belonged together. I'd long ago accepted that as the truth. Jose was part of this land. Whether he was born to it or through hard years of life had grown to become part of it was a mystery. In the predawn light, I stepped off Shade at the far edge of the herd. Slowly, my body started moving through the familiar forms. First the stretch's, then a simple workout that left me feeling awake. Over the years, I'd stayed dedicated to my routine, even added some more to them last year. A lucky encounter in Uvalde allowing me to find another teacher of sorts.

Ji Quan was someone I'd met last year. He was running a laundry, and we'd become friends when he realized I knew some of his language. After a few weeks of teaching me more of his language, he offered to teach me some new techniques. He was half my weight but could toss me around like a rag doll and made it look easy. He'd really helped push my flexibility and speed when we trained. That was another man I'd miss. The little man had a grace to him that was comforting. Every motion he made served a purpose. There was no wasted motion in anything he did. Mind, body, and spirit solely focused on the one singular task. There was a perfection about the way he did things, something almost peaceful.

The scent of Smythe's cooking drew me away from my thoughts and back to Shade. I'd taken off my shirt and was using a towel to dry off when Jesse rode up, yawning. He was my relief, so we could eat before riding out to scout. The way he was staring at me while I was drying off almost set me off. He turned away before my temper got the better of me, but I swore he was blushing. Luckily for them, this was a short trail. If not, things like that would get him killed. Everyone knew some punchers found company in their own way and most didn't care about that. That wasn't this though, this was almost like he'd never been around men before. It filt like someone who'd grown up around their momma's skirts and didn't know how to behave around men.

Maybe that was it. The kid was just green as hell and had never let go of the apron strings. It would explain both him and his pards' odd behavior. Maybe a successful ranch that went belly up, putting them on the grub line. The old man knew the work well enough, just not like they'd done it in a while. Jesse had some academic knowledge, but never really used it before. If the kid had grown up sheltered and church going, that would explain a lot. That was the only explanation that made sense to me, anyway. In the end, it didn't really matter. Maybe a year or more from now, they'd be good hands. Right now, they did their job well enough, that was enough to keep them fed.

Finally, my shirt and vest were back on, doing my best to ignore the way he had looked away. A grin snuck onto my face, wondering how he was going to deal with all the hands bathing in a river. Tipping my hat before mounting up, I turned to get some chow, but couldn't help the smile on my face. Doing my best to put thoughts about the two of them out of mind. They didn't feel like outlaws or anything else that might threaten the herd. That was all that mattered. Everything else would work itself out one way or the other, they always did out here.

After eating, Jose and I stepped onto our mounts and turned north. We'd cut east at the Nueces River, then follow it for two days. Sometime after that, we should pick up the old Shawnee trail. I'd never been on that trail, but it was pretty obvious when we found it. A quarter mile wide swath of land that was full of scrub the longhorns could feed on. It hadn't been used in years, but you could still make it out. Hard pack ground carved through the Texas landscape by previous herds. It was like the others we'd been on, a wide road through the land, made by thousands of cattle being pushed north to market.

Max had described the camp sites for me and Jose since he had ridden the trail before. Starting tomorrow morning, we would be down to just the trail crew. Bull's team and the rest would be turning back to the ranch before we got moving. They had work to get done before fall blew in. Rebuild the base herd, make sure everything was ready for winter, and do the normal maintenance every ranch needed. Temporary pens needed repairs. The last of the wild calves had to be castrated, and they had to cull some of the older bulls. Max had some sense of how many bulls were healthy to have on the range. They kept only the best of them for breeding stock. The rest were castrated if possible, if not they helped supply the smoked meat for winter.

That night, I said my goodbyes and thanked most of them for the lessons. Bull and I had gotten off to a rough start when I knocked him out that first night. He was a big man who pushed me like he had the other greenhorns. They called it checking my mud. It seemed to be a normal occurrence among the hands. It was my reaction that hadn't been normal. I'd planted an elbow between his eyes, then challenged anyone else to step up. I hadn't realized it at the time, but I was on the edge of breaking. Despite everything I'd studied, nothing had prepared me for the violence life out here held.

From Dodge City to Waco, a trail of corpses followed in my wake. It had all been done for the right reasons, but I hadn't been thinking about it while we traveled. I'd been just reacting

25

to situations, dealing with them as they came. That was before heading to New Orleans for King. After surviving the city, losing Binda, and getting to the Bar C I'd been on a ragged edge. It wasn't guilt that was pushing me, not for the killing. It was the pain of loss and guilt for still being alive that was haunting me. I'd never slowed down to take the time to grieve for them. It also felt like what called me to come out here was getting buried in blood-soaked dirt.

Jose was the first one to help me start working through everything. Riding the line quieted my mind. It made me feel the loss of Juan, Binda and so many others. The turning point came from the last thing you'd have expected. I found my peace again from more killing more men. It was the night before my first drive to Dodge City. They'd been planning to stampede the herd and kill everyone at the ranch when I found them. Their deaths had been a choice, not a life or death situation forced on me. The Bar C hands would have survived their idiotic plan and probably killed them without my help. It would have cost a few head of cattle, maybe some scrapes and bruises at the most. I'd decided to act, for the first time really making the choice to kill in defense of the brand. That night my role as a gun hawk settled on me like a comfortable shirt.

I'd protected the men around me while they did the work needed for us all to be successful. My skill set was doing what they couldn't. Kill without carrying the weight of it. That's not to say I'm some mad dog killer. No, I just didn't feel the guilt most men felt when they had to kill. There were never nightmares that haunted me with the faces of those I'd killed. Jose, the accidental philosopher, helped me more than he'd ever know with understanding that.

He was like me. Killing wasn't something that bothered him. The difference was his past. He had far more brutal experiences in life than I did. It had given him a level of comfort with our role on the ranch from the start. He'd seen the evil that men did when no one stood in their path. More importantly, he'd seen the price when good men were forced to shoulder the cost. Friends that had crawled into a bottle trying to escape the nightmares. Others who stumbled through life waiting to die because they lost the will to keep going.

When I could finally tell him about Binda and New Orleans, he wasn't surprised. He'd seen the knife scar that almost killed me, but never asked about it. Just patiently waiting until I was ready. Then he'd helped me process the pain. More than that, he helped me recognize my own guilt for not being there to protect her. He understood it after losing his family. It was the same shame he felt. That was the problem I struggled with getting past, failing to be there for her. He'd helped with that too in his quiet way. Sharing how he'd gotten over losing his family. The futility of hunting Apache, the shame of working with the bandits. How Max had found him in a cantina and showed him a better way. Finally, the realization that if he had been there, nothing would have changed except his life. He would have been just another body left to rot in the sun with the others. Admitting that last was harder to admit than anything else, I still struggled to acknowledge that truth.

Sharing our pain and guilt had brought us together. Forming a bond that would overcome any distance and we both knew it. If I asked him to come help in Montana, he would, same for him in Arizona. We both knew with an absolute certainty the other would be there, nothing short of death would change that. It was the same way we felt about parting company. Neither of us thought this was the last trail we'd share. Probably because we couldn't stay out of trouble worth a damn.

All of that and more went into the handshake I shared with Bull. The man had taught me a lot, not just about brush poppin' but also about beefs. He hated when I called them cattle, saying it made me sound like some Kansas drifter. Bull considered anyone not Texan to be a waste of time. An attitude I found incredibly funny since he wasn't born here. I'd only mentioned that once. The look he gave me made it clear what to expect if I pointed that out again.

ROBERT KNOX

"Damn it boy we ain't raising dairy cows, these here is beefs. Texans ain't cowboys. We're punchers, drovers or at least wranglers. Ain't none of us tending anything as tame as a cow."

The rest was maybe a bit more useful than his opinions on nomenclature. How to read beefs behavior so I could put my rope where they would be instead of missing completely. Knowing how to throw a rope wasn't nearly as important as knowing where to throw it. When to back off and when to charge, that was knowledge that helped when I had to cut a particular steer out of the herd. Shades cutting skills were passable, but when combined with that knowledge, we managed the job more often than not.

He was just one of the men I said goodbye to that morning. Each of them had helped me polish the skills needed for life out here. Some, like Tink, had probably taught me what not to do more than what to do. That man was damn good at his job but had a wild streak that usually left him broke and in jail every time we went to town. Not that he cared one wit. He'd told me that after the war he figured life was just chance, a twist of fate decided every day between life and death for a man. To him, how many times he could roll the dice before they came up snake eyes was all that mattered. He lives everyday like it's his last and I could appreciate that about him.

To a man they said they'd see me around. Another thing I'd learned out here. Goodbye was never said until you were standing over a grave. Jose and I rode north, scouting for the herd, but my mind was thinking about the men. They turned southwest, slowly fading from sight without looking back. I'd probably never see any of them again. They were one and all Texans. It was something about this area of the country. They wore Texan like a badge and woe to those who tried to claim it without earning the right. To them, the idea of leaving Texas longer than it took to drive cattle to market just didn't exist.

The funny was that most of them weren't born here. A couple of the vaqueros, TJ, Jose, and Chet were the only ones born Texans. The rest had come after the war or on the drift working beefs. But one and all, they considered themselves Texans or Tejanos. Each knew they'd earned the right to wear the handle. Something about them had joined this wild country on a spiritual level. They'd be buried here and to a man were happy about it. Jose was the lone stand out. He was ready to see somewhere else, telling me one night that he'd never be at peace in Texas. It had too many ghosts for him and the idea of building a future here felt wrong.

Jose and I rode on opposite sides of the trail as usual. The land rolled out ahead of us, the trail looking like a dry riverbed weaving through. Worn paths that might have carried water long ago. Now they guided herds through rough country toward the stock pens. The remnants of a trail from the early days when you had to drive your cattle all the way to Sedalia. Now it was more of a road people used to settle the area. Small farms and ranches cropped up along its route. Family working hard to secure their piece of the future.

# CHAPTER 4

The land seemed to stretch on forever when you looked at it, but I knew it was shrinking more every day. Soon the trails would fade away as the railheads moved closer to the ranches, they'd become roads or forgotten paths. Maybe a hundred years from now someone would travel them to experience the history they wrote. Already the need for them was fading. Talk about stockyards in San Antonio was common and probably wasn't far off. The days of long cattle drives were coming to an end and with it the end of an era.

There would always be cowboys working the range. Nothing could change that, but I'd come in at the tail end of the long drives. Lucky even to have been part of them, but like everything else in this country, things were changing fast. Railroads connected the east and west more than once. More and more tribes were being forced onto reservations, losing their land. They weren't being given any choice, not even one that let them stay on their land.

The Cherokee had been marched into the nations from North Carolina. More and more tribes were forced to depend on an enemy they hated. Their children are forced to learn our ways. The once mighty herds of buffalo were even shrinking. Hiders killing them in mass, usually taking nothing but the hides. I'd heard stories of skinned dead buffalo littering the plains as far as you could see. Wakes of vultures so dense from a distance they looked like ants swarming.

Some of the tribes still fought. The Apache had no interest in surrendering. The gold rush in the black hills was still causing trouble up there. Once again, we broke a treaty in pursuit of that shining metal. One we had forced them to sign not that long ago. It was going to happen no matter what. The tides of people moving west hadn't slowed. The more people who came, the more land they needed. It was the way of man, those in power pushed those without off their land. From the first days of man to the last, that power struggle would continue.

Jose broke through my musing when he whistled me over. He was sitting on a small bluff that looked out over the trail. Riding up, I could tell what it was that caught his attention. We'd found the first camp site Max had talked about. Well, he'd found it while I was woolgathering.

A small stream spun around the back of the bluff, spreading into a wider shallow pond offering easy water to the stock. There was plenty of graze for the herd and room for them to bed down. We did our normal scouting while gathering some wood for Smythe. A small grove of mesquite and alder caught my attention about a half mile west caught my attention. There might be some was fresh meat in those trees.

"Think I'll go poke around with my bow. Some fresh meat wouldn't go amiss."

"Hunt deer amigo, not the Apache." He laughed.

"One time, it was one time." I was slipping off my boots, putting on my moccasins, trying not to laugh.

Slipping into an arroyo that ran behind the grove, I started working my way through it quietly toward the stand of trees. My eyes scanned the ground, looking for deer beds or other sign when I got closer to the grove. It was an area where a decent mule deer would bed down, or maybe a longhorn or two. It made me nervous when I couldn't find any recent sign. Something should have bedded down here. It was the perfect place for a small herd to gather. Moving silently through the rough scrub, my unease grew. My eyes scanned constantly and my ears listened for the slightest sound that was out of place. If prey didn't bed down somewhere, it meant a predator called it home. If I could take a cougar, it would be more welcome than a mule deer. Their meat was prized for its flavor and Smythe loved it.

Hidden deep in the shadows of a large mesquite tree, I was shocked to find five horses. They were shod and tacked up, standing three footed in the shade with their cinches loose. I'd been right. There were predators lurking in the trees, the worst kind. Jose's never going to let this go, hunting deer and finding rustlers. Their horses never made a sound when I slipped past them toward their small camp.

Just inside the trees, four men were asleep in the shade while one man peered toward the camp. They had a couple of hours before the herd arrived, so most of them sleeping made sense. The lone look out wasn't paying any attention to what was behind him. There was a chance they had a legitimate reason for being here, but I needed to know what it was. Admittedly, it was a slim chance that they were there for a legitimate reason, but killing them without knowing wouldn't be right. We weren't on our range anymore which meant these men have as much right to be here as I did.

What I needed was a way to find out why they were hiding in the grove. Thankfully, the one on watch picked that moment to bother the man beside him. Maybe he was a mind reader with poor judgment? I watched in amazement as he knelt down and woke the other men.

"Bo. Wake up Bo."

"What the hell do ya want, Micha?" The sleeping man didn't even move his hat when he spoke.

"That other fellas disappeared. Ain't seen him in a long while."

"He see ya?"

"Ain't no way he saw me."

"Then it ain't nothin' to worry 'bout. If he ain't seen ya, then he ain't warn'n the rest of 'em."

"What if he comes this way?"

"What do ya think? Kill'em, now let me sleep."

"Fine." Micha turned back to watch the camp site. Five minutes later, Bo's snores started up again.

That was enough for me. My arm slowly pulled back on the tension in the big horn bow as I drew it back. A soft hiss was the only sound that broke the silence when I released the string. The arrow cut through the air in a heartbeat. At this range there was no question about my aim. That hiss was the only warning Micha would got, and it did him no good. My arrow pinned his head to the tree in front of him. The fletching bounced silently for a second, then silence returned. That solved all of his concerns about my location once and for all. A soft gasp, followed by a slow wheeze when his last breath escaped, was his song of death. The ferry man was already collecting his coin when I sent Bo to join him.

The rest woke up dead in hell, never knowing what killed them. I had even less concern about my actions after searching them. For some reason, outlaws had taken to carrying around their own wanted posters lately. Bragging about how dangerous they were based on the rewards. At least that was what they said when I'd ask one about it. Personally, I thought it was so they didn't end up buried without people knowing who they were. Every one of these fools had their own dodgers tucked away somewhere, a pocket or wallet. One was in their saddlebag.

Their crimes ran the gambit from rustling and horse thievery, Bo was wanted murder and rape. The men dead at my feet were worth just short of eight hundred dollars. Course there was no way I'd be collecting on that, not with Max's rule about bounties. Between the five they had just short of two hundred dollars, five good horses with tack, various pistols and rifles. The look on Jose's face when I rode up leading the horses was amusing. I already knew what he was going to say.

"Sorry, no fresh meat." I said, sliding off the palomino I'd been riding.

"Or Apache, I'm guessing."

"Nope, found a nest of rattlers in the trees, likely they ran off any game. These ponies were just left, strangest thing. Gun belts hanging off the saddle horn and all."

"Amigo, are you sure those are not the snake's horses?"

"Might have been. They don't need them anymore either way."

"Rustlers?"

"They were in that grove," I nodded, "probably scared off all the game."

"Very inconsiderate of them. You spoke to them about this poor behavior?"

"They were resistant to discuss the topic."

"You insisted, I am sure."

"I left them under a fall about half a mile off the trail. Should be enough to keep the scavengers away for a day or so."

"Five horses is a fair price for running off our dinner." Jose and I had developed this way of talking about things if no one was around. We both knew if someone else heard us they'd think we were mad.

"I thought it was rather rude and agreed to their reparations. Any sign of Smythe yet?" Just then, I heard the rattle of a wagon coming up the trail.

Smythe cut his mules off the trail before we could see him. Using a ramp to get above the graze we'd us for the herd. Jose had checked it out while I was hunting, making sure it was stable. Overgrown, and the ramp was rough, but functional. I could hear Smythe cursing before we could see him. It may have been solid, but it wasn't smooth. He rounded a soft curve with a black cloud hanging around him. We could see him moving slowly up the old path. The big man was bouncing around on the seat, cursing constantly. He didn't look happy about the rough ride. When he hit level ground and slowed the wagon, he was red faced from yelling at the mules. Finally coming to a stop on the far side of the small rise.

"Damn useless old trails. Too goddamned old to be bouncing 'round unbroken ground." The man groused as he set the brake.

"Wasn't much we could do about that." I said, reaching for the harnesses on his team. "We made sure it was solid. That was about all we could do."

"It's this damn old trail, ain't nothing to do with ya two." Smythe grumbled while stepping down from the wagon. That's when he noticed the five horses Jose was unsaddling. "Y'all keep finding more horses drives gonna need another wrangler."

"Amigo says he found the poor beast just left by a den of snakes."

"Couldn't understand why someone'd leave such fine animals like that." This was an old game we'd played several times. Smythe always grumbled about it, but kept playing along.

"Shame the way folks are nowadays, personally I blame ya damn kids." Smythe was studying us, probably looking for any sign of blood.

"Caught 'em napping." It was enough to tell him I wasn't wounded.

"Ya'll know the wranglers are the saddest to see you leave. They've had it easier every year cause you two find'n horses all broke an tacked up." Smythe still sounded grumpy. The man hadn't ever sounded any other way now that I thought about it.

"It is not our fault so many choose to donate their fine mounts to our cause." Jose grinned like a cat from where he was finishing the picket line.

I left the two of them bickering and led the mules down toward the stream. They eagerly followed me. It was never hard getting them to water. The struggle would come when I tried to get them to leave. They were a good team, but they were mules and nothing was going to change that. After the normal braying and dancing around, I got them tied into the picket line with their feedbags.

Smythe was setting up a pot of beans over the fire and Jose was looking down the trail. I could hear the bawling beefs echoing around us. The herd wasn't too far off now, dust obscuring the horizon as they got closer. Sharp whistles from punchers mixed in the noise. Slowly, like a great beast rising from the depths, they appeared through the dust. A swaying mass of long sharp horns slowly moving across the ground. It always gave me the same impression, some monstrous patch of thorns. Nothing but dust was left in their wake.

Jose met me at the horses and we rode out to help get the herd into the small canyon that would be their home for the night. I turned the lead steer toward the water and the rest followed, moving across the hardpan. Whistles and yells pushed the last of them in to the box canyon. The herd milled around, each drinking their fill, then finding a place to graze before bedding down. The dust cleared and I could see the newly cleared trail stretch out behind them. Dust still hung in the air, but the contrast between the fresh trail was strange. A line of green showing where the herd had turned away from the overgrown path.

# CHAPTER 5

The night passed, and life settled into a rhythm after that. There was a small confrontation with a rancher who tried to charge us a toll just before Waco. Local law came out and tried to back his play, but when he realized who owned this herd, they both changed their tune. The Bar C was well known. More importantly, most folk knew they weren't to be crossed. The small rancher left, cursing his luck. It had been years since anyone came up the old trail and now he'd missed his chance at some easy money.

The only other bit of excitement was a brief stampede during one of the rare Texas storms. We only lost five head because the trails path was walled in solid stone. They funneled the herd in one direction until they slowed down a few miles later. The five dead beefs either fell in the mass or didn't get up fast enough at the start. The steak was appreciated while it lasted and Max didn't get too upset about the loss.

Sooner than expected, we found ourselves riding drag as the herd walked into the stock pens. All under the watchful gaze of Max and the man counting for the buyers. Two of them had already talked to Max, trying to get a good price. Max passed them both up and found a representative for Swift. He was just waiting on the count now that the deal had been struck. The Bar C didn't have any relationship with those buyers. That's what made Max go with the company he knew. He'd been dealing with Jim Standom for years and had some loyalty to the company because of him.

The Army had come out after the herd was counted to look at the horses. They'd had a man looking over the remuda when it stopped moving. He'd make his offer, but Max was thinking about taking them back to the ranch. He'd already said it was a coin toss. Being this close to home, it might be worth it to wrangle them back to the ranch. The Army must've offered enough to make the choice for him, because I saw them shake hands after talking for a minute. Part of that money would come to Jose and me for the few horses we'd picked up along the way.

An hour later, soaking in a bath behind the barbershop, my mind started thinking about what came next. I'd get paid out with the rest of the hands tomorrow night, after that I'd be on the drift. There were things I needed, such as a packhorse, panniers, and supplies. The desire to see the ocean was still guiding me, but that didn't tell me how to get there. From here to there was a lot of wild country, and the choice of which way to drift was up to me.

Bathed and dressed in clean clothes, Jose and I found a place to eat. The food was good, but it didn't have the same feel as other eateries had. There was no sense of home or being welcomed. At first I guessed it was because we were unfamiliar faces, but that wasn't it. After watching them treat the regulars, I started to recognize it. This was just a business to them, nothing more.

It was another sign of change that was spreading across Texas. The isolation was fading as more and more people came west, each chasing their dreams. Towns were being established, the population was growing dense in the larger towns and cities. Here, where the railroad had been established for a few years, it felt like a town quickly becoming a city. There wasn't that sense of belonging I'd felt in more remote places. Safety and prosperity were creating the distance between people. Wealth and influence were the concerns and who or where you ate became important right along with them. It wasn't there yet, but in another few years a person it would be like the other big cities across the country.

After dinner, we found ourselves leaning on the bar of a saloon, each of us sipping a cold beer. The other hands were sitting at a table sharing a bottle of whiskey. The two vaqueros had joined them for the night, making it more likely Max was going to keep them on permanent. I'd heard him talking to Smythe about it a few days back and knew it was on his mind. Elias and Jesse were nowhere to be seen, but that wasn't much of a surprise. They'd kept their distance the entire drive, never socializing with the rest of the hands. If I was asked to bet, they wouldn't be at dinner tomorrow for long. They'd get paid off and be gone well before we sat down to eat.

For me, the thought of the meal was bittersweet. I'd gotten hired at the end of the drive in Dodge three years ago. Tomorrow night I'd be leaving the Bar C the same way. Halfway through my thoughts, I noticed Jose's eyes flick at some movement. Turning my head slightly to see what had caught his eye, It was three men approaching the other hands. They'd angled themselves to come up behind the vaqueros. Chet had caught the movement just after we did. His hand casually dropped down, flipping the thong off his Smith & Wesson under the table. Jose and I duplicated the movement, turning slightly to see how this developed. It wouldn't be the first time someone took issue about some of our crew being Tejanos. It had never worked out well for them.

These three looked like hands from another outfit. Probably out drinking at the end of their drive. Fort Worth was a railhead, and there had been at least three other herds in the pens. Those were just the ones waiting to be shipped, truthfully there was no way to know how many outfits were in town. There were probably a hundred different brands who drove cattle here. What was plain to see was their intent. They were hunting trouble and, for whatever reason, picked a table with six men at it. That made me scan the room with a more critical eye. It didn't take long to find the rest of them standing against the wall behind Chet. Four more men working a little too hard at ignoring the coming trouble. All four had their pistols sitting loosely in their holsters. I tapped Jose's foot, and he followed my eyes. The bartender came up about the same time to check on our beers.

"What's the story with those three?" I asked, after waving off another beer.

"Trouble hunters, the lead man thinks he's a gun fighter. The rest are just hands who like watching the show." He studied us for a second before adding more. "He'll pick a fight with one of the Mex's, did it the other night. Ain't seen him face many, but his decent fast."

"The four on the wall?"

"They'll keep the others out of it, least wise that's the usual play. Who's at the table?"

"Rest of our crew, from the Bar C." My smile wasn't friendly. Things like this tended to get a bad reaction from me.

"Think this is about ya get interesting, heard a few stories 'bout y'all."

"You don't seem concerned?"

"They'll take it outside. Most know better than to fight in here." He hooked his thumb through the lapel on his jacket and revealed his badge. "The bar owner being the law keeps most folks honest."

"Noted." I smiled, turning back to the show. We'd take our part in the play soon, but right now it was still too loud.

"He likes to fight the Mexicans?" Jose asked casually. The sheriff's smile said he knew exactly what was being asked.

"He does, seems to be one of the fools that hates for no reason."

"Gracias." Jose's smile didn't reach his eyes.

"I'll deal with the four if you want the fight?" I knew that smile. It meant someone was going to have a bad night.

"Si." It was all he had to say.

Pushing off from the bar, casually strolling toward the door, I got ready for action. Watching from the corner of my eye to be sure no one was paying attention to me yet. Sadly, for him, the trouble hunter decided to show his poor judgement by changing his focus. My braided ponytail that hung down my back must have caught his attention.

"Hey breed! Your kind ain't welcome here." He shouted across the bar. Silence followed his words like a wave. It wasn't the first time I'd been mistaken as a half breed. The insult didn't mean much to me, and I took two more steps before turning to lean on the wall beside his friends.

"Since you boys seem to be part of this, why don't you step over there with your friends?" I spoke into the silence without turning to face the loudmouth.

"We ain't..." I cut him off before he could finish the lie.

"Friend, don't make me call you a liar unless you want this dance more than he does." There was a flash of anger when he met my eyes. Then I watched the color drain from his face. It wasn't the first time someone had tried to match stares with me.

"Nope, we'll join our friends." The four of them moved across the room carefully. Not one of them looked over their shoulder and they made sure to keep their hands far away from their guns.

"You ignoring me, breed." At those words, I finally faced him.

"You're about as dumb as you look if you think I'm a half breed." The cold was running through me now. My laughing response seemed to shock the man. Maybe it was realizing that I was white, or maybe it was the way I met his gaze.

"You're not a half breed?" His response sounded as pathetic as I hoped.

"No, but since you've gone through all the trouble to find a fight, why don't you continue?" My response made him even more hesitant.

"I don't... I mean..." He was trying to back pedal now that he knew I was white and not afraid of him.

"So you wanted to fight a half breed but won't face a white man?" I laughed. There was something in me that couldn't stand a bully.

"That's not what I said." He tried to protest, but Jose decided to step in before he could say anything else.

"Amigo, I think the man would rather face me." He spoke while leaning casually on the bar.

"Now Jose, don't go ruin'n the fun." Chet piped in from his chair. His eyes never shifted off the man. "JC was in the middle of a conversation an I been watching this rattler come up with his thong off for a minute."

"He's always trying to steal my fun." I replied to Chet, then turned to Jose. "You still mad about them rustlers? I told ya there wasn't time to come get ya."

"So you say amigo. You also keep saying it was only five of them." The look on the trouble hunter's face was comical now. The poor man didn't know what to make of this.

"It was only five of them, but that ain't this. He called me a breed, not you." At this point, a few tables had caught on and were laughing at the scene. A man I hadn't noticed at one of the poker tables spoke up.

"JC, figure that must be Jose at the bar." I knew the voice, but hadn't expected to find him here. "Already figured that was Chet's loudmouth at the table."

"That you back there, Luke?" I laughed. "Thought you would be on the river this time of year."

Now the man's friends were stepping away from him. They didn't know who we were, but they must have known Luke. I'd met him the first time in San Antonio a few years back, a gambler with a reputation as a gunman. We'd crossed paths again last year when Jose and I stepped into a hornet's nest by accident. Six men had jumped him, taking his bank roll and horse. We'd found him a foot, following their trail intent on getting his back. It only took the three of us an hour to find them. He'd ridden with the Bar C to Dodge, becoming a friend to most of us along the trail. Normally this time of year, he was working the river boats on the Mississippi. Cold weather would eventually drive him west to California for the winter. That's when we usually crossed paths.

"Got a big tournament in Los Angeles, left the river a bit early this year. This ain't usually the Bar C's stopping point?" Luke smiled from behind a decent stack of chips.

"Max decided it ain't worth going to Dodge anymore." I laughed.

"Y'all from the Bar C?" The man now stood alone in the center of the room asked shakily.

"Oh buddy, you've made more than one bad choice tonight. By the by friend, where did your pards go?" Chet was never one to let someone off easy.

"They ummmm…" The man's voice trailed off when he realized they were all sitting back at their table trying very hard to not be noticed.

"I think maybe you apologize to my amigo. Then buy a round for disturbing everyone. No?" Jose was more forgiving. He would give the man a way out.

"Yeah, I'm ah sorry about the confusion, friend." He managed to say, then gulped and spoke on. "Let my buy the bar a round for disturbing everyone."

That was met with whoops and hollers as the men rushed the bar, everyone but the Bar C hands and his friends. Nothing broke a standoff like free drinks. There was still a look of concern on the troublemaker's face, but now it was focused on the bartender. I wondered if he had enough money for this. Jose walked out of the mad rush with a grin and I tipped my hat to Luke. He nodded back and returned to his game. He knew we'd be outside if he wanted to talk more. Right now, the bar was too busy and neither of us liked a crowd.

With a nod to Chet and the others, we stepped out front. Each of us packing our pipes while we walking. Stepping down the boardwalk to get away from the raucous noise before lighting them. The sun had set long ago, now the only light was streaking through the glass windows from the saloons. It painted the street in broken shadows that danced around the horses tied to the hitching rails. I watched the light of Jose's match dance off his amused eyes when he lit his pipe. He found the whole thing great sport and, for the most part, I agreed with him. We both knew it wasn't over yet. That puncher couldn't let it lie. His pride had been hurt. That devious voice in the back of his head would drive him out here soon enough. It was even money between him or Luke coming out first. The puncher who won the race, just not in the way we expected.

His body was launched through the batwing doors, sending him rolling into the street. It created an impressive dust trail, but I wasn't sure if it was from the street or his clothes. The sheriff followed him out, cussing with each step.

"No good trouble hunting bastard. You buy a round for the house. I expect it to be paid for." I noticed the gun stuck in the sheriff's back. It looked like it might have belonged in the holster of his victim not long ago.

"Guess we won't have to worry about him." I laughed as the sheriff's boot launched him further down the street. The man was scrambling on his hands trying to keep his feet under him.

"Amigo, only Chet could manage to accomplish all this." Jose chuckled.

"Looks like another one falls prey to his own short comings." Luke said, walking through the still swinging doors. He stepped toward us, taking a fresh cigar out of a holder as he moved. After cutting off the end, he took a deep pull on it striking a match.

"Good to see you again, amigo." Jose broke the silence first.

"And in a better state than the last time." I added with a grin.

"Have to admit, I was surprised when I spotted you. Hadn't figured I'd see you in this area. Maybe I should've. Think more of the ranchers are tired of Dodge and the risks getting there." Luke stared at his cigar as he spoke.

"Max didn't figure the extra money was worth the price anymore. Most of the railheads are pricing the same or near enough that it doesn't matter."

"How long are you staying in town?" Luke asked curiously.

"Not sure yet. Have to buy some stuff before I head out." I

answered.

"Max says we are leaving in two days." Jose said, answering for the Bar C. "Sunrise on Friday."

"Leaving the Bar C?" Luke asked, his eyebrows slowly raising in surprise.

"Told Max I'd give him three years. Time for me to move on." Then with a grin I pointed at Jose, deftly changing the subject. "Don't let him fool ya either, he's getting married and moving to Arizona territory before the next drive."

"Jose! Congratulations, my friend." Luke's smile split his face. "Finally found a woman to tolerate your loquacious self."

"She doesn't talk much, lets him chatter on all he wants." I smiled watching my friend. He just hung his head, smiling at our japing.

"My friend, I'm happy for you." Luke put his hand on Jose's shoulder. "I hope you've found that thing we're all looking for, someone to build a life with."

"I have amigo. She is a wonderful woman." Jose met his gaze, smiling happily.

"And going to finally get that ranch all punchers dream of." Luke nodded his approval.

"Si, that is why we are moving to the territory. The land is cheaper, so maybe I can get more."

"Will you send me your address? You can send it to the same address I used before." Luke had given us the address of a hotel in San Francisco the last time we'd seen him. I'd mailed off a third or the reward money to him when it came in. "What about you JC? Where are you heading to?"

"Si, I will my friend." Jose agreed.

"Oddly enough, I'm heading to Los Angeles." I laughed.

"Let me guess, riding that Nokota Blue?" Luke still wanted Shade. I could see it in his eyes, but he knew I'd never sell him.

"Got it in one." I knew what was coming next.

"You know there's a train you could take, right?" He laughed.

"Nope, came out to Dodge on one. I can still feel that seat haunting me. Besides, I still think it was a mistake, missed out on most of the country."

"Amigos, there is a cantina I am going to visit." The two vaqueros had come out of the bar. Jose had said earlier he was going to visit it with them.

"See you in the morning, amigo." I knew he was distancing himself by going with them.

"Pleasure seeing you again, Jose."

"Adios amigos." He tipped his hat as he stepped to join to other two.

"Where are you staying? I could use some coffee." I asked, figuring he was staying in a nicer place than me.

"The General's Mansion, it serves coffee in china cups." He looked at me knowingly.

"Right, not my kinda place. I'm staying at the cattlemen's. The coffee's good even if it's in normal cups."

"If don't mind a couple of stops along the way, I wouldn't mind sharing the trail with ya." I knew it was coming. Luke didn't like trains any more than I did.

"It won't hurt your reputation?" I laughed before stepping through the doors of the hotel. Pouring us each a cup of coffee, then we stepped back out to the porch. The evening was pleasantly cool for this time of year, and I preferred it to the lobby.

"Sure you want the eyes on you?" It was a serious question. Traveling with a known man had its downsides.

"Still mostly known as a gambler?" I asked.

"Mostly, but there's always some that hear the other half of it." Luke admitted, knowing he had a reputation with his Remington.

"Figure I can manage." I smiled, appreciating his consideration. "Sides, I don't know the way. I was just heading west, figured the ocean would show up, eventually."

"Think I might be able to find the way." He laughed at my lack of knowledge. "It's funny, but I think you were being honest about that."

"I was." This made him choke on his coffee. Once he calmed

down and re-lit his cigar, we continued our conversation.

"You'd have ended up in Mexico, my friend. You have to drift a bit north as you go west."

"I'd a still found it. Sides haven't seen much of Mexico either."

"JC, you're a different type of puncher. What's your plan after Los Angeles?"

"Not sure. Might head north up the coast, then either cut back east to Colorado or stay north to Oregon. Ain't really decided yet."

"I head to Frisco after the tournament. I'll be playing cards for a few weeks in Los Angels though. Between the tournament and the games after and before, it's usually a good pay day for me."

"Can't promise I'll hang around that long." I admitted.

"Figured, if you do we can travel up the coast together, but if not I understand. I stay in Frisco for the winter, don't head east till late spring."

"You're like a puncher." I laughed. "The season's timing out your year."

"Most folks do in some way or another."

"Seems so. You know I never thought about that until I started working beefs. Then I realized it'd done the same back east. Probably be the same when I start my ranch."

"Same dream as must punchers?" He smiled.

"Except mines already there, ten thousand acres in Montana territory, with another forty thousand available after five years." The stunned look that came over Luke made me smile. I couldn't help but tell him the rest. "I'll also have ten thousand dollar's worth of horse flesh show up shortly after I take possession."

"You're gonna have to explain all that, my friend." He finally managed to say after the shock wore off.

"Should have plenty of time."

"Reckon you're right." He spoke through a chuckle, but was still shaking his head in disbelief. "Ya know, the truth is none of that surprises me nearly as much as you having only been out here three years."

"Not the first time I heard that. Don't get is as much now that I don't look like such a kid."

"Other than that hat, ya do blend in out here well enough."

"Don't start on my hat, it ain't going nowhere." I laughed through a yawn.

"Go enjoy your bed. I have a few more hours at the table tonight before I'm done. If you're looking for me, just check The Lady's Bell. It's where I usually play cards."

"I'll get my travel gear together over the next couple of days. Already sent for my trunk, I'm going to pack my winter gear and store it again. Wells Fargo says it'll be here in two days. After that I'll be ready to go."

"Morning of the fourth day then, that'll give me enough time at the table." He chuckled through a wicked smile. "Locals will be tired of me by then."

# CHAPTER 6

I went through a limited routine the next morning in my room, using the shared balcony. Just as I stepped through the last kick and started cooling down, the sun kissed the horizon and started painting the day. Quietly leaning on the rail, I marveled at it for a few minutes. Something about the splashing color always caught my attention. Back east I'd never watched a sunrise or set, but since coming west I'd seen every one of them.

Maybe it was the change in circumstance, or maybe I was finally really living. Back in New York, life had existed in the lamp lit world of the city. You worked set hours, not dark to dark. Now my life wasn't measured by a clock or even a calendar. The sun was my time clock, that was why I noticed it. Some part of me cursed those years. I didn't take the time to enjoy it. The thought drew me into my memories, those of a five-year-old sailing out of the harbor.

I'd been standing on deck when the sun broke the horizon that morning. Watching as the ship came to life, sailors scurried up rigging, others wound ropes. Several took position on a wheel and started hauling up the anchor. Dawn to dusk they worked, the similarity of that life and this one hit me again. Sailors, punchers, and farmers didn't watch the hours of the day. People all over the world, usually the dregs of society according to the wealthy, worked tirelessly matching the sun.

Wealth was equated with freedom, but was it really? If your soul purpose was just the accumulation of more wealth, was that really living? Those men were not who I admired. It wasn't that I didn't want wealth, but rather that I wanted to be one of those few who earned it. Not through the sweat of others. I wanted it from my own effort. I admired the men in this country who were visionaries, those who built railroads and towns. They created industry and jobs for other men in the process. Often it was those men who brought dreams into reality through blood and sweat. I admired both the wealthy who dreamed of the new country and the engineers who made those dreams into reality. Finally, the hard-working men who turned that design into a reality. I'd seen the difference out here, something I'd never recognized in New York.

The schemers and manipulators were the same as outlaws to me. They all gained at the expense of others. They were truly the dregs. Draining civilization of resources and squandering it on petty wants. They gave nothing and hoarded all they could. Those men I hated because they represented the worst mankind had to offer.

The smells of a town waking drifted by my nose, reminding me I was standing on my balcony with no shirt. Stepping back into my room, I got cleaned up before putting on a fresh shirt. I didn't really have any plans until dinner. Other than spending some time with Jose before they left Friday. I was slinging my gun belt around my waist and tying it down before I knew it. My next steps needed no plan. It had been the same in so many places that it was all habit.

The sun was still low in the sky when I sat down with my coffee. Jose wouldn't be far behind me, and Max after him. Then there would be breakfast. After that I'd have to see where the day led. It was 1875, I was nineteen years old and about to set off into unknown country on a new adventure. Now I was far more experienced in life out here that it all felt normal. Part of that had been accepting how cheaply you could lose it.

Jose sat down beside me, his steps barely making any noise on the boardwalk. We sat there just watching the start of another day, something we had shared many times before. This man knew me better than anyone else. Only he knew the pain that had scarred me in New Orleans when I lost Binda. He had heard the full story in our cave and helped me piece myself back together that first winter. It hadn't been overnight, but slowly he shared all of his story. Through it I learned from his experience. The cold hollow part of me had faded, finally allowing me to let go of the rage hidden there.

I'd been with him the night he met Cassandra, recognized the look that had filled his eyes when he saw her. The man many feared for his pistol work was lost to a slip of a woman. She had defeated him with a simple smile. It took him another six months to admit defeat. He'd fought the good fight all men do, struggling to believe this perfect angel would have anything to do with him. I had watched this man who tracked Apache into the night with me tremble as he offered her the ring. Watched all the fear fade away, turning to a joy he'd long since thought gone forever when she said yes and stepped into his arms.

He had been my partner in good and bad times. We'd shared dust and blood together, knowing the other would always have our back. Our dark humor had gotten both of us some odd looks, but we'd spent more time laughing than crying. He was my partner and would always have a place at my fire, but soon we would both start new paths in life. There wouldn't be a goodbye, it would probably be said with simple nods and nothing more. To anyone watching, it would be a simple adios amigo.

Today we would be wandering around Fort Worth just wasting time. Max walked out, the creaking door preceding his steps. The sound of his knees popping when he sat down broke the silence. He joined our silence over his coffee and we all just watched the day come to life. Then, almost as one, we rose without a word, walking across the street to have some breakfast.

"Figure what you're going to do, JC?" Max asked after we'd taken a seat and ordered.

"West to start, going to see the other ocean. After that I ain't sure."

"Ought to be an interesting trip." Max nodded after a moment's thought.

"Jefe, we both know it will be interesting if nothing else." Jose laughed. "This one can not stay out of such things."

"Of that I have no doubt." Max smiled over his chipped enamel cup, laughter obvious in his eyes. "Can't help himself."

"Y'all know you're not funny, right?" I grinned, knowing this was coming. "Just means you two can retire in peace."

"We will hear stories of the nameless man in the strange hat." Jose wasn't about to give up this game so easily. He ignored my jab with that easy smile I knew so well. "The newspaper will speak of his heroic deeds far and wide."

"Think you're right Jose. God knows he can't stay outta trouble."

I was saved when the waiter set three platters of food in front of us with a basket of biscuits. It was good enough that none of us bothered to speak until the plates were clean and our coffee cups refilled. Max was the first one to break the comfortable silence. He did so while handing each of us a stack of money.

"That's for the ponies a tack y'all brought in. I know usually it isn't a thing, but figure both of you'll be needing it."

"Gracias Jefe." Jose slid the money into his wallet without much comment.

"Appreciate it, but I still want a horse from that mare." That made Max crack a smile.

"Gives ya a reason to come back down our way."

"Be easy by then, just a quick train ride." I laughed, but there was a sadness that went with that thought.

"It is true, amigo. It will not be long until everything is just a train ride." Jose looked serious as he continued. "The wildness of this place will be tamed soon. It is good you are going to see it before it is gone."

"Agreed, seen a lot of this country in my years. I'll be glad of it while sitting in my rocking chair as an old man."

"Ah Jefe, you have a ranch in the Nueces Strip. Old age may not be part of that life." Jose beat me to the punch.

Max nearly spit coffee across the table, laughing, and we both joined him. It wasn't the first time someone had questioned Max about the sanity of building his ranch there. He knew the risks and so did every man that worked for him. Most of us knew he did it by being smart. Either way, he made it work. Some of those lessons were why Jose was leaving. It would be decades before that area was truly safe for a family. That was a lesson Max had learned painfully.

"That's fair enough, Jose. You know it's going to be hard to fill the hole you two are leaving." Max sighed. "Good line riders are damn near impossible to find. Especially getting two of 'em that like the job."

"Sorry Max, nothing I can really do about it, same for Jose. For me, it's more about managing my time. I'll have to be in Montana for a few years before I start building my place. Have to learn the land and the people who live on it."

"I know all that, just like I know Jose can't raise a family working my range. Especially not when some crazy gringo built his ranch in the middle of outlaw country. Just grumbling a bit. Call it the privilege of age."

"Señor Max, there are not words for what I owe you." Jose's voice was somber and serious. "I am a good man because of you."

"You don't owe me nothing. If there ever was a debt, you've paid it back ten times over. Sides, that good man was always there. Ya just needed to listen to him. All I ever did was give ya a chance to hear his voice."

"I feel about the same, Max. Can't ever thank you enough for what you've given me. All those lessons will help me build a ranch the right way."

"You knock it off too. It's too early for all this." The older man groused, unsure of how to take our appreciation. "Smythe's got your gear separated out, he's grumbling about it being in his way. You know how he is."

"My trunk isn't in yet, but Wells Fargo said I can store things there until it arrives." I refilled our cups while talking.

"Was wondering what your plan was for all that winter gear." Max nodded his head as if a mystery had been solved. "Jose, that does mean Smythe's ready for whatever is on that list she gave you. Don't listen to him bitch bout it either, he's looking forward to cooking at the wedding."

"Smart asking him to cook for it." It was one of the reasons I thought about staying. Smythe was one hell of a cook and i could only imagine the spread he would be putting out.

"Si amigo, it was the only way I could get him to attend."

"That's about right." Max admitted with a grin, then started to stand from the table. "The man ain't exactly sociable, hell ain't even sure he's house trained. Now I need to get things ready for tonight. You two try to stay out of trouble."

"Us?" Jose feigned an innocent tone that wasn't believable at all.

"I ain't buying it." Max said, tossing five silver dollars on the table to pay for the meal. "See y'all this evening."

"Well amigo, what now?"

"According to what Max said, I figure we ought to go shopping for you or rather for your fiancé."

"It is true. I do have a list." He laughed while sheepishly pulling a piece of paper out of his wallet.

"Be happy to help."

If ever you need a laugh picture two punchers wandering from store to store looking for a specific kind of yellow fabric. Not that either of us knew what it was to start with, Jose would just show whoever was working his list. We won't even talk about me watching him turn red when he handed the list of unmentionables to the woman working that area. She let him off easy, simply telling him to pick up the package later.

I don't know how entertaining Jose found the day, but I spent most of it trying not to laugh. After eating lunch at another disappointing restaurant, we stayed the course and kept at it. He managed to get the last of the things on his list before dinner. It all got delivered to the hotel, and he stored it in his room for now. Tomorrow we'd take it to Smythe's wagon. I could pick up my stuff at the same time. It would save us some rental on the wagon we were borrowing.

Dinner was the usual end of drive affair, taking over the dining room in the hotel. Max paid everyone off before dinner. I watched Elias and Jesse disappear as soon as they got their money. No surprise there. The rest of us enjoyed steaks big enough to cover a plate with all the fixings. There was plenty of whiskey being passed around. I had one beer and then stuck to coffee for most of the night. Max did hire the two vaqueros. Both men seemed happy about it and easily joined the other hands in celebrating. I was pretty sure they'd be working the line this coming winter.

One at a time, each in their own way, the hands I had worked with came and spoke with me. Sharing a few stories and promising to meet up sometime in the future. Each of us knowing the possibility of that was thin to none. The west was a big place and none of these men would leave Texas by choice. The ones I'd known since that first year were different. Each man expressing their friendship in their own way. Smythe grumped out something about not needing as many poultices now before shaking my hand. He turned stomping out of the room without another word.    Chet cracked a couple of jokes then toasted our fallen friends with me. I told both of them if they ever needed me I'd be there, they promised the same. We'd shared enough blood to know those words were spoken in earnest. Max just said he'd see me in the morning. Something told me there wouldn't be any goodbye from the man. It just wasn't his way. The man would always welcome me at his fire, and knew I would do the same.

Hours later, I was sitting outside again, enjoying my pipe. Jose was leaning against the hitching rail across from me, smoking a cheroot. The off-key piano rang out down the street, the odd echo distorting it strangely. We'd heard the same thing in different towns across Texas. There was something familiar about it at this point. I watched the smoke trail up from my pipe, dancing on the evening breeze. There was just something comfortable about all of this. The silence stretched out into the darkness, I could just hear a coyote yip far off in the night. Quietly, almost lost to the noise of civilization, I could just hear the song, it gently drew my attention. Comforting, familiar in the way it pulled at my soul. There were still variations but I knew this song like an old friend now.

Slowly I tapped my pipe out, making sure no embers escaped. Unfolding from the bench, I nodded good night to Jose. Then dropped off my cup and headed to my room. There was one more day with old friends, then I'd be on my own again. The odd day after they left would be spent buying and packing. Traveling with Luke should be interesting but I had a feeling it wouldn't last long. Honestly I'd be surprised if he left Fort Worth with me. Not that I doubted his intent, I just understood the man. If he got an offer for a particularly good game, well that was his craft and I'd never fault a man for that. You had to take people as they came. Luke would stand by me in a fight but he'd lived by his own schedule for too long to change.

There wasn't much to be done about any of that. I'd either have his company or not. That was just the way it was, and I'd known who the man was before making plans. A part of me had been looking forward to traveling alone. If things went poorly I'd appreciate the company. I'd gotten used to being alone, except for Jose. I'd never gotten too close to the other hands. Not that there was any animosity, I just didn't feel the drive to be social like most folks. Something about me just kept most men at arm's length. Jose was the exception, probably because we understood one another's nature.

"Amigo, see you in the morning." Jose said, rising from his chair before I made it through the door.

"You will. Someone has to help ya pack all that frilly mess." I laughed over my shoulder. "If I'm lucky, my trunk will be in early."

Ten minutes later I was laying in my bed listening to the surrounding noise. It took me a while to fall asleep, my mind just wouldn't quiet down. When I did find sleep it wasn't restful. Every creaking board woke me up, but I knew that wasn't it. It was the mix of excitement for the future and sadness with leaving the family I'd built out here.

# CHAPTER 7

The predawn light saw me slowly stretching on the balcony again. This time, things had settled in me. Somewhere during the night, I'd said my farewells and accepted the change. Nothing change how I felt, but it did help ease my mind. Like most things in life, you had to settle your mind around something and that always took time. Slowly working through my routine, acceptance had found the right place to put everything. It let my thoughts focus on the future, slowly working out the complications ahead.

My feet were stretched out on the boardwalk when Jose joined me. We'd made arrangements to rent a buckboard after breakfast. We didn't need anything that big, but it would make moving everything easier. Neither of us said much as we sipped our coffee. That silence continued when Max joined us, a familiar ritual we'd long practiced. There was nothing awkward about it, just three men whose paths were diverging in the ever-changing landscape of the west.

The oldest already established ing his place and secure. Another starting a new life with a woman far better than he deserved. The last a young man just starting out, heading off to find his future. It wasn't a unique story, one that had been played out time and time again as America grew. It went all the way back to the first families in Virginia. They'd started their stories thousands of miles away, boarding a ship bound for India. The story predated even that, probably back to the first days of man.

Breakfast was filled with talk of cattle, horses and trails.

We'd all made our peace with the change. There was no need for further conversation on the topic. Moving things around that day was mundane and done without trouble. Smythe groused about Jose taking up too much space in his wagon. Then he complained about our packing job. The only change came when we had finished. Smythe spoke up before we stepped to our wagon.

"JC, you're welcome at my fire anytime. An if'n ya ever need just send word." For the normally cantankerous man, it was damn near gushing.

"Smythe, same is true for me. I couldn't have picked a better man to share the trail with." I meant it. The man had stuck through it all. Despite his grumbling, the man had been there every time he was asked.

Without another word, we shook hands and I stepped up to buckboard. During the ride back into town, I managed to wrangle the knot in my throat. For some reason, that brief conversation with Smythe that choked me up. I couldn't make sense of it at first. It took me a while to make sense of it. The man had patched me up more than once, but it was the love he shared with Tante and Binda that got me. All three of them shared a passion for making food, more then that it was part of who they were. Somehow he'd become a connection to them I hadn't been aware of. Jose seemed to recognize it before I did. He held his silence until we reached the edge of town. When he slowed the wagon to blend with the traffic, he spoke up.

"People like that are the hard ones. The ones who fight but give us more than bullets or money."

"You been reading them philosophy books again?" I let out a tight laugh, knowing he was right. I had bought him a few books on the subject and he had taken to them like a duck to water. It made me wonder what he could have done with a formal education on the subject. His mind was quick and he really did notice the abstract concepts most men missed in life.

"I much prefer being the wise old sage to the gun hawk." The grin that split his face made me laugh.

"You're gonna drive Cass insane with that wise old sage bit, but your kids will love it."

"You know she hates that name." He chuckled at the memory of her wagging a finger at me the first time I used it.

"Wouldn't say it if she was here. Even I ain't that dumb."

I got lucky and my trunk had arrived on the morning train. Jose helped me pack everything in it once we got back to my room. Most of it was winter clothes and spares I couldn't carry with me. He looked at me funny when I wrapped the scatter gun in its holster and stored it. I'd decided last night to leave it behind wrapped in wax paper and oil.

"Different trail, doubt I'll be anywhere I can't wear my Colts. If I miss it I'll send for the trunk."

"Traveling alone it is not a bad thing to have."

"That's why I'm going to pick up a new one. Can't say I won't need its effect, but I want one that does more than one thing." He understood what I was saying. The sawed off had just one use, a full-size shotgun was good for hunting as well.

"I was curious about the shells you kept, amigo. The idea of you only having four guns was a mystery to me."

"That pop gun just doesn't take up space." I patted the spot where the derringer was tucked in a pocket.

"And down to only two knives."

"Three if you count the Barlow." I laughed, pulling the wagon to a stop in front of the livery.

"Amigo, some day you will stand up unarmed and I think float away into the sky."

We returned the wagon and spent the rest of the day loafing around town. We ate dinner at the hotel and spent time at the saloon without any problems. Now we were back in the chairs out front of the hotel, sipping coffee.

"Jose, you can always reach me through Wells Fargo if you need. Might take some time, but I'll come."

"Same amigo." Was his only response before pushing off the rail he'd been leaning on. "Day starts early, amigo. I will see you again."

"You will, and I expect to find you wrangling a pack of kids when I do." I stood, extending my hand.

That was it, a firm handshake and he strode up the stairs. Watching his back fade into the gloom, wondering when I would see him again. There was no doubt it would happen. Something connected us, there was just telling when that would pull us back together. Sitting for a bit longer to finish my pipe my mind tried to picture him with kids running around. It brought a smile to my face because I knew he was going to be a happy man. It was the last time I'd see him for now, tomorrow mornings coffee would be just me. The Bar C riders would be at the chuck before dawn, getting ready to head home.

That prediction proved true. The following morning I sat alone sipping coffee for the first time in three years. It was an odd sensation and somehow the dawn didn't seem as bright. The colors still splashed across the landscape, showing off its beauty, but something about it was lessened. I couldn't throw off the slight melancholy that came over me, it just wasn't willing to fade just yet. That would take time. What shocked me was how little time it took.

By the time I walked out of the eatery, it had been replaced with a growing anticipation. My first stop was a livery at the far eastern edge of town. Luke had told me the owner was trustworthy and knew both men and horses. I noted the stores I'd hit later that day on my way there. A decent mercantile I'd been in with Jose, a gunsmith and the leather shop. The later was located right before the livery, so it would be my next stop. The sign swinging from the barn loft read Mad Mick's Livery.

"Howdy young fella." The short old man sitting out front whittling on a stick said.

"Wouldn't happen to be Mad Mick, would ya?"

"Nope, that crazy bastard run off years ago, just can't reach the sign." His cackling laugh sounded like a dry fire popping. "Names Buddy. Most folks' jus' call me Bud."

"Well Bud, I need a pack horse."

"Nope, ya want a pack mule, or 'nother horse cause yours

ain't worth a damn."

"Got a fine horse, but why a mule? I've used a few horses as pack animals before."

"True enough, horse 'ill work in a pinch, but if'n yer shopping for one then get the right animal." He spat into the dust beside him before continuing. "An that's a mule. Got a damn fine one too, some crazy fool even broke'em to a saddle."

"So you shouldn't ride a mule?" I knew punchers that swore mules were a better mount, especially in the mountains.

"Anyone with a lick of sense would know to ride a mule. Jus' learnt long ago try'n to convince a cowboy ta ride a sensible animal was like teach'n a pig to read. Waste of time an just annoys the pig."

"You've convinced me, show me this miraculous animal." I laughed, liking this man instantly.

"Good ta see a young fella will'n to learn." He stood on widely bowed legs and motioned for me to follow him around back to the corrals.

The animal that stood in the corral surprised me. I didn't have much experience with mules other than Smythe's team. They were a matched pair of brown with darker manes. This animal was a dapple grey with four black socks. The tail and mane matched the legs, but what really surprised me was her height. The molly stood almost as tall as Shade.

"That's an impressive animal." Was all I could say.

"Got one downside. Some ol' fool went an named her Wisp. Musta done it when she won't so damn big."

"How's that a problem?" I asked, thinking it wasn't a bad name. I had turned to face Bud and was a bit surprised when the animal in question stuck her nose out to snuffle the old man's hair. "I'm starting to wonder who that fool was."

"Ain't gonna comment on that, nor who broke her to a saddle." The little man glared at me then mumbled, "damn fool animal grow'd like a weed."

"How old is she?" I asked, reaching to scratch behind the mule's big ears.

"Bout five now, ain't stopped act'n the fool, but don't buck no more." He snatched his obviously already chewed on hat from the mule before continuing. "Tricky one sometimes, but she's solid on the trail an won't balk from gunfire. Don't like Injuns neither, tends ta try'n kill'em. Same for bad men, least wise the ones she 'cides is bad."

"Reckon I must pass her test." I laughed as Wisp leaned into my hand.

"Yup, can give her ta ya for sixty dollars. That'll include a pack saddle an tack. If ya want some bigger panniers I ain't got'em. Just got two smaller ones I can toss in."

"That'll be fine. Need a sheath for shotgun if ya have one around."

"I got a decent on round here. When ya want ta get it all?"

"I'm going to move my horse here, so both animals are in one place. Leaving tomorrow after breakfast unless something comes up."

"Good idea, give 'em a chance to get associated."

"How much to feed and staple them tonight?"

"Make it an even sixty-five an I'll have 'em ready for ya. Even load the packs."

"I ain't agreed to that price yet."

What followed was a dickering session that rivaled the one I'd had with Vick back in Lisbon. In the end, we settled on fifty-six dollars for everything. I had to admit the old man was sharp when it came to price. I wasn't sure who won, but I didn't feel like I lost by much if it was me. The look on his face when I rode Shade up was worth it.

"That's a true Nokota Blue." He whispered in shock. "Ain't seen one of them in years. Don't get'em this far south often."

"I picked him up in Corpus Christi a few years back. He don't try to buck me off like he used to, about the same age as Wisp."

"Seen a few of 'em back in my wander'n days. Fine horse flesh an he looks well trained." I had to admire the man's eye for horses. Stepping down and leading Shade inside to strip off his tack.

"He's a damn fine cow pony." I admitted proudly.

With his help, we got the tack stripped off in short order and turned him out with Wisp. We stood by with ropes just in case they had a real disagreement. Both of us let out a sigh of relief when the molly took to my big blue stallion. It wasn't the love affair for the ages but they weren't going to kill each other. That was all that mattered to me.

"That's settled. I'll have 'em both ready to travel in the morning." Bud said, hanging his rope back up.

"I'll have some supplies sent over today from that big mercantile. If ya don't mind, I'll sleep in the hay loft tonight and help out in the morning?"

"That's fine by me. Lock up about dark, but if the doors locked just slide in through the corral door. Don't bother lock'n it, course with you takin her I might have ta." His eyes gave away just how much he would miss the animal.

"Works for me. Any chance at some coffee in the morning?"

"Be ready a'fore the sun." He laughed.

"It's a deal then." I smiled, walking away. Since he sold me the tack there was no need to stop at the leather shop anymore.

I decided to get my trail supplies before going to the gunsmith. It wouldn't be much, just food, tobacco, and camp supplies. That was what I thought, anyway. To my surprise, I found a grill to fit over the campfire, a small cast-iron skillet, a coffee pot and a new coffee cup. I added two more canteens and some feed for the animals. On a whim, I picked up another bedroll with a tarpaulin. Replaced a couple of shirts that were headed toward worn out and picked up a new pair of Levis. The last additions were a bottle of whiskey and some plain white cloth. Smythe had taught me enough that I could clean a wound and bandage it in a pinch. I also picked up a new sewing kit, it would work if I needed to stitch myself up or mend my clothes.

The last thing that got added to the growing pile was a new pair of boots. After three years, mine were beyond broken in and bordering on falling apart. The biggest motivator was finding a pair of Hyer boots. It was a new company, and they were pretty sought after. The clerk told me another puncher had ordered them special but never picked them up. Finding them in my size made it too much of a coincidence to pass up. I already bought new buckskins not long ago and the moccasins were still good. Last year I'd picked up a new bow. It was pure luck to find another big horn bow this far south. A down in his luck miner in Dodge had it. Swore he got it as a gift from a Shoshone war chief. I doubted that but it was a beautifully made bow.

That checked off everything I would need and more from the mercantile. The only must left on my list was the gunsmith to find a shotgun. They had a new Greener twelve gauge in stock. I already had plenty of shells for it but still bought an extra hundred 44-40 cartridges. The last thing added to my bill was restocking my cleaning supplies. By the time I finished it was time to find some dinner, which meant back to the hotel one last time.

Eating there was strategic, after the meal I could move my saddlebags over to the livery. I wasn't terribly surprised when Luke come in the door looking around. Waving until he spotted me across the room, his presences wasn't really a surprise. The corners of my mouth twitched up as I watched him make his way over. For a professional gambler it was easy to read his face. I'd be going it alone after all.

"JC, glad I found ya." He said before dropping into the chair across from me.

"Change of plans?" I smiled at his surprise while calling the waiter over. "Eaten yet?"

"No, but wouldn't mind joining you. How'd you know?" The waiter took our orders, steak with all the trimmings. After switching the coffee pot on the table, the man left us to our conversation.

"Educated guess. Don't worry about it."

"Feel like I should."

"Big card game, I'm guessing?"

"Telegram just found me this afternoon. There's a big money game in Corpus Christi. Couple of ship captains that only get together every few years."

"You don't have to explain, Luke. It's how you make your living." I tried to assure him it was fine. "I take a man as he comes. You're a gambler, that's part of who you are as much as what you do."

"Can't say you're wrong, my friend. I do appreciate the understanding. That hasn't always been my experience."

"If I expect a man to accept my nature, means I have to accept his."

"I'll pick up the check by way of apology then." He laughed.

"The best meals I eat are the ones I don't have to cook or pay for."

"You sure you're only twenty?"

"Nineteen. Got a few months before twenty."

"That ain't better!" He laughed loud enough that we got a few looks.

"Let me ask you something, and you can tell me it's none of my business." This crazy idea had come to me the other night and now I had a chance to ask.

"Fair enough."

"You ever have anyone stake you at poker?" That got his attention, and he locked eyes with me.

"Once and it didn't go well. He thought of it as a sure thing, but despite what every gambler will tell you, it ain't true." He grimaced at the memory. "Cost me a good friend."

"Over losing money?" That took me by surprise.

"Found the story out later, but it was too late by then. He was gambling too, but didn't tell me that. Thought he'd staked me with extra money, the fool had done it with every dime he had. Ended up losing his ranch an family all because of it."

"That's …I just don't…." I didn't know what to say to that. It was about the stupidest thing I'd ever heard.

"Yeah, by the time the full story reached me I was just getting my stake back up an couldn't do anything for him. He went bad after that, ended up hung in the nations a few years ago."

"Never mind the question."

"Appreciate the thought." He said over his coffee cup.

I spotted the waiter coming with our food and the normal silence fell over us as we ate. It gave us time for the past conversation to fade and by the time we finished, the heaviness was gone. After dinner, Luke walked with me to drop off my stuff at the livery. He was expected at The Busted Trail tonight and I was tagging along for a beer.

"Reckon I might see ya in Los Angeles, but ain't never a guarantee." He said as we leaned against the bar. I was sipping on a beer and he was getting ready to take a seat at the poker table.

"I'll ask around, but if I don't find you I'm sure our paths will cross again."

"Till then." Luke stuck his hand out, and we shook. "May the road rise to meet ya my friend."

"And the wind forever be at your back."

My response got a laugh from him before he shook his head, walking toward a seat at the far table. Watching him was interesting. His friendly face gave away nothing about his skill at the game. A couple of men recognized him and got up from the table, but it didn't even slow the game. They were quickly replaced, and the money started moving. Tipping my hat slightly to Luke after finishing my beer, I headed to the livery. Bud had locked up not long ago, and I found him sitting on a stump in the back door sipping a cup of coffee.

"Grab ya a cup, youngster." He pointed to another stump I could roll over to sit on.

"Think I might." I chuckled, maneuvering the makeshift chair into place. After taking a sip, I had to ask about the flavor. "What's that bite?"

"Chicory got a taste for it years back. Just don't like coffee without it nowadays."

I sat in silence, savoring the flavor that called back

memories. The last time I'd had chicory in my coffee was healing from that cut back on the bayou. The subtle flavor brought back a flood of memories. Watching the stars above, I wondered that had happened to the folks who'd saved me. Things were still tense and from what I heard. They'd stopped funding the reconstruction back in '74 and things were changing again in the south.

"Didn't know you could find it around here." My comment finally broke the silence.

"Can't usually, but got a friend comes by with some occasionally. Keeps me in good supply." After that, we both sat just listening to the night.

The song was louder here at the edge of town. I could hear more of it too. Bud was listening to his own version because we both sank into a silent reverie for a while. Each man lost in his own thoughts and memories. The faint smell of his tobacco mingled with the coffee and horses didn't take away from it. There was a familiarity to those things in my mind, they were comfortable. My mind calmed, not the cold calm of conflict but the peace of acceptance.

Tomorrow I would be off on the next part of my journey. Now that everything was done, I could just appreciate that. Look forward to seeing new lands, learning more about the song that called to me so strongly.

# CHAPTER 8

In the soft light of predawn, I was up slowly working through my routine behind the livery. Bud wasn't far behind me and he started the stove to make coffee. To my surprise, he also started some bacon and eggs. Offering some biscuits that I had planned on for breakfast add to our feast. It was honestly better food than anywhere else in town. We ate in silence before getting to work when there was enough light to see.

He helped me get the pack saddle on and balance the load in the panniers. Wisp seemed to laugh at the weight once everything was loaded. She was a beautiful animal, and I was curious about her gait. Her confirmation was almost identical to Shades in many ways. Everything about her said she would match his pace all day, never falling behind or slowing them down.

"Put new shoes on her yesterday, checked his too. Ought to get ya where you're go'n."

"Thanks Bud, I meant to ask."

"All part of it to me, ain't letting an animal leave here without being damn certain they're ready for the trail. Where are ya headed anyways? Don't answer if'n it's none of mine."

"No secret. I'm headed to California but doubtful it'll be a straight route."

"Golds all been claimed, can't see a reason to go if not that. The best trails aint never straight." He laughed at the last, grinning in a way that said he knew exactly what I meant.

"Started in New York, just going to see the other ocean."

"Had that smell about ya. Goin ta see the elephant is what I reckon."

"Fiddle-footed were the words used." I grinned, recognizing the saying he'd used as something Tom had said.

"Betcha the man who called ya that been down a few trails. Prolly made a few of 'em." I was tightening the cinch on Shade as we talked. "Ya want this here scattergun on the mule ta'other side of the blue?"

"With me." He stepped forward and hung the scabbard for it before I put my saddlebags on.

"You take care of Wisp. She's a fine molly an will take care of you." I could hear a hint of sadness in his voice.

"I will." Looking over my shoulder, I caught him slipping half an apple to her.

"Got her from a fine mare, owner didn't know she was carrying when he sold her." He scratched his chin in thought before changing his mind. "Think'n back, that ain't right. He was dead, got the mare when he couldn't pay."

"Deadmen have a hard time paying bills." I chuckled, while securing the lead rope before leading them both out into the soft light of dawn.

The color had returned to the morning. They almost looked brighter now. The haze I'd felt yesterday was replaced with my desire to see what lay ahead. The array of color was slowly spreading across the town. Bright hues of gold pushing the shadows into shapes, slowly creating a second town laying on the ground. The dancing dust swirled down main street in the morning breeze. It almost seemed like the wind was calling me to follow it. Dust devils teasing me with their freedom but promising to lead the way.

"Funny how 'at works. Mind your back trail young fella an stop by if ya have a mind too."

"A pleasure Bud."

I shook the man's weathered hand before stepping into the saddle. With a quick flick of the reins, Shade stepped out into the street with Wisp pacing him. Soon Fort Worth was just another shadow in the distance and the open land of central

Texas sprawled out ahead of me. The new day's sun sparkled off the quickly evaporating water on various plants. Diamonds recreated every day, disappearing into nothing before anyone could take them. A coyote scurried from under sage brush chasing a jack rabbit into an arroyo. Small farms scrabbled out a living next to ranches where longhorns grazed. It was both new and familiar all at the same time.

Slowly, the evidence of mankind passed. Leaving only a slight road to follow in it's wake. It took longer to leave it behind now, the growing population stretching its arms out to take in more of the wild land. My plan was simple for now. Follow this trail to Fort Griffin and its more violent neighbor, Hide Town. It was one of the places I'd been warned about on the new Western Trail. I could resupply there, but it was becoming a known town. Full of buffalo hunters, soldiers, and drovers. The accompanying men and woman that came with them, soiled doves, outlaws, thieves and drunks. Jose didn't seem concerned with me going, but Chet had strong opinions about the place.

"Ya make it outta that hell hole without throwing or catch'n lead, it's by luck." He'd told me that last night.

It wasn't that I doubted his words, but it was the most direct route for now. That's what I needed for crossing Texas. After that, it would all be new land. From there I was going to make for Tularosa. After that, I'd have to see either north to Albuquerque or west to Fort Goodwin. I was leaning toward the northward route because once I turned west, it would be a direct line to Los Angeles. At least according to the map I'd studied while sending mail to my mother. Between here and there was a lot of open ground. All of it claimed by Indians, hard scrabble farmers, outlaws, and any other mix of folk between good and bad. Thinking about it all made me smile. There wasn't any fear, just the steady hum of the land and the dancing wind teasing me to follow.

I was going to take a piece of advice from Jose. When I make camp tonight, JC would take a vacation and JJ would be born.

There was a union calvary hat riding in a pannier for that very purpose. I had no doubt there would be trouble on this trip. Some of it might involve a name of one kind or another. Rather than having to adopt an alias later, I was taking one on from the start. It wouldn't be fool proof, hell it might not survive a glance. Then again, maybe it would keep problems from haunting me later in life.

That first night, I made camp at the back of a small mesa that blocked the wind. There were enough boulders around me to offer cover and let me have a fire. A steady seep not too far away left a small pool of water for the animals and myself. Having the chance for a hot meal wasn't going to happen often, so when it did, I planned on taking advantage of it. Besides, I wanted to try out my new camp setup. Using smaller rocks to build a ring around my fire pit, they balanced the metal grill above the fire. I had to admit, it made cooking a lot easier. Sadly, it didn't do much to improve my skills, but it helped not burn everything.

Leaning back against a warm rock, I ate my dinner of beans and fatback. Using the left-over grease in the pan to warm up a couple of biscuits Smythe had given me. While I ate, my mind was turning over the new persona I wanted to create. Something wasn't right with the name, not that it didn't suit me, but it felt too disconnected for some reason. I didn't want to make it easy for people to recognize me. Looking up at the stars just letting my mind wander over the problem, it hit me. I had been mistaken as a half breed twice. Why not lean into that?

My tan skin, earned from long hours under the Texas sun, and long hair lent itself to the assumption. There wasn't a single Indian that would make that mistake, honestly no white man who took more than a second to look wouldn't either. Thankfully, they usually didn't look deep enough more than willing to let their prejudice fill in the blanks. The only name I would give would be Walker. If someone like Jose came looking, he'd make the connection with Grey Walker. To everyone else, I would just be another half breed. Some might pick a fight just to do it, but most people just ignored them. To add to that assumption, I dug into the bottom of my saddle bags. For once, my habit of not throwing things away was paying off.

My new bow had come with two golden eagle feathers threaded with beads over porcupine. They had been tied to the bow but might have given away my position. They were too beautiful to just throw away, and I felt like it would have been disrespectful to throw them out. Now I had a reason to use them and hoped it wouldn't be seen as sacrilege. Using some piggin' strings, I made a simple braid around the base of the hat and attached the feathers to it. It still didn't look right, so I took it apart and tried again. This time when I braided the leather, I coated my fingers with some soot from the fire. That gave it all a properly aged look.

Finally satisfied with the hat and my new identity, I leaned back on my saddle. Absently, I took my regular hat and rolled it carefully around the black hawk feathers. Then I rolled it in with my buckskins, making sure nothing would damage the feathers. Leaning back with my last cup of coffee, satisfied with my new disguise, I let the song fill me. I hadn't intended to, but slowly it sang me to sleep. The land had tricked me into slumber just so it could kill me. It would have succeeded if not for a particular mule that hated Indians.

Waking up to a wet face wasn't pleasant. The tongue of a mule licking your face has that effect. Wisp was standing over me, silently snuffling my hair. I pushed her away, trying to figure out what was going on. She was staring at the opening between two boulders. I didn't know her well, but recognized something was going on. Slowly, I eased myself behind a boulder with my new shotgun. Silently pulling my saddlebags under my now empty blanket, then crouched back with my thumb across both hammers. It wasn't a long wait. Two shadows moved like wraiths through the opening. One split right, the other left. I couldn't get both with one blast and didn't want to risk hitting Wisp, who was standing stock still in a shadow to my left.

In one smooth motion, I locked the left hammer back, rising to my feet at the same time. The barrel swung to face the man on the right and my finger caressed the trigger. The twelve-gauge pellets spewed through the flames toward the shadow crouched along the wall. Each whistling their own song of death for half a second before they arrived at their intended target. Their impact picked up the man, launching him into the rock behind him. There was a squelching sound, and the shape fell in a crumbled heap on the ground. Even in the dark, I could see the stain on the rock.

Turning to face the other man, my thumb locking back the right hammer only to discover I needn't have bothered. He had spun to face the noise and Wisp struck from behind him. Her front hooves made contact with the back of his head and a cracking sound followed the impact. He pitched forward, a load snap echoed around the boulders just before he hit the ground. It announced his departure from the land of the living. If his skull being kicked in hadn't done it, the broken neck would.

Wisp stepped lightly back into the shadows silently. The hairs on the back of my neck stood up. I had one shot left in the Greener. There was enough space between me and the entrance to make it work. Moving to my left quietly in case someone out there had a line on my position, I waited. The barrel pointed down the narrow space. The hammer was locked back and ready to fire. I just needed a target.

Out of the darkness, Shade nickered loudly. It was evidently all they needed as an invitation. Two more figures darted through the gap. I let go with the single shot, aiming between the two shadows where the rocks narrowed. They both spun in twisting circles before falling into the darkness. I'd hit them but doubted they were dead. The echoing boom of the shotgun had temporarily deafened me, making it hard to hear anything. It was too dark to trust my eyes, and now my ears were useless. The Greener fell on top of my bedroll and my hand filled with a Colt, my thumb holding the hammer back.

This time, rising to my knees in the deep shadow of a mesquite tree, I waited. Either my ears would quit ringing or a shadow would move, giving me a target. The latter happened first. A shadow rose shakily to their feet, silhouetted against the starry night sky. They meant to stagger forward, trying to get behind cover. Unfortunately for them, it was only cover from me, not Shade. He evidently felt left out of the action.

With no warning, his front hooves lashed into the deep shadow. This time, I was glad my ears were still ringing. Watching him move, I could remember the sound from the stables at the Red. It wasn't one I wanted to hear again. Wisp stepped out of her hiding place and brayed loudly. For some reason, my mind remembered a lion roaring their challenge to anyone that might take it up. I'd seen one in a zoo years ago but could still remember that sound. Nothing answered from the darkness, but it did seem to clear my ears.

Easing out of the shadow, holstering my Colt before I tossed some fresh wood on the fading embers. A couple of breaths later, they caught on the dry wood, lighting up the small area in dancing shadows. It was enough to let me see the dead men. Four Comanche, they must have seen me earlier and trailed me here. Probably getting water at the seep, reminding me again of the old rule. You never sleep by water. It attracts predators and prey in equal amounts.

It was my fault. There had been some paintings on a rock near the water that caught my attention. I'd spent too much time copying them in my notebook. A stupid mistake and one I wouldn't repeat. I was on my own out here and made an easy target for anyone looking. The animals with me just made it a more attractive idea. Guns, food, and supplies were worth more than gold in the open country. A mule and good horse couldn't be valued, they were worth that much to people living out here.

Taking a few minutes to calm and check on the animals

while the coffee warmed up. They both seemed fine, there wasn't a lot of light but they both stood even and didn't flinch when I moved them around. I'd have to spend some time cleaning them tomorrow morning before we left. Contaminating the seep was the last thing I wanted to do. They'd have to wait until we found a stream or river to get clean.

After a cup of coffee, I set about the grizzly task of dragging the bodies out of my camp. I didn't mind the two Winchesters. They went into the packs along with their knives. Their ponies were about fifty yards away, tied in a loose group of sage I'd seen earlier. It was the first place I looked because I knew it was there. The place would be perfect for camp but wouldn't have let me make a hot meal. It was too open, and the fire would have been seen for miles. They were decent looking mustangs, not a saddle or shoe between them. Getting them back to my rock enclosure was easy. After tying them in the back near Shade, the lone stallion in the group eyed him for all of two seconds before stepping down. I had to give the little mustang credit, that was his best option. We should make Hide Town tomorrow afternoon. It wouldn't be hard to sell them there.

Using the firelight, I cleaned both the Winchesters and my Greener. One of the rifles was so dirty I didn't think it would fire at all. That didn't matter since neither of them had cartridges, which explained why they had attacked me. At least it was another reason for it. Mostly it happened because I was a lone man with two animals and made a stupid mistake. While cleaning the guns, I thought about Wisp. I had laughed when Bud told me she hated Indians, but maybe there was more to it than that. She had recognized a threat, woke me up silently and ambushed one of the attackers. I might need to rethink my opinion of mules. I'd heard stories about them being good lookouts and she had just proved that true. Sleeping wouldn't be as dangerous with her around.

The sun's first rays were slowly creeping across the land by the time I finished cleaning the guns. Climbing up on top of a boulder to enjoy the view and scan the land around took my breath away. I had meant to make sure the four dead men didn't have friends looking for them. That wasn't what stole my breath though. There was something about watching the light slowly spread over the land that did it. The dark and shadows seemed to fight for every inch of ground they gave up. Shadows slowly shrank, hiding behind trees and in deep arroyos. Far off to the west, a canyon looked like a slash of darkness across the color splashed walls.

It always amazed me, the way it all danced before my eyes. After three years, this show still enthralled me. First, the deep purples took the front lines, the deep rich color was the infantry of the sun. They began the war, so close to the shadows they wouldn't be seen. Odd dancing shades of burgundy and reds supported them as the darkness gave ground. They were the second ranks, riflemen and support. The oranges and golds held the claimed land, the picket walls of this war. Finally, the glaring yellows of the day stood fortified, commanders and generals holding power over all before them.

Before the battle was done this morning, I slid down from my perch to eat a quick breakfast. I needed to take a good look at the animal's hooves before taking care of myself. Had I really thought about it, I might have changed that order of business. Picking their hooves clean erased of my appetite for anything more than coffee. I'd eat in the saddle later, when that smell wasn't stuck in my nose. Breaking camp was quick, the slowest part was the grill. I had to let it cool off before I could pack it away. That taught me a lesson for the future. I'd have to make sure and pull it off the fire before bedding down. While waiting, I got the two Winchesters packed and made a string for the four mustangs. That took enough time for the grill to cool off and I dropped into its spot then stepped into the saddle.

An hour later, I found a decent sized stream running beside the faint trail. After starting a small fire, I set about the gory task of cleaning my animals properly. Wisp was the easy one. She hadn't stomped on the man she killed. There wasn't much more than blood splashed up one foreleg. Shade, on the other hand, had it splashed up both front legs all the way to his chest. I had to use some lye soap to get the dried blood off his coat. After ten minutes of trying, I gave up on it. He wasn't enjoying it and the last tint of pink wasn't coming off anytime soon.

I choked down a couple of biscuits with some bacon beside the stream while Shade stomped and rolled. He was demonstrating his displeasure with my removal of his war paint. The thought made me laugh. Of all the things we'd been through, I wouldn't have thought a bath would make him that mad. That laughter cost me half an apple when I had to bribe him into calming down. Wisp got the other half for saving my life. It all made me chuckle that much more. There had to be something about me that attracted interesting trail companions like these two.

After that, we covered ground at Shade's shuffling pace. The miles flew by and around noon, I noticed the small farms were getting closer together. We must be getting close to Hide Town and the fort. After watching a cloud of dust coming my way, I took my Winchester out, laying it across my thighs. There was already a round levered in, and I kept my thumb resting on the hammer, just in case.

Four riders were coming hell bent down the trail ahead of me. It wasn't anything to me, so I led my little train off to the side and waited. When I got enough of an angle, my eyes could pick out two distinct clouds of dust. One about three hundred yards behind the other. The four in the lead wore trail clothes and had the shabby look of rough living. Occasionally, one of them would lean back and fire randomly toward the cloud trailing them.

They were only about fifty yards away from me when I finally made out the other group. They all wore union blue. Evidently, whatever these four did, the military wasn't happy about it. I didn't have much time to decide what I wanted to do, or if I even wanted to get involved. After a quick look, I could tell it wasn't needed. The four horses in the lead were fading, and the army was quickly gaining ground.

The four men must have known this and thought I looked like the answer to their prayers. They veered off the trail toward me, probably counting the horses in my string. I could see it on their faces. Fresh mounts meant escaping, my opinion on it didn't matter. That poorly planned action took away any choice I might have made. With a smooth fluid motion, my thumb pulled the hammer back and I lined up on the lead man. Shade felt me shift as I shouldered the rifle and did what he was trained to do. Stood frozen in place, letting me breathe out before pulling the trigger.

My first shot sent the man tumbling from the saddle. His body tripped the horse behind him and they both went down in a heap. Levering in another cartridge, my aim shifted to the third man and fired again. A miss, but it was close enough to throw off his shot. I still heard it cut through the air beside my head. My third shot hit him clean, and he slumped in his saddle. Another bullet tried to yank my hat off before I could change my aim. I felt the cord pull tight across my throat and its weight settled on my back. Just as I cranked the lever, something punched the last man in the back. His arms went up before he fell forward on his horse's neck.

Then I was lost in a cloud of dust. Something moved past me on the right, making me wondered if I had missed one. A horse hoof flashed by and I knew it wasn't one of them. Their mounts, winded and tired, were trying to stop before colliding with my string. I felt a tug on the trail rope, but that was it. A voice cut through the dust, but I couldn't answer straight away. Not without inhaling half of Texas. Whoever it was would have to wait.

"Call out and let us know who's in there." I pulled my bandanna up over my mouth and tried yelling through the chaos.

"Walker, the one who shot three of them."

"We'll wait for this cloud to calm down, before you decide that if you don't mind."

"Might be a good choice. Ain't much else I can do in this mess."

There were some chuckles at my response. I could hear the men and their horse around me. On a guess they'd probably spread out in a fan. It was what I would have done. There was no reason to blame them for being cautious, but it didn't exactly make me happy. Finally, the dust started to settle and I breathed out a sigh of relief when I saw my animals were safe.

The three horses still standing milled around for a bit, but once the fear faded, their instincts kicked in. They had formed a small herd with my string, probably because they were calmly standing behind my stallion. Two of them still had bodies slumped in the saddle. The third had left its saddle in the mess when they fell. I could finally make out the surrounding shapes as hazy shapes. It looked like twelve men. The center most wore a different hat and a saber. An officer, probably a lieutenant at a guess.

I could sit there worrying about them or get about my business and let them figure it out. I stepped down from my saddle after putting my hat back on. Happy about managing not to flinch when I heard a rifle lever a round in. Walking back to the horses, I took the halter of the one with the body draped over his neck. I led him out of the settling cloud toward the Lieutenant.

"Ain't got a claim on this one. Your men shot him. Want the other body?" I watched the officer's mouth open and close a few times before he found his words.

"What do you mean, claim?" I could tell he was trying to bluster, but it wasn't coming out right.

"Mounts, guns and anything else I want. They tried to rob me, killed three of them. Their goods are mine. Figure the other horse is dead. I'll still take the tack and what not." My voice was intentionally hard. This was part of my disguise. "If there's a bounty on them, I'll be collecting that as well."

"They..you can't..." The man was young, well my age anyway. He evidently didn't know what to say.

"Sir, the man is right." An older man to the officer's left spoke up. He wore sergeant's strips and looked hard enough to have earned them.

"Thank you Sergeant Cook." He turned to look down at me before continuing. "These men robbed a stage. There is an army payroll bag somewhere in this mess."

"Got no claim on that." I agreed, turning to check the two horses behind me. Dumping the body out of the saddle unceremoniously before checking his saddlebags. Nothing but the normal supplies was in that one. The payroll was in the next set. I carried the two bags back toward the lieutenant and almost chuckled when the sergeant stepped down to take them.

"One of my men put the injured horse down. We'll leave the rest." The older man spoke calmly, but his eyes studied me carefully.

"Appreciate it." I met his eyes and there was almost recognition there. Not personal, but we recognized one another's character in this great play of life.

"We're always looking for mounts. If you're selling them mustangs and the rest. Ask for Sergeant Brooks. He'll beat whatever price the livery offers." He swung into the saddle after securing the money. "Pretty sure there's a bounty on all four."

"Thanks Sergeant." I kept my answers short on purpose. My eyes scanned the men surrounding me. More than one was sneering down at me.

"Form the men in a column of two, Sergeant." The lieutenant barked before wheeling his mount around. He rode to the trail without a backwards glance.

"We also always need scouts and messengers." The sergeant added before issuing orders. "Column of two, you heard the man!"

The men scrambled to fall in behind the sergeant as he led

them back to the trail behind the lieutenant. Watching them, I noted the three men who glared at me over their shoulders. I don't think they liked me claiming the horses. Either that or they planned on seeing me about their share of the bounty.

I spent the next hour stripping gun belts, searching them, and loading their bodies over saddles. It wasn't a great haul, but I'd hold my opinion until I found out about the bounties. Two Henry yellow boys, two Winchesters, three Colts, and one matched pair of Scofields. They were the new model threes, maybe a month old from the look. The new design was probably the best on the market, but Colt still dominated the market. I might keep them for a while, try them out on some targets just to see if they were that good. There was no way I'd let got of mine. Henk's work on them alone had changed their quailty, but how I got them was why I'd never get rid of them.

# CHAPTER 9

It was late afternoon by the time I rode into Hide Town. The sign outside it proclaimed it Flat Town, to my surprise. Turning toward the fort first, I ignored the town and its staring inhabitants. Marshals should be near the fort and I'd rather sell to the army, better money or not. Finding the marshal's office was easy. It was just to the left of the main gate outside the walls. A tall, lean man wearing a star stood in the door, studying me as I rode up.

"Ya must be the one Sarge mentioned. Figure ya want the bounty on them four?" He didn't have the Texas drawl I was used to, Illinois maybe. "Names Deputy Marshal Wilkens."

"Names Walker. He did mention a bounty, as a matter of fact."

"I know who they are already. Ya can leave them over there. Got a detail coming to bury them. Bounties eight hundred, two hundred per man."

"Can ya get two hundred of it to the Sergeant? His squad killed one of them."

"He's expecting ya at the quartermaster's. Give it to him yourself, just don't tell him why. Say it's in thanks for their help. Soldiers can't collect bounties." The man's laid back attitude surprised me. He never moved from leaning on the doorframe. "Dump the bodies, already got your cash inside."

I dropped the bodies where he wanted, then led my string back toward the office. The lawman was still leaning there casually. His grin was one of amusement when I walked around the corner. Something about it and him put put me on edge. When he waved me through the door ahead of him, I didn't move. That seemed to annoy him more than it should have. The smirk shifted so fast that I almost missed it.

"Just need you to sign some papers." His snake-like eyes studied me as he spoke.

"Can't write. Bring it out here an I'll make my mark. Office is too dark to see in." That rocked him back a bit. A flat out refusal might be one thing, but when his eyes shifted to look at the dark office, he couldn't find an argument.

"Just step inside and ..."

"Too dark. Light a lamp, so I don't trip over your desk." My tone was cold and flat when I cut him off.

"I don't know why you won't come in." His voice sounded annoyed but there was something else in it too. "This'll just take a second."

"Nope." I was watching him now. Something was off about this.

His eyes shifted around, studying the area around us. He was checking to be sure no one was around. That gave me a little warning. The slight twitch of his shoulder was just enough warning. His barrel made it almost level when my Colt spoke. I'd learned long ago to trust my intuition. When I stepped off Shade, my hand had slipped the thong off my gun. The first round hit him in the chest, the second in the throat. He swayed for a second, blood rushing out of his neck, then tottered forward. He hit the hard-pack like a bag of sand and the nerves in his hand finally pulled the trigger.

"What the hell is going on out there?" A deep voice came from the darkness beyond the door.

"Deputy Marshal, just tried to kill me." I responded.

"That ain't no deputy. It's the skunk that knocked me out an locked me in this cell."

I could hear soldiers coming and didn't have any idea how to deal with this. Taking the only chance I had, quickly looping Shades reigns over the hitching rail before darting inside the shadowed office. I kicked the door closed behind me and waited. It didn't take long, voices called out from outside the office. I stayed silent until it started to calm down and then yelled out the door.

"Sergeant Cook, you out there?"

"That you breed?" A voice I vaguely recognized replied.

"You ain't him."

"I'm here. What's the problem?" I recognized his rumbling voice and let out a sigh of relief.

"That deadman tried to kill me and there's another in a cell, says he's the marshal."

"An you don't know him from Adam, that about right?" He sighed heavily before speaking again. "Don't shoot, I'm coming in."

"Don't know who ya are, but I understand the problem. Sarge will get it straight." The man in the cell spoke up again.

Before Cook opened the door, I struck a lucifer match and lit the lamp on the desk, illuminating the room. The stranger was sitting on a bunk, holding a piece of cloth to the back of his head. Cook stepped through the door, glanced at the cell, then back at me. A smile spread across his face as he took in the sight.

"Don't start Sarge, this ain't funny. Sides, ain't the dead man one o' yours?"

"He is, or was. Trash an good riddance to him. Walker, that's Deputy U.S. Marshal Wilkins, locked in his own cell. We probably ought to let him loose."

"Skunk, put the keys in the top drawer." Wilkins offered.

"Sergeant Cook, report!" The commanding tone rang out from outside.

"Is that.." the deputy trailed off and Cook finished for him.

"Yup, Major Wilkins your brother." Cooks' grin reached from ear to ear. "Sir, please come inside. We may need your assistance."

This was going to take a while, mostly because no one was moving to let the marshal out yet. Thankfully, the coffee pot on the stove was full and there were a few cups sitting on the shelf. I poured myself a cup before leaning back against the wall to watch the show.

Crisp steps sounded on the porch outside before the door swung open. The man who came inside was a match for the man in the cell. That is, if you made him look like the picture perfect officer. Both men shared the same sand blonde hair, square jaw and overall farm boy build. The marshal had a bit more trail on his hide. Tanned dark by hours on horseback, he also had the feeling of death around him I'd come to recognize. His brother could have been in a law office back east. His skin was a few shades lighter and his eyes lacked the weight his brothers had. He looked at the cell and a slow smile spread across his face. The man in the cell just looked annoyed and grumpy. The major noticed the blood on the rag and immediately leaned back out the door.

"Sykes, fetch Doc." He swung the door shut and finally noticed me. "You are?"

"Walker." I answered over my coffee cup.

"What's your business here?" He was studying me carefully now.

"Four bounties, probably a fifth now." I nodded my head toward the body I assumed was still laying in the street.

"Sir, this is the man from earlier. I believe the lieutenant named him in the report." Cook offered.

"He killed your deserter, the one who knocked me out an locked me in here." Then, with an exasperated sigh, he added. "The keys are in the center drawer, still."

"Cook, please release my brother." The major said, then he dropped his hat on the desk and stepped toward the stove. "Mind?"

"Not at all." I replied, stepping out of the way.

"You two do know that's my coffee, right?" The deputy grumbled as Cook opened the door.

"You're perfectly safe, sir." The major said after noticing the thong on my Colt was still off. Then he asked curiously. "What gave him away?"

"Said the cash for the bounty was inside. Bounties are always paid by a draft." I grinned at the major. This man was sharp.

"Was a useless soldier. No surprise he was a dumb criminal as well." The Major shook his head, filling a cup of coffee. It spoke well of the man when he filled two more and set them on the desk.

"He was another one of them given the choice between prison or service sir." Cook offered from where he was helping the deputy out of the cell. Soft steps warned every one of someone else's approach.

"Major?" The voice had the confidence of age in it.

"Come in Doc." The major poured another cup and added it to the desk. "My dear brother seems to have acquired another knot on his head."

"Of course he has. It's been at least a month since I had to stitch him up for something." Doc was evidently familiar with the deputy.

"Y'all know I'm in the room? It's not like I expected one of yours to knock me out." He tried to defend himself but he was out gunned by Cook.

"Despite how many of them he has to arrest?"

"Wasn't the last time you stitched him up from a knife wound he acquired arresting another soldier?" The major offered. The Doc didn't miss a beat.

"It was, Private Lithgow I believe."

"That was him, small man, but quick." The major answered.

"Walker, your drafts will be in tomorrow. I know who the four were. That skunk had the amount right. Sent the notice off earlier when the good sergeant told me about it." The deputy decided to ignore the japing and focus on the one person not tormenting him. "Sorry, no bounty on that last one, just my thanks."

"Glad to help." I finished my coffee, turning toward the door.

"Walker, wait a minute." Cook turned toward the major. "Mind if I escort him to the quartermaster's? He's got some mounts for sale."

"Walker, despite all this, you have my thanks for helping out my brother." He didn't offer his hand, but turned to Cook before continuing. "See to him, Sergeant, and offer him one of the vacant quarters in officer country for the night."

"Yes sir." The big non-com turned toward the door, motioning me to follow him.

After collecting my string, we walked through the remaining looky-loos toward the gate. I got some dirty looks and more than one man spat in front of me. I paid it no mind, but Cook wasn't so easy going. He spun on the man and snapped out his retribution.

"Private Wells, latrine duty starting tomorrow until you learn some manners."

"Ain't nothing but a breed Sarge." The man tried to defend, but the sergeant wasn't having any of it.

"You seem to forget that last patrol when it was a half breed who spotted the ambush."

"Well no I ain't but.."

"Latrine duty." Cook snapped and stepped toward the gate again.

"Ain't nothing new." I said quietly when he rejoined me.

"I'm sure, but I won't accept that behavior from one of my troopers. Especially from the men whose lives have been saved by the Indian scouts."

"Men have short memories." Was my only comment but Cooks' next words made me stumble a little.

"Especially dumb ones who can't tell a white man who works in the sun from a half breed." When I looked over, he was grinning from ear to ear. "None of my business. Figure you ain't wanted or you wouldn't have stopped by the marshal's office."

"I knew it wasn't much of a disguise if someone looked at me with a brain."

"I'm gonna take a guess." He smiled mischievously before continuing. "Ya knew how rough some places are and didn't want to catch a name. It's not the first time I've seen an alias build a reputation, then just disappear one day."

"Got it in one." I laughed, mostly at myself. "Heading to California in a round about way and trouble just seems to find me."

"Seems so. Four bodies in a day has to be a record. Gun hand?"

"Puncher, with a bit more skill than normal with a gun." I admitted. It did make me wonder what he'd think if he knew four wasn't much to me anymore.

"Makes sense. You don't have that feeling about ya." He studied me for a few minutes as we walked toward a large building before continuing. "Ever thought about scouting for the Army?"

"Can't say as I have, right now just enjoying my wandering. Just left a ranch in south Texas, been working there for three years. Kinda figured on seeing the country before I settle down."

"That was my guess. What about courier?" He held up his hand to stop my immediate answer. "It ain't contracted or even much of a commitment. You can take a contract or not, pick one going your way if you want."

"Do they still use them? Figured with the telegraph lines, they wouldn't be needed."

"Cut lines, intercepted messages or just not getting a connection. Security is the biggest problem. Command sends orders via courier if they need to keep it secure. More importantly, they always need'em."

"Never thought about that. Can't say as I see a benefit other than money."

"Here's the trick." He smiled, knowing I was interested. "It'll take a couple of weeks to get approval because the Secret Service uses the same couriers. That's means if you pass the check, you'll get a badge. One a US Marshal won't question."

"That ain't free."

"No, you will be required to take one contract a month for the first year. Every contract will pay for that one job and your commitment ends there."

"And the badge?"

"Lifetime after the first year, so long as you don't run up against the law. Major will know more about the rules. Pretty sure I'm not supposed to even know they exist. Only thing I do know is you can't hold two badges and can't be in the military."

"So I'd have to give up to become a sheriff?"

"Yeah, but I only know that from stories."

"Might be interesting as long as I can find a message going my way."

"Right now, so long as ya want to stay heading west, that'll be easy. Ain't nearly enough of 'em." We'd reached a building and Cook pointed to a hitching rail. "Just tie up there. We can go inside and deal with the old bastard."

I tied off my string before following him into the building. There was a counter ten feet from the door with a private leaning on it. When his eyes saw Cook, he snapped upright like a tree.

"Sergeant Cook." His voice cracked and I swear he started sweating.

"At ease Piney, go get the old man."

"Yes Sergeant." The skinny young man ducked behind a door. What might have been a roar echoed out before it closed.

"He's in a mood today. Let's grab some coffee while he chews out the private for not knocking."

He casually stepped behind the counter and filled two cups. I leaned on the counter where he set them down and we listened to whatever grizzly was behind that door roar for a good five minutes. When silence finally descended, I witnessed a private fleeing for his life. His feet never touched the floor as he vaulted the counter and ran out the door.

"What the hell do you want, Cook?" The grizzly walked out of the door, half smiling.

To my surprise he wasn't a grizzly bear, but the three up and three down strips said he'd earned the old man moniker. He did resemble the grizzly I'd pictured. Standing at least six feet tall, his shoulders almost touched the door frame when he walked through. This man could have stood toe to toe with Bull and probably win the contest.

"You know you miss me if I don't come bother you. Grumpy old buffalo soldiers like you don't have any friends."

"Not when ya bring some white boy with you. One drinking my damn coffee."

"You got a brother named Bull?" I had to ask, and a confused look flashed across his face. It quickly reverted back to the glaring look of death it had before.

"Who the hell are you?" The big man stared across the counter at me.

"Knock it off, you grumpy bastard, this is Walker. He's got a string of ponies out there for you to buy."

"Ain't looking for some half dead nags." He grumbled while filling a mug. I almost smiled when he topped ours off, but managed to catch myself.

"Wouldn't have bothered with them if they were nags. Four good Indian ponies and three outlaw horses. Got three saddles, six repeaters and three pistol rigs."

"Winchesters or Henry's?"

"Mix, mostly Winchesters. Pistols are mostly Colts with a decent set of the new Scofields." I smiled, knowing this would be a challenging session of dickering.

"Might take'em. Let's go look." The big man said, trying to sound casual. "Names Quartermaster Sergeant Jackson, an if you call me that we'll have a problem. Just call me Jackson, the rest is all military crap, an I ain't got a brother."

"You sure? Worked with a brush popper down in south Texas. Names Bull, if ya ain't related, you ought to be."

We eventually landed on six hundred eighty dollars and two bits as a final price. A crowd had gathered around to watch the contest. It took almost as long and damn near as much rough language to keep Shade and Wisp. He knew they were the best two animals standing there. In the end, he insisted they stay on base while I was in town. He claimed only their stables were suited to care for them. Honestly that was more of a favor to me. Both men made it clear taking the two animals into town would lead to more trouble than I wanted.

He filled out the draft and handed it to me. The still shaking Piney, who had come back half way through our dickering, led the seven new animals to the stables. He had tried to take my mounts out of curtesy. After Wisp tried to remove a couple of fingers twice, he left them to me. Watching his face while his boss and I insulted each other had been amusing.

"This draft will cash at the commander's office or any Wells Fargo." Jackson said, handing me the paper he'd been filling out.

"Want to see the Major or go find your quarters?"

"See if the Major has time to talk about that job after stabling my animals." The thought had been in my mind the whole time. It sounded interesting, but I'd need the details.

"Like getting shot at?" Jackson laughed.

"How else would I keep you supplied?" I shot back, making the big man grin.

"Fair point. Didn't figure you made them saddles." His laughter followed us out the door.

"Ya made a friend there, an that man don't like many folks." Cook commented as I followed him to the stables. "Can't promise the Major will see you but Top will and he knows the details."

"Either way works, just need to know more before I agree to it. Also ain't sure I want to stay here for a week, not from what ya'll told me about the town."

"If ya apply, they'll put ya up in the non-com rooms while you're here. Hell, the major might leave ya in the officers' quarters."

"Think I'd prefer to stay with ya'll."

"Funny thing I didn't mention about the curriers. Technically, they hold the rank of lieutenant when they start. After that first year, they're considered captains. Something to do with security, mostly means ya get called sir and stay in officers' quarters."

"That doesn't make it more appealing." I laughed, but he didn't miss a beat.

"It fine to give away officers rank, they ain't allowed to give away sergeants stripes." He said in a deadpan voice. "Saunders, you in there?"

He might have been joking, but it was the truth. No one got given non-com ranks. Officers could be appointed in several ways. Occasionally they even forced it on non-com's. When I'd first learned that it struck me as funny, people thought of being an officer as a privilege. To me, it always seemed like that rule protected the ranks that really mattered.

Saunders turned out to be the wrangler for the fort. He took my animals without a fuss and promised to look after them. Wisp didn't try to kill him. I decided to trust him if she did. Cook caught Piney as he was leaving and told him to take my saddlebags, bedroll, shotgun and rifle to the officer's billet. They would tell him what quarters to put them in. After that, we walked across the parade grounds toward the command building.

When we entered the commander's office, Cook actually took his hat off. The corporal behind the desk glanced up and smiled at Cook. There was no race to get to his feet this time. Either this was a different environment or he knew Cook well enough not to worry about it.

"Who ya want, Sarge? Top or the big boss? Majors tied up, Tops just hiding in his office."

"I ain't hiding ya snot-nosed kid." The voice coming from the office on the left had a familiar Texas drawl.

"Right Top." The corporal grinned before continuing. "My mistake Sarge, Top is supervising the toy soldiers on his desk."

"Figure I might be able to disturb Tops critical work for a few." Cook didn't miss a beat and spoke up before the other man could.

"God damn it Cook, get in here and quit gabbing with that mouthy squirt."

"Mind your manners, ya old war horse. Got a civi with him." The corporal reached across the desk and extended his hand. "Must be alright if that oaf is drag'n ya around, names Corporal Potts."

"Walker, pleasure to meet ya." I said, shaking his hand.

"Gotta be the one that killed the fake badge totter. Got the Major hopping around like a frog in a skillet." Top yelled from his office.

"Go on before he goes horse yelling. He needs to save that for the inspection tomorrow." Potts laughed, waving us toward the man's office.

I was surprised when we entered the office. He was shorter than me, balding, with a big handle-bar mustache. There was a hardness to him I'd seen before. He had the look of toughened leather most of the old punchers had but there was another layer of hardness there. There was no give in the man, and I understood why he was the top sergeant. Sitting behind a desk that resembled controlled chaos. The look in the man's eyes announced that it and everything else around him were all under his absolute control.

"So you're Walker." He studied me carefully before continuing. "Figured you'd be ten feet tall with all the dust ya kicked up. Instead, a whip thin breed is standing here. No, not a breed...someone trying to look like one."

"Guilty as charged." I laughed.

"He wanted to know more about becoming a currier." Cook cut off the further banter.

"Suicidal then. Right, what did you want to know?"

"Mostly about the responsibility for the first year. Think I got a handle on the rest."

"Can you pass the check? If you're wanted, they'll find out about."

"Been punching cattle in south Texas for three years before that I was in New York."

"New York?" That got both men's attention.

"Came over from Ireland when I was five. Stayed in New York

until I finished my law degree, then came out west." I wasn't sure why I was telling them all this, figured it would all come out anyway.

"I ain't asking." Top shook his head before starting to explain. "You'll be required to take one job a month the first year. Free quarters and Army prices on supplies when you're working. For paperwork, you'll be afforded the respect of a lieutenant. I wouldn't expect anyone to salute you, though."

"Sounds about like what I was told."

"Contracts could be anything from a simple run between two forts or could be all the way to the capital from California. In a case like that, the sending base will cover train tickets. The rest I can't tell ya bout till you're approved. Still interested?"

"Just wandering anyway. Seems like a way to stay busy while seeing the country." I grinned.

"Mostly seems to be a way to get killed." He grumped. "You'll cross some of the wildest country alone. Deal with outlaws, Indians, an any other number of things that want ya dead."

"Was planning on doing that on my own just to see it." I couldn't help the smile that grew across my face. "Was calling it a holiday."

"Figured ya was mad. Heard enough to know you're skilled with them six shooters an your rifle. How's your skill in the wilds?"

"I can feed myself with a bow." I grinned at the look of surprise on Cooks' face.

"Spent time with the tribes?" He asked before the Top could.

"Enough. Four of them ponies were Comanche."

"You'll do, gonna need your real name though. Names Perston, Scott Preston not that it matters, you can call me Top like everyone else."

"J.C. Stone." I reached across the desk and shook hands with the man. "I'd rather keep using the other name outside of this office."

"That's easy enough. Cook, this'll take a while. You want to wait or?"

"Major wanted him put up in officers' quarters tonite but if he's stuck waiting on approval." Cook left the rest unsaid.

"I'll get him squared away somewhere until the answer comes back." Top said, then turned to look at me. "Guessing you don't want to stay in town?"

"Marshal might not like it. Got a particular way of dealing with problems. Jackson made me leave my animals here, probably better for everyone if I do to."

"See to your other duties Cook, I'll take care of him."

"Walker, come by later. Just ask if ya don't see me outside." Cook shook my hand, nodded to Top, and left the office.

"I'll get him a tour guide when we're done." Top assured the departing sergeant. "Let's get this paperwork done."

He dug out a form for me to fill out. It was six pages in triplicate, of course. I got them filled out and handed them back to Top. He read over them, nodding, then studied me again before speaking.

"Sure ya want to do this? Don't get me wrong, we need them more and more with the Indians leaving the reservations. That doesn't mean I'm going to let you walk in blind. There ain't many who make it through the first year."

"Suits my plans anyway and lets me help out the military."

"It will that. Telegraph wires are too easy to cut down or listen in on. More than one of the southern boys knows how to read that tapping mess. Shame so many of them had to turn outlaw after the war. Lincoln's assignation was used to justify the heavy-handed reunification by far too many greedy men." The man's voice had a sadness to it that I wouldn't have expected.

"All this gets sent over those same telegram lines?" I cocked an eyebrow, trying to change the subject.

"Yes, but it's sent in code. If we don't get the proper reply, we know something's wrong. Curriers are a stop gap, won't need them eventually, but right now the lines west and north are just too fragile. Once you hit the Mississippi, most of it's stable."

"Makes sense."

"Let me see if I can talk to the Major for a second, then I'll get you squared away." He stood from his chair, heading out the door without waiting for my response. He was back in a few minutes.

"He says you can stay in the officer's billet while you wait. Got more space than we got officers right now. Potts is going to give you the penny tour since he's about done for the day. I'm sure I'll see you around."

"Thanks Top." I took the dismissal for what it was and stood from my chair.

Potts met me outside. Thankfully, our first stop on the tour was the mess hall. He told me I could take mess with the officers but I passed and stuck with him. Ignoring the dirty looks some of the enlisted men gave me, we sat at the back and ate. I wouldn't say the food was good and it must have shown. Potts said that's why they call it chow. They didn't want anyone to confuse it with food.

After that, he led me to my quarters and pointed out anything else I might need on the way. They turned out to be a small single room cabin tucked in between five others. There were two slightly larger ones that belonged to the captains. Potts pointed out the non-com quarters and the larger house that was the majors. I thanked him before stepping inside.

Someone had put my rifle and shotgun on the small table next to my saddlebags. My bedroll was lying on the bed frame. There was a thin mattress rolled up at the other end. Aside from that, the room had a small stove. I'd noticed the wood outside the door. There was a desk under one of the front windows that held a simple oil lamp and a small table under a hanging lamp with two chairs.

Thankfully, on a small shelf beside the stove was a set of dishes, a pot, and coffee pot. I started the stove after opening the back door and spotting the privy. I also spotted a pump not too far away where I filled the coffee pot. Having both doors open would keep the heat down in the small space. Once the stove was hot, I started the water to boil. Packing my pipe, I pulled one of the chairs into the doorway.

The sun was starting to slip slowly below the horizon. Watching the shadows stretch across the ground gave me a sense of peace. While waiting for the familiar sound of water boiling I rocked back watching the world go by. I heard the loud chatter from the enlisted men's barracks. Far off behind that was the tinny ringing of pianos. I'd go explore Flat Town, but not today. It had already been a long day, and I was looking forward to sleep. Maybe tomorrow I'd go find a bath.

Not long after I tossed the dregs of my coffee, I rolled out the mattress, laying my bedroll on top of it. Took off my boots, hung my gun belt from the bed frame and laid back staring up at the dark ceiling. My thoughts ran through the day like it did so many nights before. I hadn't really thought about the currier job overly much, it just seemed to suit me for now. Getting paid to go where I was planning? It was too good to pass up. Sleep came for me while I was still thinking about that.

# CHAPTER 10

The soft grey light of predawn stirred me from my bed. It took a minute to stir the embers back into a fire, the gentle heat chased away the damp morning chill. I had slid the bed against the wall last night to give myself space. Now I tossed my shirt on top of my bedroll and started stretching. My morning routine left a light coat of sweat on my upper body. A bucket of cold water took care of that while the water finished heating.

When true dawn was just starting to grey the horizon, I was sitting in the open doorway with a steaming cup and my pipe. Life on the fort started earlier than towns. I could already smell the cooking in the mess hall and hear the men rousing from their beds. I was still sitting there when the Major walked by heading to his office. He caught sight of the glow from my pipe in the darkness and stepped toward my door.

"Walker." He greeted me.

"Good morning Major."

"Understand you applied for a currier position yesterday?"

"Yes, sir."

"I have a contract if you get approval. Top said you're heading west, so it should suit your plans." It sounded odd the way he talked about his men. He must have caught the look because before I could respond, he offered an explanation. "I was a field promotion. Less than three years ago I was a sergeant. Some habits are hard to break."

"That makes more sense. Your staff didn't seem to treat you like other officers."

"Yes," he laughed, "there is a certain West Point lieutenant that finds it particularly disturbing."

"I bet he does."

"Come by my office in a few days. If what I've been told is correct, I don't think your approval will take seven days."

"I will, sir."

"And please try not to kill anymore lawmen." His chuckled followed him down the street as he turned and continued on his way.

I didn't feel like dealing with the chow hall without an escort. Thankfully, my panniers had been delivered last night. I used the skillet to cook some bacon and managed a few dodgers in the grease. I wouldn't call it a particularly good meal, but it kept my stomach from rebelling. While I was drinking the last of the coffee, a few more officers walked by. Some nodded in greeting, two scowled at me. It was about the mix I expected.

After cleaning up, I decided to risk Flat Town early in the day. Finding a bath and some more supplies shouldn't be that risky. There was also a draft that needed to be deposited. I had plenty of cash, probably two hundred, and change. Most of it was mine, but close to a hundred was from the three outlaws. I emptied out most of my saddlebags, just keeping a clean set of clothes, and stomped into my boots. The last thing I did was sling my gun belt around my waist and tie down the holster.

Settling my hat on my head, I stepped out to meet the day. I didn't bother getting Shade, the town wasn't far from the fort. Passing through the gate, I noticed the private who spit at the ground was standing guard. This time I wasn't accompanied by Cook, it emboldened the man to step in my path.

"Where you goin' breed?" His sneer told me everything I needed to know, so did the hesitant look the other private had.

I didn't even break stride, knowing he'd try to grab me. When he did, my elbow snapped out and landed cleanly on his jaw. He crumpled into a heap and I stepped over him like you would a pile of horse apples. The other private was frozen. It had all happened so fast he just didn't know what to do. By the time he figured it out, I was already stepping around the corner onto the boardwalk. I'd have to deal with the fallout from that later.

I passed three saloons before finding the barber. The man standing in the doorway was too tall and too skinny to be barber from my opinion. He looked like the undertaker more then a hair cutter. When I stopped in front of him he took a long slow look down his nose at me.

"Yes?" He drew the word out far too long, like he was trying to sound aristocratic.

"Got baths?"

"Not for .." I cut him off before he could continue.

"If the next word outta your mouth is breed, I'd rethink that decision." My voice was ice cold and full of threat. The man paled, evidently catching my unspoken meaning.

"Two bits if you want hot water."

"Fine." I pulled the expected price out of my vest and tossed them to him.

"Harold, fill a bath." He called over his shoulder after he stepped out of my way. "Last door on the right."

I didn't say anything, just walked past him and down the hall. When I opened the last door, an ogre of a man was dumping two buckets of steaming water into a metal tub. It had to be Harold. At first I couldn't understand why he was working here. Then he met my eyes, and I understood. He was touched in the head.

"Done soon." He said, turning back to retrieve more water.

I was glad he wasn't hostile like his boss. My Colt might not be able to stop the massive man. Waiting on the bench inside the door while he carried in four more large buckets of hot water. Once he was satisfied with the job, he nodded to me before walking out of the room.

Pulling a stool over by the tub, I left a Colt on it before stripping off the rest of my clothes and climbing into the tub. I managed to get mostly clean before I heard steps coming up the hall. They sounded official, probably military, if I had to guess. Too light and fast to be Cook. It might be Potts, but

I doubt it. Most likely it was a lieutenant or maybe one of the captains. Quickly rinsing the soap out of my hair before picking up the colt and locking the hammer back.

His boots skidded to a stop as he strode into the room. His mouth hung open, prepared to speak, but the gaping hole at the end of my barrel froze him in place. A cold smile spread across my face as I studied the man. I had to do it so I didn't laugh. He was stuck in place, one foot off the ground mouth hanging open.

"Can I help you, lieutenant?"

"Ahhh."

"Spit it out. My water's not gonna stay hot forever."

"You're under arrest ..."

"Get out, send Top or Sergeant Cook back to get me or I'll leave a trail of deadmen back to the majors office."

"That's not how this works!" He snapped, recovering some of his bravado. It was less effective since he still had one foot hanging in the air.

"Sir, with all due respect, you can go or stay. You're here representing a private I knocked out at the front gate. He wanted to stop me for no reason other than my blood. While on duty, he decided to block my path when I left the post. While on duty he attempted to pick a fight with me."

"That's not..." he was interrupted by more strides coming down the hall. If I had to guess, that would be Top. The look of terror on the lieutenant's face told me I was probably right.

"Sir, the Major requests your presence immediately in his office." He had stopped just out of sight.

"Sergeant, I'm in the middle of something." I was impressed the lieutenant tried to debate it.

"Yes sir, I'll tell the major." I watched the lieutenant's face pale as Top started walking away. He hadn't planned on him choosing that course of action and now he was realizing how bad this could be.

The man spun on his heels, almost falling, since he didn't have both feet on the ground. Once he recovered, well I won't say he ran, but he did the very closest thing he could and still maintain some of his dignity. I did my best not to laugh as his hurried footsteps receded down the hall. I finished my bath and got dressed, tucking my dirty clothes in my saddlebags. I needed to find a laundry if there was one, if not there had to be a river nearby. Since I was stuck here for a while it was a good time to get it taken care of.

Top was sitting in the barber's chair when I walked out front. The barber was glaring daggers at both of us. That was until I handed him another two bits to make up for the trouble. He was all smiles after that. Some men were just that easy to deal with.

"Can't make it one day without causing trouble?" Top asked, eyeing me critically.

"Wasn't another choice. He was starting a fight an I didn't get a say in it."

"Ex-private Wells ain't ever been too bright."

"Is there something below private?" I hadn't missed the ex part.

"Yup, prisoner Wells. Major Wilkins can fill you in on that. He does actually need us back there."

"I just wanted a bath. Can we swing by the marshals and pick up my drafts? Save me time if they're here. I can make one trip to Wells Fargo later today or tomorrow."

"You're all scrubbed and purty probably better to see the major first. Sides his brother aint moving yet. Let's go see what fresh hell you stirred up."

"Lead the way." I grinned, following the man out the door. Five minutes later, we were walking into the command building. Potts was grinning like a wolf when he stopped us.

"Lieutenants still in there, Top. Major asked that you have a cup of coffee while he discusses things with his junior officer."

"An Wells?" Top asked.

"Still at the Docs." Potts' grin broadened even further. "He's got to wait to be arrested. Let me quote the Doc 'a shattered nose like he'd been kicked by a mule and the concussion to match.' Least that was the last I heard."

"I didn't hit his nose." I protested.

"No you did not. That would be Sergeant Jackson who did that. When Wells got up, he stumbled in to the Sergeant an made the mistake of calling him a darkie. That's when his nose got broke." If Potts' grin got any wider, I was afraid the top of his head would fall off.

"Corporal, that'll be enough. Bring some coffee into my office." Tops was doing his best to suppress his smile. He couldn't risk showing too much or we'd all start giggling like a bunch of school kids.

"Com'n up Top."

"Walker, you're still going to have to answer for your part. Just so you know Private Stern, the other man on the gate, backs up your version of events." Then he scowled, admitting the truth. "I doubt he would have if Jackson hadn't been involved."

"Don't piss off the quartermaster?" I asked.

"Not just that, Jackson's time in the field before he got promoted plays a big part. There's damn few men here that don't owe him their lives."

"He's that good?"

"Escaped slave who lived with the Crow for five years. The man has a sense for ambushes like nothing you've ever seen."

"Here's your coffee. Major says he's ready for you, Walker." Potts stuck his head in. "Said to bring your coffee with you."

"That's a good sign at least." Top grinned as I stood, taking the cup with me. We knocked on the door of his office and waited to be invited in.

"Come in Walker."

"Major Wilkins." I said, stepping into his office.

"Close the door and take a seat." The man looked annoyed, but it didn't seem directed at me.

"Sorry for the rough start to the day."

"Wells was going to be a problem no matter what. The men who've been court ordered into the military usually aren't worth the time. Another week and he would face the noose for desertion." Then he lost some of his understanding. "However, knocking out one of my gate guards isn't something I'd like to see repeated."

"Noted sir. I'll find another way if something like that happens again."

"If you get approved as a currier it won't matter, you'll be able to pull rank if need be. That's why they're given rank after all. Most of them aren't white men and there's a lot of hatred out here."

"If that's not why you wanted to see me, sir?" I thought it might have been something else, but couldn't figure out what it was.

"Oh, currently I'm chewing you out and warning you that you'll be stuck in a stockade until hell freezes over if this happens again."

"Yes, sir. I'll look properly chagrined when I leave."

"Don't bother too much. Potts and Top wouldn't buy it for a plug nickel." He laughed. "Those two know me too well. Anyone else please tell them terrifying tales of the horror I subjected you to."

"The lieutenant?"

"He won't bother you. Only reason he came to arrest you was bad information. He ain't a bad sort, just young and dumb."

"As you say." I smiled, knowing this wasn't a place my opinion was needed.

"Stop making a trouble and get out of my office, Walker." He laughed at my very obvious political answer.

I finally managed to get the drafts from the marshal late that afternoon. Too late to make my deposits today so I'd try it again tomorrow morning. Two hundred of it would go to Cook for the men who'd helped. The rest would be deposited, a little over twelve hundred in total. Then I had to find a laundry and pick up a few more supplies for my quarters. Some better food mostly, dodgers and bacon only go so far. I was surprised to find the lieutenant waiting for me when I got back.

"Walker? If I am correctly informed." He said stiffly, taking in my appearance.

"Yes sir, I probably look a bit different with clothes on." I said it with a smile, but the man sadly lacked a sense of humor.

"Yes, as you say. Major Wilkins asked me to escort you to the officers' mess this evening. I'm Lieutenant Carter."

"Pleasure to meet you formally, sir." I didn't want to aggravate the man. No sense in making enemies for no reason.

Officers' mess was better than the chow hall. Better didn't mean good, but it was enough of an improvement to deserve the upgrade from chow to mess. Mostly, it was tense. I'd say there was an even split on who thought I should be there and who didn't. As far as I was concerned, there wasn't a reason to come back. Personally, I preferred the noise of the chow hall or the peace of my temporary quarters.

# CHAPTER 11

Easily finding the way back to my quarters after dinner, I sat down to write a letter back east. I'd sent one home explaining my plans before leaving the Bar C. It was still a good idea to tell my mother and Jacob about this new job. I doubted it would help them get letters to me outside of the places we'd already discussed. They knew the only sure place to reach me was Los Angels. It was where I planned on stopping in California.

Learning Hide Town was a nickname, the town's real name was the Flats. A cow town with a reputation for a rough and rowdy crowd. When I heard the name, I remembered Max mentioning one of the main reasons he didn't like the new Western Trail. Too many towns like the Flats that didn't keep enough law on hand to deal punchers and the businesses that served them. These same towns also attracted men on the hoot owl trail looking for information about the herds. They'd find out everything they needed to rustle them. Whiskey always made someone's tongue wag too freely.

Walking around the place wouldn't be a problem, even in my disguise. Half breeds were common on cattle trails. Outlaws and trail bosses didn't care about someone's parents. They wanted men who did the job without fail, anything else wasn't their problem. That didn't mean no one would say anything, it just meant they would have to be trouble hunting. That always made them easy to deal with. You either killed them or backed them off. I'd long ago learned that if a man was determined to fight, there was no avoiding it. Your best option was to face it as soon as they started. It wasn't often you could back one off, but occasionally you could do it. Most of the time, someone would end up six feet in the ground.

Once the letter was finished, I sat on my small front porch, enjoying the cool evening breeze. Patrols of enlisted men paced around the wall. There was also a group of three that walked the ground inside the walls. Finally, sleep called to me to its embrace. Tossing what was left in my cup into the dust, I stepped inside. There was no part of the bed I would call comfortable, but there wasn't a rock stabbing me through my bedroll. I called that a win most nights. A dreamless sleep pulled me in not long after laying down.

The faint creak of a board was the only thing that saved my life. Years of waking at the slightest change around me had me rolling out of the bed before my mind was fully conscious. On the way out, my hand filled with the hilt of my knife. A quick flick sent it spinning toward the shadow occupying the doorway. Reflex making me act as soon as my subconscious recognized someone aiming a pistol at my bed. The stabbing light of flame when it fired destroyed my night vision, blinding me for precious seconds. My body rolled across the floor while my eyes tried to recover. It was the only defense I had at the moment.

My ears were ringing from the booming report in the small cabin. Changing my direction mid roll, my shoulders scraped on the bed, but I made it work. Even before my sight returned, my left hand yanked the gun belt down to me. My right hand was filled with the comfortable butt of my Colt about the same time my vision came back. The looming figure in the door tottered back and forth twice, then slowly fell backwards into the darkness. I stayed on the floor in deep shadow. My ears stopped ringing and the rapid steps of the patrol coming this way almost felt like relief.

Calls of alarm echoed around the fort and soon more footsteps raced by on the dusty path outside. Finally, someone with a lantern caught sight of the body outside my door and the voices turned toward me. I stuck to my shadow and waited with my gun in hand. My faith in these men had dropped a bit after my late night visitor.

"Walker, you injured?" It was Potts. I hated to admit how happy it made me to hear someone's voice I knew.

"Nope. Just ain't ready to get off the floor yet."

"Don't. Stay right where you are. Top an the Major will be here quick enough."

"Come out with your hands up." Someone countered Potts' instructions. When I didn't hear Potts argue, I could only guess it was an officer.

"Thanks, but no. I'll wait." I replied to the darkness. "Lot less likely to get shot that way."

"You'll not be shot, but you've killed a soldier. I am ordering you to come out with your hands up." Now I recognized the voice. It was the lieutenant from earlier.

"Stand down lieutenant." Major Wilkins had arrived before I could argue any more. "Walker, come on out, but do me a personal favor. Leave that Colt in there."

"What Colt?" I asked, slipping it back into the holster. "That's my knife sticking out of the man."

"Who fired that damn ...oh sorry sir." Top was evidently not a fan of waking up to gunshots.

"I understand the sentiment, Top. It seems someone took a strong dislike to our guest." The major responded. I was happy to note there wasn't much humor in his voice, despite his phrasing.

"That a knife?" Cook made his appearance.

"You're late to the party, sergeant. Now, would you two mind if I spoke to the owner of the knife?" Yeah, Wilkins didn't like being woke up by gunfire either. Maybe it wasn't just punchers who were bothered by it.

"I can step outside or you can come in, Major Wilkins. I ain't armed."

"Mind your eyes." He warned as the light from a lantern came toward the door.

All I could see were shapes, but one stepped forward with

a lantern and I recognized the Major. He was half dressed and had definitely just climbed out of bed. He paused over the body to study it. After a few seconds he called Top over.

"Top, who the hell is this? I don't think he's one of ours." Another shape moved into the glow and Top crouched to look at the body.

"Nope, ain't one of ours, sir." He stood up slowly, looking around the gathered shapes. "Pearson you here?"

"Whooaa Top." Someone answered from the dark.

"You spend more time in town than most. Recognize this man?" Another shadow moved into the light, crouching down in front of Top.

"Top, I ain't positive but think he's one of Dutch's boys."

"Dutch wouldn't be dumb enough to send someone on to my fort." Top snapped, the anger wasn't directed at anyone present.

"Naw Top, he wouldn't. If I member right 'at one's a pard of Smitty. Died ta other day of lead poison'n in the marshals office."

"Robbery or revenge." Wilkins said. "Get him out of my fort, wake up my brother. Let him deal with it."

"Yes sir. Pearson, grab two more men an get it done." Top ordered.

"Mind if I get my knife first?" I asked, standing up from the floor.

"Get him off the wood before you pull it out. Don't need anymore blood on my walk." Wilkins snapped.

Pearson reached down, then dragged the body out onto the dusty road for me. I followed him and pulled my knife out of the deadman's throat. After cleaning it on the man's shirt, I walked back inside the crowded cabin. Forgetting to put on my boots hadn't been the best choice, same could be said for my shirt. I heard the gasps when the lamp light illuminated my scars.

"Mind if I put on a shirt, sir? Maybe some boots?"

"Go a head Walker. The rest of you men get back to whatever

you were doing." Then he looked around the glow and his eyes landed on the only officer in uniform. "Lieutenant Martin, you're the officer on duty?"

"Yes Major."

"Get everything back to normal. I'll expect a report on my desk before noon, one that explains how that man got here. Especially how the hell he did it in a uniform."

"Yes sir. You men disperse if you're not on duty. Get this body taken care of. Pearson, ask Deputy Wilkins to come see me once he has positively identified them."

"Yes sir."

The rest was lost on me, blocked out by the log walls. I shrugged into my shirt before stomping on my boots. When I reached for the stove to stir the embers back to life, Wilkins cut me off.

"Let's go talk in the mess hall. Coffee's already done, and it has more room." Looking around at the small crowd, I realized he was right.

"Might get a bit cramped in here now that you mention it." I chuckled while slinging my gun belt on. After tying down my holster and sliding my knife into its sheath, I picked up my hat. Following the rest of the men toward the mess hall. When we rounded the corner, I could see the light cascading out of the windows around the building. Shapes moved around inside the rectangular structure. It wasn't exactly crowded, but there were more than a few people inside.

"We use the mess hall as a watch center. The officer on duty stays there except when he checks to be sure the men are doing their job." Top explained.

"Unless you need me sir, I'm going back to bed." Cook's deep voice still sounded half asleep.

"Same sir, revelry comes early." Potts added after yawning.

"By all means gentlemen, Potts report after breakfast. I won't be in before then." Both men split off as we passed the barracks.

After telling Lieutenant Martin and Major Wilkins what had happened, then repeating the same thing three more times, I was dismissed. Deputy Wilkins showed up halfway through the second round to verify the man's identity. They all asked a few questions, but before getting half way through my second cup of coffee, I was allowed to go back to bed.

The first light of the sun woke me from the few hours of sleep I managed. The familiar exercises helped wake me up. After some breakfast, I felt mostly human again. After dunking my head in a bucket and washing off, I finished getting dressed. Braiding my hair took longer than the rest, but I was still ready before the sun had fully risen. The still unsealed envelope waited on the desk, but I wasn't going into town without knowing what was going on.

It was still going to be a few hours before the businesses opened, so there was time. Even the Wells Fargo stage office didn't open for a while yet. I had another destination in mind. Last night, walking back to my quarters, I had heard a very familiar sound. The low bawling of a herd accompanied by the hum of nighthawks singing to a herd. This morning I was going to ride out to see the rolling thicket of thorns. It was unlikely that I knew the brand. It was about the middle of the drive season and there were a hundred ranches that drove to Dodge. There was something familiar about the noise that called to me. Enough so that my curiosity wouldn't let it go. That's what led me to the stables.

While I was satisfying one curiosity, there was no reason to ignore the other one. Instead of tossing my saddle on Shade, I put it on Wisp. He glared at me from his stall, letting out a snort to protest the betrayal. Soothing his bruised ego with some scratches and half an apple reminded me that I needed to find more of them. My supply was getting short, and the ones left were getting soft. They maybe had a week left before they turned, then I'd be hard pressed to bribe my persnickety animals.

The old man watching laughed at our antics, but nodded his approval when I stepped into the saddle. He'd been around long enough to recognize a good mule when he saw one. It was written all over his face. Wisp stepped off toward the gate with quick, sure steps. Her gait wasn't as smooth as Shades, but. far better than most ponies from a remuda. More than that, she had a surety in her steps that I'd never felt in a mount. Maybe Tom had been right when he extolled the virtues of mules.

I still wouldn't work long horns on one. They lacked the survival instinct that horses had. Bull preferred mules, but swore he'd never ride one to herd longhorns again. According to him, a jack would challenge a wild longhorn before retreating. He showed me a scar that ran down his leg. He'd gotten it learning that lesson. Max just chuckled and said, 'told ya it was a bad idea.' when he overheard the conversation. Now I understood the preference though, for this and up into the Rockies I'd take advantage of the molly's sure step.

Outside the gate, a slight nudge got her to step into a cantor with no hesitation. I had to admit she rode easy, not quite the speed of Shade, but close. Going up the small hill, her steps had a certainty to them I could feel. We crested the rise a quarter mile south of the fort and stopped. My eyes took in the scene and a smile spread across my face.

There was a good-sized herd below me, dappled in a mix of shadows and the early hues of dawn. The sun had barely finished chasing the darkness away. The dancing light and shadows shifted colors like a rainbow before my eyes. Light gleamed off horns that still bore to the last drops of moisture. The slowly growing dust cloud gave the herd an almost ethereal look. Like a ghost herd rising from the underworld, slowly consuming shadowed land. A scout broke me out of my trance when he crested the rise.

"What the hell you do'in on a mule JC?" It took me a second to recognize Hank. He was one of the gun hawks for the Rocking W brand. A decent sized ranch not too far from Fort Concho. I'd met him in Dodge my second year and we'd struck up a friendship of sorts.

"Passing the day away." I grinned back at the friendly man. "Nothing wrong with a good mule so long as I ain't working cattle. Shades back at the fort."

"Ain't on the trail, then? Thought maybe Max was ahead of us."

"He took the herd to Fort Worth, sold it at the railhead there. My times was up with the Bar C so I cut loose. Ambling my way west."

"Looking for work? We could always use you."

"Appreciate the offer, but want to stretch my legs out. Maybe go see California."

"Figured I'd offer, make my life easier." He laughed. I remembered him telling me they only kept one gun hawk on for the drives.

"Still just you?"

"Boss don't want to pay fer another." He spit to the side of his horse.

"Bad business crossing the nations with just one, 'specially on this trail."

"Don't matter much, the rest of the boys are quick to pitch in. Sides, the boss pays well enough." He looked around, letting out a heavy sigh. "Course we ain't staying at the Flats, so I best get moving. Adios, my friend."

"Adios. Mind your back trail out there."

He rode down the slope, speaking to one of the trail hands, then waved up at me before heading off to find their next camp. This wasn't the first year of the Western Trail, but most of the drives didn't know it like the Chisholm. They'd be depending on Hank to scout camp sites and water on top of dealing with any problems. Jose and I had more than one conversation about that responsibility when we thought Max might take this trail. It wasn't any safer than the Chisholm, just different dangers. It avoided the fake badges in Kansas, which was the biggest problem. Outright outlaws were simpler and didn't run the risk of a judge backing them.

Sitting on Wisp, watching the herd trail by then slowly disappear into a cloud of dust, made me smile. There was a part of me that had been tempted by Hank's offer. It would be familiar, comfortable despite the new trail, but that wasn't my future. It wasn't that I'd learned everything, but my education from cattle drives was complete. My future lay in a different direction now, an unknown that I looked forward to with a touch of trepidation. Three years ago, I had thought this was all just a grand adventure. Now I knew better. There was still a sense of adventure but it had been tempered through hardships and violence. This was a beautiful country but it would kill you without noticing. That wasn't even mentioning the human threats. Part of me still didn't see myself as a true western man. In my eyes, I was still a kid learning. Maybe a step closer to being a man, but not yet. It always felt like there was so much left to learn.

Finally, giving a gentle tug on the reins, we turned back toward the fort. The old soldier who took Wisp didn't pay her any mind at all when she tried to protest. I turned toward the gate, heading into the Flat. My first stop was the marshal's office to collect my drafts. It was conveniently located near the Wells Fargo office. I suspected that was done to help keep it protected. Either way, the clerk deposited the drafts and gave me two hundred back in cash. The man managed to even look glad to see me. That money would go to Cook. He'd figure out how to pay the right men. For now I tucked it into my wallet before heading further in to town. Someone had disturbed my sleep, and I wanted some answers.

# CHAPTER 12

As far as towns go, there wasn't much to this one. More saloons than anything else, which wasn't uncommon for trail towns. I counted three of them in the two blocks that was the Main Street. That only left five other businesses to fill out the rest of the space. Flat General Store was slightly better than a trading post. Gus's barber and Dentistry stood next to that. He probably worked as doctor and mortician if this place was like a million other boom towns.

Braddocks' Blacksmith looked well built. There was a small house behind the forge with two kids running around it. I could hear the ringing of steel coming from the shadowed depths. Right next to that was a livery, probably the same owner since there was no sign out front. That just left Dot's Eats. The place was small but well kept. Like most places along a trail, there were only two ways the food could go. Really good or gut wrenchingly bad.

The three saloons were separated by other businesses one way or another. Two at the end of town nearest the fort but opposite each other and the last at the other end of the street. There was Jack Mule's Aces, Miss Lucy's House and the last place was The Buffalo's Wallow. None of them looked interesting to me and I doubted they had anything close to cold beer. What did interest me was the general store.

The small bell above the door rang when I stepped inside. It woke up the man dozing on the counter. He was in his late forties, carrying more than a few extra pounds and balding. His eyes reminded me of a rattlesnake. Cold and uncaring, he reminded me of Jersey back at Caldwells. This was an ambush predator just waiting for his prey. When he spoke, his voice had the same greasy quality I'd heard from snake oil salesmen.

"Morning stranger, what can I get for you?"

"Wouldn't happen to have any apples?"

"No sir, haven't seen an apple in more than a year." He shook his head with sorrowful remorse. Part of it almost seemed genuine. "Don't even have canned peaches."

"Eggs?" I'd noticed some carrots that looked mostly fresh. They'd do for treats.

"Fresh this morning, dollar a half dozen."

"Give me a dozen, two bunches of those carrots, a couple pounds of bacon, five pounds of Arbuckles, two pounds of salt and five pounds of flour. How you fixed on 44-40 cartridges?"

"I have some. How many did you want?"

"Two boxes should do. Let me look around for a bit while you get that together."

"I don't mean to be rude, stranger, but I'll need to see some money first."

After glaring at him for a few minutes, my hackles went up after being questioned, but eventually relented. Flashing him a double eagle before turning to look around the rest of the store. There wasn't much, honestly I didn't need what I was buying. Maybe the carrots and the eggs. The rest was extra supplies that everyone used. After finishing a loop, I picked up another bunch of carrots and added them to the stack.

"Totals out to twenty-one dollars." The fact that he said it with a straight face was what surprised me. I just stared at him, letting some of the cold creep into my gaze. The sweat beaded on the man's forehead while I waited. It only took another few seconds.

"For you, my friend, how about fourteen dollars?" It was still high, but not completely unreasonable.

"Still too much, but ain't worth arguing about." I said, handing him the double eagle and waiting for my change.

"Here you are. Did you need help get'in them loaded?" I knew he wouldn't be the one helping me. There must be a boy hiding around somewhere.

"Have them delivered to the fort. I'll let the gate know they're coming. Before you say no, I'll pay for it." Flipping him a quarter, it was more than enough for the short distance.

"Yes sir." The man looked too afraid, but he wasn't looking at me anymore. His eyes were fixed on the glass windows.

Two men were passing by the window, heading toward the door. Without thinking about it, my right hand flipped the thong off my Colt. The older man was dressed like a broker from the stock exchange back east. The other was a gunfighter. There was no doubt about the man's profession. They strolled through the door like they owned the place. Barely glancing at the nervous man before locking eyes with me.

"New in town, stranger?" The fancy one asked, as if it was a normal question. His companion was slowly walking around the shop. Trying to get an angle on me.

"Don't see as that's any of your concern. What you should be thinking about is what will happen if your friend keeps trying to get the drop on me. He's got about two more steps before I kill you." The cold was flowing through my veins now, every movement caught my eye.

"You think I won't kill you after that?" The gunny said.

"Ya might, but your boss will still be dead." My eyes never left the man in front of me. I was expecting more argument, but it didn't come.

"Fletcher, come over here." The man was a better judge of character than I thought. They still stood in my way, but that didn't worry me too much. I hadn't been bothered by the one called Fletcher. He could be the fastest gun west of the Mississippi and I wouldn't care. I just didn't want to be bothered by him.

"We have business soon enough, breed." Fletcher locked his eyes on me.

"Your dance, call the tune." I smiled at the man.

"Now, now gentlemen, let's not get ahead of ourselves." The

boss was trying to calm the situation down for now. "Fletcher, please go back to the office. Wait for me there."

"Dutch…"

"Do it now." Dutch ordered. Fletcher gave me one last look before spinning on his heels and stalking out the door.

"He'll be waiting for me when I leave." I said it simply, noting which way the man went when he left.

"He'll do as he's told. Can we perhaps start over, friend?"

"To what end?" I really didn't have any interest in dealing with this man.

"Just being neighborly is all." The man insisted.

"Won't be here long enough to need that. Likely only be around a few more days, then I'll be gone." The shopkeeper had slowly slipped behind the curtain.

"Maybe I can offer you a reason to stick around longer. Reasons that pay good money." The man was persistent. I had to give him that.

"I'm not trying to be disrespectful, but I'm moving on in a few days. There really ain't no changing that." I watched as Deputy Wilkins paused outside the door to listen before turning in. The bell ringing made Dutch turn to see who was coming in.

"Walker." He nodded to me, then looked at Dutch. I was glad the man remembered to use my alias and not my real name. "Whys Fletcher standing out there."

"Waiting for me." I said before the other man could respond.

"Won't be good if ya lose another one." Wilkins chuckled and Dutch flinched.

"I'll deal with him." Dutch said, turning toward the door. Before he left, I told him the truth of it.

"Won't matter, he can't let it go. You ordering him to leave caused this, made him look weak, it'll haunt him." Dutch walked out the door, but we all saw the slump in his shoulders. He knew there wouldn't be anything he could do, worse he knew it was his fault.

"Going to face him?" Wilkins asked curiously.

"Same as him, no choice. He meant to threaten me. Guess my response wasn't what he's used to 'round here. Then his boss sent him packing. His pride won't let it go." I shrugged, knowing there wasn't a choice. "Now or later, it'll happen. Mind witnessing it so there are no questions?"

"I'll watch, but there's nobody round here to question it other than me. I don't bother with gunfights as long as both men are armed." He looked back at me before stepping outside and offered one last bit of advice. "He's too good to wound."

I knew what he meant, recognized it in the man when our eyes met. There was only one way this would end. One of us would be lying in the street dead. Old man death was waiting for one of us. Nothing was going to change things. The deputy stepped out the door next and looked down the street before speaking. I understood the gist but couldn't hear the exact words. He was trying the same thing with Fletcher he'd had with me. When he tipped his hat after shaking his head, I knew he was done.

A quick check of my holster, just to be sure the pistol moved freely. A habit I'd learned from Tom long ago. Then I adjusted my hat lower over my eyes, knowing Fletcher would be standing with the sun at his back. Walking out the door, the familiar cold calm filling my body with each step. It let me take everything in. Fletcher was standing in the middle of the street, waiting. Dutch leaned against a saloon wall, his eyes tracking back and forth between us. Deputy Wilkins was on the wall of the general store watching me walk to my ordained position.

Everything sharpened as I stepped into the dust filled street. The breeze stirred small dust devils. My eyes watched the wind move around Fletcher's boots, small twisters dancing around his ankles. His shadow stretched out to greet me but feel short by a good ten feet. The sun was high enough that the lowered brim of my hat kept it out of my eyes, negating that advantage. Finally, my eyes studied the man standing across from me.

Even before my feet stopped, I could see the fear on his face.

The way his left eye twitched from the wind. Small drops of sweat rolling down his cheek, carefully carving a path through the dust that clung to him. This hadn't been what he wanted. The man wasn't used to people calling him out, and his boss not backing him had done more damage than I thought. He thought his words would back me off, and he'd gotten the opposite reaction. I'd answered his challenge and left him trapped by his own words. He was the bull of the walk in this little piece of Texas. I was expected to step lightly around him, but that hadn't happened. Now he was standing in the street facing a man he didn't know.

Turning in the street to face him, my eyes finished inspecting him. Carefully taking in the man as a whole. I'd learned long ago not to focus on one thing or another. You had to see the entire man from the ground up because everyone had their own tell. Some, like Jose, managed to shrink them down so small you'd miss them. He'd helped me with mine, but everyone had them. Sometimes it was an eye twitch, but it might be a slight shift in their feet. Seeing everything was the only way to get that micro second of warning. Sometimes it was the difference between life and death when two men faced one another. There was a part of me that still thought all of this was foolish, but I had accepted it as part of life out here.

Your name was all you had, even with the law standing off to the side, couldn't change that. None of that mattered in this moment. Right now the only thing that held any importance was the man across from me. He broke the silence first.

"You can just walk away, kid." He had about ten years on me, enough to fool him into thinking it meant something.

"This is your dance. Sorry you're crowing like a rooster didn't go the way you wanted, but I wasn't the one waiting." My words hit the mark. I hadn't called him out, and he knew it.

"This is my town." He said it like that meant something.

"Never claimed it, but I won't be pushed." I smirked at the man, knowing he understood. He wouldn't have done anything different in my place. "Don't matter what happens

121

here, I ain't staying. I'll be down the road and gone in a week or so."

"My town, I don't step out of the way for any man." With those final words, he'd fully painted himself in the corner. There wasn't anything left to say.

His weight shifted slightly to the left and his right hand grabbed for his Remington. I watched in slow motion as the barrel cleared the holster. Watched it start to level, the gapping hole slowly rising toward my chest. My pistol bucked, my left hand flashed by, and I felt the Colt recoil again. It was funny, in these moments I never seemed aware of what my hands were doing. My body moved on its own, following the movement it had long ago memorized. M mind stayed focused on the man across from me, aware of moving but not needing to think about it at all.

His pistol was jerked out of line, the aim shifted down an inch. Flame spit from his barrel, sending the lead that might kill me through the fire and smoke. A cloud of dust kicked up ten feet in front of me. His bullet plowed a hole into the street through the head of his shadow. The oddity of it struck me for some reason, the man shooting his own shadow. My eyes never stopped watching the red stain spreading across his shirt. The pistol fell from his hand, sunlight glinting off the metal as it spun in the air. Our eyes met for just a second, his held acceptance rather than surprise. Like some part of him had known, this was the day of his death. Maybe he had. Maybe there was some premonition about it in a dream last night. If so, maybe he should have heeded its warning and stayed in bed. Then they rolled back in his head, showing the whites.

His body teetered for a long moment, then its strength fled. First, his knees gave out. When they hit the ground, his entire body seemed to crumple. Like all his bones were no longer connected, a once living man was suddenly reduced to just a pile of things. Things that were no longer connected.

Automatically my thumb flipped open the gate, my left hand worked the rod, ejecting the spent shells. Even while the sounds still echoed between the buildings, I was dropping in two fresh rounds. Before the dust from his fall had settled, my colt was dropped back in my holster. The cold slowly receded like it did every time, and that bubble of focus faded back, letting the rest of the world back in. The first thing I heard was Dutch cursing.

"Son of a bitch!" When my eyes turned to focus on him, the man froze in place. He quickly made sure he hadn't offended me. "That wasn't directed at you."

"Didn't think it was." I assured him. "Figure you'll see to the burying?"

"I will." He answered before stepping out into the street toward his fallen henchmen.

"I'll be taking those pistols, same with the rest of his gear." Dutch froze. He hadn't planned on that.

"That's all he's got." He tried to lie, but the deputy cut him off.

"He's got a damn fine black mare. She's in the stables behind Miss Lucy's. Keeps a Winchester with his tack. Warn ya, he's got one of them fancy saddles. Took it off a vaquero he killed a while back, too much silver on it for my tastes."

"I'll buy the saddle." Dutch said as soon as the deputy finished speaking. I glared at the man before responding.

"Fine! Deputy, what's the saddle worth?"

"Easy hundred dollars." That took me by surprise. It had to be one hell of a saddle.

"Take it or leave it." I cut Dutch's disagreement off before he even started.

"Done. I'll get it from the office." The man turned and walked toward Miss Lucy's.

He wasn't happy, but he really wanted that saddle for some reason. It made me wonder about it as I walked to take Feltcher's pistols and belt. He'd worn a two gun rig, but the left was set in a reverse draw. It was what had first warned me the man was good. He wasn't some kid trying to draw with his left hand. They were the new models, with a five and three-quarter inch barrel. That wasn't what had my attention, though.

They used the same 44-40s I preferred. I'd always liked the Remingtons, but the convenience of shared cartridges always kept me away from them. There had been rumors about them releasing these, but I had never seen them before. I wasn't about to swap out my Colts, they were a gift. Besides that, I'd have to retrain my draw. Everything would be different, balance, weight, even the trigger pull. It was something that would take time. All that being said, I was going to hang on to these. Maybe work with them occasionally when it was safe. Rolling them up in his gun belt for now. I'd really examine them later when i cleaned everything. Right now, there was a deputy marshal waiting to talk to me.

"Let's walk a talk. Think you might want to look at the tack before you take Dutch's money." He was right. There was something off about the man's rush. "Stables this way."

"Know anything 'bout Fletcher?" I asked as we stepped through the alley.

"Been here longer than me. I just got assigned here last year, so that ain't saying much."

"I have a feeling there is something in that saddle or the saddlebags Dutch wants or wants to keep quiet."

"Figure you're right. How you planning on playing this?"

"Depends on how quick the man is. If he gives us a few, I'll search them now. If not, I'll refuse the sale until tomorrow, say I need the tack to ride the mare for now."

"Should have time, the man's smart. He knows full well that he tipped his hand. He'll take his time, trying to keep us from wondering too much."

We'd reached the small stables behind the saloon and I got my first look at the mare. The deputy had understated how pretty she was, standing just shy of fifteen hands. Her confirmation matched Shades with little or no difference. She was deep black from tail to nose, so dark it shimmered to purple in the sun like a raven.

"Watched him ride in on her one day. Don't think I've ever seen a more beautiful horse." Wilkins spoke as we stepped to the fence.

"I'm guessing you'll want to buy her?" I laughed.

"If she's for sale an I can afford it."

"Make me an offer." I said, walking toward the tack room at the back of the stables.

"Can't afford what she's worth. Got about a hundred and forty to spare." He knew that wasn't close to her value.

"Done." I caught the surprised look on his face when I struck a match to light the lantern.

"If you're serious, we can go by the office on the way back to the fort."

"I am. She's a beautiful animal and if I had my ranch? You couldn't pry her outta my hands. Right now though, Shade and Wisp are bout all I need or want."

The tack room was small, making it easy to spot Fletcher's tack. It was stained black to match his horse, but that wasn't what drew the eye. The fender and skirts were beautifully tooled. Flowing leaves and vines almost seemed to move in the dancing light. Silver conchs glinted in the lamp light wrapped in the vines. The saddlebags matched the rest. Who ever had tooled this set made the design flow from saddle to bags seamlessly. This wasn't a saddle, it was a work or art.

Stunning, but definitely not anything I would ever ride. It was a moving target with all that silver on it. The saddlebags were the first thing I checked. They held the normal supplies mostly: a change of clothes, matches, piggin strings, spare cartridges. Nothing I didn't expect and the only thing I took was the cartridges. When my hand hit the bottom, it got my attention. It was too shallow by more than an inch.

It took me a few minutes to find the latch under the spare clothes. What was inside surprised me. Two stacks of greenbacks in varied amounts, but it looked like easily a thousand dollars. The other saddle bag had about the same in another hidden pocket. I tucked all of it into my vest pockets, then started searching the saddle. I didn't find much, but there was a hidden pocket under the back housing between the skirt.

It was probably meant to keep documents in. At the moment, it was empty.

Dutch was coming across the corral when we stepped back outside. He didn't look happy about us being in the tack room, but knew better than to say it. Wilkins had picked up a hackamore and was walking out to get the mare. I leaned back against the fence, waiting for Dutch to reach me.

"That saddles awfully pretty, thinking about keeping it." I couldn't help messing with the man.

"We had a deal!" There was almost panic in his voice.

"True, an I don't go back on my word." I held up the cartridges and continued. "Took what I wanted, the rest is yours."

"Good," he handed me five double eagles, "hundred dollars."

"Done and done." I smiled, tucking them into my waist pocket. There was no way I'd get my wallet out of my vest right now.

We made it most of the way back to the marshal's office before his cursing echoed down the street. The deputy walked with me back at the Wells Fargo with the money for the horse. The final count was two thousand four hundred and eighty-six dollars. Not a bad addition to my already healthy account balance, I'd have to ask Jacob about some more investments soon. When I walked out, it was no surprise to see Dutch glaring at me."

"You knew!" He accused

"Knew what? About the saddlebags, not until I searched them."

"You..." I stopped him before he crossed a line.

"Careful 'bout your next words." My voice had gone cold. "You were told I took what I wanted, and that rig is worth far more than a hundred dollars. You haven't lost anything, nor have you been cheated."

He stood there red faced for a few minutes glaring at me but didn't open his mouth. The memory of his gun fighter was too fresh in his mind. Finally, the anger faded, and he accepted the truth.

"You got one over on me." He admitted coldly. "Can't fault you for being quick on the uptake."

"Leave it at that, the money's out if reach. Like I said, you and I both know that saddles worth more than what you paid so you didn't lose anything. You can happily tell everyone how you got one over on me. Trust me, I won't be bragging about the cash." He eyed me carefully before continuing.

"Walker, I ain't never heard of a breed fast as you an I would've. Figure you're running under an alias for your own reasons but if ya want a job. I'd take ya on. Whatever's in your back trail won't bother you here."

"Nope, like I said, I'll be gone soon."

"No harm in ask'n." With those words, he spun on his heel and walked away. He was still mad, but not enough to risk his life.

# CHAPTER 13

I walked back toward the gate and let the private on duty know I had some goods coming. He said they'd delivered to my quarters. When asked, he also told me Cook was in the quartermaster's office. That was his usual place if he wasn't on the parade grounds. I wouldn't have called the blank spot in the center of the fort a parade ground, but no one asked me for my opinion.

Cook and Jackson were playing cards in the back. The big door was open and there was a huge piece of canvas blocking out the sun. That was what they claimed. It also stopped anyone from seeing what they were doing. None of it surprised me. What did was the amount of insults they threw at each other while playing. I waited for Jackson to pitch his hand and call Cook a two fisted polecat before interrupting.

"Cook, I need a favor. Can you split this between the men who were on patrol?" I handed him the envelope containing the two hundred dollars.

"What's this mess you're dragg'n me into?" Cook asked before looking in the envelope. When he did, the reaction was much stronger than I expected. "Are you insane? Ain't you got no idea what they'll do with this much money? Nope, ain't given it to them."

"Give it here, ya stingy old coot." Jackson took the envelope and studied it. "He ain't wrong, but I got a work around. What I can do is put it with their mustering out papers. It'll do'em more good than. Some of 'em anyway, still be a few who waste it on ladies an drink."

"Thanks, appreciate it." I left the two men to their card game and insults.

Walking back to my quarters got me the same mix of nods or sneers. That went for enlisted and officers alike. Most still considered me just a troublesome breed, not that it made any difference to me. My goods were stacked in my quarters. The delivery must have come while I was with the sergeants.

It was early afternoon, and I set about making myself some coffee and lunch. Then spent the rest of the afternoon cleaning my pistols and the Remingtons. There wasn't much difference between the two. The Remingtons were heavier because of the frame. The longer cylinder pin didn't come out and was bigger. Their grip had a slightly different angle too, it was hard to say how that would affect my drawing speed. Fletcher had modified them like most men did. The front sight was removed. Springs on both hammer and trigger had been lightened. Truthfully, they felt pretty good in my hand, but even the slight differences would slow my speed. When it came down to pistol work, things like that could be the difference between life and death.

Comparing the two, it was obvious Remington had taken the Colt as a base and addressed the shortcomings it had. Making them out of good material and probably changed just enough to avoid being sued. They were good weapons, but they wouldn't replace my Colts without a lot of work. I was still keeping them for now. They were a damn good backup and with some practice, who knows?

It was two more days of loafing around before anything happened. Luckily, I managed to trade for a couple of new books. Finished up a couple entries in my notebook, got my laundry done, ate, and drank too much coffee. I was beginning to wonder if I could last out the week before saying to hell with it and leaving. Twice today I'd had to stop myself from just saddling up to leave. The only thing that held me here was curiosity. I was a little surprised when a runner knocked on my door that afternoon.

"Major wants ta see ya Walker." The soldier didn't even wait for me to answer, just turned and ran in the other direction. I didn't even have time to see his rank.

I couldn't imagine what he wanted, but there was no use waiting to find out. Unfolding from the chair with a slow stretch, I put my hat on and stepped out into the sun. It didn't take long to reach the command building. Potts was in his usual position, hunched over several documents with a cup of coffee balanced on the edge of his desk.

"Go one through. His royal highness is waiting for you." Potts waved me toward the door behind him.

"Do I bow or curtsy?" I joked, stepping past the corporal.

"I'd say curtsy." He said over his shoulder. "'specially with all that hair."

"If it's Walker come in, anyone else can tell Potts he's fired on your way out."

"Just me sir." I smiled, stepping through the door.

"What took so long, Lieutenant?" The man behind the desk smiled at me while tapping on a telegram.

"Guess approval came back?"

"Quicker than expected. That says something about you, but I have no clue what." He laughed before continuing. "Cause anyone with the power to push this forward wouldn't want this job."

"No clue. Don't think I know anyone in the capital."

"The telegram mentions a Jacob Ellington and James Standom? They seem to have rather high opinions of you. Ellington I don't know, but Standom is high up in the Swift organization. In case you don't know, they supply a fair amount of meat to the military."

"Ellington is a business partner." I didn't see a reason to mention he was also my father. "Met Standom in Dodge when I first came out west, didn't know he got promoted. Bet he hates being stuck behind a desk."

"Near as I can tell, when those two names came up, the rest of the questions stopped and approval was sent. Which leads us to the current meeting."

"Am I supposed to stand at attention?" He waved me off before I even tried.

"The rank is a way of insuring your passage if you need it." He tossed a folded wallet of papers to me before continuing. "Those are your credentials. Rank, secret service certifications and a U.S. Marshals badge. I wouldn't go arresting folks with the marshals badge, but it has the authority. Deputy marshals won't have a clue, but the marshals will know the story."

"Didn't know there'd be a marshal's badge, figured it be a deputy's badge." I was surprised to find out about that part.

"New addition after a sheriff in Colorado held up a currier for four days. They may not know about the rest, but they'll know that thing. More importantly, they know you can yank them out of office. I'll let you know some of the marshals aren't happy about that being added."

"Bet not." I could imagine they weren't.

"Fortunately for us, Fredrick Douglas, or Marshal Fredrick Douglas doesn't seem to care what they think. You'll notice that badge makes you one of his direct subordinates. Believe me when I say this: there isn't a marshal out there who will argue with you. You've also been approved by the Attorney General and President Grant."

"So wait, do I have the authority of a marshal or not?"

"As far as anyone out here knows, you do. Anyone who knows how the curriers work might try to argue, but it don't matter. You have it if you want. Unlike other lawmen, you have the choice to walk away if need be. That being said, the law out here is usually done on an as needed basis. If you step in with a badge, I doubt anyone will mind. I doubt anyone west of the Mississippi would challenge you about it either way. They still couldn't stop you, not without direct approval from Marshal Douglas."

"You sure you want to give me that much authority?" I laughed, but to be honest, the idea scared me a bit.

"You'll be fine. You're only required to use the authority to accomplish your mission. Anything you do outside of that is up to you. Far as your job goes you can ride through a bank robbery and act like it's just a normal Friday. No one's going to hold you accountable. It's not your job."

"Don't see how it makes a difference, then. There an oath or something we need to do?"

"The short answer is no, but you are legally bound to report from one base to another. That means even if you get robbed and can't recover the messages, you still have to report. Failure to do so can result in your arrest. Reading or distributing classified material will likewise land you in jail or hung."

"Seems reasonable."

"One other thing they changed, pay by the delivery. Headquarters sets the price. Orders arrived today with your packet on the stage. The one I need you for is from here to Fort Sumner. It's to be handed directly to Lieutenant Colonel Hughes."

"Was debating between there and Tularosa anyway, so it suits me."

"Pay is twenty-one dollars. There's a bit extra there since you'll be crossing Apache lands."

"If it's ready to go, I'll plan on leaving tomorrow morning."

"It's been ready for a week or more." He laughed. "Meet you here after breakfast?"

"Before, I'll be down the road a bit before I stop to eat."

"I'll be here at first light." He nodded in satisfaction. "Enjoy the rest of your evening."

"Dinner and a last night in a bed, that's the vast majority of my plans. One thing though? Keep it quiet that I'm leaving."

"Spies?"

"No telling what Dutch would do if he knew. Probably nothing but better safe than sorry."

"Fair enough JC and thanks. You'll likely never know what happens, but I promise you this matters."

"My pleasure Major."

My mind was mapping out my route by memory while working through my morning routine. Darkness still dominated the land outside, but in my mind's eye, I could see the map clearly. One of the new punchers said there was a new crossing of the Red, but I didn't plan on drifting that far north. I'd turn west at the Brazos River, then cross the Staked Plains until I hit the Pecos. Once I made that, Fort Sumner shouldn't be too far north.

Course, it would take me through Comanche and Kiowa territory. Most of that fight was over, and I'd probably run across army patrols more often than the natives. There were a few bands still raising hell, but most of the fighting had been done for a month or more. I'd still need to stay alert, but with Wisp to watch at night, it shouldn't be a problem.

The first rays of the sun found me walking Shade across the parade ground. Wisp was trailing behind with her packs loaded. Major Wilkins was standing outside of his still dark office. He held a bundle about the size of a saddlebag, it was wrapped in a tarpaulin bag, locked with a small padlock. He also had a set of saddlebags hanging over his shoulder, which made me curious. They were a plain brown and looked pretty close to mine. They even had some wear on them. It might take a day or two in the sun, and they'd match mine perfectly.

"Morning Major." I greeted him, hitching Shade to the rail as I spoke.

"It's almost that." He admitted looked at the faintly lit horizon. "Ready to learn of our trickery?"

"Educate me, oh great coyote." I could tell right away that he didn't get the joke.

"What the hell does a coyote have to do with it?" The look of confusion turned my chuckle into a real laugh.

"Nevermind, just fill me in."

"Simple really, take this official-looking bundle of babble and stick it in your pannier. Then swap your saddlebags for these. You can leave yours behind, this set is yours now."

"False bottoms?" I asked, remembering Fletcher's.

"Yeah, thinner than most, since they only need to carry documents."

"Seen a set recently and heard of folks using them to hide cash." I started transferring my gear to the new ones while we talked.

"You'll find these are more subtle than most, very thin at the bottom, about an inch. Now if you get stopped don't die for that, it's a false trail." He motioned toward the fake bundle. "As far as we know, the saddlebags are still secret."

"Ain't looking to die for any of it." I was packing the new set carefully now that I had everything laid out. The major took note of my gear with a smile. It was probably the buckskins and two Apache knives. He hadn't exaggerated. I could barely tell there was anything off about the bottoms.

"Someday I'm going to remember to ask you about your past." He chuckled after noticing my bow. It was sticking out of my bedroll slightly.

"Aint much of a story."

"Another time, maybe. When you reach Fort Sumner, you'll take those saddlebags to Lucian Maxwell. Only when you are in his office and only when it's just you and him do you open them." He motioned to the saddlebags I was now attaching to d-rings. "If anyone wants to argue about that, arrest them. That's where the marshal's badge comes in. No matter what fort you're at, the commander must back your decision."

"Got it." I finished tucking the last of my possibles into the new bags. "Lucian Maxwell doesn't sound like a rank?"

"He isn't. In this case, it's not a specific military matter. It goes without saying you're expected to endure whatever you have to. Protect those papers with your life."

"Figured that was the deal."

"One other thing, not every officer you'll deal with is going to be as lax as I am. Some will try to command you like a normal officer. They can't, any of them you'll be dealing with should know that. Sadly, it won't stop others from trying."

"What if the man's unavailable?" I meant dead, but didn't need to say it.

"You'll never release those documents to anyone below the

rank of captain. No one below that rank even knows curriers exist." He chuckled and added. "That's not counting some of the senior non-com's. There's nothing those men don't know but they also know to stay out of it. If no one is of sufficient rank, got to the next fort."

"Got it, sir."

"Save travels Lieutenant." He laughed before turning toward his quarters.

Stepping up onto Shade after unhitching him, we set off on a new adventure. It struck me as funny when I turned north on the flattened ground of the trail. I could have taken up Hank's offer for a job, it would have been ideal cover. There was a part of me that liked the idea of working for the Army in this capacity. The childish part of my mind painted ideas of sneaking around enemies in the night. Fanciful thoughts created by that small part of me that still remembered dreams of being a pirate.

I couldn't help my imagination following the idea. Painting the rolling flat land ahead of me into crashing waves that broke across Shade's chest. The image lasted for just a moment, but it was enough to make me smile. Soon the rising sun stretched my shadow out. The heat rose with the sun, reminding me of what lay ahead.

# CHAPTER 14

The next day found me eating lunch where the Brazos left the Western Trail. The land changed ahead of me, a basin of life spreading out ahead. I was going to follow the river until the Double Mountain Fork. It would give me the shortest path across the Stacked Plains. It also increased my risk of running into other folks, but good water was worth the risk.

That first night I cooked some dinner under a mesquite. It scattered the smoke, helping hide my presence. Before dark, I cut down a small creek to make camp. Wisp had proven her capability to keep watch, but announcing my location with a fire and then sleeping by it? That would be asking to die. A tight group of Texas Ash shielded my cold camp from view. They would also break the wind at night. Shade and Wisp had access to decent graze and water, so I'd left them near the stream. I laid out my bedroll close to them, trusting both not to step on me by accident.

Coming awake in the dark wasn't out of the ordinary, but I couldn't understand why for a minute. Laying in the darkness trying to understand what had woken me when my mind finally caught it. Silence, deathly silence, hung on the night like a blanket. With no fire to steal my night vision, I slowly looked around. My ears struggled to find any hint of what had made the animals go quiet.

My right hand tightened around the butt of my colt, my thumb automatically perched on the hammer. It would come up ready to fire once I found the threat. Slowly, my eyes scanned back and forth, taking in the surrounding ground. There! My eyes caught the movement, a shadow slipping through the trees. It was a mountain lion. There was no other creature that could ghost through the shadows, like one of them. That quick glimpse put the hairs on the back of my neck up. It had been a big cat, one that could kill me faster than any man. Good or bad, it wasn't hunting me.

My eyes traced its slow stalking steps, working out its target. It was after Shade. The apex predator had picked its target and ignored the warning scent of man. That wasn't its worst mistake. It also ignored the other animal who was frozen five feet from Shade. It seemed Wisp disagreed about who was the hunter and hunted. I'd give even odds that the molly could take the cat, but I couldn't afford an injured animal. Watching and waiting, finally the big cat crouched, preparing to leap. It would land on Shade's back, claws digging into his hide to hold it in place. Then it would sink two inch canines into his neck and wait for the horse to die. When its rear legs shifted, I knew the time had come. My hand came up, finger already pulling the trigger as the hammer locked back. Flame spit out the end of the barrel, stealing my sight for precious seconds. Wisp brayed her war cry, ready to back up my attack. Luckily she wasn't needed, the cat's carefully planned leap failed. It's heavy body crashing to the ground in a heap. Not knowing much about the cats, I waited for it to move again. Guessing from what little I'd seen, the cat had to be a hundred and fifty pounds at least.

My position was given away with that shot and I'd need a fire to see now. Gathering wood was easy among the aspens. I'd done it before going to sleep. Being prepared for the morning was just being smart. After checking my boots and stomping into them, I put my gun belt on. Lighting the fire took moments, then I checked on the animals. Shade was calming down and Wisp acted like nothing had happened. Truthfully, she glared at me like I'd stolen her fun. Her blood lust made me laugh, crazy mule.

"Sorry my lady." I bowed to her. "Couldn't afford to have you hurt."

I filled the coffee pot but didn't put it on the fire yet. I wasn't going to miss the opportunity to harvest the cat. Tom swore that they tasted better than any beef. I wanted to know if he was right. Fishing out a small lamp and the short piece of rope I used to hang game, I got to work. It took a few minutes to find my skinning knife, after that it was time to get dirty.

When the light revealed the cat, I let out a long, slow whistle. My shot had been lucky. Hitting the chest, my bullet had punched through the heart, killing it instantly. This was no young cub. If I had to guess, this was the dominate male in the area. His paws were bigger than my hands, easily exceeding my guess of 150 pounds. My shot had left the hide clean except for the one hole. There was no way I'd leave it or the meat laying here. That meant I'd be camping here for a few days to tan the hide and smoke the meat. I had some supplies in the pannier. There should be enough to get everything done and not run short.

First, I had to harvest the meat and get rid of the offal. By the time that was done, dawn was breaking through the trees. Using the creek to start the soak, weighing the hide down with rocks. Next, I started putting together a makeshift smoker to preserve the meat. The sun was fully up by the time I started my coffee, but except for some back-strap, the rest was already smoking. It was in a skillet, waiting to be cooked. While more coffee water boiled, I did my first scrap of the hide and put it back in the stream to soak.

I had to admit Tom was right, the backstrap had been better than beef. After breakfast, I sat down and did a real scrap of the hide, stretching it across a frame made from the aspen. Using the cat's brain to mix up the tanning solution. That was rubbed into the coat, then rolled up in a tarpaulin. Throughout the day, I'd take the hide out and reapply the mix after wringing it out. By late afternoon, most of the meat was done smoking. I was also scrubbing the hide clean in the stream, using some lye soap to get it completely clean before starting to dry it. I had enough daylight left to get it softened and smoked. Tomorrow

I'd probably spend most of the day repeating that process.

The morning of the third day, I was finally done with the hide. Tossing out the dregs of my coffee, I started breaking camp. I collected the claws that were left to dry on a rock while the hide was tanned. It had come out better than expected. I'd been careful and worked on it slowly. Now it was rolled up tight and tucked in a pack. The smoked meat was stored, split between panniers with some in my saddlebag.

I was back on the Brazos before the sun fully rose that morning. My eyes marveling at the beauty that spread out around me. I did my best to ignore the three braves watching me. They'd been doing it since the first morning. None of them had left, and they hadn't done anything but watch me. So far, they hadn't given me a reason to confront them. That changed this morning. The time for watching must have passed because they stepped into the trail a head of me. Shade stopped with thirty feet between us. My Winchester sat across my thigh ready to fire. They stood watching me, probably hoping my fear would show. I stepped out of the saddle to stand in front of Shade. Wisp was dancing around, expressing her displeasure at their presence. Speaking in Iroquois and using the generic hand signs, I broke the awkward silence.

"Fight or speak?"

"I do not know the language you speak." The middle brave stepped forward and spoke in English.

"It's the language of a tribe far to the east."

"You killed the cat."

"I did."

"We watched you. You did not waste it like so many white men do." I didn't bother to answer because there hadn't been a question. "Who are you? The feathers are Shoshone, but you are not."

"I am Grey Walker."

"The people know that name, but he is not Shoshone either."

"You are Comanche." It had been a while since I talked to the People. It was strange remembering to speak directly without

139

many questions. "I am Grey Walker. I have many hats."

"But you do not have many black hawk feathers."

"No, but that medicine is known to many bad men. Men who do not care about its medicine. Now I travel as Walker." I could see he didn't understand and truthfully, I knew why. The entire concept of lying was still a mystery to them. They had learned what it meant from the treaties that had been broken but it still didn't make sense to them.

"White mans business." He grumped, losing interest in the subject. "The people will let you pass. You are welcome at our fires."

"I thank the people for their hospitality." I moved to take about half the smoked cat meat out of my pack. "My way of feeding the old and young."

He nodded, appreciating the gift for what it was. Every man was expected to help feed those who couldn't hunt. The man next to him took the meat and packed it in his bag.

"I am Swift Rabbit." Like his name was a farewell. The three men disappeared into the brush.

I didn't bother wondering about it, just stepped back into the saddle. They were never what a white man would call chatty or even polite. The fewer words you spoke, the more strength they had. With a light touch, Shade got moving again. Taking a cheroot out of my pocket, I struck a lucifer on the saddle horn and brought it up to light the tip. The smoke filled my lungs as I rode, my eyes studying the land ahead of me. That had gone far better than I feared. The Comanche could be tricky sometimes. One day friend, the next day foe but being welcomed at their fire was different. There wouldn't be any attack so long as I remained respectful.

The days passed peacefully. I'd take a grouse or rabbit with the bow for dinner just to vary my diet. The jerky was good, better than most, but the same thing every day got boring. Besides, hunting got me back in the habit of stalking through the scrub silently. I'd made the turn to follow the Double Mountain Fork around noon after taking a rabbit by throwing my knife. It was just another way of keeping my skills from getting rusty. They were all perishable and needed constant work.

That turn marked the beginning of a change in the land. It started to flatten out. The scrub was still present, hiding wild animals and more than a few long horns. But off in the heat hazed distance, I could almost see the staked plains stretching to the horizon. The long stretched out flat land wasn't going to make for a fun ride but at the same time I was looking forward to it. It was a change and might hold something new.

Following the fork for the next few days was pleasant. I shared a camp one night with a small hunting party of Comanche. They gave me more information about the staked plains and what lay ahead. Thier tribe had taken the land from the Apache for hunting grounds. Buffalo grazed across the plains, making this area incredibly valuable. They warned me about the buffalo hunters who were known to shoot anyone they thought might be taking their kills.

The day I rode out of the basin and started across the long flat plains was hot. The only markers I had were distant mesas that stood like sentinels watching over it all. Pointing Shades nose at the largest of them, we set off through the tall grass. That night I stopped at the foot of it. There was a spring on one side with fresh water. While the horses drank, I made myself some dinner, slowly roasting a rabbit over the fire. I'd passed a decent spot for cold camp before the spring. It was far enough away that we should sleep peacefully.

The false dawn woke me up the next morning. After my morning rituals, I led the animals back to the spring so they could drink while I rinsed off. Starting a fire for breakfast back at the cold camp, I ate the last of my bacon with some fried dough while watching the land come to life around me. After filling all four canteens, I picked another mesa as a marker and started west.

Mid-morning, the dark spots started to appear at the edge of my vision. Soon the dots blended together, forming a moving brown forest of fur and horn. The breeze carried the smell ahead of them, heavy musk and the dung of grass eaters. The buffalo herd in front of me seemed like an ocean of great shaggy beast slowly washing across the plains. A slight touch of my heel guided Shade to the left. There was no way I'd risk riding through that ocean. It took the entire day to move around the edge of the herd. The mesa I had picked was an open space in the flank of the herd. Like one and all, they had decided to only pass it on the right side. The sun was starting to fall, and I wasn't going to sleep anywhere near the herd. Unless a better answer showed itself soon, I was going to spend the night in the saddle. It wouldn't be a new experience, just not one I liked. Especially on land I'm unfamiliar with and a massive herd of buffalo sleeping nearby.

Riding nighthawk on a herd wasn't like riding through unknown ground. A herd flattened the land, made it almost safe for a horse. This would be dangerous. Unknown gully's, gopher holes, buffalo wallows, and anything else that could hurt a horse. That's not even mentioning how hard it was on the horse to not get any rest. Shade could do it for one night. After that it would start effecting his health. Even just one night would mean slowing our pace until he recovered. There were some who didn't care and would push their animal to exhaustion. To me those men deserved to have that done to them, then be beaten until they couldn't walk.

In the slowly fading light, I spotted a trail winding up the mesa. Wide enough for a horse but not big enough for a buffalo. Sleeping up top safely was possible, but there was no way I'd have a fire. It would be seen for miles from up there. A cold camp better than sleeping in the saddle, for me and the animals. A slight shift in my weight turned Shade up the trail. After the first thirty feet, it opened up enough to move easily. Something seemed off about the way it looked. Studying the trail, it took me a few minutes to realize what it was. That first thirty feet where the trail narrowed wasn't right. The outside edge of it had been intentionally narrowed. My eyes could make out pick marks along the edge where it had fallen below. That told me someone had wanted to keep the buffalo off the top. It also meant no wagons were making it up this trail. That ruled out hiders. They'd never leave their wagons below.

The pick marks looked old, the work had been done years ago. That created more questions than answers. Indians wouldn't have done this, the army might, but why? That was the only answer that made sense, well that or outlaws but they usually wouldn't put in that much effort. Either way, I needed to be careful going up this path. There was just no way of telling what might be waiting up top. Hopefully nothing but out here you just never knew.

About a hundred feet from the top, I tied the animals off on a small piece of rock. The rest of the way would be done on foot and moving quietly. By the time I reached the top I was bellying crawling to keep a low profile. The sight that met my eyes in the fading sun seemed unreal. The top of the mesa was maybe a hundred yards across. The far eastern corner had rocks jutting up that broke the smooth top, giving me cover from one side.

None of that surprised me, not even the small pond in the center with a small gentle water fall coming from the rocks. What completely stunned me was tucked back in the shadow of a cliff. A small adobe house, not much more than a hut really, but its very existence on top of this mesa was insane. There was just no reason a house would be up here. Everything was dark and nothing moved around it. I watched for five minutes before finally accepting it was abandoned. I was alone up here with a small house that had no business being here.

I still approached it carefully, trying my best to stick to the few shadows that stretched across the top. Slowly, I crossed what seemed like endless open ground. A blind man could have picked me off easily anywhere along the way. There wasn't even a small rock for cover. Someone had made sure no one would approach this place unseen. Finally making it to the door of the small cabin, I crouched there, listening for any signs of life. Nothing but echoing silence and the soft sound of falling water met my ears.

When I slowly reached out to push on the door, it swung open easily. The cloud of dust stirred up by that movement helped quiet my fears. In the feint light left, I could just make out the heavy layer of dust covering the floor. No tracks, human or animal, marred its surface. Sighing heavily, I slipped my colt back into the holster before stepping inside. There was a lantern covered in dust just inside the door. A quick match lit the wick and exposed the rest of the place. It was a small one room building, well built and at some point in the past it was lovingly maintained. Outside of being dust covered, everything looked solidly built. Someone had taken great pride in crafting all of this. There was a table with two chairs, in one of them a skeleton sat. The pose looked like whoever it had been was sitting there and just fell asleep forever. A piece of paper held under its hand caught my eye. What mystery was this? I had stumbled into something interesting again.

I'd unravel that after seeing to my animals. There was a small stable and functional corral off to the side of the house. The grass was tall enough that they'd have good graze for the night, honestly there was enough for a few days easily. The best part was the water trough on the side. Filling it would be easy if the pump beside it worked. An hour later, listening to the water fill the trough while Shade and Wisp explored the little space I smiled.

After finishing my chores, my feet carried me back inside the cabin. A quick examination of the fireplace verified the chimney wasn't blocked. I started a fire with some of the wood left beside it. Like everything else in the place, it was a well designed with a small grate I could use to cook on. An hour spent using the broom I found behind the door, got a fair amount of the dust out. I wouldn't call it clean, but it no longer left streaks when I touched things. I hadn't touched the skeleton yet. Now it was finally time to address that mystery.

"What's your story, stranger?"

I didn't know why I spoke, it just felt right. Picking up the note was the only way I'd learn anything about my companion. It was a struggle to read the Spanish. Between my lack of knowledge and their penmanship it took a while. I was surprised at the clean flowing script the man wrote in, sadly it didn't make reading it easier. It did tell me that whoever this man had been, he came from money and had some education.

*Amigo,*

*If you are reading this, I can only hope you are a friend. My name is Manuel Fagas, welcome to my home. I have lived here since the Americanos took my home. They told me that since I was a Mexican, it didn't matter that I had a deed.*

*In truth, they did me a favor, so there is no ill will toward them. The past twenty years living in my small hacienda has been bliss. That was until my Teresa passed away last spring. Since then I have only been waiting to join her. That is why I am writing this letter.*

*I ask you for only one thing, my friend. Bury me next to her. You will find her headstone behind our home. When I placed her marker, I planned ahead and carved mine as well. If you would lay me there and place my headstone, I would be indebted to you.*

*Yours in death,*

*Manuel Fagas.*

I wasn't looking forward to digging a grave in what was probably mostly rock, but I would do it tomorrow. It might delay me another day, but it just seemed like the right thing to do for the man whose house was sheltering me. The lonely open land didn't always grant folks grace when they passed. More than once, the Bar C had buried entire families killed in horrible ways. It usually delayed us, but no one ever questioned doing it. It was just one of those things you did for folks when you could. Rather than risk losing a bone, I laid out some tarpaulin I found on a shelf and gently let him fall onto it from the chair. Then folded it around him, making a bundle that was easy to move. There hadn't been any sign of animals up here, but I kept him by the door rather than risk scavengers. He'd be laid to rest tomorrow properly and my debt for the cabin would be paid.

My bedroll fit nicely over the leather stretched bed frame. Luckily, the straps hadn't dry rotted, and the bed was still solid. I managed a decent stew with some jerky, wild potatoes, and onions that I found out back. They'd been in what was probably a garden before my friend Manuel died. The remnants of a fence still wrapped around it. There was an old dutch oven in the cabin that I managed passable biscuits in. To be honest, passable might be over stating their quality. Edible was more accurate.

The house stayed cool over night and I slept comfortably. The morning showed every sign of a bright, clear day. My ears could still hear the distant bellowing of the buffalo echoing up from the plains below. After starting some coffee, I checked on the horses. Then, taking full advantage of the open space, I did a full work out for the first time in days. The freedom of movement and something about this place made everything just flow. Every stretch and step seemed effortless, but by the end of it I'd worked up a good sweat.

# CHAPTER 15

Frying some of the jerky with the eggs add come flavor to them, a few more potatoes sliced into the pan rounded out my breakfast. Taking my last cup of coffee, I walked around the back and found a headstone laying next to an older grave. There was a hammer and chisel set aside to carve the last date. A pick and shovel waited beside them. All the tools were coated with a heavy oil, probably linseed, to keep the rust off. I took the pick in hand and started working. I hadn't bothered to put my shirt back on after exercising and saw no reason to now. The ground was easier to work than I'd thought it would be. By early afternoon, I had the grave dug. Carving the year on the marker only took another hour and tested what little skill I had with a hammer and chisel. This was probably the second time I'd ever used them.

Back inside, I carefully moved Manuel out to his final resting place. Lowering him in alone, even wrapped tightly, was challenging. Luckily, he didn't weigh much anymore, making it more awkward than anything else. It did involve me climbing into the man's grave and picking him up on the edge. Not a comfortable feeling if I'm being honest, but it was the only way to do it. There was just something about standing in someone's grave that felt wrong. The sun was just starting to set when I finished filling it back in and placing the marker.

I stood for a minute when it was done, silently saying a prayer for a man I'd never met. It struck me how odd this all was, being out here in the middle of nowhere, burying a man I'd never known. There were so many strange occurrences out here that some of the shock had worn off, but this would likely stand out for a while. Laughing to myself, I stepped around the man's grave to get my hat. It was sitting on a boulder behind the gravestone. I almost tripped in a small hole that had been under the headstone. What saved me from a twisted ankle was a leather wrapped bundle. Curiously, I picked it up, trying to understand what it was. Something was wrapped inside. Realization hit me like a bolt of lightning. The only way to find this was by fulfilling the dead man's request and placing his marker.

Thoughts of buried treasure and lost fortunes flashed through my mind. They were quickly washed away by reality. No one with a fortune would have spent their life on top of a mesa. Well, maybe they would. There was a part of me that could see the appeal of it. A small part, but I recognized the worth of a simple life now more than ever before. I left it and my hat inside the cabin and went to take a cold bath in the pond.

On my way there, I got sidetracked by some paintings on one of the natural rock walls. It covered the back part of the pond. There was enough room between it and the water for a small camp. My imagination filled in the space in an instant. A small fire banked against the wall to reflect the heat. Three natives sitting around it, one roasting meat, another marking the wall while the third man recovered from an injury. After a quick run to get my notebook, I spent an hour making notes. Recording the drawings, even sketching the area around them. There were notes about what I thought they meant and where I found them. My notebook was almost full. I'd have to get another one soon. Places like this decorated almost every place we camped. That wasn't a surprise. Water always guided the path of life.

This one was different somehow. It stood out because of where it was more than anything else. This was the first one I'd found in such an isolated location. True, it was a beautiful place, but not something you found by chance. Another story played out in my mind, one similar to my own. People fleeing or hiding from something or someone. It was the only reason they'd climb that ledge. Once discovered, it was no mystery why this place would become a prized location. Shelter, safety, and water, there wasn't much more you'd want in a camp.

Restrictive access made it ideal for defense. Easy water and wild food made it perfect for a hunting party. In times of war, it would be a place to watch the enemy from. It would let you track them without being seen and attack from seemingly out of nowhere. It fascinated me how useful a place like this could be to the tribes. Still, how had Manuel found it? Did the tribes tell him, or did he find it like I had? There wasn't a definite answer, but it all went into my notebook. The cool waters call couldn't be denied any longer, or it was the stink of my own body. Either one finally pulled me out of my thoughts and reminded me why I had come here. After carefully wrapping my notebook, I put it away and went to wash the stink off.

Discovering life here in the small body of water while bathing made this place that much more interesting. Luckily, there was a small fishing kit in my pack. It was another part of my kit that I always kept with me. It had only been used a few times, but it still got the job done. Four or five pan fish was a good change of pace for dinner. Adding a few sliced potatoes and onions in the skillet with them inspired me to dig out some of the spices I had. As bad as my cooking skills were, I managed to make a good meal and didn't over season the food.

Dessert was the mystery bundle I'd found under the tombstone. Childish thoughts still raced through my head. Maybe they were the thoughts both men and boys shared across the world. Treasure maps, gold, or jewels could be hidden in the little bundle. Fantastic dreams inspired by Jules Verne danced across my mind as my hands opened the bundle. What I found took me a few minutes to understand. It was that far outside of my expectations. Wrapped in layers of paper was a small carving.

Stunned, I sat there, studying the small piece of black wood in my hand. It was heavier than expected. Understanding took longer than it should have. This was petrified wood that someone had painstakingly carved into a raven. The detail was amazing. The craftsmen had carved every single feather with some small tool. Its head was tilted back, delicate feathers around the head flared out. Its beak was open, cawing into the void. I could almost hear the call emanating from the little black figure.

I've never seen something so beautifully done. The entire figure stood four inches tall, each wing was slightly flared, matching the neck. Small ridges in each foot tapered down to talons that dug into its perch. Even that was carved painstakingly detailed. Each crack in the bark looked natural, duplicating the life it once lived. The whole thing shimmered in the flickering lamp light. I could see the dark wood shift from black to shades of purple. Finally tearing my eyes away from the bird, I noticed the piece of paper. It was the last piece I'd pulled off, and it had writing on it. The same flowing calligraphy gracefully filled the paper.

*My friend,*

*If you are reading this, I can only pray that you discovered it after burying me next to my beloved. I was nothing but a lucky man who found a good woman. I have no riches to leave you. This small thing represents my only talent.*

*I began carving when I was young. This is the culmination of sixty years. My final piece, done in a piece of petrified wood I found many years ago. Please take it with my thanks and maybe in some small way my name will live on.*

*Sincerely,*

*Manuel Fagas*

That was it. The rest of the bundle was soft cloth and shredded paper meant to ensure the raven wouldn't be damaged. It all fit into a small fur lined leather bag. His name would live on, not only in this carving but in my telling of this story. Anyone who saw this piece would hear his story and know the master craftsman's name. I recognized the artistry in this piece and saw no reason to doubt his word. The simple life of a man who had somehow managed to capture the beauty he saw in a physical form.

I'd buried the man with no expectation of gifts or wealth, but he had surprised me. The skill on display was amazing, but what really made me admire him was the planning. He had buried his wife knowing that he was alone out here in the middle of no where. Carved his own tombstone, then placed this under it after wrapping it carefully with the note. After doing all of that, he had lived for who knows how long while looking at his own grave. Topping it all off by knowing when the time of his death was coming, he'd penned his last letter. I know he'd written it ahead of time because the quill, the only one in the place, was across the room on the small desk.

This was no simple man. His penmanship showed a fine education. The skill he displayed in the carving showed not just an artist's touch, but also the passion he had for his craft. You didn't just carve something like this without spending hours studying the subject and material. Only after long hours of study would you begin to understand both well enough to create the masterpiece on the table before me. That's not mentioning the skill needed to understand working petrified wood so delicately.

Of all the mysteries I'd run across the since arriving in America, this one was the most amazing to me. In my mind, he somehow defined the multitude of people I'd met. From the punchers quoting Shakespeare to beefs while riding nighthawk to Tom, a simple man who knew this land before anyone else. The native people who lived with their world, existing in peace with the untamed country around them. Even those lost legends I was trying to decipher from aged paintings. There was something about this land, this country, that inspired people to greatness.

With almost religious care, I wrapped the small figure back into its bag. Keeping the man's last words wrapped around it first. This would have pride of place in my home someday. It would be the symbol of my time learning to be a man. Every time I looked at it, my mind would think of the many faces who taught me. Of the men and women who showed me, through their actions, what it meant to stand for what they believed in. After carefully packing the leather bundle in to bottom of my saddlebag, I sat outside smoking my pipe. The last rays of the sun slowly disappeared below the horizon, ending a long and interesting day. My brain was still running in circles, contrasting my sore muscles that protested every motion. There was something about digging graves. It didn't matter how good of shape you were in, it always hurt.

Slowly I stood, stretching my shoulders and made my way to the bed. Tomorrow I'd ride back down the trail and like as not never see this place again. It would always be a part of me, another marker on my path. There was something about this place that made me wax philosophical. Maybe in some way this place marked the change in my life more than leaving the Bar C. I might forget that last drive, but this place would always stick out in my mind. That was fine for now, but tomorrow I'd have to be alert and ready for what lay ahead. It was time to sleep, then get back to life, with all of its complications and challenges.

Days later, I finished crossing the Staked Plains. It had been an experience I'd never forget. Finally, seeing the herds of buffalo people talked about made it easy to understand the stories. That first herd had been small in comparison to the last one. It had covered the land like a tide of locust, taking two full days to ride around it. I couldn't even guess how many animals were in that one herd. The comparison to an ocean of brown fur and horns was even more accurate than before.

Now I was looking at another herd a head of me. It was smaller than the others, but was about to demonstrate the power they held. I'd found my way to the top of another mesa for the night. Now I was getting ready to leave, but my plans changed instantly. Something spooked the herd and suddenly the ground I stood on, two hundred feet above them, shook under my feet. The smallest of the herds was literally giving me my first taste of an earthquake. The sensation put every other stampede I'd experienced to shame. Nothing could survive that formidable tide of fear and rage. Being in front of that was death. It would swallow up and leave nothing but a red stain behind.

After the dust cleared, I rode down the trail to start across the rest of the plains. My plan was still to make camp on the Pecos tonight if nothing delayed me. Fort Sumner wouldn't be more than a few days past that. Turning west, I saw what had spooked the herd. Dead buffalo dotted the land in front of me. Mounds of fur scattered around as far as the eye could see. Weaving my way through the mountains of flesh, doing my best to ignore the coppery scent of blood that hung heavy in the air. It mixed with the musky scent of the herd, creating something that pressed down on me. A sharp whistle passed by my ear, reminding me of an angry hornet. Something splattered the side of my face, wet and sticky. The boom came a second later. Instantly I recognized the report of a Sharps big fifty.

My eyes barely saw the plum of smoke some five hundred yards away. It was enough motivation for my spurs to touch Shade's flanks. He responded immediately, leaping to the right, taking what cover was offered. A dead bull laying just ahead of me. Before he stopped, I was out of the saddle, holding my Winchester. It didn't immediately strike me as odd when I looped his reins around the buffalo horn in front of me. Later, I'd think back on that act and laugh at myself.

None of my guns would reach as far as their Sharps. With this many dead animals, there had to be more than one shooter. Worse, these were men used to shooting moving targets. Admittedly, they usually shot things a bit bigger than me, but that didn't offer much comfort. Even a grazing shot from one of those could take off a limb. I took off my hat and left it with the panniers on Wisp. No need to make it too easy for them. Peeking out around the front of the massive beast, I took in the area around me in a quick glance.

The grass was trampled flat by the panicked animals, so it wouldn't offer any cover. The dead beasts scattered around the area did, thankfully. The head of the beast I was hiding behind jerked. A wet sound preceded the boom of another shot. I didn't waste the chance. Darting forward and to my right, I moved toward the next animal. A second and third shot boomed out, but I had no idea where they hit. Cutting back left to a further animal on a guess that everyone had taken their shots, reloading would give me a few extra seconds.

The disadvantage of Sharps was exactly that, the time it took to reload. I had to credit these men for their skill. Just as I slid across the blood-soaked grass into cover, another shot whistled by. They knew their weapons well and unfortunately, that wasn't good for me. Two more shots hit the body I was hiding behind, sending me off and running again. I zig zagged, moving toward the cloud of smoke that hung in the air ahead of me.

Falling into a small gully that appeared out of no where, I slid to the bottom laying flat. Just as I dropped, another shot zipped by overhead, close enough that I felt the heat pouring off it. Close enough to hear their cursing didn't mean it was time to shoot back. There was no way I'd pop back up where I fell. That would only result in my death. Low crawling through the rough grass, moving north while listening to them yell at each other. I slowly worked around the edge to flank them.

"Goddamn it! Stagger yer shots 'at damn fool keeps waiting fer us all ta be reload'n." The voice was harsh, probably dry from the powder smoke.

"Ain't me at missed an give'em a chance." This voice was just as scratchy but sounded younger.

"Let dem skinners go fetch'm up. Tired of wastin' shot." The third voice had just a hint of a French accent.

"An if he kills 'em? Ya skin'n all of them beasts?" The first voice growled. It was followed by two more new voices.

"Hell no!"

"We ain't goin out there. Ya didn't hire none of us for kill'n"

While they argued, I'd worked my way around to their right. The gully had backed on a slight rise, but I didn't peek from the top. Working a bit further around before peeking out from behind cover. The cold was slowly calming my breath and that strange delay in time stretched out, giving me time to think.

Two men sat around a fire near a half skinned buffalo. Three others were laying flat on a small rise scanning the ground while arguing. I was trying to figure out how to kill three men before one of them brought their Sharps to bear. The answer came pretty quick thankfully. Staying here long enough for them to see me was a bad idea.

The man closest to me was wrapped in a heavy buffalo hide coat. The only reason I could see around him was their staggered position. If I shot him first, the other two would have to move before they could line up on me. That few seconds would be the difference between their Sharps and my lever action. Accuracy was always a question, but speed and men's natural fear of flying lead could decide things in the first moments.

I didn't bother to consider anything else. My sights settled on the big man's head. He was still a fair distance off, so I'd have to take my time. First, I calmed my breathing, then locked back the hammer. Slowly I exhaling, then started applying the gentlest pressure to the trigger. When the stock kicked back into my shoulder, it came as a surprise. Exactly like it's supposed to. Through the smoke, I saw the man's head pitch sideways. That was all the time I gave him. My eyes were already lining up the iron sights on the next man. He swung his Sharps my way but jerked the shot, fear making him shoot too fast. At such close range, his dead friend was almost launched into the air by the heavy impact. Blood sprayed across the grass as the body rolled. Half of his chest was turned into a fine mist.

My Winchester bucked into my shoulder again, but it only

kicked up dirt a foot short of his bulky shape. The third man's big fifty hummed by me as I levered in another round. Taking a second to aim and slow my breathing, slowly centering my sights on him again. He was struggling to feed another cartridge into the breech when my 44-40 slug found his throat. This time it punched through, spraying the third man's face with blood. He fumbled his reload in shock, giving me enough time to lever in another shot. Time slowed further, letting me watch his every action. He jammed a new round in just as my sights lined up on him. Slow breathing, ignore the barrel slowly pointing my way. Easy pressure on the trigger, breath held. The kick hitting my shoulder just as the gaping maw of that big fifty lined up on me.

Suddenly it was jerked back. His head rocked back, a neat red hole appearing just below his right eye. My sights shifted to the men at the fire. Both of them were standing with their hands up, eyes squeezed shut. My lever worked again, making both of them jump. I had to slow my self back down to avoid shooting. It took long seconds to regain control.

"Jeezus mister don't shoot we didn't want no part a that mess." The older of the two said.

"Yeah, they jus hired us ta skin for'em."

"Just stay real still. I'll kill the first one that twitches." My voice still had that cold edge to it.

"We ain't even armed." The older man proclaimed. "They made us leave our guns locked up in the wagon."

"Ya kill'd all three of 'em!" The younger one's eyes were fixed on the bleeding corpses.

"Seemed fair to me, figured they had enough chances to kill me." I was walking toward the men now. "Lift them shirts up and each of you do a spin. I want to be sure nether of ya has a gun."

They did as I ordered and if they had a gun, it wasn't anywhere they could reach easily. I left them standing there while checking the three others for any signs of life. They were all well and truly dead, but I only trusted that after checking in the tried-and-true way. A swift kick to the ribs of each man quickly verified their departure from the mortal world. Having a wounded man try to kill me once was all it took to learn that lesson.

"You two walk ahead of me. We're going to get my animals." I motioned for the two men to move.

"Mister, we ain't got nothin…" I cut him off before the excuse started.

"Don't care. You can either walk ahead of me or I can shoot you where you stand. Either one can be done without chatting."

They did as I ordered. It took thirty minutes to get back with Shade and Wisp. Part of that time was spent tying their hands. They protested, but not for long. Staring down the barrel of my Greener usually makes people stop arguing with you. I sat them down by the fire and told them not to move before going back to the three dead men.

Searching them, I collected a little over three hundred dollars. Each of them had their Sharps, two had Colt new armies, and the last had an older Dragoon that had been converted to take cartridges. They also had a collection of knives, more than any man had a need for, but with their line of work, it made sense. Hiders had a reputation for solving problems with blades.

One of the Sharps was the latest model, an 1874 chambered with the newer 45-70 cartridge. If I remembered right, this was one of the higher end models. Double set triggers and adjustable sights marked it as the best of the three. The other two were older and chamber the big fifty caliber. That 45-70 would be going with me, the other two I was still undecided about. First, I had to figure out what to do with the other two.

"Where you two out of?" I asked, while setting a big coffee pot on the fire. "Just one of you speak an tell me your names."

"Names Jake. That's my cousin Milo." The older man spoke, leaving the younger one to stare longingly at the coffee. "They hired us out a Tularosa. Didn't hire us for nothin but skin'n."

"Take it you ain't mad about them being dead?"

"Not if you let us get to work. Don't care none 'bout them, but 'em hides sitting out there is money rotting in the sun." Then he eyed me suspiciously. "Less'n ya want that wagon?"

"Don't care about the hides or the wagon." I believed him. The way they were eyeing the buffalo was unmistakable. It was like watching a starving man stare through the window of a diner. "Stick out your wrists."

After cutting both men loose, they got back to work without another word to me. Carving off a chunk of meat, I sat down for a pleasant lunch of buffalo steak and coffee. I had to give the two credit, they knew their business. It impressed me how fast they peeled the hides off. They had seven or eight of them finished by the time I finished lunch. Their Winchesters and pistol were locked in the wagon. I'd given them the key with a warning to wait for me to be out of sight before getting their weapons.

The three Sharps and pistols, along with the ammo, were added to Wisp. She didn't seem to mind the weight. I'd found thirty-three rounds for the 45-70 and close to a hundred of 50. I left the rest of the supplies for them, minus some salt I used to store some fresh buffalo. Looking around, I spotted fifteen Comanche waiting a few hundred yards off.

"Jake, ya'll care about any of this meat?" I called out to the man. He turned and looked around, spotting the Indians.

"If they leave us be, they can have it. Can have some of the hides to if'n they want."

"I'll tell them." Turning Shade toward the group, I rode toward them.

They knew my name and agreed to leave the two white men alone. I had to assure them they hadn't been the ones who killed so many buffalo. When they found out, I'd killed the three men, they promised to pass the word among the People. After that they descended on the dead animals, starting as far a way from the skinners as they could. They worked just as fast, using a few hides to build quick travois. They were quickly loaded with meat and ready to be hauled away. As the plain of death faded from sight, more of the tribe arrived to help. It made me smile, knowing that at least the meat wouldn't go to waste.

# CHAPTER 16

I didn't make the Pecos that night, partially because there had to be enough light for me to clean my weapons. After finding a suitable spot, I stopped well before dark for dinner. It was a risk, but I needed to take a few shots with he '74 to familiarize myself with it. After ten rounds, I had a good feel for the weapon. Comfortable enough to hit a target at five hundred yards. Its range was much further than that, but it would take me a lot of time and practice to develop those skills. After cleaning all the guns and eating another buffalo steak, I moved camp again. This time a good three quarters of a mile further west near a small stream. There were enough dried buffalo chips to make a fire in the morning. Going to bed on a full stomach of fresh buffalo made me sleep like a baby under Wisp's watchful eyes.

I rode across the Pecos in the early afternoon the next day and turned north to find Fort Sumner. Most likely, the fort was still a day or two away following the river. After that, unless something led me elsewhere, I'd head to Albuquerque. That was my plan anyway. The first part of it went perfectly. Fort Sumner rose out of the landscape just before lunch the next day. My course must have drifted a bit more west than I thought crossing the plains. At my current speed I should make it by early evening, just in time for dinner. It was a luck on my part but I'd take it.

Riding into the fort revealed a flaw in my thinking. It was more of a settlement than fort. A few of the buildings looked like they had been military at some point. Now they had been repurposed for civilian use. Stopping someone to ask about Lucian Maxwell, they pointed me toward a massive house at the edge of town. The place was a mansion, but I was pretty certain it had started life as a military building. The older lady who answered the door seemed surprised at my appearance. That's when things started to go wrong.

"May I help you, young man?" She didn't sound off put by having me there, but something was wrong.

"Yes ma'am, I need to speak with Lucian Maxwell."

"You're a few weeks too late, sir. He's no longer with us." I should have recognized the downcast look.

"Ma'am, I mean no disrespect, but it's on official business."

"You misunderstand, sir. He was buried three weeks ago." Her tone was sharper, understandably so.

"Pardon my ignorance, ma'am. It's been a long day on the trail."

"Is there anyone else you'd like to talk to?"

"No, ma'am, sorry to bother you." She came as close to slamming the door in my face as you could without actually doing it.

Stepping back into the saddle, I turned Shade away from town. I'd camp on the Pecos again, then figure out where to go from here. There were several choices, but I didn't really know enough about any of them to do more than guess. Fort Stanton to the south, Fort Craig was southwest, and Fort Macy to the northwest. Staton was the closest, but it would take me dead south. Macy was near Santa Fe. There would definitely be someone with enough rank at that one.

My safest bet would be to make for Fort Macy, but that meant resupplying. Then a conversation I'd overheard came to mind. Albuquerque was the supply point for the military across the New Mexico Territory. There would have to be someone with enough rank stationed there. Besides, it was the direction I wanted to go and my supplies should get me there. My packs would be running on empty by then, but it was still my best option.

Tomorrow morning I'd head west until I hit the Rio Grande, then follow it north. After a look at the deflated panniers, I amended my plans. Tomorrow I'd ride back into Fort Sumner and resupply what I could, then head west. When I reached for the coffee pot to refill my cup, part of my soul sang out. It matched the song of the land for just an instant, almost confirming my decision. Something was calling me west, a part of me was driven that direction for some unknown reason. This felt like whatever it was agreed with me about making for Albuquerque.

It took me longer than planned to make the outskirts of Albuquerque. The open land was broken by mesas and canyons. Following the river had worked, but it wasn't the most direct path. I'd met a few parties of Comanche and Kiowa on the way. Nether had been actively hostile, but they weren't friendly either. Both preferring to keep their distance. One night I did spend at a Kiowa village after I met their hunters skinning a lone buffalo. They took my appearance as a good sign for their hunt and welcomed me to the feast. That night spent in the buffalo hide teepee brought back long forgotten memories. Sitting in the door with my belly stuffed full of meat. My ears just listening to the life around me. Dogs fighting over scraps, women and men celebrating their life by creating more. The heavy smells of sage and smoke filling the crisp night breeze. It all made me feel like I was at home, a home at least.

There was some part of me that truly felt alive here among the people. With no real connection to this tribe, there was still a deep feeling of attachment for their way of life. I knew it was dying. In fifty years there wouldn't be a wikiup or teepee left on open land. That thought brought a very real sense of loss with it. Part of me didn't know if I wanted to be here when that happened. Something would be lost from the world when that happened. Those melancholy thoughts were washed away when I spotted three older boys slip into the shadow of another teepee. Tracking their path with my eyes, I realized another boy, closer to a young brave, was hiding in another shadow watching them. Training themselves, three hunting one who was in fact hunting them. Cycles like this would always exist, time would change them, but it would still exist. Young men doing all they could to rush into manhood.

The next morning, the leader of the hunting party gifted me two crow feathers adorned with beads on a leather thong. I gifted him one of the better Apache knives from my collection. Its sheath was colorfully decorated with intricate bead work, making it a suitable gift for the respected man. After locking forearms, I rode west back toward the Rio grateful for the night. It had refreshed me in some way that I'd never understand. That night I put the feathers on my hat, the Shoshone feathers were carefully packed. It felt better wearing a real gift, more honest.    Smiling at the memory from two nights ago, while sitting beside my fire, it was another part of my story. One that may never be told but it would always be a part of me. I was a mile or so outside of the settled land near Albuquerque. Earlier in the day, I found the heavy wagon tracks along the river. Wagons that had left their mark not only in the deep ruts but in the discarded broken wheels along the route. Now sitting off the trail just enjoying my evening meal of fresh caught catfish. It had been fried in some buffalo fat I'd saved for the purpose. A duck egg, the last of my flour and the few spices completed the recipe. Some fried wild potatoes cooked in the same grease with a few wild onions were a nice addition.

The next morning, after my routine and a quick bath in the river, I started planning my day. After making some coffee, I started getting my gear ready to go. A few fried dodgers from last night would be my breakfast with the last of my salted venison. It wasn't as good as the catfish, but still better than most of what Jose and I ate that first year. My cooking skills couldn't stand up next to Smythe, but they'd definitely gotten better on this trip. Tante and Binda had given me the foundation and out of respect for them I'd done my best to

163

improve.

My mind wandering like this wasn't unusual when I got to the civilized parts of the country. My wariness didn't fade, but the focus changed. This close to a settlement, I had to worry more about white men. They were easier to see coming, which let my mind wander a bit more. It was a strange kind of relaxed, wary, but alert. That's how I spotted the two men. One of them moved a few hundred yards ahead of me.

The choice of what to do was simple. Dismounting and retrieving the Sharps from Wisp I studied the situation. Standing in the middle of the road, I looked at the brush, studying it carefully. The distant rumble of a heavily loaded wagon was echoing in the canyon. That made me pause. My first thought had been they meant to jump me, but suddenly I knew that was wrong. They wouldn't be waiting here for a lone traveler, not enough money in it. For a wagon loaded with military supplies? That meant there were more than a couple of men.

I'd been standing there long enough that if I was their target, they'd have taken a shot. Well, if they had a long rifle they would have. Crouching down to really study the narrowed spot in the road proved worthwhile. On a small overhang above the road, I spotted the other man. He did have a long rifle but was so focused on watching the wagon through field glasses he hadn't noticed me. His rifle told me what his job was. Either shoot the driver or the mules. Most likely the driver, since mules were worth money.

Kneeling in the road, I laid my Winchester on the ground beside me after locking the hammer back. Then I sighted in on the man above with the Sharps. My mind was still wondering why the other men hadn't warned him. I didn't do anything other than wait for the next five minutes as the rumbling wagon drew nearer. When he put down the field glasses and started to prepare his rifle, I had to make a decision. The dust from the wagon was getting closer to the narrow spot. They were already in range of an expert, soon they'd be close enough for any decent shot.

It didn't take me long. The blue uniforms driving the wagon made up my mind. The first trigger clicked back when I'd settled the sight. Slowly my finger eased back on the firing trigger. The echoing boom of my shot started the violence. The mans prone body jumped with the impact then rolled over the edge. A single scream followed his body down, finally silenced by the sound of flesh impacting hard rock.

Vaguely, the yells of the soldiers pulling the wagon to a stop bounced off the rocks into my ears. Drowning out most of that were three men bursting from the brush, already mounted with Winchesters pointed my way. There wasn't time to take another shot with the Sharps. I carefully swapped it for the Winchester at my feet. The cold filled me and again everything seemed to slow. Just as my iron sight centered on the first man, my finger caressed the trigger.

His hands went up, flinging his rifle in the air. My mind noted it was a yellow boy when the sun shined off the side. Even as his body rolled out of the saddle my sights shifted, my right hand working the lever. Hot brass spun out of the ejector as another 44-40 slid into place. The hammer clicked down a half second later, sending another bullet toward the man on the left.

Through the flame I watched the man's shoulder come apart. Blood sprayed up his neck and across his face. His body tilted in the saddle and he dropped his rifle to make a desperate grab for his saddle horn. He missed and started to fall, his right boot hung in the stirrup. If the man was lucky, the first impact killed him. A Dutch ride was a terrible way to die.

A bullet creased my left leg, but the cold shut the pain down before it affected me. My right hand worked again, another round seated, ready to fire. My sights settled on the last man, his red headband identifying him as Apache. Flame blossomed from the end of his Winchester, but firing from horseback never helped anyones aim. The extra second I took paid off, my bullet took him just left of center in the chest. He was dead before his rifle hit the ground.

The paint dragging the second man slowed when he got close to my animals. Herd instinct calming his fear. The other two mounts did like wise. The sound of approaching horses told me the escort for the wagons wasn't far behind them. I put the Sharps back on Wisp and checked the new animals. None of them had been hit. Shade had a small scratch from a rock shard. He didn't seem bothered by it, only twitching slightly when I cleaned it.

The soldiers had stopped where the men lay dead. They were looking around the scene with two watching me warily, their Springfields held ready. Not pointed at me, but prepared if I gave any sign of aggression. I had to put the Winchester away to get the poor man's foot loose, that seemed to make them relax. When they saw me start making a string to tie up the three horses, it was enough to break the stand off. Three of the six rode forward, calling out to me when they got a hundred feet away.

"Mind talking to us while you work, friend?" I had finished tying the string to Wisp and was crouching down beside the dead man.

"Nope, figured ya might have questions."

"My name is Lieutenant Smith. If my sergeant reads this correctly, we owe you a debt."

"Just don't like Bushwackers, and they usually have bounties." My answer seemed to have caught the man off guard. I'd pulled off the deadman's gun belt but his gun was somewhere between here and where he fell.

"Still, I'd like to thank you. Most likely, that rifleman would have killed one of my men." That got me to stop and look at the man curiously.

He sat upright in his saddle, like there was a metal rod up his spine. Maybe twenty-four at the most. His brown hair was tucked neatly under his hat. What gave him away as a greenhorn was the pale skin. He hadn't been out here for more than a month. Any longer and the sun would have started darkening his skin. The sharp green eyes studied me with more than a little condemnation.

"Woulda killed the wagon driver, that's what they wanted." I said simply.

"May I know your name, sir?" He was using respectful words, but the tone told me what he thought of me.

"Walker." I opened the wallet I'd found in the man's vest and smiled at the wanted poster it held. You had to appreciate these men carrying their own posters. It made life so much easier. He was worth a hundred dollars, enough to bother wrapping him up for the local sheriff. Looking back at the lieutenant, I asked for the information I needed. "Who's the commander in Albuquerque?"

"That would be Colonel Granger. I can't imagine what business you would have with him." Still polite, but definitely looking down on me while trying to figure out why I'd ask about his commanding officer.

"I'll clear off the road as quick as possible." He wanted more information, but I wasn't interested in talking to this popinjay.

"Ahhh yes, thank you." The man was happy to get out of a conversation he considered below him, but annoyed that he wasn't getting the information he wanted. Jerking the reins of his gelding sharply, he turned back toward the wagon. The two men with him didn't say a word, but both touched their hats in thanks before turning to follow him.

I rolled the man up in his bedroll and went to get the other two. One of them had a dodger in his wallet for two men, but it didn't match the one beside him. Maybe it was the man who'd fallen? If so, it was another hundred dollars for the two. The first one I shot was younger than the rest. Maybe he didn't have a reward yet. I collected the rifles and lost Colt from the first man. After rolling them to the side of the road, I gave a quick wave, letting the wagon driver know the road was clear.

It rolled by and the driver thanked me with a quick nod. He knew the way of things out here and recognized I had saved him. The lieutenant was leading, flanked by the two privates that had been with him before. A sergeant trailed behind the wagon in the dust. He stopped in front of me.

"Figure we owe ya a bit breed. Ain't my way normally, but ya have my thanks." He didn't wait for me to respond, just tipped his hat before speeding after the wagon.

I started climbing through the brush toward the last mans shooting position. Luck was with me. His horse was tied not far from the corpse. When I went to get his body, it followed me willingly. Unfortunately, his Springfield and field glasses hadn't fared well from their fall. He was the other half of the bounty, which made this worthwhile at least, brothers according to the poster. I rolled his pistol belt up and tucked it in his saddlebags. Wrestling him over his saddle wasn't bad, thankfully he wasn't a big man.

I took the time to search them all throughly before tying the men over their saddles. I found eighty-three dollars between them and about a hundred rounds of 44-40. That was always good to have, but didn't add up too much as the sum total of four men. It took me over an hour to get everything repacked, including the bodies. By the time I rode into Albuquerque, it was just short of noon. A few people stared at my sting of bodies. One of them happily pointed me toward the sheriff's office.

I wasn't surprised when the sheriff and two deputies were standing on the boardwalk waiting. He was a big man, about half way between working muscle and comfortable life starting to soften him around the edges. The first touches of grey were streaking his black hair. Sharp eyes peered up at me from underneath his hat. The man took my measure in an instant.

"Step down and tell me what happened. Damn fools can't tell a half breed from a white man." He grumped, glaring at one of his deputies. "Names Yarbrough. Most just call me Sheriff, rolls off the tongue easier.

"They only see the feathers. Walker, pleasure to meet you."

"John, go get the undertaker. Figure they have paper?" He

looked back at me expectantly.

"Three, the youngest either doesn't or was smart enough not to carry his own poster." I knew this man, not personally, but he was the same type that rode with me on the Bar C. A true western man who knew the way life worked out here.

"See if I can help." He stepped over to the paint with the younger mans body tied over the saddle. He lifted his head by the hair and studied the face for a minute. "Don't strike me right off, but might be on one. Got coffee inside."

Stepping out of the saddle I looked at my packs and the Sharps for a minute, thinking. The sheriff seemed to read my mind and solved my worries by telling the other deputy to stay out with my animals. He also added to be sure the undertaker didn't take anything but the bodies. Then he turned into the office, expecting me to follow. Inside was like every other lawman's office I'd been in. A stove sat in the corner with a burnt coffee pot on it. The low heat still made the small office stuffy. A battered desk sat toward the back of the room with two rough cut chairs in front of it. Wanted posters decorated the one wall, the other held a rifle rack. A single door was open at the back. I could just see three cells back there.

"Here." The sheriff handed me a battered tin cup full of coffee before taking his seat behind the desk. "Got them dodgers?"

"Let me dig them out." I sat the hot cup on the desk before digging into my wallet for them. He skimmed through a few newer ones on the desk while waiting.

"Don't think that young boy has one yet." He admitted after sorting through the stack. "Those others are accurate, though. The undertaker will verify them for us. Didn't look under that wrap, his face recognizable?"

"Good enough to identify. Foot hung in a stirrup when he got hit."

"Never a pretty sight, appreciate you covering him up. Figure I ought to ask how they found their way into the next life."

"Won't mind the abbreviated version? I can come back and give ya a full written report once I get some sleep."

"At'll do I reckon."

"Was coming up following the Rio maybe an hour or so out. Spotted one of them in the bushes when he moved. Thought they were there for me, but I heard a wagon rumbling along. Guessed that was their target an decided to interfere. First was their long shooter. He had a Springfield up on a ledge where the trail narrows."

"I know the spot." He nodded.

"Waited for him to sight down at the soldiers before I fired. After that I opened the dance, the other three charged. Winchester took them down."

"Four men an you didn't catch any lead?"

"Got a nasty burn on the side of my leg, but you know how shooting from a galloping horse is."

"Bout as useless as fish'n in a dry stream." He barked out a laugh.

"I was kneeling and prepared."

"That's how ya come out above ground most of the time." He studied me for a minute, like he was comparing me to the wanted posters. "Take a day or two ta get those drafts. Mind sticking around for a bit?"

"And to verify my story?" I laughed. He smiled, acknowledging the truth. "Planned on staying a couple of days anyway, so it's no bother. Lieutenant Smith was leading the wagon. He and his men saw most of it. Need to meet with Colonel Granger while I'm here. Hopefully, that won't take too long."

"Not sure that'll go like ya hope. Man still thinks he's in the capital. I know Smith's team, they'll be back in three days."

"I'll stick at least that long. Either way, I don't mind waiting on your okay." I shrugged, not seeing a reason to leave anytime soon. "Decent hotel around?"

"The Grand is pretty high end, couple of the others are decent but it's worth the money. Don't let the name fool ya, it ain't a fancy place. Take my meals in their dining room. They know they're in the west an still don't mind the dust."

"Thanks, I'll try there."

"Got a bath house out back an a Chinaman that does the laundry."

"I'm sold." I laughed. "The laundry alone would have done that."

"Come by tomorrow an file the report, that'll be fine. Jackson's livery is just down the street. I keep my animals there, if that's a recommendation for you. He'd likely take them extra off ya for fair price, too."

"I'll be by after breakfast." I hesitated, then asked carefully, not wanting to offend the man. "I start early. What times your breakfast?"

"Their dining room opens at sunrise. I'm usually there wait'n." His laughter made me relax. "I'm still a dark to dark man on my working hours."

"Probably see ya for breakfast."

"Just no conversation' til I get my first cup."

"Understood." I grinned before sticking out my hand to the man. He returned it with a firm grip before walking me outside. The undertaker was loading the last body into a cart as we walked out.

"Phil going to need the older three verified." The sheriff spoke to the man.

"Who's paying for this all?" Phil was a sallow, pockmarked man.

"County, so don't make it fancy."

"Just don't check their feet." The little man mumbled as he led his cart off.

"Don't buy boots from undertakers who own general stores nether." His deputy mumbled just loud enough for me to hear it.

# CHAPTER 17

"In the morning Sheriff." I said, tipping my hat to the man. Shade was tired from standing in the sun and nudged me to hurry up. "Don't worry, you're heading to the livery."

Stepping up into the saddle, I turned my little train toward the livery down the street. I had to circle around the town square to get there. Unlike most, this one was full of bawling oxen, cussing drovers, and a mix of men loading wagons in every direction. Wagons came and went almost constantly. It looked like chaos, but somehow it was all getting done without any major collisions.

Jackson's livery looked like the type of place you'd pick on sight, well cared for and clean. There were three corrals out back, all freshly mucked and not too crowded. The hostler looked a few years older than me. That caught me off guard at first. Seeing someone my age running a business wasn't that common, much less a livery.

"Reckon ya might be looking to sell a couple of 'em." He stated it like he'd been waiting for me. Despite his age, I could already tell the man knew his business.

"The four, tack an all."

"Can't take 'em guns, but Harper'll be over shortly. Heard ya come in trailing bodies, so's we been wait'n." He was stocky, maybe 5'6" but walking around at two hundred pounds easily. His skin was a deep black and his eyes were sharp.

"I'm here now." A bookish looking man said, coming around the corner. "Not much time. What do you have?"

"Yellowboy, two 73's, three Colts and a Remington. All the pistols have belts." The little man stared off into the distance for a minute, counting something in his head before he looking back at me.

"I can offer two hundred for the lot."

"Works." I agreed, stepping down. "Got a couple of Sharps big fifties that I might see you about later."

"Leave them here. I'll have my man pick them up later. Come by my shop when you're done and I'll pay you." With that, he spun away. Quickly disappearing back around the corner.

"Man's efficient, if nothing else. Figure we should talk horse flesh. For that, let's get them two taken care of first, do the rest in the shade." He motioned for me to follow him inside the stables. "Just hang your tack on the rail for now. I'll look over these four while you see to yours."

I didn't bother to respond, recognizing he wasn't interested in small talk. It was better to just started stripping off Shade and brushing him down. When he was done, and in a stall with fresh hay and water, I started on Wisp. She got the same treatment, but I made sure she got along with Jackson before putting her in a stall.

"She can be funny." I explained to the man.

"Ain't funny, prolly jus' smarter than most. If she was mine, I'd trust her 'bout folks."

"I do." The admission made the man smile before he went back to the horses and tack.

"Tack rooms back there. Ya can leave them buffalo guns and the rest in there. It stays locked up." I'd been cleaning my tack while he finished up.

"Need to clean them."

"Tables in there, most supplies too, ought to give me time to finish check'n these ponies." He nodded toward the back room. I gave both rifles a good cleaning before storing them with the rest. He finished with the four horses and tack about the same time.

"Got a price in mind?" I asked, walking back to join him just as he turned out the last horse.

"Ain't enough. Three of 'em are damn fine bits of horse flesh.

Don't change the fact that I can't do more than five hundred for the lot."

"Throw in those two staying here and we'll call it done." It wasn't uncommon for the property to be worth more than the bounty, especially not with horse prices still being over a hundred dollars for a middling one.

"Done. Draft from the bank work?"

"Ain't like I can't find ya if it's a problem."

"That's for truth." He laughed.

"Can ya point me to the Grand?" I asked when he handed me the draft. He'd already told me where to find Harper's gunsmith. It was right around the corner, the Grand was basically across the street from it.

The little gunsmith paid me with a draft from the same bank, adding another hundred for the two Sharps. I'd deposit the drafts once the sheriff had the bounty. Once the little man realized I was happy with my guns and wouldn't be buying anything, he went back to his work. It was almost rude the way he did business, but as I watched him work, it made sense. Some men were gunsmiths because it made money. This man was like Henk. He did it out of love for the craft. That separated him from the rest of us in some ways.

Maybe I'd tell him Henk had worked on my guns later. Right now, I wanted to get my room sorted and a bath. After that, I'd try to catch Granger before he closed his office for the day. It was still early afternoon, and I'd rather get that taken care of. The young man working the front desk eyed me carefully before agreeing to rent me a room. I'd already seen the sign that said no Indians, Irish, or Celestials allowed.

"Yes, sir. Did you want the first floor?"

"Got any with a balcony?" I asked because they always had room for my morning routine.

"Two suites, sir. Both on the second floor. They are two dollars a night." He watched me for a reaction. When none came, he smiled.

"I'll take it for a week." Fishing out the money to pay for

them. "The sheriff said you had a bathhouse and laundry?"

"Yes sir, baths are out back, hots two bits. Laundry, you can leave outside your door. The bill will be here when you're ready." He handed me the key to room 204 as he spoke.

"Thanks." I said, shouldering my saddlebags to walk toward the stairs. After a thought, I changed course. The bath first, I was past due.

An hour later, I felt ten pounds lighter. it seemed like washing off the trail dust made me lose weight. I'd met the laundry man coming out of the baths and gave him my dirty clothes. There was no reason to drag them up to my room when I could just to leave them there. With nothing else to do, I dropped off a few things in my room, then I started walking toward the commander's office. The clerk at the front desk told me where it was.

Walking around the square again, the mad pace had slowed somewhat, with fewer wagons leaving as the day drew on. The massive adobe building that dominated it was where I could find Granger. A private working at the door stopped me when I turned to go in.

"Sir, this is a military building. Can I ask your business?" He wasn't overly polite but did manage to hide the sneer that started to creep across his face.

"Is Colonel Granger still in?" I'd prepared for this ahead of time. Using some paper at the hotel, I'd written a simple note. It said one word on it 'Currier'.

"He is, but the colonel doesn't take visits from strange people." Another soldier had come up while the private questioned me. He was a corporal.

"Just give him this. I wouldn't recommend reading it yourself. It's a serious matter, I assure you."

"I can't ..." the private started, but the corporal cut him off.

"I'll take it to him, sir." The private looked at the other soldier oddly, not sure why he was speaking respectfully to me.

"Thank you corporal, I'll wait here." The private was truly confused now, but he was smart enough to keep his mouth shut. Two minutes later, when the corporal came back a little out of breath and told me to follow him, the private was at a complete loss.

"Right this way, sir." The corporal waved me through the door, then led me upstairs.

The man sitting behind a massive desk looked tired, but one look into his eyes revealed a sharp mind that was far from drowsy. It was all part of aging out here in the rough country. His body had been put through its paces and they had taken a toll. All of those hardships had been used like a wet stone to sharpen his mind, giving it a razor's edge. When the man stood, his straight back showed a man who would never bow. It gave me an immediate respect for the man.

"That'll be all, corporal." The man's voice was rich and full of power.

"Yes sir." The corporal didn't hesitate and closed the door.

"The documents?" Now the man's sharp eyes turned on me.

"I was meant to deliver these to Lucian Maxwell at Fort Sumner. When I arrived, he was dead. You were the closest place I felt sure of finding a man with sufficient rank, sir."

I didn't need to add the sir, but this man obviously deserved that respect. Putting the saddlebags on a chair, I carefully removed the false bottom and withdrew the papers at the bottom. I set each unopened package on the desk, then waited for the colonel.

"Well done, young man. I didn't expect to see you for another week." He took the papers and put them on the desk. Managing to keep my mouth from hanging open was an accomplishment I still take pride in.

"Sir?" It was all I could manage.

"I received word of Maxwell's death soon after it happened. You have made me a bit of coin because there was a small bet amongst those who know about the curriers." I couldn't help it. Laughter escaped my lips.

"How did you know I'd come here?"

"Simple logic. Please sit down, relax. I don't expect military formality from my officers, much as it annoys some of them." He sat back in his chair after waving me down. "I asked myself what I would do. That left only one option. Only here could you be certain to find an officer of significant rank. Fort Macy probably did, but that's still a chance."

"Fair enough Colonel, glad to contribute to your finances."

"It's more the pride of being correct." He chuckled before waving me to the worn pot on the stove. "Coffees there, but it's probably closer to mud if you're not used to it."

"Been punching south of Uvalde for three years. Mud means it's about right." Pouring myself a cup, I sank into the chair.

"Haven't been past San Antonio, but I understand the sentiment."

He looked thoughtfully out the window, memory filling his eyes. This was a man who suffered life in the office but still longed for a good horse under him. A long silence stretched out as we sat there, both of us recognizing the siren song of the land and its pull. He knew her song, probably better than me. It had obviously grabbed his soul long ago when he first ventured out here.

"What are your plans now, my young friend?" He broke the silence first, his eyes shifting back to me.

"West, no particular pace or reason other than to see the ocean."

"Might I impose on you for a bit?"

"How so?" Something about the way he said it told me this wasn't a currier job.

"You are one of two curriers whose background was verified. You may not know this, be we haven't had a marshal in the territory since last year. I have already been told a new marshal will be here after January." He was watching me for a reaction as he spoke. "Several territories are dealing with the same problem."

"Go on." I didn't know about staying here that long, but I'd hear the man out.

"I've also received permission to make you the U.S. Marshal

temporarily for this territory."

"It's not the time. Like I said, there's nothing waiting for me. How would this work?"

"The marshal's office is here. You'd have no deputies but could hire a jailer and a driver for the jail wagon. They'd have to know there was no promise of the new marshal keeping them on, of course. The office has an attached living area. Food would be in the officer's mess."

"I won't say no, but who would I answer to? There is, of course, the matter of pay."

"You'd only answer to me in this case. Pay is a hundred dollars a month and found, you do keep any bounties as well." That amount of money set off warning bells.

"What's the full story?"

"The papers you delivered refer to the Maxwell Land Grant Company. There is a war of sorts brewing in Colfax County. Rumors of corruption and pending violence are filtering in."

"And you want me to deal with it?" This was out of my league by leaps and bounds.

"Yes and no, I wanted to you to stall it. I realize this isn't something that can be solved by a lone marshal. My only hope is that we can hold off the violence for a few months. After that, the weight of the government can be brought to bear through a fully trained marshal."

"Not sure what I can do honestly, but I'll give it a try." The words surprised me when they came out of my mouth.

"You will?" It evidently surprised Colonel Granger. "Wait before you agree, I need to explain further."

"Go ahead."

"What I want you to do is information gathering. Go talk to Reverend Tolby. He can talk about the settlers that feel under attack. Try to make it clear that things will change when the new marshal arrives. The law in the area, Sheriff Rinehart, is following the law as he understands it. He's in over his head but, as far as I can tell, is working legally."

"What exactly is the problem?"

"Maxwell sold the land before he died to a group of English investors. Their company is the Maxwell Land Grant and Railway Company. Lucian had allowed settlers to build on his land with nothing more than a handshake agreement. He also let the Ute and Jicarilla hunt freely. The new owners consider the settlers' squatters and have been behaving aggressively toward the tribes."

"The courts?" I asked, hoping the answer in my head was wrong.

"Silent so far, but that's being addressed by other people. It's part of what Rinehart is struggling with. The simple legal answer is the company owns it."

"I'll take your money, but ain't sure what can be done."

"Ride there, be seen, talk to people. Even if that's all you do, it'll help. That and deal with a few hundred other duties that are far more straight forward." He laughed.

"Now I understand the pay."

"Cimarron can wait for now, or rather, it will have to. First, you'll have to catch up on the other duties. You'll need to find a driver for the jail wagon quickly. There's seven deserters that need to be brought back for trial in Las Cruces. That has to be your first job. There's a back log of prisoners waiting to be picked up all over the territory."

"I'll do what I can."

"You might find a drover at the Rolling Wheel Saloon, most of the men there are experienced. Take this and get situated. Your animals can be kept here or tell whatever livery you pick to send their bill here." He laid a heavy envelope on the desk and slid it toward me. "Inside you'll find the territory marshals badge, keys to the office, and a receipt book. Your expenses will be reimbursed so long as you have a receipt."

"What do I pay the driver and jailer?"

"Jailers pay is twenty-five dollars a month, the driver makes fifty plus expenses. The jail wagons behind the office, its mules are kept here. When you hire them, send word to me with their names. I'll make sure they can get the mules. The Jailer gets a small room at the office, comes with the job. They eat and fetch meals from the enlisted mess."

"If there's other questions I'll ask and there probably will be. The deserters go to the jail?"

"No, they come directly to my stockade, as do any other military prisoners. One last question. Are you going to keep the alias?"

That I hadn't considered yet. Acting as a lawman when people thought I was a half breed would make things harder. I'd been dodging a name for a long time, but didn't think having one as a lawman would be as bad. It would still be a thing, but it was different from being a gun hand. US Marshals especially had a reputation for being smart men who knew how to use firearms.

"I'll use my name, JC Stone." Saying it out loud made me wonder if I was making the right choice.

Stopping by the Wells Fargo office on the way to the Grand, I deposited my drafts and paid to have my trunk brought here. After getting my gear from my room and canceling my reservation, I walked to the marshal's office. Thankfully, my brain caught me before I made it too far and went back to the desk. It took a few minutes to have my laundry delivered to the office instead of my room and cost me another dime. They did promise it would be there in the morning.

After that, I walked down the street to the office. It was a squat adobe building like most of them. Built to survive a siege if need be. Unlocking the door, I stepped inside. My eyes scanned the front office, taking it all in. There were two doors, one right, one left with the desk between them. Out dated wanted posters dotted the right wall, the left had a small stove, coffee pot and collection of tin cups. The right wall held an empty rifle rack. It all looked solid, and it was a safe bet the rifles were with Granger.

The left door led down a short hall. There was the door on the right that opened to reveal a small bedroom. The jailer's room was my guess. At the end of the hall, a heavy door opened to reveal six cells. Three on either side of the long room. After checking them to assure myself they all worked, I walked back to the front office.

The other door lead to a decent sized office. The desk was backed by a bookcase, one wall had an empty gun rack and ammunition box. Beside the desk was another door that led to a small apartment. The main room was a comfortably furnished sitting area. There was a kitchen of sorts on the far wall. Two more doors were in the room. Behind one was a furnished bedroom. After tossing my saddlebags and bedroll down, I went to check out the last door. It opened to a walled area behind the building.

The space was large enough to hold the jail wagon and team when transporting prisoners. A small corral next to a well with a newer pump and outhouse. The back wall had heavy wood gates beside a normal door. A quick peek told me it opened onto the road out back. It would be plenty of room for my morning routine. The rocking chair beside the door was a welcoming sight. A part of me knew I wouldn't be spending much time here, but I'd enjoy it whenever possible.

There was some wood for the stove, both outside and stacked beside it. The real surprise was finding a pump inside. In the cupboard, I found the expected dishes, plates, silverware, enamel cups and such. On the stove was a skillet, coffee pot, and a cast iron Dutch oven sat on a shelf nearby. I wouldn't need my camping gear here. That could all stay with the panniers at the livery.

It was still too early to look around for a teamster, so I wasted a few hours setting up my bed and cleaning the place. Mostly just poking around, taking a quick inventory of what was there. The Greener, Sharps, quiver, and bow went in my office. After checking the ammo box, I made a quick list of what to get from Harper tomorrow. It was always better to have it at hand when you needed it. The last thing I did was change back into clothes that made me look like a white man.

That was really just changing the hat and vest. It still

amazed me that people would just assume someone was a half breed or a white man based on a few feathers and a buckskin vest. The hanging crow feathers and beads made me a breed. A Black hawk feather attached to the band on my hat, and suddenly I was a white man with a strange hat. It made no sense to me, but that's the way it worked. The last thing I did was pin on the territorial marshals star, my other one I left wrapped in my buckskins. There wasn't much difference between the two. The one I wore had 'New Mexico Territory' engraved across the bottom, where the other was blank. It was still early, but I was bored. Rather than get lost in a book I'd swing by the sheriff's office. Might as well let him know I'd be in the area.

# CHAPTER 18

A few people noticed the marshal's badge as I walk around town. Tipping my hat and saying hello to people got a mix of reactions. Most ignored me, uninterested in the stranger with a badge. The rest seemed friendly enough, but it was likely out of politeness more than anything personal. The majority of men were rough looking wagon drivers. Either waiting for a load to get finished so they could leave or looking for tomorrow's job. A few covered in dust groused about the trail or this mule, that river. They had just finished a job, some maybe for a day, others coming back after a week.

Dodging a few wagons as I crossed the street to the sheriff's office, there was a strange sense of familiarity in the act. I'd been dodging across streets most of my life and compared to New York, this wasn't worth noticing. Opening the door, I saw one of the deputies behind the desk, John, if my memory served. He looked up, then did a double take, studying me more carefully. When he looked at my face, I saw the guess at my age come to his mind. He was easily ten years older than me, but somehow I outranked him.

"Ya wasn't wearing a badge earlier."

"Nope, wasn't a marshal then." I grinned back at the man. "Sheriff Yarbrough in?"

"Yup." He knocked on the wall behind him. A chair scraped on the floor when someone pushed back from a desk. Soon a door opened, followed by the big man's steps echoing down the hallway.

"What the hell John?" When he rounded the corner, glaring at his deputy. His eyes almost casually studied me until he spotted the star. "Marshal?"

"Good to see ya again, Sheriff." He studied me for a bit. The questions were easy to read, but he managed to push them down.

"Can't say as I expected that." Had to give the man credit, he adapted pretty quickly. "Mind sharing the story?"

"Sure, ya want it out here?"

"Na, got coffee in the office. Come on back." He turned back to the door behind him, motioning for me to follow.

Once we were seated in his office, I gave him the story Granger and I had come up with. The Colonel knew me when I was a deputy marshal in the nations. He'd pulled some strings to get me temporarily assigned to New Mexico until the permanent marshal got here. Mostly, I was going to pick up prisoners and transport them for trial.

"Makes sense. Had more than a few sheriffs reach out about the men they've been hold'n." Yarbrough laughed.

"Just need to find a jailer an a teamster."

"Teamster, ya can take your pick. Jailer, I can help you out with straight away. Willie knows the drill, did the job afore."

"Know where I can find him? Much rather have a man who knows the job."

"Likely I do." He laughed and banged on the wall. John appeared soon with a questioning look on his face. "Fetch Willie. Should be sleeping in the second cell."

"What's he in a cell for?" I asked, curious about the man and why the sheriff would recommend someone locked up.

"Let him sleep there. He cleans my cells in trade for the bed and a meal. He's a good man, don't worry. Caught an arrow in the knee a few years back, can't ride long or work cattle anymore. He did some time on a chuck but didn't have the skills for cook'n."

"I know the story. Knows his way around firearms?"

"Wasn't ever a gun hand but he can mange his own well enough, prefers a shotgun."

The man who appeared in the door looked somewhere

between fifty and a hundred. Leather like skin stretched over a wire thin frame, his face was like a road map of every trail in Texas. The long white beard that covered everything from the bottom of his nose to mid chest bounced as he scratched his chin. There was a twinkle in his lidded green eyes when he looked me up and down.

"That's cause anyone with sense don't want ta face a double barrel." His dry, cracked voice reminded me of hard leather scraping over rocks. "Don't even look old 'nough ta drink boy."

"Call me boy again an you better know how to use that." My voice had just a touch of ice. The gun in question was a dragoon. On the short, thin frame, it looked like he had a cannon strapped on his hip.

"Don' get yer hackles up, don't mean nothing by it." He stepped forward and extended his gnarled hand. "Names Willie, an I can watch yer jail."

"JC Stone, figure you're hired then." I handed the jailer's keys to him after shaking hands. His gnarled hand didn't lack strength, I could still feel the calluses from hard labor on them. "Sheriff says you know how it works."

"I do. How long I got this time?"

"Few months, get ya through the first part of winter. Can't say if it'll have much weight, but I'll recommend ya to the permanent marshal when he comes in."

"Til he goes corrupt or gets run off." The old man growled. "Figure 'at'll do."

"If the new man don't want ya I'll try the council again Willie. Towns grow'n an I'm gonna need a jailer." Yarbrough broke his silence.

"Hell, maybe I'll get myself killed first." He said it with a grin, showing off a full set of perfect white teeth.

"Always good to have a goal." I laughed, liking to old timers' pessimistic attitude.

"Enough jabber'n. I'll get my stuff an move in. Figure I need ta clean up 'round the place 'for it's fit for liv'n."

"Need anything, just let me know." I took twenty-five dollars out of my wallet and handed it to him. "Get coffee and the like to have at the office, along with whatever you need."

"Chow still with the soldiers?" The grimace on his face told me how much he liked that idea.

"Unless you want to cook." I laughed.

"Only thing worser than the mess is my cooking boss." His cackling laugh joined mine. "Figure I'll see ya at the office if'n ya don't get killed 'fore then."

"He always looks on the sunny side of things." Yarbrough offered with a grin.

"Appreciate the bunk sheriff." Willie's voice carried into the room from down the short hall. it was followed by the sound of a closing door.

"Willie's a good sort. Glad to get him working again. Mind you, as soon as the town council approves it, I'll be stealing him."

"Good to know you think that highly of him. Appreciate the loan as long as it last. About time to see about finding a driver. Need to start working soon, I reckon." Standing from the chair, I extended my hand to the sheriff.

"If ya have a question' bout any of... no, scratch that. You need help. Just let me know. If you're checking the Rolling Wheel, ask Moe. He's the big guy behind the bar, knows the drivers better 'an most."

"I'll be around if ya need my badge for anything." Pausing before walking out the door, I added. "Forgot my other reason for stopping by. Probably miss breakfast, but I'll come by for the paperwork."

"Understandable. Just come by when ya can. Drafts should be ready soon. If you ain't around, I'll leave'em with Willie." I tipped my hat in thanks and headed to find a drover.

The saloon was easy to find. It wasn't far from the square, unsurprising since most of the men started and finished there. It was still early, but the place already had a decent crowd. Most were eating what smelled like good stew with coarse bread. A few tables had bottles of whiskey, but most were beer or coffee.

These were men who worked every day, hard drinking wasn't a luxury they had often. They all looked rough and ready. Like punchers, teamsters dealt with many of the same dangers. More so in some ways because wagons were hard to move and slower than a horse. All wore guns and more than one table had a shotgun laying on or leaning against them. The big difference was the boots. Teamsters preferred the heavy boots of miners with reinforced toes over the heeled riding boots.

Behind the bar was a bull of a man. He stood close to seven feet tall and looked to have been assembled from stone. The salt and pepper mustache balanced on his face was so heavily waxed it looked carved from the same rock. His eyes constantly scanned the room and paused when he spotted me. Slowly, he nodded to me after his examination, deciding for himself that I would be allowed in his world. The badge didn't have anything to do with his decision. This was a man who knew how to judge people. Clothes, badges, guns, none of that made a difference. His eyes judged and weighed, then decided.

Walking to the end of the bar, I angled my self to face toward the door with a wall to my back. The position let me see most of the room with an eye on the swinging bat wings. The big man watched me with that knowing smile most western bartenders had before heading my way.

"Marshal, hadn't heard there was a new one." He stuck out a hand that looked like it would swallow mine. "Names Moe, though most will say Big Moe. Always figured it over stated the obvious."

"Might be meant as a warning." I smiled, shaking his hand. "Names JC."

"What can I get ya?" I'd noticed condensation on the mugs and knew the beer was cold.

"Cold beer wouldn't go amiss." He stepped down the bar and pulled a draft before handing it to me.

"Be dime."

"Need a man for the jail wagon. It won't be permanent, least wise I can't promise it will be."

"So you're looking for someone good with team an guns, maybe a bit of cooking thrown in?"

"For my sake, switch the last two on importance and I'd take that version."

"Particular 'bout the way they look?"

"Not a bit, only thing I'd want to avoid is a man who feels the need to fill the silence."

"Think I know a man, but ya won't find him in here. Names Moses, most who'll talk ta him just call him Mos. If he's got a last name, I ain't heard it." He rubbed a thumb across his jaw, thinking for a minute before he continued. "Ain't like ta see him in here. Last I heard, he had a camp set up 'bout a half mile west of town. You'll see an old lightning split tree beside the road. Turn left there. Likes ta keep to himself. Most folks agree with him on the subject."

"I'll take a ride and see if I can find him. Sounds like we might get along."

"Be sure ya sing out loud when ya see his fire. He ain't one for surprises." Moe's laugh was a deep rumbling roll like thunder.

"I'll do that." Another man stepped to the bar requiring his attention, and Moe left me to my drink.

It was a good beer, cold with a hint of sweet to the taste. Loud conversation filled the room with a constant drone. The smoke from pipes, cigars and cigarettes drifted lazily around the room, adding to the haze. There was no off key piano banging in the corner. I'd learned long ago that no piano west of St.Louis had ever been tuned. No saloon girls wove seductively between the men, trying to tempt a few dollars from them. There were five waitresses deftly flowed through the crowd. They varied in age from maybe twenty to forty-ish. These men didn't want ladies or poker, they wanted food, a decent drink, and time to socialize.

After finishing my beer, I walked back to the livery. Shade fussed a bit when I took Wisp out, but I still needed some time riding her. There was also the scratch that needed to heal. It wasn't bad, but there was no need to risk pushing him. Every animal was different: temper, gait, all of it. The vaqueros back at the Bar C had hammered in the need for a rider to know their animal. According to them, it was the only way to be worth a damn in the saddle. After bribing both animals with carrots, I tacked up Wisp, doing my best to ignore Shade's accusatory glare.

Wisps' light, fast gait took me west out of town in no time. Two wagons passed us on the road before I spotted the tree Moe had mentioned. Keeping to the west of it, I started searching for a camp. A little over a hundred yards ahead of me, I spotted the glow of a fire. Remembering the advice, I slowed my pace. When I got within fifty yards, my voice broke the serenity of the area.

"Hello the fire!"

"Ain't noth'n here ta steal." The answer had the strangest accent I'd ever heard. Southern drawl mixed with an Indian dialect, not sure which tribe, but I did recognize the inflection.

"Looking for Moses." I had stopped Wisp before calling out and now sat waiting.

"Ain't nothing a law dog wants wit me, ain't even been ta town." I still couldn't place the accent and it was starting to bother me.

"Moe at the Rolling Wheel says you're the man to see 'bout driving a jail wagon."

"Ride in, ain't got much but chicory ta offer."

"Won't be the first time I've had it." The accent made more sense once the man came into view.

The man standing beside the fire was a bit shorter than me, solidly built but not big by any stretch. His build reminded me of Red Wolf, lean and meant to run for days. Dressed in buckskins that looked worn and comfortable, like me, he wore no adornment on them. His skin was a smooth brown with the first hints of age starting to show around the eyes. The long braids, rolled in the Cherokee style, hung down to his chest. I saw three feathers in the back and beads woven in the braids glinted in the firelight. The accent made complete sense to me now. The man was a half-breed. Black and Cherokee was my guess. Moe's question made more sense now. If people didn't like white half breeds, I could only imagine how they treated this man.

"Seen me now. Ya can ride on, won't take no offense."

"Rescinding your offer of hospitality?" The anger that flashed across his face told me I'd hit the mark. He'd grown up in the tribes, rescinding one's hospitality once offered was a serious thing.

"Step down then, white man." He snapped, but the anger faded and he studied me carefully. "Just answered a question for you, didn't I?"

"Haáhe." I greeted him in Cheyenne. "I am called Grey Walker."

It took the man back, making him take a good look at me. The black hawk's feather in my hat, the long braid hanging down my back. Then he stared at the marshals star pinned on my chest.

"You ain't Cheyenne." He stated flatly

"No, I'm white. JC is my Christian name." I switched back to English. "I am a friend of the People. Maybe not with the Apache. They have always been my enemy."

"They are enemy to anyone who ain't Apache."

He stepped back and sat down across the fire, motioning for me to join him. I took a cup out of my saddlebags with a small bag of coffee and sat down opposite him. The small bag was one I always had ready as a gift when I shared another mans fire. I tossed the bag to him and saw the faint hint of a smile. After another minute of studying me, he filled my cup, then topped off his.

"My thanks." I said, after sipping the scalding brew.

"What is it you came here for?" He was curious, not concerned.

"Like I said before, I need a driver for the jail wagon. Someone who can handle four mules, shoot if need be and, more importantly, cook. Also, have to help deal with the prisoners. Pays fifty a month and found."

"Why me?" His blunt question wasn't meant as a challenge.

"Big Moe recommended you when I asked about finding someone who wouldn't fill the air with noise. Can't promise the job past December."

"You got a wagon an team? I'd want to study them before agree'n." He didn't seem to care about the time limit.

"Wagons at the office, teams at the military livery. Truthfully, I haven't looked at them yet."

"I'll do it tomorrow."

"You fixed for guns?" I noticed the cap and ball pistol he carried. It and the shotgun looked well maintained, but they'd seen some use.

"These and a yella' boy."

"Won't work for this. After you look at the mules, come talk to me at the office. Should have something more suited to the work for you. Make it around lunch after you get a supply list together. We'll be leaving the following morning."

"I don't need..." This wasn't up for debate, so I cut him off.

"It wasn't a question, not betting my life on something getting fouled." I realized how that sounded and tried to soften the blow. "I'm not saying those are bad weapons. Simply that for the work we'll be doing, I don't want to risk a fouled cap or wet powder."

"That's fine." He got a slight smile that almost looked painful. "I just don't know when I can pay you for them."

"I have a feeling that won't take long, found includes bounties. When we happen to run across wanted folks on our travels, you'll get half. Provided you lend a hand 'course."

"Think I'll like working with you, Marshal."

"Just JC, see ya tomorrow. Right now my social skills have 'bout hit their limit."

"I'll be there at first light."

"Might be out to breakfast, but I'll let Willie know to expect you."

Willie would probably be at the office and I hadn't been

kidding. My social skills were about finished for the day. It's funny how that had changed since leaving the east coast. Too many days with Jose spend in silence or alone riding the line. I didn't hurry Wisp, and we made it to the livery with the last bit of light. Jackson was just closing down. I helped him get Wisp taken care of before leaving. I didn't feel like eating with other people, so I took a few supplies with me to cook. Tomorrow I needed to pick up some supplies to keep at the office. Beans with some jerky would due for now, it wouldn't be flavorful but it would fill the hollow spot in my stomach.

The light was still on in the office and when I opened the front door, Willie came out from the back. The man had been busy. The front office was neat and the wood stove radiated heat. From the smell drifting around the room, the coffee was still fresh.

"Can't stand a mess where I work, 'preciate ya keep'n that in mind."

"Works for me. Let me go throw these bags down and I'll come have a cup of that coffee with ya. You tell me how you'd like to run this."

"Go ahead, be a new experience hav'n a marshal ask me." He chuckled as I walked back to my quarters.

I dropped the saddlebags on the small kitchen table and put my Winchester in the rack. After taking my coffee cup out, I walked back up front.

"Tell me the way you'd like this to be done, Willie. I got my office and no deputies, so most of the day to day will be up to you."

"Bout time one of ya'll badge totters recognized how this ought ta work." He laughed. "Keep it simple enough for ya. Don't worry 'bout the jail or 'em fools locked up in there. Ya kin leave 'em ta me, jus' don't make me a mess out here if ya kin help it."

"Seems fair to me." I took a sip of the coffee and let out an appreciative whistle. "You make some good coffee."

"Learnt it from an old mountain man. Add some chicory

while it's boil'n then mix in the secret ingredient whilst it cools. Find ya a wagon driver?"

"Moses, he's coming in to check out the mules and wagon tomorrow."

"Good man, he'll stand." That was high praise from someone like Willie.

"Seems like. You fixed alright on what you need?"

"I'll get what I need from Nickles tomorrow."

"Nickles?"

"Quartermaster Sergeant. He's got the office guns and what not. Don't worry none, we know'd each other a while."

"I'll leave you to it then." The man knew this job better than me, so I had no reason to interfere."

"Mos know the score?"

"Same as you. I'll recommend, but can't promise." Then I added with a laugh. "Just get him to taste that coffee and you'll be hired."

"Ain't the first time I heard that." He laughed with me and pulled a worn pipe out of his pocket with some tobacco.

"I need to eat. My stomach thinks my throat's been cut. Be gone before first light to meet the sheriff for breakfast. Let me know if you have any problems. Can you let Nickles know about Moses?"

"They won't bother him none. Like him or not, they know he won't do nothing he ain't opposed to. Sides Nickles likes Mos, trusts him to run payroll if the commander ain't look'n."

"Good to know." I said, turning toward the back, but he stopped me.

"Marshal, ya ought to make it to the officer's mess." He studied me for a moment, then explained. "Them officers will wanna know who this fancy new marshal is. They're bout like a bunch of hens. If'n ya don't go a bunch of 'em likely come here to see the elephant."

"Why?" That didn't make any sense.

"A breed had a meet'n with the colonel then goes and turns inta a white man tottin a badge? Can't imagine why they'd be curious." He laughed.

"I'll give you that." I agreed, chuckling. I did wonder how he knew so much, but was too done in to think about that right now. "Where's the officer's mess?"

He gave me directions after assuring me they were still serving. What followed was the most trying meal I'd had in a very long time. Military officers couldn't understand the hair, my age, or how I'd been trusted with the badge. One even swore he was going to send a telegram to his family in New York to check after questioning me.

The man didn't look pleased when I asked him coldly if he was calling me a liar. A major had stepped in, making him apologize for his careless words. He did, but I could tell by the look on his face he still planned on sending the telegram. Not that I cared one way or the other. Being questioned by the pompous ass just bothered me. The major was decent enough and knew what I really was. He turned out to be the executive officer. Smiling, he tried to explain that most of the junior officers had no clue what it meant to live out here.

The food was much better than my planned meal would have been. Aside from the one lieutenant, most were just curious about me. Life out here was months of boredom followed by ten minutes of gut wrenching excitement. Anything new that wasn't trying to kill you was a novelty they couldn't pass up. By the time I escaped, the major assured me I'd given them enough for the evening. When I mentioned Moses to him, the man looked unhappy, but said he'd make sure there were no problems.

I made it back to the office and sat out front with Willie for a pipe before finding my way to bed. It had been a full day with far too many people, and I doubted tomorrow would be any better. After that, I'd be out of the city on open land again. I had to laugh at myself again. Most of my life, I'd been surrounded by people. Now even a few days of it grated on me. The last thing I did was pen a letter, letting the folks back home know where they could reach me for a while.

# CHAPTER 19

I was rinsing off after my morning routine when I heard a knock on the back gate. Moses was standing there when I opened it. He looked at me funny before walking over to the wagon. That was fair considering I'd opened the door shirtless, with a Colt in my hand. Leaving the man to his work, I went inside to get dressed. When I stepped back out, he was just finishing his inspection using a lamp he'd found by the wagon. The sky was just starting to show color. It was a good sign that he got started this early.

"Coffees on the stove if you want it." I said, sitting in the chair beside the door.

"Willie's?"

"Sorry it's mine." He shrugged and stepped inside to get a cup.

"Wagons good, needs some grease. That's about it." He said, walking back out with his cup.

"How many manacles are in the box?"

"Twelve full sets."

"Ought to be enough. You going to draw supplies from the quartermaster, or do you need money for the general store?"

"Mostly from the army. Might need a few from Murphy's."

"I'll set up an account after breakfast. You'll be able to draw on it. Make sure you get a hundred each 44s and two hundred 44-40's. Add fifty twelve gauge to that an get whatever else you need."

"I'll bring the mules over today, test out the rig picking up supplies. There's enough feed here. Be ready at first light."

"Ain't got a spare bed, but you're welcome to the floor if you want." He studied me for a minute, almost like he didn't believe me.

"Mind if I camp under the wagon?"

"Suits me fine. You're welcome either way."

"Used to being outside."

A comfortable silence fell over us as he watched the light start to fill the sky. I couldn't see it but the smells of life were beginning to fill the air. Willie came out not long after with his own coffee.

"Hope ya don't mind boss, figured ya was out here." Despite the limp, he had come up silently. Only the slight scoff of one boot had given him away. "Mos good ta see ya, coffees on the stove out front."

"Thanks, my friend. Been missing good coffee." Moses smiled and shook Willie's hand before going inside.

"Refill this, will you?" I asked, after tossing out what was left.

"Got a taste of his coffee already?" Moses laughed, taking my cup.

"Last night."

"Y'all heading down the trail tomorrow?" Willie asked once he'd eased himself down to the bench.

"First light."

"Figure I won't have much ta do till y'all get back. Gimme me plenty of time ta get things set to right."

"All of them from this run will be going to the stockade. You'll have an empty house for a while yet."

"Got a stack of telegrams from sheriffs wait'n on ya. They'll fill quick enough." Willie grinned as I took the cup Moses held out.

"Colonel said we'd keep busy just catching up." I admitted, inhaling the smell that drifted up from my cup. Moses walked back to finish whatever he was doing with the wagon, ignoring the conversation.

"I'll map out good routes for y'all. That way ya ain't try'n ta run this way an that."

"That'd be a big help."

Silence fell across the small courtyard, broken by the creaking leather and jingling metal as Moses laid out his traces. Finally he seemed satisfied and walked back toward to two of us. With a grunt, he announced. "Going to get the mules."

"Want me ta bring chow back for ya?" Willie offered. His joints creaked and popped as he stood. None of it slowed the man down, and he never showed a hint of discomfort. Moses didn't speak, just nodded his acceptance before disappearing inside. He was back out, striding toward the gate minus his coffee cup a minute later. Willie nodded to me before ambling back inside to see about his business. That was my hint to be about mine.

I stopped by the hotel and officially checked out. The star pinned on my chest was the only thing that got the balanced refunded to me. That much I figured out because the clerk said he couldn't do it last night. I'd need to speak to the manager. Across the street at Wells Fargo, I sent off my mail and caught a bit of luck. My crate would be in later this afternoon. It was coming in with a shipment for the general store. It cost fifty cents to have them deliver it to Willie, since I wasn't sure where I would be when it arrived. For what I was going to be doing, the return of my scattergun would be a welcomed addition.

My stomach demanded attention before I made it much further. The officer's mess was still busy, and I got more than a few stares. They got more subtle when Colonel Granger asked me to join him at his table. He introduced me to Major Collins, his executive officer or XO. We'd met the night before, but I hadn't remembered the man's name.

"Moses is a good man but not well liked." Granger commented after we'd all finished eating.

"Any particular reason besides the obvious?" I asked.

"Mostly his heritage, half black and half Commanche. He's also not shy about telling folks the tribe treated him better than the civilized world." That tidbit surprised me. I hadn't thought of Commanche, but it made sense out here. To my surprise, Collins spoke up in response.

"He's not wrong." He said it quietly enough that only we heard him, but Granger still glared at him.

"I'll not debate the topic, especially not when others can hear us."

"Yes, sir." Granger sighed before soothing his obviously annoyed XO.

"I don't disagree and you know it. The man saved fifteen of our soldiers and paid a heavy price for it. For not having to write those letters, we will both be in his debt."

"Any chance of sharing that story?" I asked, curious now that I had a hint.

"Not much to tell from our side. Few years back he got fifteen of our soldiers free after they were captured. It cost him his home. They considered it an act of cowardice, but he knew what would happen if we had to ride in there to fetch our boys back. He'll never have problems with my older soldiers. Some like Nickles were among those captured." Granger told a very brief version.

"Ask him about it. The Colonel makes it sound very cut and dry. It was not, not at all, and for a young greenhorn captain it saved me a lot of pain. Very likely my life and career as well." Collins solemnly added.

"You'll have to get the details from the man himself. He's been very reticent to offer them for a formal report." Granger laughed. "As I'm sure you've noticed, the man isn't very chatty."

"Main reason I hired him. Can't stand someone who feels that silence is a personal affront." This statement, of course, brought the expected awkward silence.

"Well, yes." Granger finally broke it. "I'd expect that's a precious thing to a young man from New York."

"Or punching longhorns." Collins added, laughing.

"True, in both cases, gentlemen." I smiled, unfolding from my chair. "We'll be gone at first light. Shouldn't be more than a week to make it back with your prisoners."

"I'll have the trial ready." Granger looked up at me over his coffee. "Good travels Marshal."

"Colonel." I nodded to him and then to Collins. "A pleasure seeing you again, Major."

"Same Marshal." A porter was already clearing my plate after refilling their cups.

I managed to get out of the mess hall without further conversation. Checking my Colts before stepping out into the street, a habit that had been drilled into me. I walked toward Harper's Gunsmith, but changed my plans when I remembered the sheriff still needed my written statement. It was tucked into my wallet, ready to be delivered. It was the last thing I'd done last night before going to sleep. Somehow I escape without getting trapped in conversation and soon I was opening the door at Harper's. The man was behind the counter when I came in. Working on one of the Sharps big fifty's he bought off me. He didn't move toward the counter, but looked up at me curiously.

"Need a good Winchester '73, nothing fancy. A Greener of you have one. Hundred Schofield 45's." I'd already learned the man didn't like to chat, so I dove straight in. True, Moses was picking up some ammunition, but there was no such thing as too much.

"Used '73 will save a few dollars, only Greener I got is new, though." He set down a good-looking Winchester. There was a lone scratch on the stock, but the rest looked perfect. "Got all the ammunition. Call it seventy-four dollars for everything."

"Fair enough if ya throw in a sack to help me carry it all."

"Did you need any work on the Schofield?" The man asked almost longingly. "Or those Colts you carry?"

"Henk in Dodge did the Colts, not sure who did the Schofields, but someone did them right."

"Henk did those?" He'd stopped moving and focused on me, well on my guns anyway.

"Back when I first came out west, first ones he ever did."

"May I?" The tone of his voice reminded me of a soiled

dove flirting with a customer. It was almost enough to make me uncomfortable. Rather than answer, I drew my cross draw and unloaded it. After handing it to the man, he seemed to disappear into it, but quickly looked up in shock.

"Wait, these are chambered for the 44-40. Where did you get them?"

"A gift from a friend. He owns some stock in Colt."

"I'd heard rumors but didn't expect to see them. Not yet, at any rate." He mumbled the last as his attention was drawn back to studying the gun. Finally, after ten minutes of standing there listening to the man mumble under his breath, he handed it back. Reloading it automatically before sliding it back in place, I waited for him to speak.

"You have my thanks. The man is a genius. It's such a rare pleasure to see his work." He finished getting my order together, but stopped me when I reached for my wallet. "Forty dollars. The rest is my thanks for letting me examine that fine weapon."

"That seems like a pretty big change for just that."

"I got a small hint of how to do something I'd been working on. I'd give you it for free if I could afford it."

"Won't argue with it too much, but I'll add to my side of it." I picked up the bundle and two rifles without explaining after handing him the money.

Ten minutes later I walked back in, handing the stunned man my Winchester. Once he saw Henk's mark, a grin split his face. He left me standing there for the next twenty minutes while he studied it. When the man handed it back, there was a glazed look on his face.

"Simple amazing. If you handed that to its maker, they wouldn't know recognize their own work." When I looked closely, I had to smile. The man looked shell-shocked.

Leaving him staring off into space, I walked back to the office. The jingling of harnesses told me Moses was back with the mules. I dug out one of the Schofields and tucked it behind my belt. Harper probably had a good custom pistol, but these were free. I'd still have one left unless Moses wore two guns.

Stepping into the courtyard, I took in the four mules. They'd been curried to a polished shine. Moses probably did it while examining the animals. They weren't exactly matched in appearance. All four were brown, but that's where it stopped. They were a consistent size, that was the important thing. I'd leave them to Moses. The man knew his business according to everyone I'd talked to. He was currently putting the rear two in their traces.

"Come inside before you leave. Got some new weapons for ya." He didn't even look away from his work, just grunted his agreement.

A while later, Moses walked in the back door. He stopped to fill a tin cup with water before sitting with me at the table. His eyes flicked at the guns laying on the table, then the bag. I could see him fighting internally. He liked what he saw but didn't like the idea of owing anyone.

"Winchester 73, there's a hundred rounds in the bag for that. The Greener has twenty rounds." I watched him pick up the lever action first. He worked the action and dry fired it a few times. When he was satisfied, he set it down and picked up the Greener. Opened the shotgun, checked it then closed it and tested the pull on the hammers. After dry firing it a few times, he grunted out his response.

"Still don't want to owe you."

"Ain't done." I said, pulling the '75 Schofield from behind my back. "Hundred rounds for that in the bag. After you pick up the supplies, go out a ways and fire them. Aint worried about owing me. I'm more interested in both of us stay'n alive."

He took the pistol and worked through it. I could just see his lips twitch up. The weapon had been worked right. I didn't know who'd done the work, but someone had known their craft. The front sight was shaved off, the hammer flared just a bit to make it easier to catch with your thumb. They had also smoothed out the cylinder action.

"Can't owe you this much."

"Twenty dollars." That made his eyes snap up from the pistol in his hand and lock on me. "That and two small pieces of lead is all I paid for them."

"How?"

"Schofields are from a bounty. Harper charged me twenty for the rest cause I let him look at my guns." There was a look of disbelief on his face, but he was still debating it.

"Why would he do that? Just to study your guns?"

"Both my Colts and my Winchester were redone by Henk in Dodge City." That made his eyes go wide. Maybe Henk was a bigger deal than I thought.

"I'm not fool enough to turn down that deal." He finally cracked a smile. "Got a holster for this?"

"Fool who had it wore two pistols, but we can slide the other one off."

"You wear two." He observed.

"Not set up to use my left hand. Only met one man who could shoot worth a damn with his left hand." I laughed, remembering the man who'd taught me to fan that second shot. "Even he admitted it was stupid outside of a show tent."

I'd gotten up to retrieve the gun belt while talking. Thankfully, the second holster floated, and we were able to get it off easily. He didn't bother hiding his smile now, fitting the rig he tested the draw a few times. He wasn't trying to show off, but his movement was smooth and clean. I'd bet even money on his speed against most men.

"I'll get in some practice with all of them. Thank you, Marshal." He left carrying the bag and weapons. I figured that was a gushing response from him.

Watching him pack them away in the box under the seat of the wagon made me smile. He knew the value of good weapons and it showed in how he cared for them. I opened the gate letting the team moved out. After locking it back, I went inside just in time to hear something banging down the hallway. Willie was dragging my trunk, steadily cursing my existence.

"Damn useless lazy no good sons of ...oh didn't see ya there

Marshal." Willie looked a bit embarrassed. "Wells Fargo driver wouldn't help carry this damn'dable trunk."

"Grab the back." I said, stepping forward to grab one end.

"What the hells in this?" He asked.

"Clothes and a couple of extra guns." I didn't mention the amount of ammunition that was in there. It wasn't much, but enough to add some weight. "Also a small collection of Apache knives. Habit I picked up in Texas."

"Did'ja buy in bulk?"

"No, it's just the ones I killed."

"Any of 'em left in the whole damn state?" He grumbled, letting his end drop to the floor near the small dining room table.

"Figure I left a few still wandering around." I laughed before opening the trunk.

I took out the clothes and put them in the small bedroom with the clean clothes. The laundry had dropped them off at some point. Willie watched me curiously. With each knife I laid on the table, he let out a low whistle. It wasn't all of them. Some had been traded or gifted. Truthfully, I didn't think about it until they were all laid out on the table. I might need to stop collecting them.

Twenty-four buckskin sheaths covered most of the table. There wasn't one I couldn't remember exactly where it was taken. Each one had a story tied to it. That didn't change the gruesome reality that was spread out in front of me. Each one was from an Apache I'd killed, either by blade or gun.

"You ain't old 'nough for that." Willie finally breathed out. Then his eyes took in my sawed off. "Where the hell did you find that nightmare?"

"Caldwells not long after I came out from New York. The old owner didn't have much use for it anymore. It's saved my life twice now, once against some Arapaho braves that tried to raid a trading post I was in. The first time was in New Orleans."

"It's a nasty piece of work, an that holder looks a bit off."

"It's for my saddle." I laughed. "This side ties off to D-ring on the right side, the other one hangs on the left."

"Be a nasty shock for folks with bad intentions." He let out one of his dry, cackling laughs. "Guessing at one's fer carry'n it under a coat? Fancy bit a leather there."

"I wouldn't say it's fast, but you get the idea."

"Ya know I wasn't 'xactly certain bout you. Mean no disrespect, just kinda young. Looking at this, I ain't got no doubts."

"You're not the first one who wondered about my age." I laughed before packing the knives back in the trunk. "Doubt you'll be the last."

Absentmindedly, I took out my first gun. The Colt navy in its shoulder holster. Still rust free, liberally coat in oil and wrapped in cloth. Studying it, my mind went back to the hours of practice I'd spent with it. It had been carried every day for years and never once used. Those years had taught me lessons that helped keep me alive out here, not in killing but in judging men. I carefully repacked the gun, then nestled the bundle holding the raven beside it in the trunk. They were two things that would stay, following me until my ranch became a reality.

Willie had gotten up at some point. I could hear him out front working on something. Repacking my saddlebags with clean clothes so they'd be ready for the morning was done without much thought. It was my normal load: two shirts, pair of pants, lucifers, piggin strings, spare cartridges, some jerky, and my ever present buckskins. There were several swaths of clean cloth wrapped around a bottle of corn liquor for wounds. A sewing kit finished off the medical kit. My fishing gear was packed beside that.

I'd repack my bedroll in the morning, wrapping it carefully around my bow and arrows. Hunting with it drew less attention. It also served the dual purpose of keeping my skill up. I spent the afternoon cleaning my weapons. On a whim I took the Sharps over to Harper's. He said fine tuning it was all he could do. He'd have it done by the time I got back. That worked for me, besides I wanted someone who really knew those weapons to go through it. Being able clean it was one thing, but anything I was going to keep it was worth having a gunsmith check out. That was another habit Tom had hammered into my head.

Moses made it back that night and set up a simple camp near the wagon after turning the mules out. The only thing I asked him about was coffee. He assured me he'd gotten enough for the trip. With a smirk he specified that it was enough for the two of us He wasn't sure about anyone else. He'd put the ammo in the office before setting up his camp.

Dinner was uneventful except for the lieutenant. He came up and apologized for his behavior last night. Collins told me quietly that he had sent a telegram to his family and gotten a reply. He didn't know what it said, but the man had been walking on glass all day waiting to see me. I had no idea, but could only guess they found out about my relationship with Jacob.

Moses joined me for my evening pipe. The silence of it assured me I'd found the right man. Watching the light fade from the day was familiar. Shadows slowly reaching their fingers out toward the dying light, gave me a peaceful feeling. I watched the light gradually recede, slowly changing from gold all the way through the spectrum to black. By the time I got up to go inside, only Moses' fire cast any light in the small enclosure.

# CHAPTER 20

The next morning, while I went through my workout, Moses started laying out the traces without giving me a second glance. Willie brought coffee out before the sun broke the horizon. After cleaning up, I walked to the livery and got Shade saddled. I was back and tying my saddlebags on when Willie reappeared with a sack.

"Bacon biscuits, had the mess hall pack'em."

"Thanks Willie." Moses said, taking the bag.

"'Enough in there for both ya." He added, eyeing Moses suspiciously.

"You think so little of me, old man?" Moses japed, making Willie bark out his harsh laugh.

"Nope, but figure ya might think I'm smarter than deserved an woulda packed two bags." That dry laugh filled the area while he walked to open the gate for us.

I finished tying down my bedroll and stepped up into the saddle. Shade danced a little, but it had been a year since he tried to buck me off. With a tip of my hat to Willie, I rode by as Moses rolled the wagon out. I stopped outside the gate until hearing it lock, then turned and rode beside the wagon.

"You were on a mule the other night." Moses studied Shade.

"Wisp, she's still at the livery. Shade's been my pard for a while now."

"Nokota?"

"Got in one."

"Biggest one I seen." He said thoughtfully. "Looks pure though."

"That's what I was told. Don't change much for me. He's been trained to work beefs almost as much as I have."

That was the end of our conversation until we stopped to rest and eat breakfast. Moses was leading and setting the pace. He'd been down to Las Cruces before and knew the way. I'd studied the maps, but there was no sense in letting pride blind me. We talked about the route while the animals rested. He didn't expect any trouble along the way. Usually, it wasn't worth the effort to attack a jail wagon. There was nothing of value, and it would bring the marshals down on you with a vengeance.

We turned into Las Cruces in three days later in the afternoon. The morning of the fourth day, we loaded seven ragged looking prisoners into the wagon. Each wore wrist and ankle shackles, they'd stay in them the entire trip. As deserters, these men had nothing to lose by taking a chance at us. Each man knew the likely sentence waiting for them: death by hanging. If they were lucky, they'd spend years making small rocks out of big rocks. Either option made it worth the risk of trying and escape.

We took no chances with them. Anytime they weren't in the wagon, a shotgun covered them. They were never let out of sight, which was as much a punishment for us as them. The return trip was dragged out because caring for them slowed us down. We pulled into Albuquerque late in the afternoon on the eighth day. Granger sent a corporal to deal with the men when I walked into his office. Moses left as soon as they were out of his wagon. He needed to get the animals and wagon taken care of. He'd be camping with the wagon again and already knew my plan. Resupply tomorrow and leave again the day after.

Giving my report to Granger only took a few minutes. He asked about my immediate plans and I told him Willie was mapping out the best way to get caught up. I knew what he was asking. I'd be heading down to Cimarron to poke around right after I got caught up with the other duties.

"Getting caught up first is a good idea. Judge Bristol is not happy about you being appointed without his consideration."

"Whose Judge Bristol?" I was a bit annoyed, and it came out in my tone. The idea of being used in a political game, one that had nothing to do with me, put me on edge.

"He's the Territorial Circuit Judge. I should have told you about him, but things needed to happen."

"He's here?"

"No, but he's due for trial in six weeks. He isn't bothered as much by you personally, more by the way I got you appointed. The man's the oldest sitting judge in the territory. Hates anything not done in what he considers the right way."

"Great." I growled.

"He's a fair man, don't worry. Just do your job and he won't find fault with anything. Just have his court docket full, he hates delaying justice."

"Colonel, I mean no disrespect, but is there anything else I need to be made aware of? I have a strong dislike for being in situations I'm unaware of."

"I meant nothing by it." Granger waved off my anger. "Truthfully, this will come back on me, not you."

"I'll have to take your word for it."

"Believe me JC, you're not being hung out to dry here. If it eases your worries, think about it this way." He leaned back in his chair before continuing. "If I threw you in a hole back in Washington, my name would be destroyed. If you're unaware, curriers are rarer than hens teeth. Colonels, on the other hand, aren't worth a plug nickel right now. True, I had enough power to get you assigned here. If that costs the military a qualified currier? I'd be quietly retired."

"That's a lot of value to put on someone running messages." It did take my anger down a bit. This man was risking his career because he really believed in what he was doing.

"Just fill the man's court. It's what you were planning on doing anyway."

"Fair enough. Best get on with it." I smiled, standing from the chair. We shook hands, and I left to find Willie.

The next six weeks went by in a blink. We were constantly on the trail either going to get or bringing back prisoners. Willie knew his business, in that time we brought back sixty-five prisoners. Most of them were in the stockade because we couldn't house them all. Only the worst stayed with Willie in the cells.

One of those lucky few was the lone attempted escape. His name was J.M. Vialpano, a member of the White Caps. Five other members of the gang had tried to jump us on the way out of Chama. Three of them never made it back and the other two were bleeding when they ran. It was the first and only bounty Moses got paid from. It wasn't a bad one, though. Each of us made $275 from the three dead men and another $150 for the horses, tack, and guns. For me, it was another draft for deposit. For him, it meant paying me back and having enough money to live on for a while.

When we dropped off the last wagon load, they all went to the stockade. Most of the men there were charged with theft, rustling or the odd killing. Willie met us out back, opening the gate for us after we pulled around. He'd been dealing with six hard cases for the last two weeks, and it showed. The man looked madder than I'd ever seen him.

"Glad ta see y'all. Means them evil bastards will be done soon."

"Given you any trouble?" I asked. Moses was already stripping the traces off the team.

"No more than lip, nothing I ain't heard before. Ya also got a message from the Grand earlier. Judge Bristol would like ta see ya this evening fer dinner."

"Glad to hear he made it." I meant it too. His arrival meant we could clear these court cases and get rid of the prisoners.

"Yup, need that scum outta my cells. Gonna take a month ta wash the stink out."

I could understand his sentiments. The six he was dealing with were all men who shouldn't have been alive to be arrested. They were charged with multiple counts of rape and murder.

Two of them had spent the last six months of their freedom butchering their way across southern New Mexico. Those two weren't the worst of the lot, either.

"I'll find out when he is going to start court over dinner, most likely." I assured the man.

"Best get a bath, got bout an hour afore dinner. Johnny Chen dropped off yer laundry a few days ago." That was good. I'd hate to show up at the Grand covered in dust and wearing dirty clothes.

"Thanks Willie, I'm headed to get a bath and a shave."

"Cut that damn hair too." He groused.

"Nope." I laughed, stepping inside with my saddlebags.

Dropping my dirty clothes out of my bags in a basket for the laundry, I packed a clean set for after my bath. Climbing into the saddle again, I pulled Wisp around to head for the livery. I'd drop her off and stop at the barbers on my way back. I'd been alternating mounts this whole time. That way, one animal was always fresh if I needed them. Jackson took good care of them, always made sure they had good shoes and were ready to go. He waved me off after I helped strip the saddle off.

"I'll take care of her, Willie, tol' me not ta let ya get to mess'n about with 'em."

"Thanks Jackson." I left, shaking my head.

Willie really had become my right hand here in town. Supplies were always stocked, little things like the laundry had been arranged. The man knew his job and quickly learned how I wanted things. Sadly, he still wouldn't teach me his coffee recipe and the old man was cagey when he made it.

Murphys was quick and easy. As quick as any bath is after a few weeks. It took three tubs of water before it stopped turning to mud. The fourth finally got me clean. As always, Murphy grumbled about cutting my hair while he shaved off a week's worth of patchy beard. I'd already braided my hair and made sure to keep it tucked away from the man. He had very strong opinions about white men having long hair.

"Like a damn injun, just ain't right." He groused constantly.

Why did I keep coming here? Simple. He had the best baths in town, not to mention the steadiest hands I'd ever seen with a razor. Walking back to the office, part of me was watching the people around me. The rest was just happy to be clean. Willie was sitting at the desk in eating his dinner when I walked in. Leaving him to it, I walked back to drop the last of my dirty clothes off with my saddlebags. By the time I got back to the front, he'd finished eating and had a cup of coffee waiting for me.

"Got a few minutes 'afore ya met the judge."

"Enough time for coffee." I agreed, sipping the rich smooth brew, then sighing heavily. "Damn that's good. Mos makes good coffee, but nothing beats yours."

"Good for sumthin more than jus' feeding hogs." He grumped, but I could see his lips turn up in a smile. "If ya can get a sense of when them six are gonna be on his docket, I'd 'preciate it."

"I'll ask." Finishing the last swallow, I set the cup down and checked my guns before walking out the door. The Grand was still just as impressive and the clerk on duty recognized me when I came in.

"Marshal, the judge is already in the dining room."

"Mind telling me what the man looks like?" I asked.

"I'll do one better." He turned to the page that was waiting to help clients with bags. "Mark, take the Marshal to the judge's table."

"Follow me sir." The boy hopped up and led me into the dining room.

He took me through the dining room and then down a short hall at the back. When he opened a door on the left, it revealed a small dining area that might hold eight people. Inside was an older man with a neatly trimmed goatee and thin mustache. Beside him was a younger man, clean shaven with slicked back hair. Nether of them wore their coats, they hung on the back of their chairs. Both men had their sleeves rolled up to the elbows and were sorting through papers.

"Marshal Stone?" The younger man looked up from his work.

"Yes sir."

"Afraid you caught us off guard." He laughed but looked a bit embarrassed about his appearance.

"Balderdash, we've work to do and from the amount of it, I'd say the marshal understands." The older man slowly rose from his chair to greet me. "Judge Bristol and this fastidious youngster is my clerk, Ethan Pease."

"JC Stone, pleasure to met you both. Just call me JC, please." Shaking both men's hands, I took off my hat and hung it on the rack. "Arranging your docket, I'm guessing?"

"Warren and Ethan, when not in court please. In court, it will be titles and formality of course." Warren said before sitting back down. "Mark, that you hiding back there?"

"Got it on the first guess this time, sir."

"I told you to stop that sir nonsense. Tell Penny to bring more coffee and another cup for the JC."

"Yes boss." Mark said with a hint of mischief before dashing down the hall.

"Rascal." Warren grumbled, but I saw the grin on his face. This wasn't what I expected from the man, but I found myself liking him. "JC join us, please. I wouldn't mind your input either way."

"Thanks." I started to study the papers as I sat. They were a mess. "What are you working on?"

"Right now, organizing the witness statements to match the trial they go with." It was all copies of the various documents I'd brought in with the men.

"How's they get like this?" When I brought them in I'd organized them all into case files. These were all the loose copies that had been sent before I picked the men up. The originals were at the office.

"The usual. This is what we were handed. A giant stack of papers." Ethan said unhappily.

"It's normal. The sheriff saves the copies he's sent, eventually sending them on. When we arrive, this is what we get. We have to organize them and get ready for court. It's all part of the judicial process. Each case has to be separated and copies given to the attorneys as well as one for the court." Warren explained it like I had no idea how court worked.

"Yes, into case files. I assumed they would be organized before you received them. Each assigned a case number."

"Sadly, no. We have to do it ourselves." Ethan said, still studying the document in front of him.

"My copies are already organized." My response made them both stop and look at me.

"What do you mean JC?" Warren asked.

"I wouldn't accept the files from the various sheriffs until each was separated and organized with three copies. I assumed they needed to be ready for court before taking the prisoner." Ethan froze and slowly looked up at me.

"Are you saying that you made each sheriff give you the original case file with three copies for each prisoner you picked up?" Ethan asked with a slight tremble.

"Yes, I didn't assign a docket number, of course, but each one is numbered for easy reference." I hadn't understood why the sheriffs balked at the demand. To me, it was their responsibility. I wasn't the one charging the prisoners. "I have them all at the office."

"They are all done?" Ethan asked, like he couldn't believe what I was saying.

"JC let's be clear. You have them separated by the case number associated with each prisoner and have kept them organized?" Warren asked.

"The case numbers aren't effective. Two different counties will each assign the same case number without knowing it. I used the legal code of New York for each violation, then the prisoners' initials and an associated number for each county. That was all it took for each file to have a unique identifier."

"Legal code of New York?" Ethan was staring at me without blinking now.

"Yes, I studied law there and still remembered the numbers."

I was surprised that they didn't have a system like this in place. When I thought about it again, wondered why they would. This was still a territory. Organization like that was the product of formalized judiciary in big cities. I actually felt foolish now that I thought about it.

"Mark!" Warren yelled. The door swung open as he yelled and a small older woman came in carrying a large pot with a lone cup hooked on a finger.

"The boy ain't deaf." She snapped after the shock faded. She sat the cup down in front of me, refilling the other two on the table before leaving the pot.

"Ye sir?" Mark stuck his head in a little out of breath. I had an idea what the man was thinking and cut it off before he sent the boy snipe hunting.

"Judge, Willie won't let the files leave unless I'm there. Besides its sixty-five files in triplicate, we'd need a wagon.

"Very well. Mark, Is that cart you used earlier still out back?"

"Yup." Mark was almost bouncing on his feet now.

"Marshal, would you go get those files with our young friend?" He wasn't really asking.

"Yes, your honor. Take me bout fifteen minutes or so." I replied, eyeing the mess on the table meaningfully.

"That will give us time to clear this out." The judge quickly understood my meaning. 'Get rid of the chaos if you want my organized files brought here.'

"Show me this cart, young man." I turned to Mark and noticed that Ethan was still in some sort of shock. It took twenty minutes to get them and the file boxes to the Grand. The look on the judge and his clerk's faces when they saw the file boxes with tabs noting each number was priceless. I had to explain my system again, but they understood it quick enough. Once it all made sense, the judge started laughing.

"So let me understand this. You're almost twenty, educated as a lawyer but now working as a U.S Marshal. You used that knowledge to not only get all this put together, but to have each file separated into folders. One for the defense, another for the prosecution and the originals for the court? You did all this while collecting sixty-five criminals scattered across this territory? AND managed to get file boxes made to order by a carpenter?"

"Seemed like the way it ought to be done." I really had done it because it made sense to me.

"Not only that, but they are ordered in the crates by date of arrest to help ensure the fastest trial dates for each defendant?" Ethan asked, looking through the crates.

"I wasn't sure that was right and know Willie wishes I'd put the ones he's got first." I reached for the pot filling my coffee cup while answering.

"JC I don't know if you're aware of this, but I wasn't pleased about your assignment." Warren leaned back in his chair, watching me while he carefully rolled a cigarette. "Let me say now that I was wrong. I will be sending a letter to that effect back east. There will also be a recommendation that you be hired to train new marshals."

"Now don't get carried away. I still have some other plans once this is done."

"If nothing else, the way you did this will be used as a standard at some point. Not only that, but if I have my way, you'll keep that badge no matter what you choose. I've not met a man yet that deserved it more." He wasn't going to be deterred, so I gave up the argument.

"Does this mean we can have dinner now?" The easy smile that spread across my face made them both laugh.

"It does, and that was a very deft change in subject." Ethan rocked back in his chair, laughing.

"One last thing, my young friend. Soon enough Ethan will be done clerking. If you have any interest in becoming a judge, I'd take you as a clerk gladly." Warren smiled warmly as he spoke, then a grin split his face. "That's neither here nor there for now. Food sounds like the best course of action to avoid being politely told no."

Penny appeared as if by magic. She took our orders, heading

toward the kitchen immediately after. While we waited conversation was light and friendly, the three of us doing away with all formality for the evening. We ate and shared news, mostly about the country and its rapid growth. Finally, as the evening was coming to a close, Warren asked one more question.

"It's not truly important, but do you have a suit, JC?"

"As it happens, I do." It had even been brushed out and hung up in my room.

"Would you mind standing in as my bailiff for the trials? I'm assuming you know the process."

"Be my pleasure." There was no way I'd pass up the opportunity to see how a courtroom worked in the territory.

"We'll be using the military courtroom. It's attached to the stockade. Most of the prisoners are there, so it will keep it simple. The military will handle the jailer's duties. If you'd like, we can settle the six you have first?"

"Take them in order. I think the first of them is twenty-first on the docket." They'd decided to use my system to set the docket. It was legal and already organized that way. "Don't want to over crowd the stockade, not with those six. If anything, put them all on one day so we only have to move them once."

"You think they'll be a problem?" Ethan asked nervously.

"None of them has anything to lose. They'll all hang. Why wouldn't they? Men who know they're going to die are always dangerous." I said it casually, but had already made sure the colonel would loan me a full platoon to escort them.

"In that case, I think we can start hearing cases tomorrow at 9am sharp. Meet us here for breakfast please, as bailiff you will be escorting us to the court. If we're lucky, we can get through these in a little over a week, maybe two if someone stretches it out."

"I'll be here bright and early. If you'd prefer, I can stay in the hotel?"

"No need for that. I'm sure you prefer your own room."

Warren was right. I liked my space but would have moved to accommodate them.

"I'm going to see if I can catch Major Collins at the mess. Get a few soldiers to help transport the files tomorrow." I said, rising from my chair.

"Good idea better than us hauling them. See you in the morning." Warren said from his chair.

"Night JC." Ethan nodded to me from his seat. He was leaning back, puffing on a cigar.

# CHAPTER 21

I found the XO lingering in the dining hall over coffee. We worked out the details for court and to transport the documents. I figured if the judge had me working as a bailiff things like this were my responsibility. Maybe it was overstepping, but if the judge told me I was responsible for their safety, then it would be done right. He'd have four men meet me at 8:00 to help with the files. We also agreed on four soldiers in the courtroom as guards, with another two assigned to each prisoner. They would rotate, each pair escorting the accused to and from the stockade. That would put two men on the door checking for weapons, one in each back corner. That would leave me up front near the judge. We also decided the two at the front doors would also be taking weapons from anyone coming in.

For the six in my cells, a full platoon would be available to escort them from our cells to the stockade. Three squads would cover the route while the final squad would escort the prisoners with me. It may sound excessive, but at least three of them were from various organizations that might try to break them out. Two of them were probably in the gangs they claimed, the last one I doubted. Something about the man was just off.

I'd seen posters for the James-Younger gang like everyone else, he wasn't even mentioned on them. That wasn't the only thing that put me off about him. There was something about him broken inside, the piece that made him human wasn't working anymore. His killings showed that according to witnesses. Six families over less than a month, he'd killed the males and then played man of the house for a few days. Eventually, something would change and he killed the rest before moving on.

The only reason he'd been caught was a lucky neighbor showing up. The prisoner hadn't known the man and tried to act like the father, even tried to invite him in for coffee. The neighbor had knocked him out when then tied him up. He didn't know what was going on, but knew something was wrong. The sheriff had found evidence from the other farms in his packs. If he'd been back east, someone might have argued that he was insane and needed to be committed. Out here? He was the hangman's noose.

Those merry thoughts had been playing across my mind while walking back to my office. They might not have been comforting, but for whatever reason they occupied my mind. Maybe it was the contrast between how the man would be treated, depending on where he was caught. It might have been a way to sidetrack my mind from worrying about the next day. Either way, the thoughts fell away when I sat down out back with my pipe.

The next morning I was just cleaning up when Willie walked in with coffee for me and Moses. Both men had long gotten past what Willie referred to as 'that weird celestial dance.' They just figured it was part of my overall strangeness. Willie started cursing after I told him the six guests would be around for a while yet. Moses just sat cross-legged on the ground, silently sipping his coffee. None of it was his problem. Once he finished turning the air black Willie calmed down and accepted the situation. After I explained the reasoning, he understood. Not that it made him any happier, but it stopped the cursing at least.

My pocket watch told me I had to get moving. Getting churched up in my suit to meet the judge for breakfast took a minute. Wearing black trousers, my dress boots, a white shirt with a narrow ribbon tie and a black vest. The darker grey long jacket hung low enough to keep my guns out of sight, but still easily accessible. I kept my regular hat with the black hawk feather proudly on display since it was a better choice than my other one.

Breakfast was served in the same room we'd used for dinner. Just as we finished the last sip of coffee, Mark stuck his head in to announce that four soldiers had arrived. The judge told him to send them in, then he quickly set them to the task of moving the crates. He never questioned how they knew to be there, which made me feel better about taking action. Five minutes later, we stepped out of the hotel on our way to the first day of court.

There were no problems on the way there. The courtroom came together quickly, Ethan started setting up the documents for the day. The prosecuting attorney was a man named Thomas Carton. I'd heard a few stories about the man. He liked to puff up his chest and put on a show. Thankfully, he knew full well that Warren wouldn't tolerate his behavior in his court.

"Mr. Carton, here are the first five case files." Ethan called over and handed him the files.

"Any defense?" The man's voice made my skin crawl. Not in tone, but in the way people who thought too highly of themselves did. It was like every word was meant to remind you how far beneath him you were.

"Pollard will stand for them if we need him." Ethan answered, nodding to an older man asleep at the table. "Nudge him awake, please."

"Huh cough uh yes yes." The man woke up with a start when one of the soldiers nudged his shoulder. He looked around for a few seconds before remembering where he was. "Ethan a pleasure, Mr. Carton."

"Mister Pollard, please stay awake for the proceedings." Ethan snapped. "You know what the Judge will do otherwise."

"Yes sir." The man stood, straightening his wrinkled suit. He still looked disheveled and reeked of who-hit-john.

"I'll give you files as needed. The standard court fee will be paid at the end of the day." Ethan glared at the man in warning. Ten minutes later, I was standing behind the bench and Ethan nodded to me.

"All rise for the honorable Judge Bristol. The circuit court for the territory of New Mexico is now in session."

Other than breaking for lunch with a similar speech, that was all I said that day. At the end of the day, we'd made it through the first fifteen cases. The most serious sentence anyone got was one year at the territorial prison. The rest were fines, times served, and one man found not guilty.

"We can leave the files." Ethan told me as we wrapped up the day. "The Major will have a guard posted over night. Join us for dinner and your day is done."

The next three days passed much the same. After four days, we'd finished forty-eight cases. Pollard had been called on once the second day, despite my initial opinion, he mounted a decent case. His client's charge was dropped down and instead of ten years, he only got one. The next couple of days went by following the same pattern. Everything moved along smoothly, with no hiccups. The trouble started on the morning of the fifth day when Pollard didn't make it to court.

After a quick conference, Ethan juggled a few classes around and we made it through five more cases before hitting a snag. They took longer but didn't need an attorney since the accused plead guilty and offered explanations. The extended time was for Ethan to read the witness statements out loud for the court. Two of them were dismissed as self defense, the other three were convicted and sentenced. The last man of the group was sent down for ten years. He didn't argue, just apologized constantly and looked ashamed. He'd gotten into a bar fight that turned serious. He was drunk when the guns came out and missed the man he was trying to shoot. Sadly, the bullet had found a target of its own in the chest of a local miner. The man died instantly, never knowing what had killed him.

The sheriff had arrested him at the livery, thinking he was

getting ready to run. The truth was discovered when a deputy took the livery mans statement. He'd been selling everything he owned. His horse was the last thing left after selling his claim to the bank. He went willingly with the sheriff but insisted that all of it be given to the man's widow. He'd even sold the small piece of land he owned in Indiana. According to the sheriff's statement, she received a little over four hundred dollars. That act was what saved the man from a hangman's rope.

Mistakes out here are always expensive, even the smallest lapse could cost you everything. Watching the man as he was led away, I knew he would never leave that prison. His guilt would kill him long before he finished serving his time. Whiskey had tallied up another victim, successfully killing two men that night. Sadly it never showed up in court to face the accusations.

The next morning, Pollard didn't show up again. The sheriff's arrivale said enough for me to know there was a problem. He looked annoyed when he walked up to Ethan. They had a brief conversation before he left. I couldn't catch any of it but Ethan looked annoyed. He spun on his heel and walked back to talk to the judge. A few minutes later, he came out waving for me to follow him.

"Marshal, we have a problem." Warren was sitting behind a small desk covered in folders. "One I must ask you to assist with."

"Pollard?" I had a feeling about what was going on.

"Dead drunk and locked up for swinging a bottle at a deputy." Ethan didn't hide his disdain. "I knew we shouldn't have paid him until we finished."

"Be that as it may, we are going to need you to stand in as the defense attorney. We have six cases today. One of them will need you for certain, maybe two."

"I've never dealt with an actual case judge, much less one out here." I wasn't sure about this. It didn't seem like a good idea, considering my lack of experience. "What about one of the officers?"

"We checked before asking Pollard. None of them are educated on the subject. Ethan, go get Mr. Carton. We'll need to involve him in this." After sending Ethan, Warren looked back at me. "You're capable of this, I'm sure. Most law out here is quite a bit simpler than the laws back east."

"I'll do whatever I can, might have to be patient with me." Ethan led Mr. Carton back into the office and closed the door.

"I'm guessing there is a problem with the defense, your honor?"

"Astute as always, yes Pollard is in the sheriff's jail. He tried to hit a deputy with a bottle and can't be released."

"I'm guessing we need a defense attorney for some of today's cases?" I had to give the man credit, strutting peacock or not he caught on quick.

"What I'm going to need is some patience from you today. Our young marshal here has a law degree and is, or rather was, approved by the New York Bar Association." I could see Warren studying the man's reactions. "However, he's never worked out here and is not as familiar with our laws as Pollard."

"I didn't actually sit for the bar exam, Judge. Clerking seemed like a better choice and it completed by the last six months of school."

"Taking the exam or clerking accomplishes the same thing." Ethan smiled when he spoke. It was true, especially out here where taking the bar wasn't really an option.

"Truly? I had assumed he was just another law man, young and industrious, but not much else. It appears I under estimated you, sir. My apologies for the assumptions." Mr. Carton looked genuinely surprised. "What cases do you suspect needing him for?"

"There is a horse theft charge that seems questionable. The defendant, a young man with no criminal past, swears he bought the horse from an unidentified man. The sheriff in the area believes him, but the owner is wealthy so he couldn't just let it go." Warren read from a note on his desk before finishing.

"The other is a killing that the witnesses are divided on. Some say the defendant drew first, others the opposite. Again, the victim was a rich man's son and we all know how that can go."

"The sheriff managed to get him here for trial. He stood off a lynching the first night." I added. "Picked him up two counties away from where the crime took place. The sheriff had a deputy get him out of town. Vega's his last name if I remember right."

"Manuel Vega, you remember correctly." Ethan said, reading the file.

"What's your take on the situation, Marshal?" Mr. Carton asked curiously.

"Honestly, the witnesses saying the other man drew first is a deputy. I think his name was Cardoza." I flipped through the file and found the statement I was looking for. "Here it is. He was the one who got Vega out of town, but he wrote his statement the night it happened."

"According to?" Mr. Carton asked. The man was sharp and didn't want to be caught off guard.

"The sheriff pointed it out to me. I picked up the statements where it occurred before picking up Vega. The deputy was still with the defendant and hadn't been back in town."

"If that's the case, then we can dismiss the murder charges on that one." Carton spoke casually while looking at the judge. "Of course, with your agreement, your honor."

"Marshal, you'll stand for the defense. After Ethan reads off the witness statements, you repeat all of what you said for the record. Mr. Carton, you agree when he asks for the charges to be dismissed and we're done. Agreed?"

"Yes, your honor." Both me and Carton spoke.

"As to Christopher Gaines, the horse theft. Any opinions, Marshal?" Ethan asked.

"That one's harder, but I believe the accused." I put up my hand to stall the questions. "Let me explain why. It's not just a feeling, but rather experience with punchers. First the man didn't run, he was arrested in the town where the horse's original owner lived. They arrested him as he was checking into a hotel. The clerk's statement said he was prepaying for a week."

"Criminals are not always the smartest bunch." Carton commented.

"True, but this one is. He's a puncher on the drift to Arizona territory after finishing a drive to Dodge City. He had enough money on him when arrested to buy land and stock for the ranch he wanted to start. Close to three thousand dollars. That tells me he's been working in Texas for a while. There isn't a puncher alive that doesn't know how horse thieves are dealt with."

"Who can make that kind of money?" Ethan's suspicious nature wasn't wrong.

"True, that is concerning, but the sheriff verified his story with the law in Dodge City. He had a good night playing poker after a drive. You'll see the telegram in the file. They had to clean up the mess when a few of the drovers thought the man was cheating."

"They verify that he was not cheating?" Carton asked.

"They say if he was, no one could prove it." I admitted. "Innocent until proven guilty, as they say."

"Quite right." Warren agreed before pushing us past that topic. "Where the money came from isn't important. Its only purpose is to help with the matter of the horse."

"Yes, your honor." I agreed before continuing. "According to the sheriff and two others, it wasn't just the one horse. Gaines dropped off a string of five other animals at the livery. One, a mustang, was the horse he'd left Kansas with. The other five were all stolen in the area, four were returned to their owners and they didn't want to press charges. Their statements are included but offer only that they believed Gaines story."

"The last man?" Carton asked.

"A Mr. Angel Quinonez, he is one of the biggest spreads in the area. The stallion in question was one of his prized studs. Even according the Gaines, the stallion is why he bought the other horses. After seeing it in person, I'd have likely done the same. It's a pure Andalusian imported from Spain as a foal."

"Gaines didn't question it?" Warren asked.

"Took it as his luck holding. He also didn't get them cheap, according to him. The man he met wouldn't take less than six hundred for the string and he had to buy them all." I held up my hand again to forestall the comments. "Yes, that's still a deal, but he swears the man had a believable story. It's all in the statement, probably more accurately worded than my memory."

"Give us the basics, if you will, Marshal." Warren insisted.

"He said the man looked rough but not rustler rough more like he'd been on the grub line for a while. His story was that one of the associations had pushed him off his land and all he could take were the horses. After traveling for days, he realized if they kept going he'd ruin the animals. No money for good feed and no land to let them rest. Gaines said the horses looked rough, not run out but just unkept."

"The other reason you believe him?" Carton asked.

"The way he acted at the time. According to the sheriff's statement, when they arrested him, his first thought was giving up the horses. He wanted nothing to do with stolen stock, didn't make a fuss about the money at all. Said he'd deal with that."

"Deal with it?" Ethan raised an eyebrow.

"Knowing punchers, he'd have tracked the man down himself and gotten his money back. More likely he'd have tried and gotten killed." I laughed before explaining the last. "The biggest reason I believe the whole thin is Willie, my jailer. One of the hard cases we have at the office was particularly loud about the money in his property. Five hundred and forty-seven dollars, to be exact. His mistake was not watching his tongue, bragging to the other men. According to Willie he said and I quote, 'got that offa a fool ain't gonna have 'nother one steal it with a badge.' I didn't think about it at the time but later I wondered about Gaines story."

"That's a lot of assumptions, marshal." Warren looked suspicious but he was willing to hear me out.

"One that's easily dealt with. Leave Gaines until tomorrow. We are moving the hard cases to the stockade tonight. Might be interesting to see if he recognizes one of them. At the same time, I don't want to contaminate any possible ID by telling him my suspicions."

"That's well thought out. What would you have done if Pollard had showed up?" Warren asked, his mind trying to puzzle out my thoughts.

"I watched him the other day. Drunk or not, the man's sharp. I'd have nudged him to look at it."

"He's right, your honor." Carton laughed. "Pollard is many things, but a bad lawyer isn't one of them. He's beaten me more than once and never misses a trick when sober."

"That's the only reason I use the man. That and some sense of sympathy."

"It was a tragedy that could break any man." Ethan's voice held a somber tone, he looked away when I tried to meet his eyes.

"Either way, I agree with your plan. It won't change much timing wise and may clear an innocent man." Warren agreed. "Any objections, Mr. Carton?"

"None, your honor." Then he turned his eyes to me. "My young friend, you are wasted behind that badge. Very few people would remember everything you just said and don't think I didn't notice. Not once did you open a statement to check something to bring the facts to mind. You did that all from memory."

"Agreed." Warren said, smiling at me. "I may not have liked the way you were thrust on me, but I must admit to being impressed. I'm more certain that you should clerk for me when Ethan finishes. You'd make an excellent judge in a decade or so."

"Thanks, but there are other things in the works." I laughed politely.

ROBERT KNOX

# CHAPTER 22

Court proceeded as planned. We finished early enough that enacting our plan regarding Gaines could be done today. I watched as the platoon split off, finding positions to fire from on the route from the office to the stockade. Willie was surprised to see us but happily helped get the prisoners ready. All six were shackled wrist and ankles with a long chain connecting them. The shuffling steps meant we moved at a snail's pace but it was worth it for the security. None of the men spoke after the first one tried in the jail. Willie had a doubled him over with the butt of a shotgun to the belly.

Finally, we made the stockade, and each man was sorted into their individual cell. Gaines had done exactly as I hoped. Standing at the door of his cell, watching the parade of men. The plan was for me to be the first man in. That would let me stand by the door, supposedly to watch the prisoners. In truth, I was watching him. The moment he spotted the man, a sharp intake of breath gave him away. Slowly, a smile spread across my face. I expected him to yell, accuse, or even try to reach for the man, but he didn't. He fell back on his small bunk with his head hung in defeat. That didn't make sense to me. Why wasn't he yelling or making a ruckus? Curiosity drew me to his cell.

"You alright Gaines?"

"Fine marshal." Then, under his breath, I barely heard him mutter. "Just doomed to hang."

"What changed?" When he looked up and met my eyes, the barely contained rage was obvious.

"The one man who knows the truth is going to hang." His words were a hiss.

"Explain on the way to court." I motioned for the sergeant who was in charge to get him out and manacled. "Just his wrists will be fine."

"No problem, Marshal." The soldier went about his work efficiently.

Soon Gaines was walking beside me down a hall at the back of the stockade. I did notice when he slowed walking past the other man's cell. He carefully studied the man lying on the bunk then let out a heavy sigh.

"That's him, ain't no doubt." He mumbled. I didn't ask him about it until we reached a small room outside of court. It was a holding room we used to prepare the prisoner before going in front of the judge. What Gaines didn't know was currently court was in recess. This had been arranged beforehand.

"Spit it out. Who's the man back there?" I broke the silence.

"Ya ain't gonna believe me. Hell, I can't believe it myself, but that's the skunk who sold me them ponies."

"Any way you can prove that?"

"Nope, just my word. I mean, unless he still had the money on him."

"How would that do it?" That got my attention. The other man's money was locked in a safe currently.

"Some of the bills was marked. One of the fellas at the table was betting greenbacks. Well, none of us trusted they was real and made him have 'em verified." He laughed, thinking about it. "We tried ta get him to swap 'em for eagles. Said he didn't like how heavy they was."

"Known a few punchers like that. Folding money fits in a money belt easier."

"Well, I meant ta get 'em switched but never got round to it cause of the trouble in Dodge. That skunk took'em without question, probably shoulda been a hint. Every one of 'em will be marked with a W.F.D.C. stamp. Wells Fargo Dodge City. Guess it's something that comes up from time to time cause they had a stamp an all."

"Wait here." I said, standing up and calling Willie in to watch the man.

All the prisoners' possessions were locked in a safe with the judge. There was a chance they might be the evidence we needed. After Ethan invited me in, I found all three waiting on me but I waved off their questions. Picking through the statements until I found the right one. 'Mica Wilson-charged with rape, murder, horse theft, rustling and armed robbery.' This was the guy Gaines had identified.

"Mr. Carton, as the prosecutor, would you come with me while I question this man?"

"Of course, Marshal, or is it Mr. Stone for this?"

"Reckon Mr. Stone for this." I smiled, leading the man back to the stockade. We left Ethan and Warren with curious looks on their faces.

"Mica Wilson," I said, stepping to the man's cell.

"Whatcha want, law dog?" The man growled out when he saw me.

"We maybe adding an additional charge. Were you in Kansas last year?"

"Hell no! Ain't been ta Kansas in ten years." It might be a lie, but we'd take him at his word for this.

"Ten years?" I asked, but made sure that my tone invited questions. It was enough to make the man study me carefully.

"Well, not ten maybe, 'least four. That damn Sheriff Brooks busted my head for a little fracas an took all my money. Lit out after that, an ain't be back. Didn't wanna kill a law man. Course my opinion on that's changed 'ere recently." He sneered through the bars at me.

I didn't bother to respond, just waved for Carton to follow me back. Once there, I pulled out the envelope that held Wilson's property but didn't open it. Instead, I handed it to Carton.

"Don't open that yet, but we might have gotten lucky." He raised an eyebrow questioningly, but nodded his agreement.

"Tell us what you've found out." Ethan was on the edge of his seat with anticipation.

"You want me to tell it or hear from Gaines?" I asked, looking at Carton, then the judge.

"You'll do." Warren answered.

"Agreed." Carton nodded.

I repeated what Gaines had told me, carefully recalling every detail. When I finished, Carton opened the envelope and started sorting the bills. Five hundred and twenty of them were stamped with the initials, just as Gaines had said.

"How do we know this is legitimate?" Carton asked. I couldn't blame him. The only reason I knew was having seen it once before.

"Wells Fargo will verify folding money, they do that for greenbacks. I've seen different bills with various stamps. A lot of people still don't fully trust the new money."

"Your word is good enough for me, but if Wilson got them four years ago?"

"Remember he said Brooks had taken all of his money? Bill Brooks was run out of office in '72. I was there when it happened."

"I'll be damned!" Ethan swore, then started laughing.

"This maybe the first time so many things have come together like this to save one man from the noose. The very idea of using paper money to prove someone's innocence seems so far-fetched." Warren laughed with him.

"I don't know about being a judge, but you'd make one hell of an investigator." Carton sat staring at the bills, shaking his head. He met my eyes and added thoughtfully. "Probably a difficult opponent as a defense attorney as well."

"Gaines got lucky." I down played my part in the process.

"True, but you put the pieces together. Pollard would have fought, but I doubt he could have put all that together. Even going so far as to make me, the prosecutor, your witness." He started chuckling at that. "Should we tell Mr. Gaines?"

"Still have to do it formally as the charges were brought before the court." Ethan said.

"Let's get it done. Plan on joining us for dinner tonite JC, you as well Tom." Warren said rising from his chair.

"A pleasure." Carlton replied. I nodded my agreement before stepping out to call the court into session.

"One more thing JC, please return this to Mr. Gaines after he's released." Ethan handed me his property envelope after dropping the five hundred and twenty dollars inside with the man's gun. "Tell him we apologize about losing his mustang."

"He didn't." I cracked a slightly shameful smile. "It's a trained cow pony. No way I was leaving that behind. Paid the sheriff for her and brought her back with us. She's in the livery with his tack."

"He can settle with you about that." Ethan laughed.

To say Gaines was surprised by his change of fortune would be an understatement. Especially when I returned all his money, including the five hundred and twenty. His biggest shock was finding out his pony would be released to him. He asked about a place to stay and without any hesitation, I suggested the courtyard behind the office. It'd keep him out of sight and let him relax. Moses said he didn't care so long as the man wasn't a chatterbox. Willie agreed to bring meals for both of them from the mess. After he got settled in I went to join the judge for dinner. It wasn't a mystery what they wanted me there for.

Most of dinner was spent with the three of them trying to convince me to start practicing law. I had to explain my long-term plans to them. Even that didn't make any difference. Warren just changed tact and said if I started now, he could get me appointed as a circuit judge in the Montana Territory in seven years. I had to give the man his due. Nothing deterred him once he got a hold of an idea.

Trying to change the subject failed when they assured me that tomorrow Pollard would be in court. That made me relax a little because I didn't trust any of the six men left in the stockade. After the meal, I made my excuses and fled back to the office before they could start in on me again. Stealing some of Willie's coffee, I sat outside watching the stars for a bit. My mind was actually working out what could go wrong in court tomorrow.

Gaines thought my morning ritual was funny, but it wasn't the strangest thing he'd seen. Most of the punchers I'd worked with said the same thing. He was already packing up, planning to be back on the trail before court started. He was going to grab some supplies and leave this morning. Last night he'd insisted on paying me for his mustang. We shook hands before I left for court and he rode out the back gate shortly after.

Soon I was calling court to order. Mica Wilson was the first case on the docket, Pollard didn't have to do much. He didn't blink at the added charges, probably because they wouldn't make a difference. The evidence and statements against the man were beyond question. It took just twenty minutes for him to be sentenced to death.

"Mica Wilson, this court finds you guilty of all charges. You're sentenced to be hung by the neck until dead. The execution will take place in three days."

The man promised vengeance on all of us while the soldiers drug him out of the courtroom. One of them quietly told him that he'd happily be there to drag him up to the gallows. Reality seemed to hit Mica all at once and he suddenly went pale. His feet forgot how to work and he stumbled through the door, mostly being dragged by the soldiers. Every man knew they were going to die, but knowing the date and time could be its own form of torture. That's not mentioning the terror dancing from the noose held for most men.

Movement at the back of the court caught my eye just then. It was Gaines. He was talking to one of the soldiers at the door. It almost looked like an argument, but it quieted before I got involved. Gaines came in and took a seat in the gallery which struck me as off. When I met his gaze, he mouthed one word to me, 'Danger' and then he sat there. He seemed to relax when my thumb casually flipped the thong off my Colt. Gaines had been planning on leaving before court started. I couldn't think of any reason he'd stay, much less be here unless something was very wrong. When I saw Moses at the back of the balcony, I knew something was going on.

My eyes started studying anyone in the room who looked like they might be trouble. I didn't find any that stood out enough to remove. There were two half way up that I'd keep my eye on though. The next man up was one from the John Kinney gang. They operated locally and were the most likely to attempt a jail break. The two looked similar to men listed as members of the gang but I wasn't sure.

Watching the man as he came up to the defense table, his smirk told me enough. The cold slowly filled me, calming my mind and letting me focus. His eyes told me which one of the two men it was. They locked eyes, and the stranger gave the slightest nod. Edward Hart, the man on trial, wore a slight grin on his face when he sat down. I knew what was coming and kept his pard in sight as I called court to order. It was a trick I'd learned long ago, watching someone without keeping my eyes focused else where. People could feel your stare if you weren't careful. I'd felt it myself more than once.

Just as the judge opened the door, the man in the gallery moved. His hand flash to his boot and before he could get the pistol leveled, my Colt spoke. All hell broke loose then, wood splintered next to me as someone took a shot from the other side. I'd crouched slightly to get my shot off. It was the only thing that saved my life. I could feel the splinters stuck in my face, but kept moving toward Hart.

Acrid smoke hung in the air, but those were the only two shots I heard. Now the room was full of noise. Chairs falling and men yelling as they rushed for the doors. I saw Hart rear back to hit Pollard, who was just standing there, stunned by the sudden violence. My fingers just managed to catch the chain when he started swinging forward. He screamed in pain as I yanked him to the floor by his cuffs. Something snapped when it happened but couldn't take the time to find out what. Besides, I didn't really care about what happened to Him.

The floor felt like there was a stampede. I was standing on

the chains, ensuring Hart couldn't move. I couldn't see Gaines through the chaos, but knew he was out there somewhere. Moses was kneeling down behind the half wall in the balcony. Carton was under his desk, Ethan was in the same pose under his. The judge I could only hope had stepped back through the door into the protection of the soldiers. Finally, most of the people were out and I could hear soldiers yelling at the crowd. Gaines was crouched near a body with blood spreading in a puddle at his feet.

"Gaines you hit?" I made eye contact with him first, hen I yelled up to the gallery. "Mos you?"

"Ain't my blood." Gaines said, wiping his blade off on a dead man's coat.

"Deadman up here, but ain't me." Moses called down. It was just in time.

"This is Major Collins of the United States Army. Put your weapons on the floor..." I cut his speech off.

"Major Collins, this is Marshal Stone. Everything's handled in here. You can come ahead." A moment later, the major came in, flanked by two men. Four more followed them closely. It was the four men that had been in the court room. I finally looked around for the two that were supposed to be guarding Hart. They were unconscious on the floor. "Need a doc for your men, think Hart knocked 'em out with his chain."

Hart wasn't moving either. When I looked down, a slowly spreading pool of blood under his head explained that. None of this was his problem anymore. Deadmen didn't care about the complications of the living. He'd landed badly when I jerked him down. His neck was at a bad angle, must have hit the chair on his was down.

"Private Tompkins, fetch the doc." The major looked over his shoulder at a young man who dashed off without a word. "What the hell happened, Marshal?"

"The defendant was a member of the Kinney gang. Think those three tried to bust him out of the court room. I got that one, Gaines got one and Mos got the one up there with him."

"Sorry couldn't get him 'fore he took that shot." Moses called down. "Folks was in the way."

Before I could respond, the door behind me open. Warren walked out a second later, scowling at the surrounding chaos. He immediately took charge of the situation and started things moving. "Major, get this courtroom back in order and figure out how those men got guns in here. I want a report of what happened in ten minutes."

"Yes sir." Collins almost saluted.

"Yes, your honor." I sighed, knowing this was going to be a pain. "Mos, Gaines, fill me in on what you know. Guessing one of you caught wind of this since both of you showed up to lend a hand."

I turned, leading them into the small room I'd used when acting as the defense. There was no coffee, but at least there was a pitcher of water. The major was barking orders in the courtroom. Thankfully he'd noticed the pieces of wood stuck in my face. He asked Doc to come check on me after his men. The splinters were starting to get annoying.

"Look half porcupine boss." Moses japed. "It ain't too bad though, want me to get'em out while ya talk?"

"Got anything to clean the wounds with?" I asked.

"Doc will. I'll just get the wood out."

"That's fine. Who wants to go first?"

"Reckon it's mostly my story." Gaines spoke before dropping into the chair across from me.

"Let's have it. Thanks to both of you, by the way."

"Ain't paid me yet, can't have ya killed." Moses laughed, easing the splinters out with a Barlow.

"Figure I owed ya for saving me from the noose." Gaines grinned back at me. "Pretty simple, overheard that gent up top gabbing with his pard. He's the one I got. They mentioned a third, but I didn't know who he was. Figure it's the one you got."

"Ow damn it." I grimaced as Moses cut out a longer one.

"They was talking about shooting up the court, get'n that

Hart fella freed. I found Mos, but we got here too late ta warn you. Just had ta play it as it came." For the first time, I noticed that Gaines looked a little pale. He wasn't used to violence like this.

"Still wonder how they got guns in." I spoke, not expecting an answer.

"They been here every day, figured out them soldier boys don't bother checking boots." Gaines supplied. He was saved from further explanation when a middle age man walked in. Going by the bag, he must be the doctor.

"Let me look at those Moses." He stepped by just as Moses got the last piece of wood out of my hide.

"Think I got'em all Doc, just ain't had nothing to clean it with but water. JC this 'here is Doc Drummond."

"Pleasure Doc." I said just before the man started dousing my face with liquid fire. "Damn it! Give a man some warning!"

"You'll live. Keep them clean and come see me if you start getting a fever. Sorry for the lack of bed side manner, I have two heavily concussed soldiers waiting in my surgery."

"I understand, Doc. Thanks for taking the time." The man was busy, I couldn't really blame him. He was out the door before the last word left my mouth.

"You two stay here an write out statements. You can write Gaines?" I looked over at the man cautiously. "I'm guessing both you killed them with blades?"

"Can, can't promise anyone can read it. Call me Chris, will ya." He paled a little again before adding. "Ya stuck him good enough, I reckon."

"Same." Moses said without much feeling.

"Chris, it is. Thanks again. Both of you probably saved more than just my hide." I had reloaded my Colt before we came in but double checked it before walking out the door. Collins was waiting outside for me. I had to credit his men. The bodies were gone and the two injured soldiers were taken to the Docs. Now there were four men cleaning up the blood.

"Figure you need a report too. Follow me, I'll give it to you and the Judge in one breath."

"Thanks JC." He dropped in behind me as I opened the door to the judge's chambers.

Warren, Ethan, Carton and Pollard were all sitting when I came in. Each man except Pollard held a glass of whiskey, the latter was trying to force down some coffee. Ethan was still a bit pale, but Warren just looked mad. Carton was mostly disinterested, like this wasn't anything new and that told me a lot about the man. Maybe there was something more to him than originally thought. Pollard's hand wasn't shaking from fear. My guess was Ethan had refused to let me have some whiskey.

"Marshal, are you okay?" Warren asked.

"Yes sir, just some splinters. Hurt more when Mos took them out, then the Doc cleaned them and the real pain started." I was trying to lighten the heavy cloud that hung over the room.

"Then please tell me what the hell happened." He demanded.

"Mind if I grab a cup of coffee first?" I asked, already reaching toward the tray.

"Sure you don't want something stronger?" Ethan asked.

"Coffee will do just fine. Need a clear head for this." I poured a cup and took a long, slow drink before speaking. "It appears we owe Mr. Gaines our thanks."

I told them the story, then what I had seen and done. Warren waved off apologies for killing Hart saying only that I 'saved the territory a hangman's fee.' Collins jaw clenched tight enough to crack teeth when he heard how the men had gotten the guns in. He didn't say a word, just spun on his heels and stomped out the door. You could hear the snap of his boot heels on the hallway as he left.

"Couple of soldiers are going have a bad time of it." Carlton chuckled once he was sure the man was out of earshot. Then he turned his eyes on me. "Marshal, I've never heard your name before but I was facing you when it all started. Hell, I think everyone was. That pistol was just suddenly there and spitting fire. I never saw you draw."

"That's owed to Hart." I explained, shrugging. "He locked eyes with the man. That let me be prepared. Sides, the man had to reach for his boot, which still makes no sense."

"What do you mean?" Warren asked.

"They'd been here long enough. Why didn't he move the pistol beforehand? There's no way I could've made that shot if he had it ready."

"Fear? Lack of forethought? Who knows why a man would try to disrupt a court in the middle of a military compound." Carton mused, sipping his whiskey.

"Smart outlaws are rarer than hens teeth, thankfully," Warren joked, then leaned forward resting his elbows on his desk. "Should we try to finish the rest today? Is it safe?"

"Safe sure, but I don't think you'd have much of a gallery. Folks'll be pretty leary about coming back today." Then added with a laugh. "An you can bet the soldiers will be taking their time searching people after this."

"Damn!" Warren swore. "You're right, of course, but I wanted to get this done. Perhaps it is rushing things to expect more for the day. I wouldn't want anyone who came seeking justice to miss out on witnessing it."

He was referring to the family members who traveled to witness the law at work. They had come here hoping to see some sort of justice. To be present when the person who commited such vile acts was held accountable. Seeing the killer convicted might somehow help the grief they felt. The idea didn't make sense to me, but I'd never been in their situation.

"Warren, I'd say leave it for today." Carton offered. "It seems like too much."

"Agreed. It's the best course of action. JC, could you let anyone waiting outside know?"

"Yeah, I'll go take care of it. Then I'm going to check to make sure Mos and Chris's statements are done before writing my own. They'll be on your desk by the morning. I'll get a copy to the colonel as well."

"Very well, and please tell both of them the court appreciates their assistance."

The reports took another hour. A corporal was stationed outside, letting people know court was done for the day. I managed to catch the colonel at dinner and gave him a copy of the report. He questioned me while we ate, but seemed satisfied with the answers. He apologized to me about his men and I told him not to worry about it. They did what they thought was right. I could understand how it wouldn't seem important. Honestly, I felt responsible for it. I should have warned them to pay more attention today.

Sunset found me sitting out back of the office drinking coffee with the three current residents. Willie and Moses could tell Chris needed to talk. They wandered off to give us space. It still took him another ten minutes to vocalize his thoughts. I waited patiently, knowing this was hard for him.

"JC, ain't ever killed anyone like that before. I mean, sure Indians and rustlers before...least I shot at them." his voice trailed off, trying to find the words.

"You mean where there's no doubt, no wiggle room that it might have been someone else?" He nodded numbly, just waiting for me to continue. "Taking a life is never a good thing. You end all the potential that man might have had. Each time you have to weigh that into your actions. Sadly, most often you have just seconds to act."

"How do you do it?" His voice was hollow. He was a man looking for reasons, or maybe some way to justify what had happened. I didn't think my answer would help him much, but I'd give it a try.

"Tell ya what I was told. Think about the nighthawks and guards you knew on the ranches you worked."

It suddenly hit me how odd this was. This man was at least a decade older than me. How had he not faced this before? Then I thought about the way people thought about things. In a big gun fight, you didn't always see the man you shot. Even if you did, there was always a question about whose bullet had killed them. The mind could believe its comfortable truth in those cases. Not with this, there was no way to shroud the truth.

"Yeah, I know a few that remind me of you, some others remind me of Mos."

"There is a difference between them. You're right in thinking that. I was told there are basically three types of men. The first, like you, carry the full weight of their actions. They feel the responsibility and guilt if they're forced to kill. If you take that too far, it can ruin you. You're going to have to let that go, my friend."

"How?" There was a pleading tone in his voice.

"Don't take the easy answers like whiskey. Time, it's the only thing that's going to help. Would you like to know who the man was?" I'd gotten their names earlier this evening.

"Did he deserve it?"

"If he'd been taken alive, we'd have hung him." I already knew he wouldn't take the bounty. It was written all over his face. The money would just haunt him if he took it.

"That helps some."

"No living family either."

"Thanks for that." He took a slow sip of his coffee and I continued.

"The second type is like Moses. They're pragmatic. They accept that sometimes killing is what needs to happen, but they still feel every death. It can get to be too much for them, too. Ever heard of a successful rancher who just sells out and moves back east?"

"Yeah, a few."

"That's them. They can't pay the price anymore and make the choice to leave before it crushes them."

"And the third? They're like you, aren't they?"

"Like me and some of the gun hands you've known, even some outlaws. We don't feel any of it. No grief, no guilt. Shooting a good horse bothers me more than killing a man does."

"You're saying there's no difference between you and them?" He scoffed, not believing me at all.

"The difference is our rules or code, if you will. Only my sense of right and wrong stays my hand. I've done things that are technically illegal, but to me and those with me, it was justice." I met his gaze evenly, hiding nothing from him.

"Not gonna lie, the thoughts a bit terrifying."

"It is, but don't get to thinking one is better or worse than the other. Every man finds his own way an someday none of it will be needed. There'll be law and police. Men won't be so quick to sell their lives cheaply." Then I thought about it and changed that last. "That's not right, they'll be fewer. Sadly, I think they'll always be those who would rather take from the world. The idea of working for things is something they'll never understand."

"It does help, if nothing else just knowing I'm not the only man who feels this way." A slight smile broke his grim visage.

"Time and happiness, my friend. You're going to start your ranch, find a good woman, and raise you a family." He was going to make it. He'd find his way through and get back to building his dream.

"Thanks JC. I'll be leaving at first light, but you'll always be welcome on my range. Whenever I find it anyway." He laughed, and I watched the darkness recede from his eyes the slightest bit.

"Same, it'll be up in Montana territory, but you'll be welcome on it." I shook his hand before standing to go inside.

# CHAPTER 23

I spent the next hour cleaning my pistol and checking the other one, just to be sure. Automatically switching one for the other to be sure they got used evenly, I hung the belt near my bed. After that, I was asleep before my head hit the pillow. A deep dreamless sleep that left me no more time to wonder about the events of the day.

The next day was uneventful. The remaining men were sentenced to hang without much fanfare. No one tried to free them, no one took a shot at anyone. Gaines left before dawn. Moses rode out at the same time, saying he needed some space. I knew where to find him if need be, he'd leave sign for me to follow. Probably starting where I'd found him that first night. I understood his desire for open country. My own feet were starting to itch.

Dinner was with the judge again, mostly them still trying to convince me to stick around. Carton was leaving for Santa Fe in the morning. He had some business there that was waiting for him. Warren and Ethan would be staying until after the hangings, which meant I would still be assigned to escort them. After that, I'd be going to visit Cimarron, hopefully to get some answers for the colonel.

Given a choice, I wouldn't have attended the hangings. There was something about the almost festive nature that surrounded them. It turned my stomach more than the actual hanging did. Thankfully, we didn't have to be down among the crowds. Warren had accepted this as part of his job long ago. Ethan knew it was part of the process and suffered through it. I could tell it bothered him.

The death didn't bother me, but the mob did. Perfectly normal people who would be at church tomorrow suddenly became part of a mob celebrating death. There was a darkness that seemed to come over them. Cheering someone's death was acceptable in that shadow, but it felt wrong to me. Wrong to the core of my being. Death was never something to be celebrated it was the end of all potential. A final decision that couldn't be changed, it just never seemed like something to celebrate to me.

I knew it was somewhat hypocritical of me to look at the crowd that way. It was still hard to put in words how I viewed life and death. The word personal comes to mind, death should be private, not something cheered by a crazed mob. Especially when that mob would shrug off the finality of it. Justifying it as deserved. They were bad men, no question about it. Nothing would change that. They would offer nothing of value to the world except as an example. Still, I felt like that needed to be respected.

Existential crisis aside, the three days passed and the executions were done. I collect rewards for the men in the courtroom and, as promised, split them with Moses. Willie had another route worked out and this time it would take us to Cimarron. Finally letting me get that mission out of the way.

There were a total of eight new prisoners in the northeastern district of the state that needed to be brought back for trial. Five were deserters. They would be turned over to the military. The other three would be held in our jail until the last court of the year was held. All three men were part of an outfit who had been lucky enough to have a law man catch them. If it had been the ranchers, they never would have seen a courtroom. Law and order were coming, but rustlers still faced a rope without ever seeing a judge.

We left a few days later when Moses returned. We had to travel in a wide loop and this trip would be at least two weeks. First, we'd travel out to Agua Negra Chiquita, then loop up to the Colorado border. Two of the deserters made it to Dillon before they got caught. After that, we'd pick up the last two in Blossburg. Turn south to stop in Cimarron, then get the rustlers in Loma Parda. What I was looking forward to this trip was finally seeing the Rockies. The last leg we would be following the foothills south. I was tempted to go by Hot Springs, but it seemed like a bad idea with eight prisoners.

It felt good to be out of the city. The open land sang to me as we traveled, instantly reminding me of how much I'd missed it. Ranging out hunting or scouting as we traveled east let me feel more relaxed than I had in days. The second afternoon, I took a decent javelina, and we stopped for a day to smoke most of it. Some Jicarilla Apache showed up the third day out, but the small hunting party kept their distance from us. Their presence made me stick closer to the wagon, not wanting either of us to be caught out alone.

Agua Negra Chiquita wasn't much, a small settlement just starting out. They'd caught the deserter stealing food and locked him in a smokehouse. I was pretty sure the church was the only reason they hadn't killed him. He was the first man I'd ever seen that was happy to climb into the jail wagon. Evidently, spending the last week locked in the small building was enough for him. Even the prospect of death didn't bother him anymore.

I got my first look at the Rockies not long after that when we headed to Dillon. Our travel slowed, but it was worth every minute. Part of me wanted to turn north and continue to explore. There was something about the shining blue mountains called to me. Whatever was calling me west was going to be replaced. Colorado wasn't calling yet, but I could feel it. The rest of the trail to pick up the deserters the mountains held my attention. There was just something about them that stole a part of me.

Five days later, Cimarron rose out of the land around me. I had to admit if staying here was an option, this place wouldn't be a bad choice. Not that the town was particularly nice, but the surrounding area was amazing. The river cut through the foothills like a knife carving a path filled with green. It was a meandering branch of the Canadian, its soft rippling water shimmered in the sunlight. The town was split across it, connected by a ford that probably flooded out in the spring.

When a man stepped out to stop us, I almost missed his arrival. The sun reflected off the star on his chest, finally getting my attention. He was tall, lean and looked to be in his thirties. Clean shaven and dressed nicely, there was something tired in his eyes. Like a weight that bore down on him relentlessly. I had a pretty good idea what that was.

"Marshal, welcome to Cimarron. Names Sheriff Rinehart." The man's voice sounded as tired as he looked.

"Pleasure to meet you. Still getting used to the marshal's title and likely won't have it long. Name is Stone."

"New to the job?"

"Temporary, just doing it until the permanent marshal gets here next year."

"Damn." The man quietly swore. "Was hoping for some help."

"Well, the Colonel did ask me to talk to Reverend Tolby about keeping the peace."

"That's gonna be hard unless ya got a spirit walker with ya. Found him dead yesterday."

"Guessing that's not a good thing?" For a county looking at a land war, I knew this could be the tipping point.

"Nope, it aint. Folks already convicted a man, but I don't think it was him." The man watched as I stepped out of the saddle to talk to him.

"Walk me through it. Looks like I need to get back to Albuquerque and fill the Colonel in."

"Clay Allison has a group of vigilantes looking for a man named Cruz Vega. His family has a reputation. That's about all the proof they have or want."

"What'll they do when they find him?"

"Ain't sure, but it won't be pretty."

"Think that'll light the fuse?"

"Likely, tell the Colonel I'm gonna need some help. Already sent a message to the governor, but ain't sure what it'll accomplish." Quietly, so only I could hear him, he added, "Feels like there's some big money in this fight somehow. I just can't puzzle it out."

"I'll tell him. Maybe he can apply some pressure from his end?" I had a bad feeling about this, but wasn't so foolish as to think I could do much.

"Hope so, cause I ain't gonna be able to stop this once the ball gets rolling."

"I'll do what I can. We'll push our speed."

"Oh looky, a marshal showed up!" A man yelled from the boardwalk. He had a crowd around him and looked like he was trying to rile them up. "He ain't noth'n but a kid."

The cold filled me as my feet started moving toward him. He stepped forward, prepared to exchange words. Unfortunately for him, I wasn't in the mood for it. Spinning on my left heel, I used the momentum to whip my right heel into the man's jaw. The bone snapped as my foot finished its arc and the man fell unconscious at my feet.

"Anyone else want to say something?" My voice carried enough cold threat to freeze the crowd where they stood.

"Marshal, he didn't mean.." I cut the new man off before he could finish.

"Any man who wants to speak disrespectfully to me gets that, or worse. I don't give a damn what he thought. Anyone who pushes won't like the response."

"I ain't saying that, Marshal." The man who stepped out had jet black hair and a full beard. His eyes were sharp, taking in the scene. "I ain't pushing either."

"Get him to the doctors." The sheriff walked up and faced the man. "Clay, this is Marshal Stone."

"Appreciate you not killing Jimmy." The man recognized that the thongs were off my Colts.

"Not worth the lead." I muttered, watching two men from the crowd half carry, half drag the man down the street.

"Clay, I know ya'll feel like you have to do something and think you know who did it but I'm asking you to leave it for the law." Rinehart spoke over my muttered comment.

"Sheriff, I ain't trying to be rude, but you're the only law here. You can't even get them to pay for a deputy." Clay wasn't being confrontational. It was plain to hear his dislike for whoever 'they' were. "You're a good man. I don't doubt your intentions, but that doesn't change the truth. You don't have the man power or time. Hell, can you even do anything that far out of town?"

"You're not wrong." Rinehart admitted. "But you and I both know this could spark bigger trouble."

"That troubles coming no matter what you or me do." Then he nodded toward me. "If he's staying to investigate, it might buy time."

"Can't. I'm not the permanent marshal. Just filling in mostly for prisoner pick up." I admitted the truth. Both men seemed to deflate at my words. "I will tell you the Colonel is paying attention to what's going on up here. The mans fair, if you have an honest grievance you could talk to him. I give you my word he'd take the time."

"Best I can do is try to keep the anger focused on one target." Clay said, shrugging his shoulders. In his way, the man was trying to keep the violence down. "Far as talking to the Colonel, I appreciate the effort and his willingness to try. Courts already ruled. If nothing changes soon, it'll turn violent."

"Just bring him in to me if you can." Rinehart finally accepting the truth.

"Can't promise that. Don't know if I'd even try. Franklin was a friend, the Cruzs betrayed all of us." There was real anger in the man's voice. It was driven by pain. This was all personal to these men.

Before the Sheriff could say anything else, Clay walked back into the saloon. I could hear angry voices inside, spurred by whiskey and grief. Rinehart sighed heavily. He knew he was losing what hold he had on the town and wasn't sure what to do about it. I could stay, send Moses back with the prisoners, but that would be a fool's errand. One more gun or calm voice wasn't going to help much. Not to mention these men didn't know me and had no reason to trust me. The only thing I could do was get back to the Colonel and hope he sent men to help the sheriff.

The colonel had been right. This place was a powder keg. It was going to get bloody long before a full time marshal could get here. We did what we could, Moses and I pulled into Albuquerque three days later with exhausted mules. The prisoners were not any better off, we'd barely stopped to eat from dark to dark. Only stopping to water the animals and ourselves just enough to keep going. I could have left Moses and made it back  faster. He had offered that exact thing but it didn't feel right to me. Leaving him alone with eight men wasn't a good idea. Aside from that it was my responsibility to see it through. Moses hadn't argued and seemed to appreciate the decision. Most would have left him, figuring if he got killed it was no big loss. That way of thinking had never made sense to me, especially not when it came to good men like him.

"Go to the Colonel. The soldiers will deal with theirs. Willie can help me get our folks taken care of." Moses offered when we reached the stockade.

"Thanks Mos, I'll met ya at the office." I said, turning Shade toward the command building. The private on guard just stepped out of my way without a word. Something warned him I was in a hurry. Major Collins was sitting at the desk outside the colonel's office and looked surprised when I came in.

"Willie said you weren't due back for three or four more days."

"Bad news. Is he in?"

"He is, been cursing all day." The major was already knocking on the door when he spoke.

"What?" The voice growled through the door.

"Marshal Stone is here, sir."

"Both of you in here now." Granger barked.

"Colonel, you're going to need to get some help to Rinehart."

"What do you mean?" Whatever else was bothering the man faded immediately.

"Reverend Tolby was killed. A man named Allison is leading a group of vigilantes hunting for someone they think killed him."

"Son of a bitch!" Granger roared and slammed his fist on to the top of his desk. Collins stared in shock at his superior, unused to hearing the normally calm man angry. Granger took a slow, deep breath before continuing. "Apologies gentlemen, this couldn't have come at a worse time."

"There's never a good time for a situation like this sir." Collins admitted.

"Worse now, Major. I have to send our currier to Arizona. Which means we lose our marshal." Granger sat there for a minute thinking, then seemed to make a decision. "Major, send a telegram to the governor."

Attention Governor Giddings.
Santa Fe
Tolby killed stop
Trouble coming to Cimarron stop
Federal troops available Fort Union upon your request stop
Colonel Granger
Albuquerque

"Yes sir." The Major took the message and walked out of the office at speed.

"Arizona sir?"

"There's a mess there. They need to get cleaned up and you're the only one who can deal with it. A rogue deputy US Marshal is causing problems. These orders come from the top. There's no choice. Deputize Moses for now and Willie can handle the jail until the new marshal gets here."

"A rogue deputy?"

"He was a stop gap left there to deal with things. Just like here, there's a new marshal coming out next year for the territory. Country is growing faster than we can keep up with in many ways. The law is just one of them."

"Guessing he wasn't answering to anyone?"

"They just got the territorial government formalized in Tucson. The governor, Stafford something or other. He has some four word name I haven't bothered to learn. It doesn't matter, the fool hasn't dealt with the man, blames it on the marshals and says he can't exceed his authority to arrest the man. Your orders are simple. Arrest him if at all possible and deliver him to the territorial prison in Yuma. They'll transport him east for trial."

"Take me a day to get outfitted and rest my horse. I'll be gone the next morning. My badge still good?"

"Leave that one here. Your other badge has been activated with no assigned location, that's per Marshal Douglas. You're his problem solver right now. Telegram him personally when you finish there. It does mean your short-lived career as a currier is finished."

"Didn't take long to get fired!" I barked out a laugh. "Any hints about where the man might be?"

"He's been sticking around the Colorado River. He'll go into a town, collect a 'marshals fee' along with anything else he can get. The man's name is Jack Almer, goes by Red Jack. Best I can tell you is start in that area, find a town he frequents and wait if need be."

"As good a place as any to start."

"Let me deal with this other mess. JC, it's been a pleasure and I do appreciate the help. You did quite a bit in the short time you've been here."

"Same sir, appreciate the work." I smiled at his look, then chuckled. "Well, it's been interesting."

"Good luck, young man." He laughed while shaking my hand. "I expect to hear stories about you."

"Hope not!" With a quick grin, I walked out of the office to go confuse Moses. I wasn't sure the man wanted to be a deputy US marshal.

It turned out I was both right and wrong. The man didn't know how to feel about it when asked. By that evening, he was wearing his new star when we went to the officer's mess. That had been my idea. If someone was going to give him trouble, I wanted it done now while I was here. A few officers glared, but when Collins invited us to join him, most got the message.

After dinner, we walked around the town and I introduced him to the sheriff. That had been a waste of time. They knew each other and got along fine. It did make me feel better about leaving the man in charge. I knew he had the skills and temperament for the job. He just had to do it.

The next day I told Jackson to check my animal's shoes and tack. He promised they'd be done and ready to go the next morning. Another forty-three dollars in supplies, including plenty of coffee and tobacco. The mercantile had a tasty blend of pipe tobacco and some good cheroots, so I bought plenty of both. The last stop was to restock my ammo and pack my shipping crate back up. Wells Fargo said they'd pick it up the next day.

Riding out of Albuquerque in the early light of dawn the next day was a mixed bag for me. There were good folks here, and I felt lucky for the experience. On the other hand, I was more than ready to be moving again. Willie and Moses saw me off from the back gate. Before the sun had full risen, the city was just a shadow in the distance. I was moving west again, getting one step closer to California. I was happy with the way this was working out, but couldn't help but wonder how long I'd keep this badge.

# CHAPTER 24

I enjoyed being on my own again and resumed the disguise of Walker before leaving New Mexico. Stopping for two days in the Zuni mountains after taking a good sized buck. Using the excuse of needing to smoke the meat, I took the time to let myself feel the land. After finding a decent cave and building a primitive smoker, I spent time just exploring the area until meeting a hunting party. I traded some of the meat with them for some herbs they had gathered. They invited me to travel with them to their camp, but I politely declined. My smoker was already working, and I'd set up a good camp. Normally, I wouldn't have stayed there after they left, but they knew Grey Walker and welcomed me to their lands.

It's a subtle difference, not something I'd have bet on with every tribe. Some would trade with me, then come back for my scalp if the notion struck them. The Zuni and Pueblo were different, not that they weren't dangerous. More than one man had made that mistake. In their lands, they were unmatched hunters and warriors. They knew these mountains far better than any traveler could ever hope to. The truth was, if they meant me harm, there wasn't much I could do about it. The real difference was that they didn't view us as a threat. Settlers didn't stay in their lands, not yet at least. While there was still plenty of easy land to work on offer no one would take theirs. That would change eventually. Someday soon, all land would become precious. Sadly, that realization would come too late for many of the tribes. They wouldn't be able to stop the tide and would be swept away with the rest.

After three days, I left their range behind me. Riding mostly west toward my next destination, San Juan. It was a small ranching community that was built around a crossing of the Little Colorado. I didn't even stop in the town since my supplies were still good and made camp across the river for the night. I wouldn't need to resupply until Flagstaff just before crossing the San Francisco range. After that, the hunt would start for the rogue deputy.

Flagstaff wasn't much more than a wagon stop on the trail to California. A town was starting to show signs of growing here, but it still wasn't much more than a trading post. A general goods store, saloon, and a blacksmith with a livery attached. That was it, just the basic things a wagon train would need.

I happened to arrive just after a wagon train. It wasn't one of the big ones, there was only seventeen wagons parked in a neat circle. Beales Wagon Road was well traveled. To be honest, I was surprised to see only one. Then again, it was late in the season. Some of the mountain crossings would be snow covered already. The only thing I could do was hope their wagon master knew his business.

Ignoring the general store, it was currently packed with people from the wagon. I headed to the livery. Leaning back in a chair outside was an ancient looking Mexican. Dressed in the traditional loose white homespun clothes with a straw sombrero tilted over his face. I wasn't sure if he was awake or not.

"Amigo, you want to leave your animals?" He spoke from under his hat, never looking up. Guess he was awake after all.

"I would, my friend. Maybe get the smith to check their shoes if he has time?"

"Chico!" He yelled without moving. "Si, my niño will look. If they need them, it will be some time. The smith is busy with the wagons."

"Si, I can check them." The young man who walked out was a little younger than me.

"Gracias." I said, stepping out of the saddle. "The molly can be difficult, just watch her."

"No problem." Chico walked up and spoke in rapid Spanish to Wisp. It was soft enough that I couldn't catch it, but Wisp seemed to get the meaning. "Check back in an hour. I will have them fed and curried, amigo. I can tell you about their shoes then."

"Thanks." Tipping my hat to them before walking toward the saloon. Not sure what to expect, I checked my Colts on the way.

The saloon was a short, squat adobe building. It was more of a cantina honestly. Inside wasn't much to look at, a rough cut plank bar across three barrels, six tables with a variety of wobbly chairs. The only furniture in the place that looked fully finished was the poker table at the back. I stepped to the left of the door as I entered, letting my eyes adjust to the dim light.

Taking that moment to survey the room, I studied the occupants. Three of the tables were full of men from the wagon train. This wasn't a guess. They stood out in contrast to the men who lived out here. There was the obvious clothing, but that alone wasn't it. There was a presence they lacked, some toughness that made men stay in these harsh lands. It just wasn't there. They didn't pay any attention to me. The other three men did.

They looked like punchers for the most part. They all had that dark leather skin from working in the sun, marked with scars and still healing scratches. These were men who didn't follow the road. They chased cattle or horses out of the harsh terrain, paying its price in blood every time. Their eyes didn't miss my appearance and, with almost universal understanding, we all nodded to one another. There were two men at the bar and I made sure to give them space. Waking past, I caught only part of their conversation. It was enough to pique my interest.

"Deputy, I just don't see why you think I'll pay you for crossing the land. There's never been a toll on Beales road." The man speaking wasn't a settler or a puncher.

Older, maybe in his fifties, he had the lean muscle of a man who worked for a living. That matched a puncher near enough. What marked him as different were his hands. They lacked the built up the calluses you'd get from working a rope. He wore a single Colt high in his right hip, out of place for a gun hand. Clad in a buckskin shirt with his pants tucked into high calvary boots. From what he said and his appearance, I'd guess he was the wagon master.

The man he was talking to was different as well, but his type I knew. Lawman or outlaw, the two were interchangeable a lot of the time. Dressed like any puncher, it was something in their eyes that gave them away. A watchfulness that only comes from being in danger much of the time. He wore two Remingtons tied down and hanging low. Both were well cared for and used.

"Don't matter if it ain't had one before, it does now. You can pay it or deal with being arrested." The man growled out. He wasn't used to being challenged and didn't care for it.

"What's your name, deputy?" The older man asked. I watched the deputy tense up as I leaned on the bar near the bartender.

"Beer." I said, simply trying to listen to the other conversation.

"Jack Almer, deputy US Mashal." I almost laughed. Of all the places to walk into. Someone up there was looking out for me.

"Names Blake Killinger. This is my twelfth trip on this route and I ain't paying an illegal toll deputy marshal." The man nearly spit the last two words out in disgust. The bartender collected his dime. When he looked away I slipped my badge on.

"You'll be arrested then." Red Jack growled, but even I could hear the hollowness in that threat.

"Doubtful." Killenger snorted before turning to walk over to his charges.

Red Jack turned to follow him with his eyes. His hand dropped to the butt of his right-hand pistol. The man almost vibrated with anger, his eyes burning holes in his back as the man walked away. That stopped when the barrel of my Colt smacked the back of his head. He crumpled to the ground in a heap. Before anyone could move, I stepped back, watching to room. There hadn't been enough time for me to really look around the room.

"I'm U.S Marshal JC Stone. This man's wanted to impersonating a deputy US Marshal, theft, extortion and murder." No one moved, but I heard Killenger laugh.

"Knew there wasn't a toll." Then his eyes met mine. "He's alone Marshal, saw him come into town this afternoon."

"Thanks. What did he ride in on?" I holstered my pistol and quickly disarmed Red Jack. While I was searching him no one moved. I used the man's own manacles to lock his hands behind his back and the tension left the room. I found two knives and a holdout colt in a shoulder holster along with seventy-three dollars.

"Paint, leading a mouse grey pack horse. They should be at the livery." Killenger offered. "He shook down the bartender before he tried me."

"How much?" I turned to look at the bartender.

"Five dollars, his usual for the month." He looked shocked when I handed him a double eagle.

"Ought to give ya some back." I grinned, picking up my beer. It wasn't exactly cold but tasted fresh enough.

Just as I finished my last swallow, the lump on the floor groaned. Jerking him to his feet when he started to struggle. A grin split my face when his eyes widened. The first thing I did was take the star off his vest. His eyes were locked on my marshal's badge. The fear that danced in them made me smile. I didn't bother to speak, just spun him around to look at the goose egg on the back of his head. He wasn't bleeding and seemed to be aware enough.

"What the hell, marshal?" I plopped his bowler back on making him wince when he started to speak.

"Jack Almer, you're under arrest and will be turned over to

the new territorial prison in Yuma. That is until such time as you can be transported to stand trial in federal court back east."

"How d'ya find me?" The man knew the game was up, didn't even bother trying to deny anything. He'd known the outcome when he saw my badge.

"Luck. Just happened to stop here for supplies. If it helps your pride, my only reason for being here is to find you." I chuckled at his look of surprise.

"Musta been that one fella." He grumbled.

"You'll have plenty of time on the way to Yuma to figure that out." I noticed his mouth twitch when I said that. It wasn't a to me mystery why. The road to Yuma wasn't a short one. That long on the trail, he'd try to find a chance to escape.

"We'll see how that goes, Marshal." He said under his breath. Turning to the bartender with a question. I'd need a way to secure him while I got ready.

"Is there anything resembling a jail around here?"

"Smokehouse out back. It's got a good lock on it. Used it a few times ta lock up troublemakers."

"Mind if I use it?"

"Help yourself." He slid a key across the bar to me. "Long as it's for him."

"Whipple, you'll pay for 'at." Red Jack glared at the man, but the bartender just smiled back. The first thing I needed to do was secure him with my manacles. I was pretty sure he didn't have another key, but it was better to be sure.

"Come on." I yanked him back from the bar by his wrists.

It didn't take long to get him secured in my manacles, tossing his to the side. I added leg shackles for the night and attached them to a post in the middle of the shed. After telling Chico I'd be leaving in the morning he smiled. He'd watched with some amusement when I switched the chains. First, I put on the ankle set, he tried to kick me but I'd expected that. As soon as he drew back his foot, my right elbow drove into his crotch. He didn't try it again, to be honest he didn't manage to get back on his feet for a while after that. It had the intended affect, he seemed much more agreeable.

Chico told me I could sleep in the loft and he'd help get all the animals ready in the morning. The offer included using a small campsite outback for cooking and such. He also told me the shoes on all four mounts were good. My total cost was a dollar fifty. I paid him two dollars out of Red Jacks money with a smile.

An hour later, I was in the general store stocking up on supplies with my prisoner locked in the smokehouse. With two pack animals, there was no need to be shy about buying supplies. The only thing the store didn't have was cheroots. Thankfully I still had plenty. I was floored to find out he had a few cans of peaches left after the wagon train. They got added to the smile pile on the counter. The last thing was thirty feet of rope. Jack didn't have any and my riata was too expensive to cut up. Jack graciously paid for all our supplies despite my attempts to disagree. He insisted it was only fair since he'd use some of them. The owner, a man named John Smith, said he'd have everything ready in the morning. I was just stepping out of the store when a familiar voice hailed me. It was Killenger.

"Marshal, a minute please."

"What can I do for ya?" I asked casually, leaning in the shade outside the store. I struck a match on the rough cut wood and lit a cheroot.

"Just wanted to thank you for arresting that man."

"Just doing my job."

"All the same, I'd like to offer you dinner if I may?" Now that was attractive, someone else's food always tasted better. "Of course not cooked by me. The ladies of the train do that thankfully."

"Sounds better than my master plan of beans and bacon." I laughed, exhaling smoke.

"How is it that's all we ever learn to cook?"

"I can cook more, but usually don't bother. Mind if I ask, you folks are late for the trail aren't you?"

"Let's walk toward the wagons, an I'll explain."

"Long as there's coffee."

"There's always coffee." His voice was solemn, but the big grin that split his face said he knew the joke. "Ever cross the Mojave?"

"Can't say as I have."

"I've learned to do it late in the year. Nights are damned cold, but the days aren't as torturous. Easier on the settlers and the animals. This is my thirteenth time crossing it. Painful experience has taught me the best time to do it."

"Hadn't thought about that." I answered honestly as we reached a small camp site set up near a wagon.

"This is Paul, been my wagon driver for the last two trips." He introduced me to the short stocky man as we approached. "Paul, this is Marshal Stone.

"Please call me JC." I offered my hand to the man as he stood. His heavily callused hand gripped mine firmly.

"Welcome Marshal, most folks just call me darkie." He laughed and no matter how I tried, I couldn't help but the join him.

"Paul will you ever stop telling that joke?" Killenger didn't find it funny. "One man called you that and I quickly corrected him."

"Ya did boss, that don't keep folks from thinking it. I can either be mad or laugh' bout it." I recognized his accent, Louisiana. Not New Orleans, further back on the bayou somewhere.

"Touch of the swamps in your accent?" I asked, changing the subject.

"Been round my folk before, eh?"

"Spent a few months down that way. I was privileged enough to find good friends among the Creole." It didn't hurt as badly to think of Binda anymore. Now I just remembered her smile and the way her hand felt in mine. There must have still been something in my tone, because Paul studied me carefully.

"Truly ya been round da swamps, can see it ya eyes."

"A traiteur saved my life."

"Ya truly know da real people den." As he thought of home, his accent got a little thicker. "Miss running dem swamps. Don't miss da hate though."

"Plenty of anger down there."

"Nough of dat, coffee?" He changed the subject, knowing that neither of us wanted to talk about the subject.

"Always." I grinned, smelling the chicory in it. "Good coffee at that."

"Gotta carry it wit me. Can't stand the stuff without the proper makings."

"Mr. Killenger. Will you be taking dinner with us?" A female voice broke into our conversation. She looked to be in her late twenties, pretty enough with her blonde hair in a neat bun. Her eyes spotted me and she almost took a step back in shock. I was still dressed like Walker and she thought I was a half breed.

"Mrs. Watkins, this is Marshal Stone." Killenger introduced me and I stood tipping my hat to the lady. "Marshal Stone, this is Mrs.Watkins. She and her husband manage the wagons for meals and other such things."

"Pleasure to meet you, ma'am." I tipped my hat to her after rising to my feet.

"Ummm yes Mr. Stone." She still looked nervous. I heard Paul chuckle softly from where he still knelt by the fire.

"I was hoping he could join us for dinner. I happened to meet him while dealing with that deputy 'bout the fake toll. He arrested the man and will be taking him to the territorial prison."

"Oh!" She sounded surprised by the news. I knew why, but Killenger seemed to have no clue. First she assumed I was working with him. Now she didn't know what to make of a half-breed marshal. "Umm yes, of course."

"Ma'am, the good marshal is a white man." Paul said, doing his best to look studiously at the fire.

"What?" Killenger seemed stunned by his statement. Not

that he didn't know, he just couldn't understand why Paul had said it.

"Yes, of course he is." Mrs. Watkins tried to recover, but I could see her embarrassment. "I'll hope to see you for dinner."

Then she spun in place before almost running back into the center of the wagons. Paul managed to keep his laughter quiet until she was far enough away. Then I joined him and we both had a good chuckle while Killenger stared at us, confused by the whole thing. Finally, he seemed to understand what was so funny.

"Did she really think you were an Indian?"

"Yeah boss, she did. Course she did. Long hair, feathers? Gotta be a savage injun." Paul tried to explain.

"But anyone with eyes can see he's a white man." The man just couldn't see how someone would be confused.

"These people haven't seen what life's really like out here," Paul explained. "Even wit all the miles behind us, 'em folks still figure the world is simple. If ya has long hair an wear feathers, You's an Indian. Every'thang else be told by skin color."

"That doesn't make sense." Killenger muttered. "Course you're right. Seems to always take me by surprise."

"I'm guessing you've been out here for long enough to know some of the People." I was giving away information about my knowledge with that statement, but it didn't matter. "If you know them, you recognize them. A half breed might fool you sometimes, but most of the time you can see the traits. Especially if they grew up with the tribes."

"You know, in all my trips, I've never run across this. Maybe I'm keeping these folks too safe." He admitted, rubbing his chin in thought.

"Told ya boss, you always see the good in folks. That's why ya don' see the way dey look at me. Sure, they gets better as we travel cause they see me being useful an folks start mix'n a bit more. That don't change the fact that none of them gonna invite me ta dinner." Paul spoke into his coffee, keeping his voice gentle. Trying to point out something to the man, not scold him for something that wasn't his fault.

"Most people out here don't care about color." I waved Paul down before he could reply. "I mean punchers and ranchers, folks who really live out here. Saw it working the ranches in Texas. Hell, my foreman at the Bar C used to be a slave. That being said, there's many a ranch where folks aren't allowed in the house for Sunday dinner."

"I never thought about it like that. Fought for the Union in the war, helped the Underground Railroad before that. Guess my father taught me better than most."

"Ya told' me your pappy came over from Germany if I 'member right?" Paul asked.

"Came over when he was a youngster. His father wanted a shot at owning his own land. My older brother is still on that farm in Pennsylvania."

"Bet yer paw couldn't own no land cause he weren't from the right family?" Paul filled his cup again as he spoke. "Raised y'all not to treat folks like he was treated."

"Of course." Killenger admitted.

"Most folks ain't raised that way." I held my cup out and Paul refilled it as he spoke.

"Guess I should pay more attention to that truth." Killenger laughed at himself. "I apologize Paul, I'll try to be more aware of the differences."

"Ain't nothing to worry 'bout boss. Just the way folks are, least out here folks ain't as likely to kill me just cause."

"Marshal, if we want to join the others, we'd better wander over that way. You joining us, Paul?" I rocked up from my toes and downed the last of my coffee. I had to admire Killenger's deft change of subject while showing his willingness to push people toward change.

"Think I'll enjoy my dinner here boss, ain't much in the mood for socializing."

"Before we go, I have a question for you Marshal." Killenger looked at me carefully before asking. "What's your plan after Yuma?"

"Find my way to Los Angeles. After that, I don't know."

"The train will make Kingman in about two weeks. You're welcome to travel with us across the Mojave if you can make it by then. We're actually short a scout."

"Long as he makes the coffee." I agreed, nodding toward Paul.

"He does if I can avoid it." Killenger laughed.

"An if I wanna drink anything other than his mud." Paul shot back.

"I'll leave word at Casters Dry Goods when we leave. That way you'll know you missed us." Killenger smiled before stepping toward the circle of wagons.

The meal was pleasant. Folks mostly kept their distance, not sure what to make of me. Only one of them stood out, a small man with piggish little eyes. He seemed to go out of his way to avoid my notice, which had the opposite effect. There was something about the man that made me want to keep him in sight. I didn't know why. Maybe I just didn't like him. Either way, something about him made my skin crawl.

I didn't over stay my welcome, using the excuse that I still needed to set up my camp as an excuse I left. Stopped by to say adios to Paul, assuring him that if at all possible I'd meet them in Kingman. He told me there'd be coffee ready at false dawn and I was welcome to join them. After nodding my thanks, I left their small camp, walking back to the livery.

Sleep came fast in the hayloft. I was up and moving before the first light. There was no way I was trying my routine up here. There wasn't enough room or privacy to even consider it. After stomping into my boots and slinging my gun belt on, I climbed down and left my bedroll near my tack. Take a few minutes to stretch lightly before walking toward the fire not far away. It's dancing light calling to me.

# CHAPTER 25

"Hello the camp." I called out after getting close enough to not yell.

"Coffees' bout done. Come on in JC." Paul answered.

The rest of the morning was pleasant. Paul turned out to be an amazing camp cook. Chico met me at the livery and between the two of us we got Wisp and Jack's pack horse ready to go. He'd get the other two ready while I was getting the supplies loaded. The store's owner pitched in and the sun was just showing when I left them at the livery to get Jack.

"Get up." I kicked the man's boot to wake him.

"Ya ain't human, leaving a man in here with no food." He complained.

"You can have some jerky once we're on the trail."

"How bout some coffee?"

"You missed out this morning." I said, pushing him toward the livery. "Here's how this is going to work. You make my life easy, you get the same food and coffee I do. Give me trouble and I'll drag you into Yuma half starved."

"Ya can't…" I cut him off before he could start.

"I can and will, because I don't care about this badge. If Marshal Douglas wants to fire me, he can. Won't matter to me."

There must have been something in my voice. Maybe the cold I had let seep in caused it. The man shivered like someone had stepped on his grave. I used part of the new rope to tie him into the saddle, then attached the trail rope to Wisp. His pack horse was behind me, which pissed Wisp. She expressed this by trying to take off my fingers when I tried to calm her down.

Bribing her with a piece of the penny candy helped and she stopped trying to kick me at least.

"Now pay attention Jack, I'm gonna tell ya about Wisp. She don't much care for people, as you can see. So if you decide to yank on these reins, she's likely to kick your horse." I smiled while explaining the last part of the threat. "I'm guessing that'll make your horse either drop or rear up."

"Bucky would rear up an fight." Red Jack said proudly.

"Good, a solid animal then. Problem is that won't be good for you. See how I've only tied in one leg?" I grinned up at him and let the cold fill my voice. "Now, with one foot tied into the stirrup, what do you think'll happen?"

"That ain't right, no man oughta face that." His voice was tinged with panic.

"It won't happen so long as you don't piss off Wisp." Like she'd been trained for it, she looked over her shoulder to glare at him. "I'd like to deliver you in one piece, but it's not a requirement."

Red Jack, for all his bluster, knew when he'd been beat. His head sagged and his shoulders slumped. There was just the barest hint of a nod. I didn't need anymore than that for now. He could try whatever he wanted. I'd just have to be prepared for it. During the day while we traveled, doing what I did created an impossible situation. It should make my life easier during the day.

"This trip is going to happen. It can be easy or hard. That's your choice." My words carried the intent I wanted. Not a threat, but an offer. "You'll have a chance to fight the charge in court. A real court back east. All you have to do is go along with the program. Fight me and I won't have many options, make it easy, then get a good lawyer. Nothing you've done is a hanging offense, far as I know."

"Figure you're right, marshal."

We both recognized the lie. He'd test me, probably try to escape. Not from the saddle, not when it was rigged like this. Too much risk of a bad death. When I stopped to rest the animals and eat some breakfast would be his first chance. I cut that thought out of his head quickly. When I untied his boot, I left the rope attached and him in the saddle. I took the far end and tied it to a tree. Only then did I let him dismount.

I felt his body tense just before he tried to hit me with his wrist shackles. It was enough warning to yank him out of the saddle. He hit the hard packed ground with a whomp, the air leaving his lungs instantly. Standing over him, I just shook my head before walking away. He laid there for a while, collecting his thoughts before struggling to get up.

"That ain't right, marshal." The rope stopped him ten feet from the fire.

"Just have a seat. Coffee will be done soon."

"Jus' ain't right." He grumbled, but sat down on the ground.

Before I set his coffee and biscuits down, my right boot stepped on the chain connecting his wrists. This brought more grumbling, but let me set his food down without risk. He ate in sulky silence, but I caught him looking around. Studying me, the animals, and his shackles. When I caught his eyes resting on the panniers, it almost made me laugh. He'd seen me put his guns in them earlier. The corners of my mouth twitched up knowing what he'd try next.

The pannier was just within his reach. He'd have to lay out flat to reach it, but he could. None of that worried me. He wouldn't get far with that plan, either. There was no need for me to tell him that, let him learn it the hard way. I drank my coffee and ate the cold bacon biscuits, doing my best to hide the grin. When I was done and started breaking camp, the inevitable happened.

"Need to make water." I'd been waiting for that one.

"Fine." I casually rose to my feet. He studied me, waiting for a reaction. "What? Go, that rope will let you reach the buses. You run with no guns and no mount. You'll die an I'll drag your carcass back with me."

My answer caught him off guard. He hadn't thought about that, but now that I said it, he couldn't avoid the thought. Like most of the wild lands, a man without a horse was just waiting to die. Now the fear of that slow death wouldn't stop running through his mind. I'd just removed one plan he had by pointing out the obvious.

His next move would be finding a weapon while he was out of sight. The man was so easy to read, I almost felt bad for him. A lazy man assumed everyone else was lazy and acted accordingly. He wandered off to relieve himself and I waited. He wasted five minutes before coming back out, the hint of a smile on his face. He'd found something, a rock or sharp piece of wood, was my guess. I didn't need to guess where it was. His right pant leg was just slightly out of place.

When I cut the rope at the base of the tree and started pulling it tight as I walked toward him, he laughed.

"Didn't want ta get your hands dirty?"

Without warning, I yanked the rope hard. Dumping him back to the ground again. For the second time today, he was left gulping for air. I held his legs up in the air and dug into his right boot. What I found inside was a short piece of mesquite that had broken off with a sharp point. It wouldn't cut anything, but the tip was sharp enough to stab me.

"Warned ya bout this. Didn't I?" My voice was cold and his eyes widened in fear.

He only threw up once before lunch. Most men who spent a few hours tied across a saddle like a bag of flour would have done it more. He did complain throughout, but I'd expected it and just let the words wash over me. When I stopped for lunch, I let him drop to his feet. As expected, both of his legs folded under him. Tying the end of the rope off on another tree, I left him there to take care of the animals. After rubbing some feeling back into his legs, he managed to sit up without grimacing.

"Ain't right treating a man like that."

"True, I wouldn't do that to a man." I said, setting down the pannier just close enough that he could reach in it. Then I walked over to take the saddle off Shade, turning my back to the man.

"Careless marshal." He growled, and I heard the hammer fall on an empty chamber.

"Careless would be trying to shoot a man in the back without checking the load." Another click as the hammer fell again. "Course now I could just shoot you and save myself a lot of trouble...."

The gun hit the ground. I had to prepare myself for whatever came next, probably groveling. Turns out not yet, he was searching the pannier for cartridges. There wasn't a single piece of ammunition in them, I'd made sure of that. It did mean I couldn't kill him, unfortunately. Really would have been easier but just knowing that he wasn't armed stayed my hand.

"Careless to keep the bullets with the gun, too." I set my saddle down and slowly turned to face the man.

All the color had drained from his face. Realization turned to terror. Much like the rest of him, his perspective on the world was tainted. He'd kill me in cold blood without hesitating. Every part of him just knew I'd do the same. Now he did what I'd expected earlier, started begging.

"Please Marshal, I won't give ya a bit of trouble jus' don't kill me."

His eyes followed my hand as my Colt slowly rose. The gaping maw at the end of the barrel seemed to draw his eyes into it like a black hole. There in the dark hole, he saw his doom. The end of whatever life he had. The sound of the hammer locking back made him open his eyes wider. When I saw the wet spot spread down his legs, I knew my point had been made.

Slowly lowering the hammer, I holstered my Colt. The man on the ground kneeling in front of me was broken. He'd never stand up fully again. That truth was written all over his face. I'd seen the same look in men before, men who crawled to avoid death. Something in them broke that would never heal. It just took all the fight out of them, afterwards they'd do anything to avoid facing their death.

"That was the last of my patience. Next time, I will leave your corpse for the scavengers." The cold filled my voice with icy shards, stabbing every word into the shattered man.

"Yes, sir. I won't never give ya no trouble again." His voice quaked. The man he had been was gone. Whatever this was wouldn't give me or anyone else a problem again.

Five days later, we rode into Gila Bend. I'd skirted the Big Horn range from here. We'd be following the Gila River to Yuma in a couple of days. The Crossroads of the Southwest was a busy freight town that was trying to become something more. There wasn't much to the town itself yet, the basic stores and goods. I'd heard it was growing, and the railroad was likely coming soon. Right now I was tying up at the local sheriff's office. Jack didn't move to get out of the saddle.

"Come on, let's find you a bed for the night."

"Sure marshal, be nice to have a bed." The man climbed down and even opened the door in front of me. The deputy behind the desk look up casually at Jack, then caught my star and shot to his feet. He finally realized Jack was manacled at the wrist, understanding filled his eyes.

"On the way to Yuma Marshal?" I gave him credit. He either didn't care or knew I wasn't a half breed.

"Got it in one, but I couldn't use a good night's rest. Any chance I can borrow a cell for the night?"

"Sheriff's out of town, chasing a killer, so as long as he ain't a problem, sure. Old Gus watches the drunks at night, he ain't much for real hard cases."

"He won't give him any trouble. Sides, I'll see to his meals and what not. Just need the cell."

"Come on back, we can put him in the far cell and I'll let Gus know to leave him be." The deputy stood, letting me get my first real look at him. Mid twenties, shortcut, sandy blonde hair. It all fit on the tall lean frame, giving me the impression of a future politician.

"Thanks, decent place to get a bath around here? Maybe a

shave?" I still grew the thin wispy hair that marked my youth and it was getting out of hand.

"Right down the street, the only place in town that ain't a bawdy house. Trevor's place is clean and the waters hot." He answered the rest of my unasked questions easily. "Eatery across the street is good. It's where we get our meals. Hotels right next to that and the livery's at the end of the street. Javier will take real good care of your animals. Man's got a knack with 'em."

"Been asked all this before?" I chuckled.

"Had a few folks come through." He grinned, opening the cell for Jack who stepped in as soon as he could. The deputy stepped back without me asking and covered me while I unlocked the manacles. Jack didn't move until the cell was closed, then he rubbed his wrists, shrugging his big shoulders to stretch sore muscles.

"Thanks marshal." Was all he said before sitting down and kicking off his boots.

"I'll bring ya some food before I go get cleaned up." I said, following the deputy back up front.

"I gotta go eat soon. I'll get him some food while I'm there. We feed em well and they only charge us a quarter." Then he seemed to realize he'd forgotten something. "Damn sorry Marshal, names Bug, well that's what everyone calls me."

"Pleasure Bug, names JC." I shook his extended hand. Already deciding to get rid of the alias since I was wearing the badge. "Bet there's a story 'bout that name."

"Tell ya about it over a beer after my rounds if you're out later." He laughed.

"This'll cover his lunch." I said, fishing out a quarter. "I need to go wash this dust off after I get my animals takin' care of."

The livery man was a middle-aged Mexican. True to the deputies' word, he had a way with animals. Even Wisp seemed to like him. With a quick smile, he promised to take care of them and I could store everything there until I left. I planned on staying two nights. The animals needed the rest and so did

I. He curried each animal while I stored everything in the tack room. By the time I walked out carrying my saddlebags and Winchester, he was already checking their shoes.

"Can ya change'em if they need it?"

"Si, señor. It will be no problem." I left the man to his work and headed to the hotel.

A room with a balcony on the second floor cost me a dollar for two nights. They had a laundry service outback, and I planned on dropping my clothes off after the barbers. Everything got left in the room except a change of clothes before walking down to find a bath. It ended up costing me almost as much as the room. The man charged by the tub and it took three of them before the water stopped changing color. That was after crossing the Gila earlier today. A pleasant surprise was finding someone to polish my boots while I bathed. I'd almost forgotten the true color of the leather. It was good to see them looking clean again. Had to admit, I'd be looking for this book maker to order more. Most comfortable pair I'd ever owned now that they were broken in.

I had the same argument with Sam about my hair, seemed like barbers everywhere had united against long hair. No, I didn't want a hair cut. Just a shave nothing more. Changing hats after the bath, I borrowed some of the oil they'd used on my boots to treat the leather. I left clean and feeling more like myself.

It was past lunch but not quite dinner yet by the time I was done. It gave me some time to buy supplies and check out the town. After dropping all my laundry off to be washed, I looked for the general store. It wasn't anything special, but he had everything on my list. My order would be ready at first light the day after tomorrow. Unsure how it would be after Yuma, I'd restocked everything so as not to get caught out. It was still too early for dinner, but a beer sounded good. Especially if it was cold. Removing my star and sticking it in my wallet, I wandered toward the saloon. There were two at the edge of town, one more of a gambler's place, the other a bawdy house.

For my own sanity, I picked the gambler's place. The sign swinging in the wind read The Lucky Draw.

It surprised me when I walked in. The place was fully built out, complete with a big mahogany bar. It even had a polished brass rail running around the base. There were ten tables scattered around the center of the room. Three clean poker tables lined the back wall, two had games going already. Even this early, a man sat in the high chair watching the room with a shotgun across his lap. The bartender, whose most distinguishing feature was not having one, greeted me when I stepped up.

"What can I getcha?"

"Got cold beer?"

"Coldest in the territory." He smiled, pulling a draft to fill a clean mug. The quick condensation on the glass made me smile. "Be a dime."

"Thanks." I handed him the dime and took a long drink of the cold beverage. He wasn't wrong for all I knew. It was the coldest thing I'd had in more than a few days. "That's cold alright."

"Names Issac, welcome to Gila's Bend." He smiled and stuck out his hand.

"JC." I shook his proffered hand. "Only be here a day or so, just resting my animals."

"That's what I figured when you rode in." He nodded toward the big window. "Lawman?"

"Marshal, figured wearing a badge drew too much attention." We both knew I'd taken it off to avoid making anyone who might be wanted nervous.

"Figured, but round here you don't have to worry 'bout it. Sheriff Drew runs an honest town. That man don't tolerate trouble hunters or owl hoots."

"That's a change." I admitted. Most local sheriffs didn't worry about things out of their jurisdiction.

"Place was plenty wild when he got hired. Town council wanted to do everything they could to attract the railroad.

They hired themselves a damn fine town tamer."

"I'll keep that in mind. Hopefully, I can meet him before I leave."

"Might find him on the way to Yuma. Damn fool he was chasing ran that way." He laughed and walked away to serve another man down the bar.

Before he could make it back, someone stomped in the door. They came in fast enough to slam the bat-wing doors into the wall on both sides. The left door broke a hinge and hung sideways now. I didn't stare, but did take time to study the man. Early twenties, a filthy beard hanging down to his chest, dressed in filthy trail clothes. The echo of twin hammers locking back broke the silence that followed the man's entrance.

"Ya know better than ta use that, Ike." The man growled up at the bouncer.

"You know better than to set foot in here, Boullin." Ike growled from his chair. He wasn't a small man and the shotgun helped him measure up a bit more.

"Sheriff Drew ain't here ta stop me." He growled. While he was focused on him, I slipped my badge back on to my vest. "An you won't like my Pa if you pull 'em triggers.

"Boullin, you know the rules." The bartender said casually. "You also know what the Sheriff will do if you push it in town."

"He won't do noth'n if he knows what's good for him." The man was done talking and strode toward the bar. His eyes study everyone around him and eventually landed on me. "Who's this?"

"None of your concern." The cold crept through me, calming my nerves. If this fool was smart, he'd recognize that.

"Don't get mouthy, I'll whip you good." I heard the board behind me creak as he stepped on it. Then his heavy hand fell on my shoulder, intent on spinning me around. It was a poor choice on his part, Isaac tried to warn him.

"Boullin don't..." that was as far as he got.

Using my left hand, I grabbed his wrist and ducked down,

taking two steps back. The twisting of his arm with the force of my movement taking the big  man by surprise. His chest smacked into the bar hard enough to steal his wind. Before he could recover, I kicked him behind the knees. Keeping my grip on his wrist, pinning it behind his back. My right hand grabbed a handful of filthy hair and bounced his head off the hard wood.

The meaty thunk seemed to take everyone by surprise. While the man was unconscious, I stripped his gun belt off and bound his wrists. Then tossed the last of my beer in his face to wake him up. Slowly, the light came back to his eyes. He stared up at me, trying to figure out what happened.

"What the hell?" I saw him wince, his head not liking the volume of his own voice.

"Arresting you." The man finally saw my star and cringed. "Walk or be dragged. Don't matter to me."

"I'll walk. Someone coulda warned me ya was a marshal."

"I tried, but you didn't want to listen." Isaac said sadly.

"Guess that's fair." The change in the man had me confused. He'd come for a fight, that much was obvious. Maybe now that he'd found one, it scratched the itch?

"Considering I'm passing through anyone want to fill me in?" I couldn't help my curiosity.

"Boullin comes in once a month or so. Visits the ladies, then comes in here for a fight. He's probably got enough money to pay for the door and his fine." Isaac filled in the blanks for me.

"Course I do. Wouldn't be that dumb. Might piss off the Sheriff." I just shook my head and untied the bandana.

"Use the money to get a room. You'll sleep better than in a cell." I couldn't help but laugh.

"Can't, the door's two dollars, fines five dollars. I only got seven."

"Wasn't a fight, so no fine." That seemed to stump him for a minute, then he started laughing.

"Reckon that's true. Wouldn't call that a fight for sure." His laughter was genuine and matched the smile on his face. "I'll try it your way marshal if ya let me buy ya a drink?"

"Fair enough, since you're wearing half my beer." I smiled, handing him back his gun belt. Maybe I should have been worried, but something about the situation told me everything was fine.

"Explains my desire for one!" He laughed even louder and slung his belt back on. "Having a taste always makes me want more."

The patrons seemed to completely ignore it all and went back about their business. Boullin was the son of a local rancher. He was only allowed in town once a month to cut loose. Somehow, he had gotten stuck repeating the cycle every time he got into town. He was good company now that he'd changed the habit, and it took me longer to leave than I'd planned. Finally, I begged off and headed for the diner the deputy had mentioned.

With a stroke of luck, they were serving pork chops that night. I had to admit, it was a tasty meal. Not nearly at Smythe or Molly's level but still damn good. When they cleared the plates and refilled my coffee, I ordered some for Jack. I did ask them to cut out the bone. The man was still an outlaw and I wouldn't make a mistake that could get someone hurt.

Bug was just leaving when I came in. He introduced me to Gus. The wiry man looked tougher than leather. Jack managed to clean up a bit and thanked me for the food before digging in to it. Gus said he'd be fine, even offered to get Jacks breakfast in the morning so I wouldn't have to rush. Agreeing only if he let me pay for a drink, I gave him enough for breakfast and a whiskey. After that I made for my bed. It had been calling me since that fourth biscuit.

# CHAPTER 26

The first hints of dawn found me leaning on the railing of my balcony, cooling off after my workout. Finally, having a chance to do my full routine felt good. Sweat was slowly dripping off my nose to fall on the wood below me. Slowly the light was stretching across the land, birthing a new day. Even now, the sounds and smells of life started to drift across the town.

The animals were starting their day first. Milk cows bawled in an alley somewhere not to far away, ready to be milked or searching for her calf. A rooster proudly declaring his right to rule echoed down the street. His challenge was answered by another further down the road. Horses nickered from the livery and the few small corrals around the city. Somewhere, a drunk was roused from his night stupor and broke into song.

The air began to smell like humanity. Scents of coffee mingled with bacon on the soft morning breeze. Outhouse doors slammed shut in the faint light. Another town in a different place doing the same thing so many others were across the country. People starting another day just like the last one. Ready to keep building their future.

After washing up and getting dressed, I found myself on the porch below. Smoke drifted up, mingling with the steam from my coffee. Joining in the cycle of life with my own repeating behavior. How many times had I done this exact thing? How many places? I thought about the folks in Dodge City. Randy had married Millie. Was he at the dinner with her? Or sitting with Vance and Travis drinking his own coffee in the sheriff's office. Maybe they were at the Duece, talking about the night before.

Jose was probably married by now or getting ready to be. I knew he was sitting somewhere doing this very thing, maybe wondering the same things. Max and Smythe would be back at the Bar C, dealing with another winter. Moses was probably sitting at a fire somewhere, his prison wagon close by. It was just as likely that he and Willie would be sitting out back of the jail sipping the chicory infused brew.

I was just starting my journey, but had met so many incredible people. Folks I'd killed and bled with. Men and women who dealt with the swinging reality of this country. One day filled with joy, the next brought the crushing pain of death. Sitting there watching the shadows recede made me think about the changes I'd been through. My body had more than a few scars that were already telling my story to anyone who saw them. It had also been reshaped out of stone and leather. Back east if they saw me, I doubted anyone would recognize me with just a glance. I'd carried the west with me now, both its beauty and terrible cost.

For some reason Elias and Jesse crossed my mind, the mystery around them still crept into my mind occasionally. They'd become somewhat of a hobby, or maybe a mental puzzle I could gnaw on. The mystery of their behavior was something that still didn't make sense. Something about that pair I couldn't let go of. Isaiah had been oddly particular about anyone talking to Jesse. Maybe he was his father trying to protect a growing son from the punchers' sins? That still didn't explain the strangest thing I'd heard about. Jesse had a tendency to disappear a few times a day, especially when they crossed a river. Just another strange bit of behavior from the young puncher that made me wonder what their story was.

Jesse was a bigger mystery. He did his job, sure, but what kind of puncher didn't socialize at all? Some of the other punchers hadn't ever heard his voice above a whisper. Hell, I'd only heard it a few times. Even then, it had been so soft I'd had to struggle to hear it. There was just something about him that kept popping up in my mind. That night he got startled it had sounded so odd even for a young man. Somehow, both of them were part of a story I couldn't figure out. I was like a dog with a bone, something that kept my mind busy for a bit. There wasn't anything about them that would cause me problems. Maybe that was why it kept popping up. It was a simple puzzle, but not a threat. This morning it only filled a few minutes. My mind seemed to be determined to recall all the past few years.

There was a trail of bodies in my story. Friends and enemies buried behind me, parts of some kept alive in my memory. Juan's gentle nature, the way he'd be worried about being a coward after Caldwells. Trent's slow drawl when he poked holes in Chet's stories. All the men who'd helped teach me about life out here, good lessons and bad examples. Each one was a part of me now, just like the men who'd taught them.

Binda my first love, lost to hate and greed. She'd taught me so much more than how to make coffee. Her sharp wit paired with a generous heart, happily sharing both with me. She let me glimpse what life could be for me someday, the feeling of love and family. Sharing both with me, inviting me in without a thought. She'd always be in my heart. The debt I owed her could never be paid. The best I could hope for was to pass it on in some way.

They all lived in the stories we told about them. That was the immortality of the west. That was the mark you left on the world. Most often they were your only gravestone. The physical bodies buried beside the trail were lost. Any marker left washed away with a storm. There was every chance I'd end up the same way. Dead and buried, never collecting on my bet with Vick or finding my ranch.

Slowly, I unfolded from the chair, tapping my pipe out into the street. I'd heard the door open for the diner and my stomach was demanding action. The smell wafting out the door wasn't bacon, but the peppery smell of sausage gravy mixed with something sweet. It was time to sample another cook's biscuits and gravy, but that wasn't what really drew me. That faint sweet smell was one I recognized from that first ride to the Bar C. It was the doom of every puncher on the trail, bearsign.

They rated about middle of the road on the main course, better than most, but not coming close to the top. Nothing compared to Smythes, who still held the crown in my book. The bearsign was something different. They were magical, and I ate far too many of them. Don't get me wrong, too many was two after the biscuits and gravy. It was all I could mange to get down before I had to wave the white flag. It took a good two hours laying in my room before the over stuffed feeling left me. After that, I wandered around town just window shopping.

The Sheriff found me sitting in the Lucky Draw mid afternoon. Honestly, I was bored and would have been getting ready to leave if it wasn't for the animals. Supplies were bought and everything was ready to go tomorrow.

"Marshal." The man was taller than me and lean like a hunting cat. His every move was smooth, but you could see the speed that came with it. If this man wanted to move, you'd have a hard time tracking the motion.

"Sheriff Drew I'm guessing?" I stood to shake the man's hand. "Appreciate you letting me use a cell."

"Not the first time it's happened. Didn't think we had a new marshal yet?"

"Join me for some coffee. I'll fill you in." I motioned toward a table and waved at Isaac for more coffee.

"Sounds good." He was still a bit suspicious, and I couldn't blame him.

"I'm not assigned to the territory." I started explaining once we both sat down, taking the documents out of my wallet and handing them to him. "Marshal Douglas back east is my direct superior. He sent me to arrest Red Jack. The man had been made a deputy marshal and was abusing the power since no one was here to oversee him."

"That's who's in my jail? Heard he was a bad man, that don't fit what I saw this morning." He commented casually as he read over my paperwork. Once he was satisfied, he handed it back.

"Made one too many mistakes on the way. He's broken now." Most law men knew what I meant by that and the sheriff nodded his understanding.

"Had a couple do that a few times over the years. Deputy said you're headed to Yuma tomorrow?"

"First light." I agreed, sipping my fresh cup of coffee.

"I'll make sure Gus has everything ready for you. Where ya headed after Yuma?"

"California most likely, unless there's other instructions for me at Yuma. Left Texas a while back heading that way. This badge kinda fell into my lap along the way." That got a raised eyebrow from the man.

"Just happened to become a nomadic marshal?" The man's lips quirked up slightly at the statement.

"More truth to that than you know. Was doing some work for the army, a colonel in Albuquerque asked me to help him out." I wasn't going to tell him about the curriers, it was still a secret the military protected. "He was the one who brought me to Marshal Doulas's attention. They're in the same state as you, no marshal until after the first of the year. I was just collecting prisoners around the territory when the telegram came that sent me here."

"You really did just stumble into it." He laughed. The first real smile splitting his face. "Pardon the question, but ya seem awfully young for this type of work?"

"Doubt it'll last long, I hear that often enough for it to be a problem. Think I was just the one standing there who could pass muster."

"That'd make sense. Age don't mean much out here. If ya can do a man's work, you're a man."

"Seen that truth more than once. Had a drover work with us up to Dodge year before last. Damn good hand at fifteen years old, carried his own weight and stomped his own snakes."

"Few towns east there's a sheriff who's about that age. Man runs that town properly an most have learned not to argue with him. I've dealt with him a time or two. He's one to ride the river with."

"Now that's one I ain't heard in a while." I laughed, thinking back to hearing Tom say that.

"Got it from an old mountain man who decided to stick around here. Lives back in Eagle Tail now, used to trap up north back in the day. Check in on him when I can, that old mans tougher than leather."

"Got lucky an had a teacher who was the same. Helped educate me before I came out here."

"Bet that was an odd education." He laughed.

"My mother knew I was coming out west an did her best to prepare me for it. Got lucky and found a few people to help educate me. Tom took one look at me and said I was fiddle footed."

"Bet there's a story there, sadly I need to get home before the wife comes to fetch me." He stood, extending his hand. "Been a pleasure meeting you JC. If you're back this way, I'd like to hear that story."

"Pleasures mine. I'll look forward to it."

The sheriff was one of the good ones, that much was obvious. Enough backbone that he'd stand, but smart enough to work with folks around him. Not long after he left, I went off to find some dinner. After some to Jack and reminding him we'd be leaving in the morning, I wandered back to the saloon. Out of boredom, I wound up at a card table for a few hours. All skills need to be practiced after all. When I realized the man across from me was a professional, it reminded me painfully. Pretty sure he had twenty dollars of mine before I left. Back at the hotel, I enjoyed a pipe on my balcony with the stars dancing above me. Sleep came easy. My body knew the trail was coming and had to be prepared for it.

Three days later, I rode into Yuma Territorial Prison. The trip had been uneventful. Other than the landscape, there wasn't much to see. That had been beautiful. Someday I hoped to come back with time to explore it more. The prison itself was still under construction and I wondered why I'd been sent here. That mystery was answered when I rode up and two marshals stepped out to meet me.

"Marshal Stone? Names Nemo. This is my partner, Banks. Marshal Douglas sent us out here to take your prisoner back." Studying the two carefully, I figured they had to be telling the truth. These two were not western marshals. Both of them were dressed for working in the crowded streets of a city. Nemo's accent said Virginia unless my guess was off.

"Suppose I'll need to see some documentation." I said casually, but neither of them blinked.

"In the office, there's also a small block of cells that have been finished. We can lock him up there." Banks spoke for the first time. His accent was from further north, but I couldn't name it.

"Jack, you can step down." I stepped down at the hitching rail and looped Shade's reins over it. After checking the string, we all walked inside.

They put Jack in a cell while I checked out their paperwork. They had my next set of orders too. They were simple enough to understand. I was free to be about my business for now, but the badge was mine. I'd need to telegram back periodically to a specific destination and could trust any orders that came in response. Don't wear the badge unless I have to and only exercise my authority if absolutely necessary. They also had a draft for three hundred dollars to pay me. I hadn't asked and knew I wasn't going to be paid for just wandering around the country.

The message was simple: check in for work, stay out of trouble and don't expect them to save me. That was all fine by me. Nemo agreed to send my destination, San Diego, with their report that night. Checking in wouldn't be a problem. I'd do it anytime I stayed in a town for more than a day. That way, they'd have time to respond if need be. For now, my plans were simple. I was going to spend the night in Yuma and sell the extra horses before I left. It wasn't much of a plan, but that was the point.

"Before you go, I have to ask." Nemo spoke as I turned to go. "What happened on the trail with Red Jack? The man in the cell doesn't seem like who we expected."

"He made one mistake too many and had a good look at Old Scratch's eye. Some men can't take the glare and break." They both looked confused. "He faced death and the fear broke his will to fight."

"That can happen?" Banks asked like he'd never heard of such a thing.

"Talk to him, you'll see. There's no fight left in him."

"That had to be some scare." Nemo whistled.

"Stare down the barrel of a man's gun an listen the hammer lock back. It'll change your perspective on things quick enough." I said the last stepping into my saddle. "He won't give you any trouble. Trust me on that."

They still seemed confused, but took my word on it. Tipping my hat to them, I turned Shade back toward the city of Yuma. I'd passed a decent-looking hotel on the way here. The livery was my first stop. Bryan Jackson, the man who owned the livery, bought both animals, tack, and guns for two hundred and forty-five dollars. It only took thirty minutes of haggling to get it done, a personal record for me.

The Yuma Grand Plaza wasn't all that welcoming at first. I couldn't really blame them. I had several days' worth of trail dust decorating my clothes and saddlebags. Their attitude changed when I paid for a suite with a balcony. Money always seemed to erase folks concerns. The clerk actually grinned when I asked where I could get a bath. He directed me out the backdoor where they had a decent set up for hot baths. This time, it only took two tubs to get clean.

Dinner was passable, and the bed was comfortable, but at first light I was already crossing the Colorado River. Breakfast an hour later was the first thing I did in California. I'd debated the night before if I wanted to head straight to Los Angels or cut toward San Diego for the hundredth time. Having sent word back about San Diego wouldn't cause a problem if I changed my mind, but in the end, riding up the coast won the argument. It sounded better than edging around the Mojave to see the mountains.

# CHAPTER 27

Actions followed thought. After putting out the fire I pointed Shades nose west, making for San Diego. The land around me changed, growing richer and more lush as I gained distance from the Mojave. Trees dotted the mountain slopes like patches on a quilt. Mesquite changed to sycamores and then to pines as the elevation increased. Bushes replaced the cactus mixed with rich green grass that blew in the wind. The land around me hummed with life again. Farms and ranches dotted my view, people carving their future out of the rich land. Wagons and carts were more common, vaqueros rode horses pushing cattle across pasture land. Life seemed to burst from around me as I traveled. The song was less lethargic, its tempo nearly matching my heartbeat.

Three hunters from the Kumeyaay showed up at my camp a few nights later. I'd killed two decent sized rabbits and was roasting the meat when they carefully came out of the dark. Wisp had warned me long before they got there, but she hadn't sounded alarmed, more wary. One of them spoke English. Coyote Walking told me I was on their hunting ground but it didn't sound like a threat. Sharing my meat and offering them some tobacco as my thanks seemed to take care of that concern.

They watched me with interest the next morning as I went through my routine. Wild Coyote asked if it was my war dance. Telling him that it was the way I welcomed a new day made him smile, he could understand that. It was near enough the truth and reminded them of the padre calling people to prayer every morning. We shared breakfast when I was done. It cost me the last of my flour but I managed some passable biscuits to go with the bacon.

"You are different from others." Coyote Walking said over the fire.

"We are all different." Shrugging because I couldn't think of another answer.

"You hear the land."

"Don't all who listen for her?"

"White men do not listen." He was right. Most didn't ever hear the song, too focused on the next thing. Her song was like an unspoken secret among punchers. We all heard it, but never spoke of it.

"It's a sad thing."

"Do not forget to listen, friend. She knows you and will be unhappy if you stop."

All three of them rose to their feet, signed farewell, but didn't speak again. They disappeared into the trees like ghosts, fading from sight like mist. I could still see their sign, but this was their land. The only it existed was because they meant to leave it. They knew every twig or branch around them. If they didn't want to be seen, they wouldn't be.

San Diego started growing out of the land later that day. First was the cultivated fields pushing the trees back, creating a boundary between the wild and the civilized. Those farms gradually changed to small homes, but they looked older. Still well cared for, but there were years of life on the sun baked wood. Like there was an outer ring around the newer part of the city. As I moved with the now constant traffic, the age reversed. Old homesteads were slowly replaced by new.

When I got within site of the harbor I started paying more attention. More businesses and newer homes filled the streets. A grand looking brick hotel near the business district caught my attention. Three stories tall, it stood out even in the modern city growing around it. A stable boy ran up when I stepped down and greeted me.

"Welcome to the Star sir, will you be staying with us?"

"Might be if there's a room." I grinned down at the enthusiastic youth.

"I can take your animals around to the stables and have the bags brought in." Before agreeing, I looked at Wisp. She'd already decided the kid was okay. To demonstrate her approval she snuffled his hair.

"Looks like Wisp agrees." I laughed at the boys look of displeasure. "His name is Shade, take care of them both. Need me to come get the guns?"

"No sir. Did you want them in the room or locked in the tack room? The hotel insures their safety." The boy was even happier when I flipped in a silver dollar.

"I'll take the Winchester with me. Don't worry about the Sharps or Greener coming to the room." I said, pulling my Winchester out of its boot. "The shotgun and bow are in the bedroll, so mind them."

"They'll all be safe, sir." He assured me, leading my tried animals off to their comfortable rest.

Walking up the steps to the front door, it struck me that the boy hadn't even blinked at my trail dirty appearance. Then I remembered the gold rush. They were used to rich men coming out of mines covered in dirt. Comparatively, I was damn near clean. Chuckling to myself, I walked in as a man at the door held it open for me.

The clerk behind the desk greeted me with a friendly smile. After taking ten dollars for two nights' stay, he said my bags would be up soon. The money didn't bother me. I'd been warned how expensive this town was before coming. What did make me smile was the indoor plumbing, including a bath attached to the suite. Laundry was done over night and would be left at my door the following morning. The bellman who led me to the room assured me it was no problem when he took my clothes. I did tip the man generously for it.

By the time I got cleaned up, the day was fading into evening. I didn't feel like exploring the city just to find dinner, not today. It made my decision to eat in the hotels restaurant easy. They had offered to have it brought up to the room, but I declined. Eating in the dining room was a good way to get a feel for the people around me.

My quiet night of observation was foiled when someone across the room called out my name. A man stood up from a table on the far side of the room. Four others looked back at me, curiosity painted across their faces. They all looked like older wealthy men, all in their later thirties, early forties. When their eyes fell on me, it wasn't with appreciation. Whatever was going on, it didn't seem like I was a welcomed interruption. That didn't stop Jim Standom from waving me over.

To say I was shocked to see him would be an understatement. The smile on his face and laughter in his eyes said he was just as surprised. I weaved through the crowd, making my way to the table. When I got closer, he stepped around the table to shake my hand.

"JC, what a pleasant surprise!" The man hadn't changed much over the years. Dressed a little better, but he still had the same welcoming presence.

"Jim, it's good seeing you. Been a couple of years."

"The boss made me start staying at the office. Thomas took over the operations in Dodge." One man in particular looked chagrined at the words. "But please join us? I need someone here to temper these outlandish ideas. Someone who knows what it's like in the rough country."

"Jim, I don't think we need another voice to debate our choices." The man sitting beside Jim grumbled.

"Let me introduce you. Then maybe I can explain why this young man might have something useful to offer on the topic gentlemen." Jim didn't give them a chance to object, quickly pulling a chair over beside his.

"The man with the grumpy look is my boss, Gustavus Swift. To his right is Franklin Adams. He's one of the heads for the Central Pacific. To Gus's left is JB Killian, a successful rancher who has more money than god currently. The last man and most vocal in his disagreement about your presence is Joseph Nash, one of the founders of the San Diego Bank."

I shook hands with each as they were introduced. Swift was an earnest-looking man, balding with a neatly trimmed beard. Adam's reminded me of most railroad executives, cleanly shaven and neatly dressed. Killian, I had heard of, he wasn't the biggest rancher in California, but his investments had paid off more then any ranch could. He was a hard man, someone who'd carved out his piece of the world and meant to keep it. Not like Max or the other men I'd met in the west. He was a different kind of hard, more civilized but no less deadly. Nash was a purebred east coast businessman, from his polished shoes to his smoothly greased hair.

"Not sure what this young man can offer." Killian complained. "I mean no disrespect."

"Since I have no idea what Jim thinks I can help with, how could I be offended?"

"A pleasure. I believe Jim has spoken about you before." Swift's eyes studied me as he thought back. "Yes, I remember now. You have a law degree but left New York to pursue a ranch, if I remember? Seems there was something about a wager in his story."

"Yes sir. The land for the ranch is there, but I wanted to know the business first hand before taking it on." I was surprised Jim had mentioned me to his boss.. Seeing no need to discuss money, I hoped to derail talk about the bet and what I had gained. "The proceeds of my wager are being handled by a trusted associate back east."

"Don't handle your own finances then?" It would be the banker who caught that. Nash's eyes studied me carefully as he spoke.

"Communication from the trail are slow. I'd miss too many opportunities if I did it myself." Again trying to sidetrack the topic. "My associate deals with it from the city. For me, that means rather than sitting in a bank, it's being put to work."

"Smart decision, uninvested money creates someone else's

ROBERT KNOX

wealth." Adams said, smiling at Nash with a bit of mischief dancing in his eyes.

"Sit down JC once they get going, it takes a while." Jim laughed and motioned for me to take the seat next to him before signaling the waiter. "Coffee drinker if I remember right?"

"Hasn't changed." I smiled, hanging my hat before sitting down. "Have you ordered yet?"

"Just got drinks." Swift assured me over the now bickering Nash and Adams. "It'll be a few minutes before they call a truce again. Maybe in the mean time Jim can fill you in on our current discussion."

"Of course." Jim shifted toward me as the waiter filled my cup. "These fine gentlemen have a taste for hunting. Now myself and JB have spent our time under the stars but the others, I'm afraid, are about like you on your arrival to Dodge City."

"They ain't left their comfy beds and think the tall and uncut is safe." JB's version was a bit less polite, but it got the point across.

"You're talking about around here?" I didn't think much around here was too dangerous, but that didn't mean it was safe.

"Santa Rosa range, not as bad as the territories, but it still ain't exactly tamed." JB gave me a bit more information.

"If we take enough experienced men, it'll be safe." Swift didn't insist, but neither was he willing to give the idea up easily.

"That's dependent on a lot of things going well. First hiring men who wouldn't sell you for a double eagle." I didn't think before opening my mouth, it was the first thing thought that crossed my mind.

"What do you mean by that?" Nash had evidently tired of his argument with Adams and caught my statement. Everyone but Jim was looking at me in surprise, like the thought of men betraying them never crossed their minds. Jim looked like the cat who ate the canary.

"I don't know any of you, but I'm guessing between the four of you there's enough wealth to buy a country?" I didn't wait for an answer. "Well, getting a piece of that wealth from ransom wouldn't bother a lot of men."

They all looked like I'd said something ridiculous, everyone except Jim. He still wore that same grin. I must be telling them something he'd been waiting to spring on them. The man looked absolutely pleased with me filling in the missing pieces.

"That couldn't happen, we'd take enough security." Adams declared. It made sense the railroad man would think of that. It was no secret that they dealt with the Pinkertons often enough that he'd be comfortable with them.

"You talking about Pinkertons?" I asked, already knowing the answer.

"Of course." The man said proudly.

"Didn't the Ross's use them?" Adams visibly paled at the reminder of the child kidnapping. "Don't get me wrong, the Pinkertons are good, but no one can beat a loaded deck."

"What do you mean?" Nash looked more interested now.

"All it takes is one inside man to undue all the security in the world, if that man in charge has any sense. Just one porter or guide telling his partners where and how many men there are and it will all fall apart."

"So we are supposed to spend our lives in the gilded cage we built?" Adams demanded.

"There's a way, but you won't like it." I admitted, and Jim's grin just grew. JB seemed to know where I was going, but was perfectly happy to let me lay it out.

"Spit it out man." Swift demanded. He wasn't speaking harshly, but the man was sharp enough to know when he was being led.

"Go as is, just you five and truly rough it. JB knows the area?" The big man nodded, agreeing with my words. "No one else, that is assuming you all trust one another. That means camping, hunting, skinning, cooking all of it falls on you."

That sat them all back, everyone but Nash. Something about the way he looked made the hair on the back of my neck stand on end. I didn't know these men and knew nothing about their situations, but something was wrong with him. It made me wonder if Jim knew what was going on but couldn't say it. When I looked at him curiously, the slight nod he gave me said there was more he'd tell me later.

"Even that it would put you at risk. If say the man selling you supplies knew someone who'd pay for the information? They could easily track you until you were far enough and take you then. Basically gentlemen, your success will make you targets. With as much open country? If it were me I wouldn't risk it."

"How old are you, young man?" Swift asked, but I had a suspicion that he already knew.

"Twenty or near enough to it." I admitted and was saved by a waiter approaching from looking at their shocked faces.

"Would the gentlemen be ready to order?" Everyone ordered and the coffee pot was replaced with a full one before the conversation started back up.

"That all sounds very terrifying, JC," Nash said with a slight tone of mockery, "but aside from the security risks, Jim was telling us of the more physical dangers."

"That's another bit of trouble. The land can and will kill you without warning. You don't have to do anything more than leave your horses hitch a bit loose. A man on foot out there? You're dead unless you get very, very lucky. Bears, cougars, stampedes, snakes, bad water, bad meat... anything really."

"It can't be as bad as all that. It is a civilized area."

"The Modoc war wasn't that long ago." JB added solemnly. "There are still some braves taking scalps back in the mountains."

"That's not mentioning the outlaws." Jim finally added his two cents.

"I simply can't believe in this day and age it's unsafe to go on a simple hunting trip." Nash insisted, To me it sounded like there was a hint of desperation in his voice.

"Agreed!" Adams declared.

"I'm game for it gentlemen." Swift assured but he added some words for thought. "It must be done as safely as possible."

"Ain't my first trip, so I'm happy to go along." JB was supremely confident. "Course I do have the home field advantage in a way, so I wouldn't expect you to manage as easily."

"You've all decided on this foolishness, so why discuss it?" Jim threw up his hands in surrender. His arm nearly dumped the tray our waiter was carrying. "So sorry my good man."

"No trouble, sir." The man said with some understanding. "May I serve the table?"

The conversations were diverse but sparse with the introduction of food. Pipes, cigars and to my surprise, Adams rolled his own cigarette while the table was being cleared. I stuck with coffee but the rest of the table switched to cognac or whiskey. Taking the opportunity to study Jim while I packed my pipe, I could see concern in his eyes. When he met my gaze there was definitely something he knew about this.

"I've had enough of the indoor air for now gentlemen. Please excuse me." I said, unfolding from the chair. "I think I'll take my pipe to the porch. Please allow me to take care of tonight's meal for foisting my company on you."

"That's not necessary JC." JB looked surprised by the offer.

"If I remember right, I owe you a meal JC. You picked up the last one in Dodge." Jim presented an argument I couldn't win. He was right I'd bought the last time. "But I will join you for some air, if you don't mind?"

"You win." I laughed, signaling my surrender. "Your company is always welcomed. Again, gentleman, my thanks to you for a pleasant evening."

After shaking hands with the four men who were already resuming their talk of hunting, I led Jim outside. The night was beautiful and I finally got to see my first sunset on the Pacific Ocean. The reflected light was a dazzling array of colors, each dancing through various shades with the rise and fall of the waves. The sight nearly took my breath away. From the front of the Star I couldn't see the actual beach but this was enough for now. I stood in awe, just watching the light play off the water until Jim broke the silence.

"First time?"

"Yeah, it's amazing." I breathed out.

"A good night for it. Sometimes if a storm is timed right, it will leave you speechless."

"Going to fill me in?" I asked before striking a match and puffing my pipe to life.

"Caught it already? Knew you would." He smiled, lighting his cigar. "Got any plans?"

"Not anything that can't wait."

"I have no evidence you understand and might be asking you to live rough for no reason."

"Jim, you introduced me to Max. Just ask and it's yours. No need to break a confidence or speak out of turn. All you need to do is ask."

"Thanks for that." I could hear the relief in his voice. Whatever he suspected, it wouldn't be comfortable for him to say it. "They're going hunting. The whole debate thing was just a way to pass the time. What's more, they'll go alone. Well, alone for them which will mean at least two Pinkertons, Adams can't move without them."

"Noticed them two tables away, didn't look like they approved of me." I smiled, remembering the scowl on their faces.

"You're not that kid I met anymore." He laughed, smoking drifting around the disturbed air. "Can you track them from far enough back to help but not be seen if I'm wrong?"

"Easily, 'specially if I know roughly the area they're heading."

"I know it's the Santa Rosa range, not sure where specifically. It's a good sized range."

"When will they go, do you think?"

"It'll have to be within a week. Swift has to be back in

Chicago in three weeks for a meeting, one he can not miss."

"Delay them leaving for four days, anytime after that will be fine. Can you do that?"

"Why four days?"

"Three days for me to get out there and scout it out. Two days to find a safe place to use as a base, then one day to get out and be ready to follow them. With a day allowed for me to enjoy this hotel. I already paid for the room." I chuckled at the admission.

"Indoor plumbing means that much to you?" He japed back before agreeing. "I can do four days but not much more."

"I'll leave at first light day after tomorrow."

"You really aren't worried about the why?"

"Jim you're a friend, a good one. If you need something, all you have to do is ask."

"Moments like this, I miss being out on the range. No politics or back room deals."

"Horse shit!" I laughed. "You're rich enough you could quit working and wander for the rest of your life."

"Fair point." He admitted before slowly puffing his cigar back to life. "Sadly, the allure of bathing has trapped me in its civility."

We spent the evening like that, talking casually of life and its doings. Swift came out with JB and joined us after a while. I liked Gus. He was a good man and I could understand Jim's loyalty to him better now. JB wasn't a bad sort, a bit arrogant, but not a bad man. His biggest problem was still thinking he was young. Age hadn't taken much yet but comfortable living had slowed the man. If you combined that with his forty-plus years of hard living, there was always a price.

Adams and Nash never did make it outside. Gus said they had found a poker game and would be there until tomorrow. Some hours after the sun had fallen from the sky, I made my excuses and wandered up to my bed. It was strange, but my thoughts never went back to the favor Jim was asking. Trail tired was evidently an effective cure for my imagination.

The next day wasn't what I had planned. My original plan had been seeing the city, just exploring it. Sadly, my day turned out more mission oriented. General goods to stock up and arrange for them to be picked up at first light. Restock my ammunition and pick up a heavier coat. Aside from being in a trunk, my sheepskin was too heavy for this area.

I did find time to shop for a few things that were luxury items, two new books that caught my interest. 'The Way We Live Now' seemed to be an amusing take on the literary world. Best of all, I found a copy of Verne's third book in the Nemo series 'The Mysterious Island'. If nothing else, I'd be able to read. The last thing I picked up was a lucky find, a new Taylor Sheffield automatic blade. I'd seen one years ago and never thought I'd find one for myself.

I ate at a place down the street. It wasn't better than the dining room and cost almost as much. When I slipped into my room, I found a folded piece of paper on the floor. A smile crept across my face when I opened it. Somehow, Jim had gotten more information and had sent me a map of their proposed hunting area. That would make this much easier.

# CHAPTER 28

First light the following day found me on the trail beside a stream with the small coffee pot boiling while my animals grazed. The song was still muted this close to the city, but her steady hum still called out to me. It was comforting, welcoming in its way. The threat was always there. Danger always gave the song an edge that was invigorating more than threatening. It was there to keep you alert, never trusting enough to fully relax.

Over the next two days, the song grew in volume and depth. The further behind I left the trapping of civilization, the more she called to me. Riding through a pine forest in the foothills of the range, I was enjoying the world around me. Shade moving silently over the pine needle floor when Wisp stopped suddenly. Twisting the saddle to look at her saved my life.

It felt like a mule kicked my left shoulder. The force of it rolled me across Shade's neck. Warm liquid was spilling down my chest. The world tumbled in front of my eyes, but I couldn't make sense of it. Shade jerked sideways, dumping me to the soft floor of the forest. I heard Wisp bray, then her hooves were receding, but it all sounded muted. Distant for some reason that I couldn't understand. Why was she running? That was my last thought before my vision closed in around me.

I woke up in darkness. Only the soft light of a crescent moon lit the forest around me. When I tried to move, dark spots filled my vision, threatening to pull me back under. Pain screamed from my shoulder, informing my brain how bad of an idea that was. Focusing my will, I ignored it. Pushing the pain down so my mind could process information clearly. Sweating,

I managed to sit up, a slight wet feeling tickled down my back. It wasn't sweat, too warm, it felt to thick. It was blood from a wound, a gun shot wound. That realization finally broke through the haze.

Slowly taking stock of my situation didn't help much. With no clue how long I'd been unconscious, it couldn't have been more than a day. Any longer, and the scavengers would have finished me off. Using my right arm, I felt my shoulder. The wound burned, but by a miracle called Wisp, the bullet hadn't hit anything vital. It had cut through my trapezius muscle, missing my arteries and bone. It was still bleeding, and I'd lost a lot of blood, which explained the wooly feeling in my head.

The rest of my body hurt, but wasn't injured. Nothing felt broken or out of place. There was a lump on my head that was still tender. The best explanation for that was hitting my head when I fell out of the saddle. My gun belt was gone. Both Colts and the Bowie Tom had given me. Same for the blade at the back of my neck, wallet, and my hat. They'd missed the new knife. It was tucked into my boot. I was honestly surprised they didn't take those. More than one man had come to after being robbed missing his boots.

Moving carefully, I inched around until a tree was in easy reach. Using the knife, I cut into the bark, peeling it back. It felt like it took forever. My vision faded in and out, but if I passed out again, it would be the end of me. The wound on my back would bleed me to death before I ever woke back up. Slowly I cut into the tree's flesh, digging out a hole.

The next part would be the worst and knowing that I took several minutes to focus. Forcing the cold through me, I'd have to rely on it to keep me conscious through the pain. With my right hand I found my bandana, carefully cutting it in half I used part to gather the sap and slowly reached back. With a shaking hand, I pressed the sticky cloth into the wound. Lights strobed behind my eyes, the pain blinded me, but I fought back against the closing darkness. It felt like it took years for it to recede, but eventually the world came back into focus.

The pain was still there, but using my fingers I was relieved to find the bandana managed to cover the wound with the sap. That just left the entry wound on the front. The thought of having to do that again made tears trail down my face but crying about it wouldn't get it done. Carefully, I repeated the process, ensuring the wound was covered. Leaning back on a tree panting, my mind slowly started to focus back on my situation.

While my body tried to recover, my mind replayed what I remembered. Shade had stood where I fell, at least to the best of my recollection. Wisp had run off, braying as she went. The only guess I could make was Shade had been taken with the rest of my things. Wisp might be closer, they wouldn't have bothered chasing her just for the supplies. She was my best hope because the thought of going after the men unarmed wasn't a pleasant one. It might have been what I wanted to do very badly, but that didn't mean it was the right choice.

Wisp had the Sharps and other supplies I needed. If I was lucky, she might not have gone that far. What made it my best option wasn't that. It was simply that she wouldn't have covered her tracks. Follow a running mule might be hard in my state, but tracking men who would try to cover their trail would be impossible. The coyotes would be feasting on my corpse sooner than I'd like. That all required light. Right now my body needed rest.

Slight hints of dawn stabbed through my eyes and woke me. Using a branch that had been laying nearby, I started to stand. Using it and painfully leaning on a tree, I struggled to my feet. Bouncing from tree to tree, I started to move, following the signs Wisp had left. Pain racked my left side with every step, but I didn't feel any blood running down my back thankfully. The pine sap burned when it pulled, but it was almost soothing compared to the rest.

I don't know how long my feet kept moving. It's all just flashes of visions, a stream of cool refreshing water, more pain. Tripping over a root, the jarring pain flared again, blinding me. A raven followed me through the trees, waiting to take my soul every time I stumbled. The burning sensation of a sharp broken branch slashing my arm. A fallen tree filled with grubs, the tasteless things quieting my empty stomach. Then the scent of smoke filling my nostrils, fear waking my fevered mind. Voices as I fell, my face nestled on quiet pine needles, then silence. Half dragged, my heels bouncing behind me, punctuated by a familiar braying then darkness.

The next thing I knew was warm soft fur inside a woven dome of greenery. Soft voices close to me speaking a dialect I didn't know. Cold wet cloth washed across my face. My eyes traced the arm to see an ancient woman kneeling beside me. She was obviously native, but I didn't recognize the tribe. Her face split in a grin and her haggard voice broke through the murmuring distant voices.

"Welcome back, boy." She studied me carefully. A small cup appeared and she tilted my head to pour some bitter liquid down my throat. "Swallow it."

There was no way I'd survive trying to fight or argue the topic, so I did as ordered. Before anything else was said, she made me finish the cup one bitter gulp at a time. Finally, the last swallow full of gritty ground herbs went down. It wasn't a magical cure, but it did dull the pain.

"Where?" My ragged voice cracked, but I had to know.

"My kish, you're among the Cahuilla people. You followed your mule would be my guess." She spoke English fluently and the surprise must have showed on my face. "Don't be too shocked. I'm no fool. Speaking your language makes life easier for my people."

"You speak it perfectly."

"Spent more time using it than most."

"How do you know she is my mule?" I don't know why that question popped out.

"Because she won't leave the front of my kish." She cackled. "Feeling better?"

"Much. What was in that medicine?" I did feel better. The

pain was still there, but the burn had faded.

"Things that should be used to heal the body, better than pine sap." She clucked her tongue. "Using it did save your life but you may still regret it."

"It was all I could do." I knew using raw sap wouldn't be easy, but it would clean the wound and keep it from bleeding.

"There is a proper poultice on the wound now."

"How long have I been here?" Panic filled me.

"Only a few hours. The men found you when your animal ran to you. She seems attached."

"Do you know what day it is?"

"By your way, it's Sunday." Relief flooded me. I'd only been out half a day, there was still three days. "Sleep and we will try food later."

"Agreed, but one last question. Are my packs still on the mule?" This made her laugh.

"Yes, I've had to treat two of our men when they tried to remove them. She won't let anyone get near." My body gave up the fight and I gladly surrendered to the darkness.

Again, the light broke through the opening above me. Without thinking, I sat up. A small groan escaped my lips, but the pain wasn't nearly as bad. A hiss was all the warning I had before the ancient medicine woman was back by my side.

"Fool boy." She grumbled while fussing over my bandages.

"I'm fine. Okay, not fine, but I fell much better." I tried to reassure her.

"You make blood fast for white man. You feel better because it's mostly back inside you. Stop moving fool boy, so it stays there."

"I need to see too Wisp." Standing slowly with her grudging assistance.

"Fine, you keep her from killing me and I'll do it."  The old lady wasn't happy, but did understand the need to care for my animal. The pannier had to come off the animal or she would get sores. Mistreating an animal was something both our cultures found wrong. Between us we managed to get it all inside her home. Some dried grass worked for a quick curry and Wisp shivered at the relief before moving to a nearby stream. Two men watched as my panniers were moved inside, they're eyes fixed on the Sharps. The older of the two stepped forward to speak.

"You hunt buffalo?" His tone was almost accusatory, and I knew why. Buffalo hunters stripped the hides and wasted the rest.

"No, I took it from one I killed." That was evidently an acceptable answer.

"I am chief here. You can stay until you are healed." With that, he walked away never giving me his name. I wasn't welcome, but they'd let me stay until the old woman chucked me out.

"Sit, you must eat and drink more of the medicine. The sun will help heal you." I could see the amusement on her face, but wasn't sure what it was. Either at my not so warm welcome or something else.

"Thank you." I said to her back. She'd already turned back to her house. She was working a mortar, probably making the bitter brew for me.

By that evening, I felt well enough to sort through my packs. The first thing I did was take out an Apache knife and belt. The one I'd taken that first year at the line cabin. After lashing the belt around my waist, I sat and started sharpening the knife. It didn't need it, but the motion let me think. Doing my best to keep my left arm still, just using the muscles to hold the stone still.

Who had shot me? Were they part of some kidnapping plot or something else? It didn't really matter, they were walking deadmen. Deadmen with my guns. I'd get them and Shade back if I had the bury this place under a mountain of corpses. Rest tomorrow and the night after, then I would start hunting. They must have the same information I did, or they did now since they'd taken my map. They'd taken my badge too. That was another reason I needed to find them.

While we were eating, I asked the old woman about it. She thought my timing was too fast, but said she knew a trick that might help. She did warn me I wouldn't like it, still when she told me I agreed. She was right. I wouldn't like it but also knew it as the best answer.

The next day, laying on a clean hide, the old woman used my sewing kit to close both sides of the wound. She used boiled pine sap to coat the stitches after cleaning it all with the whiskey I had. She thought I was mad when I soaked the thread and needle in it instead of drinking it. Half way through the process, I started to agree with her but knew it was a better choice. The piece of leather stuck between my teeth kept me from screaming that and bravado.

Once the sap was applied, the burning pain eased enough for me to spit out the leather. I drank two more cups of her vile brew, finally recognizing one of the ingredients. Calendula flowers, another lesson from Tom about wound care surfaced. Brewing a tea from them would help fight infection. There were other things in her mix but I couldn't identify them for the life of me.

My left arm was better, but there was no way I'd be using that Sharps anytime soon. True, I could fire it, but the kick would rip this wound open, even the opposite shoulder. The greener wouldn't be any better. I might be able to draw my bow, but it would be  shaky. I'd have to use every bit of woodcraft to deal with these men. Cut back on my supplies and leave the panniers with the tribe along with the supplies. On the subject of the Sharps, my mind went to trade. Part trade and part payment for the care.

"Old woman?" I spoke into the tent. She still hadn't told me her name.

"What boy?"

"I want trade that rifle to you. I want a good tomahawk for it."

"Fool, to trade a rifle for that? And what use do I have for a rifle?"

"I want to trade it to you in payment for your care, but I need the weapon."

"Humph! Fool boy, that's still not enough. I'll add in some of my tea. You drink it twice a day."

"Fair trade." I agreed.

She walked out and returned in a few minutes. She set an iron forged tomahawk beside me on the fur. It was one of the better ones I'd seen. There was no way it'd hold a real edge, but you didn't need to shave with one for it to kill. I had to admit to being amused by the irony. Having one of the cheap trinkets we traded to the natives traded back to me for a rifle? There was no way to avoid seeing the humor in it.

"Done." She smiled at the deal.

The next morning at first light, I was getting ready to leave when the older man approached me again. He didn't seem any friendlier, but there was no hostility in his eyes.

"You trade rifle and leave food. Make debt must be fair trade. People who shot you are here."

He knelt down, drawing a rough map in the dirt. The stream I'd been using flowed through a forest, then split. Part of it sinking into a cliff. If I read his drawing right, it then came back and fed into a pond on the other side. He marked that as the place they had gone.

"Fair trade." Raising my right and pointing down with my index finger to show agreement.

He turned and walked a way without another word. I could see the old woman standing by her door laughing, but had no clue why. They'd helped me and that was all that mattered. There was no debt between us, so there was no reason to come back. That was why the man had come to me, he didn't want me coming back. A smile crossed my face before turning Wisp to follow the stream.

Riding bareback with just a blanket to protect her back, I was happy for her smooth gate. The panniers had been modified to resemble open saddle bags and my bedroll and slicker sat behind me. The bags had my basic supplies and small coffee pot. My bow was still rolled up with my Greener, but there my arm was no where near capable of using it. If things went badly, they'd still come in useful no matter how much it hurt.

I rode easy on Wisp and didn't rush. I had a lot riding on the men still being where the tribe said they were. I didn't have another lead to follow right now. If they were gone, it was still my best shot at picking up their trail. We found the cliff in late afternoon and I had to make grab for Wisps nose to silence her. Evidently they were still there and so was Shade. His nicker echoed in the canyon on the other side of the cliff wall.

There was no way with my arm to climb that cliff, so I moved back deeper into the shaded pine forest. Under the boughs of a massive pine, I staked Wisp and made a small camp. After choking down some of the tea, I dug out the extra buckskins that had been in the panniers. Getting them on was a tricky adventure, but eventually I managed it. Dressed properly, I ghosted into the shadows after checking my blade and tomahawk. Killing time was coming and the cold filled my body with energy.

Just before sunset, I found the opening into the canyon. It was a tight small space covered with pine boughs someone had piled up. They'd done a decent job of hiding the entrance. Unfortunately, like most western men, they'd done everything to hide it from someone on horse back, never thinking about a man on foot. To any skilled woodsman, it stood out in the natural world. They hadn't even staggered the boughs, crawling under it was simple. Voices made me freeze in its shadow and creep forward slowly until I could see them.

Laying there watching the five men inside, a slow grin spread across my face. They sat around a rough lean-to with a fire out front. The canyon was small and their voices carried around it, making it easy to listen in. I wasn't sure if there was a man above me or not, but that didn't matter. I wasn't moving until well into the night. By then I'd know if they were five or six deadmen. As luck would have it, the information I wanted was shared far sooner than expected.

"When them rich fellers com'n?" A thin man in a slouch hat leaning against a tree asked.

"Bout tomorrow, I reckon. Long 'bout noon or so." This one was lying on a bedroll with a big sombrero over his face.

"Bout time. For an easy job this sure has stretched out." A younger guy crouching near the fire this time. Across from him was the most dangerous of the bunch. He looked like the only experienced one of the bunch. He also wore my gun belt.

"This is easy money. The bonus for that pony will make it worth the effort."

"That dude didn't want nothing but that horse? " The last man was leaning on a tree near their picket studying Shade. "Don't make no sense."

"Doesn't matter why. We'd already been hired for the other job. That kid was just a bonus." He patted my Colts and smiled. "Damn nice bonus too."

"Ya still sure just us will be enough? Ain't there four of 'em coming?"

"Three of them is city folk. The last man might be a problem, but I'll deal with him."

The older guy was the leader, no doubt about that. He'd revealed enough to make me wonder. Two people hired them? Nash was the obvious choice for who in the group. But who was it that wanted Shade so badly? He was a rare but not that rare. Just how had they known about my part in this trip? That was an even bigger mystery. I hadn't been here that long and didn't know anyone but Jim.

I had the first part of the story. Now they just needed to sleep. The last few hours of waning light I spent trying to see where they'd set a watch. What truly stunned me was when they didn't. They must have a lot of faith in their little canyon to not have someone out there. Just before the sun faded completely, I saw why, a dog. It was tied by the horses and the only reason I saw the beast was it moved, making the horses shift. I couldn't get a good look at it, but that didn't matter. Any movement would start it barking long before I got close. Or it would have if I hadn't seasoned my buckskins well enough. That wasn't a sure thing by any means, but they might buy me just enough time.

Four of the men laid out the bedrolls under part of the lean-to, using their saddles as pillows. The leader laid out under the stars near the fire, which suited me perfectly. He was the one I wanted alive. That man had the answers I needed. He'd live, at least until I knew the full story.

I waited, listening to them snore, taking quick cat naps myself so I wasn't too tired when the time came. Just when I was getting ready to move, about two hours before dawn, the man at the fire stirred. Watching as he stood without putting on his boots, and shuffled toward me. I waited for the sound I knew would come. He was fumbling with his pants. My hand shot out grabbing his ankles. My left arm screamed at the fast movement, but I had to take advantage of this. He went down with a whomp, all the air left his lungs and I climbed on top of him cat quick. Before he could get his wits back, the hilt of my knife slammed into the side of his head. I watched the lights go out and hoped it hadn't been too hard of a blow.

Quickly using the piggin strings to bind his wrists and ankles, then hog-tied them together. His bandanna and sock made a decent gag. Just as I finished the dog stirred near the horses. I heard him move, and the horses voiced their displeasure, but he didn't bark. Slowly crawling forward unwilling to wait, I reached for my Colts. The weight told me it was loaded and ready for use. That's when I stood up and waited.

# CHAPTER 29

It wasn't a long wait. The dog barked suddenly. Almost instantly, the men under the lean-to started to stir. One came up instantly, looking around to figure out what was going on. He spotted me and it took him a second to realize something was off. When he reached for his pistol, I shot him. Then the dance really got started.

The other three came up fast. The next two barely got their weapons out before I put them down. The last man, the youngest, managed to get a shot off that whistled by my ear. He joined his buddies in death a second later. A neat red hole reflected the firelight for just an instant before he fell back. It was dead center of his head. For some reason. I noticed his eyes cross for an instant, like they were trying to look at the hole. Silence fell in the canyon when the last echo faded away. The acrid smell of gun smoke and death filled the air.

The dog wasn't barking anymore, scared quiet by the abrupt violence. I started dragging bodies out to the fire, no need ruining the gear. Laying them on the far side away from the animals so the scent didn't bother them. Then I pulled down the pine boughs blocking the entrance and went to get Wisp. My left arm was screaming by the time I made it back and the sun was starting to break the horizon.

Wisp went to Shade as soon as her packs were off. Before my shoulder started throbbing again, I used the boughs to block the entrance again. I wasn't going near the horses until getting a look at the dog. It didn't make a sound when Wisp came over. If it made a move toward her, she'd kill it. All I could do was hope it had enough survival instinct to not make me shot it. Right now, that wasn't my concern. Getting some much needed answers was. Luckily, I knew just where to find those.

Dragging the bound man up to the fire, I sat drinking their coffee and waiting for the sunlight to creep into the canyon. When it was finally light enough to see, the first thing I did was recover my Winchester and hat. The hat was hanging on a branch near the lean-to. Either they didn't want it or hadn't bothered with it yet. My Winchester was laying near my gun belt, which I immediately slung around my waist and tied down. The familiar weight sat comfortably around my hips. Reloading the colt took longer with my arm, but I got it done. My wallet and badge were in the pocket of the unconscious man.

Rummaging through their supplies, I was pleasantly surprised to find a few sausage links that were still good. There were also four eggs, with those and a Dutch oven full of biscuits it made for a fine breakfast. That was until the dog started whining. There were two sausage links left, and it seemed like the right time to sort this out. Looking that way, the animal that met my gaze surprised me. I'd expected a big cur, or maybe half wolf with the way it sounded. What I got was a cattle dog tied on a short rope to a tree. When I approached, it bared its teeth and let out a ferocious growl. That was promptly cut off when Wisp stamped forward. She backed the dog down, then just stood there waiting.

I took that moment and shot forward, a quick slash and the rope fell free. It shook hard, shedding the loose tie around its neck, and without a second glance bolted through the opening and disappeared. Guess it didn't want breakfast, or maybe it did? I heard the rustling when it reappeared under the pine branches. A grin grew while I waited across the fire, holding one of the sausages out. After ten minutes of creeping forward, it leaned toward the sausage. I didn't move, letting them come to me. Ever so gently, they took the meat from my fingers, then dashed back to the entrance. They repeated this for the second one, but it didn't take as long this time. They didn't seem aggressive, so I ignored them after that and got to work.

Using their own ropes and one of their horses, I hung all four of the deadmen up by their ankles after searching them. Making sure the last one alive could see his pards dangling in the air. He was conscious by now and just playing possum. They had four hundred and thirty dollars each, which struck me as odd. The leader had more, but most of that was mine. Despite that, all of them having the same amount told me quite a bit.

"I need information. That's about the only thing keeping you alive. The only question you need to concern yourself about now is how you die, cause death isn't negotiable." I spoke, undoing the bandanna.

"Why should I tell you anything?" He barked out, but I could hear the fear behind it. He did his best to hide the truth behind bravado, but I wasn't buying it.

"Cause death can take a long time or be quick. Who hired you to steal my horse?"

"Ain't tell'n ya nothin." He growled, but I knew this would be easy. This was a man with no heart. I could see the truth of that written all over his face. All it took was fishing a coal out of the fire with his knife. The man folded like a poker player holding deuce seven off suit.

"Some gambler, that fella Nash owes money. Names Luke something." I hadn't even started moving toward him, but the words stopped me in mid-step. Then the cold rushed through me, feeding off my building anger. Luke? Luke had hired men to kill me for Shade? That didn't make sense. It was three years ago why would he do it now?

"You're sure about that?" He met my eyes and whatever he saw there made him talk.

"Truth, I swear it! He was at the meeting when Nash told us 'bout you. He wasn't sure if you was coming but thought you might. That fella Luke laughed real funny an offered us an extra hundred for 'at horse. Said it was a nice bonus for him since he had ta wait for his money. We just had to be dead certain ya wouldn't come looking for it." Then, quietly enough that I could barely hear it, he added. "Reckon I know why now."

I sat back on my heels, Luke Short. The snake had acted like a friend. All the while, he was ready to strike me the minute my back was turned. He was going to travel with me but now paid to have me killed as a bonus? I couldn't believe it. I'd been so throughly fooled by the man. Was his plan back at Fort Worth to kill me on the road? None of that mattered now. They were all just lessons I needed to learn. Proof that I wasn't done growing yet, but this betrayal would never leave my mind.

"Tell me the plan."

"Once we capture 'em four an took care of you..."

"There should be five, including Nash." I cut him off because four wasn't right.

"Supposed to be, but he figured it'd make more sense for him to collect the ransom. Being such a good friend an all." He snickered at that, but when he met my eyes, it stopped. "Once he got the money, we'd met up ta get paid. He'd pay the gambler an get on a boat for France or some other such place."

"The hostages?" I knew the answer, but needed to hear it.

"Killed or left out here to die, didn't matter none ta them. We had to be sure you was dead though. That Luke fella was real specific 'bout that. Thought ya was too, sure was covered in enough blood ta be dead. Reckon we shoulda put 'nother hunk a lead in ya."

"Ain't Hindsight a wonderful thing. Where are you meeting them?" The cold was running through me now, slowly gathering into a tight ball that I'd felt once before. Back in New Orleans, when Binda and Tante had been killed, there wouldn't be any escape for either cowards. Not for Nash and not for Luke.

"Supposed a meet Nash at the Star in his suite once all ya'll was dead. Don't figure they trust each other much. That feller Nash wanted us to take Luke his cut an never see him again. Luke stomped on that idea from the start. The three of us meet

313

in the same place. Pretty sure Nash is afraid of 'em, same way I figure 'at gambler afraid of you."

That was all I needed to know. Before the man could utter another word, I shot him. Two rounds neatly tucked in just above his left pocket. He was dead before his mouth closed. He'd been far too obvious about trying to cut his bonds. Carefully, I took my hidden sheath off his corpse. If he hadn't thought there was a chance of escape, there wouldn't have been any reason other than fear to talk. Fear made a man tell you what you wanted to here, not the truth. You always had to give them hope if you wanted the truth. They wouldn't risk a lie cutting the conversation short while the worked. After checking the blade and sliding it home, I tossed it beside my clothes. I'd put it back on when I changed clothes if my shoulder wound didn't stop me.

I left him hanging with his friends and went to start putting the horses on a string. It was time to go met the hunting party. It took an hour to get them all saddled and loaded. Pistols were rolled in saddlebags, Winchesters stored in sheaths. Getting them down from where they hung and tying them over their saddles was another hour. Hanging them before made it easier because I lowered them across the horses instead of trying to lift them. It was the only way to do it with my shoulder. That's why I'd gone through the trouble of stringing them all up.

They had a mule and panniers full of supplies, those went on Wisp. Their mule went on the string behind her. Before noon, I'd bathed in the stream and got back into my trail clothes. It felt good having my weapons back in place, comforting in a way. Clearing the entrance for the last time, I rode out to find Jim's friends. I'd need to find a local sheriff or marshal's office to collect the bounties. Funny enough, this group was different. The boss, whose name turned out to be Black Frank Willis, had the bounty posters on everyone else. All totaled, it was six hundred and forty dollars. I'd wondered why he had them all until I read his description. The man acted as a bounty hunter off and on. He planned on turning the whole gang into a sheriff he was on friendly terms with. He'd keep the money and collect the bounties after paying a cut to the lawman he worked with.

There was no way to know for sure that was his plan, but it made sense. Men like him never knew a friend they wouldn't betray. Which brought me back to Luke, my personal betrayer. The reality of it made me question everything I knew about the man and my judgement. Did he plan on killing me back in Fort Worth? Was that why he offered to travel with me? All for a horse?

I just couldn't get past that. It was another lesson in life for me, one that hurt. Taking a man at his word was one thing, but Luke was different. He acted like a friend, but never truly stood by me. From now on I'd have to watch people more carefully. Making sure I knew someone before putting my trust in them. I'd been naïve, still was in a lot of ways. Knowing this didn't mean I knew how to fix it, not straight away. It took painful lessons that you could only hope didn't kill you to learn.

This was all part of what I'd come out here to learn. To be able to see a man for who they really were. In hindsight, I recognized things about Luke that should have warned me. That first day at Iron Mike's saloon, he'd pushed until Mike warned him off. That should've alerted me to his character, unwilling to face a risk. Then, in Dodge two years later, there was a fight. He'd stayed out of it, never warned me about the man behind me with a knife. Then in Fort Worth, say one thing and do another. I knew it was his character, even knew in my mind he wouldn't keep his word, but ignored the warning. This was my fault, in a way. Luke was being exactly who he was. It was my mistake in expecting him to be different. A snake's never not going to bite you. The ones on two legs will just pick their moment.

Spotting their fire just as the sun made its turn in the sky, shifting the shadows to reach the other way. I assumed it was them because no one with any sense would have made that fire. They made no effort to hide it using the terrain, and the amount of smoke it was producing could only come from using wet wood. I shook my head, riding up. These men would die out here if left on their own. Another thought did creep into my thoughts. Maybe it was intentional, meant to advertise the location to a particular group of men. Was Nash with them?

"Hello the camp." I called out as I approached.

"Come in if you're friendly." Adams called out with a slight slur.

I tied the string off a fair distance from their camp and rode Shade forward. No need to bring in the bodies and tell Nash he'd been found out. Jim was the only one with any trail sense. He'd at least stepped back from the fire. The other three were sprawled out around the fire, passing a bottle between them. I met Jim's eyes and gave him one brief nod. He read that and the disapproval in my gaze when I looked at the camp.

"I know. It's the first night out and there is a small town half-a-mile back up the trail." He tried to explain. "It's still safe."

"Perfectly safe from the other, the normal dangers are still about. Got a lawman there?" Maybe I could get rid of these bodies without riding for days.

"Deputy US Marshal. He covers most of the Santa Rosa and San Jacinto, names David North. Why?" JB answered from where he lay.

"Tell ya when I catch back up tomorrow, should be back before ya break camp."

I hadn't bothered to dismount, just waved over my shoulder after I turned. The trail they'd followed was easy to read. More and more the men coming out here acted like it was all tamed land, it would cost more than one their life. Riding into the small community leading a string of horses and bodies meant I didn't need to search for the deputy. It wasn't really a town, more of an overgrown trading post named Brookstone. The deputy found me before I made it to his office. He took a quick look at all five before sending me to the gravedigger's shack.

"You're gonna have to pay for the burying. I can approve

the bounty for collection with an affidavit, but that's it." He explained while walking with me toward a small shack.

"Law in San Diego take that as verification?" I asked.

"Always have, the sheriff anyway. The town marshal could be a problem. The man doesn't care for most bounty hunters. He likes some well enough, like your friend there. Man's just fine with him." He motioned toward Frank's body as he spoke. That tidbit told me a bit more and gave me some warning about where to collect from.

"Your boss isn't bothered by it?" I asked, curious.

"He's in Los Angeles and the man's not corrupt enough to warrant our attention." He laughed and called out to the cabin. "Jeremiah got some work for ya."

"Dollar each, no box. Five dollars if'n ya want 'em in a box." The big man who walked out of the shed wearing nothing but dirty overalls was obviously simple. That didn't mean he lacked the understanding of money and its value.

"Doubt any of 'em need a box or deserve one." I said, stepping down from the saddle.

"Five dollars, drop'em by the dirt pile. Plant 'em tomorrow." He reached a grubby finger up to scratch at his chin as he spoke. "Ain't stink'n bad yet."

"Just get it done tomorrow please, you'll get paid..." I said, but the deputy held up a hand, stopping me from continuing.

"Ain't right ta do me like 'at Davey." The big man complained.

"Pay after work. That's how it works for a man." The deputy said it softly, like he was reminding Davey of a previous conversation.

"I member, just need some crunchies." The big man pouted.

"Get it done early. I'll give you some of the money to get crunchies and hold the rest for you." I watched the conversation starting to fill in some of it for myself.

"Fair 'nough, Davey. Find ya when they planted." Without another word, the big man shuffled back into his shack.

"I can explain." North started to explain, but I stopped him.

"Pretty sure I got it, no need." I smiled at him while leading the string over to the dirt pile. I started cutting the ropes that held them on, letting them fall by the pile.

"Appreciate the understanding. I started helping him out when I got stationed here."

"Just gotta ask. What are crunchies?"

"Penny candy. He'll spend all of it on them if I don't step in." He smiled warily at some memory. Probably occurring after a certain young man ate five dollars' worth of penny candy.

"Don't need to say anymore." I chuckled, dropping the last body. "Place I can stay around here?"

"There is, but if I'm being honest, finding a camp outside of town would be better." He looked a bit ashamed but was telling me the truth.

"That bad, huh?"

"Celestial house rents rooms, but the place always feels off to me."

"Opium?"

"No, nothing like that, least not that I've seen. It's hard to explain an maybe it's just me. Old man Kwai is a nice enough, just something dangerous about the man."

"Think I'll take your advice." Part of me was curious about this dangerous old man. Not curious enough to mess around too much in another law man's area, but still curious.

"Got coffee at the office and can write up that affidavit for ya."

"Works."

I made it out of town and found a decent camp about half way back before all the light was gone. Two big pines against a cliff with the boughs cut clear at the lower part. A clean stream ran close enough to get water and there was good graze. After caring for the animals, I gathered some wood for a fire. Just managing to get set up before the last traces of light disappeared.

Some beans and fatback with a few left over biscuits made for a quick meal. When a small shadow slunk toward the fire, I managed to stop myself before grabbing my Colt. The dog crawled out of the shadows toward the dancing light, looking miserable. I'd finally managed to see enough to tell it was a bitch. She looked exhausted, which made me wonder if she'd been following me all day.

"Ain't naming you yet. Stick around long enough an we'll get there." Her ears flicked forward when I spoke.

I scraped half the beans to a plate and added a few chunks of jerky before pushing it a few feet toward her. Her eyes flicked back and forth from the plate to me. Speaking in low soft tones, I called to her, whistling quietly. When her ears flicked at the sound, a thought crossed my mind. I'd seen cattle dogs used a few times. They were controlled with different whistles. A man sitting on horseback could use two dogs at the same time. Both animals responding to different whistles.

Quietly, I started trying different whistles, noting the ones that made her twitch. There was no way to know which ones did what, but I was trying to find the one that called her. How had this dog come to be with those men? She was obviously a herding dog, and they were definitely not punchers. They must have taken her from a ranch somewhere. That didn't explain why they kept her, but anyone who knew that was dead.

Finally I hit the right tone, a single high pitched short whistle. She got up like it was just another day and sat in front of the plate, waiting for my permission to eat. A sharp snap of my fingers seemed to be enough, or it at least it conveyed my meaning. Her head went down, and she started eating. Slowly reaching my hand toward her, she looked up, meeting my eyes. I froze, letting her decide. Slowly, she leaned forward, ducking her head under my hand. Two scratches were all she allowed before ducking back to the plate of food.

When she finished eating and walked over to the stream to drink, I watched to see what she'd do. After drinking her fill, she walked back like it was the most normal thing and flopped down beside me. When I started petting her, she rolled under my hand, letting me scratch her belly. Evidently, I had a dog now and she needed a name.

"Gonna have to see who you are before naming you girl." She turned at the sound of my voice watching me. There was that same look of intelligence in her eyes I'd seen several times now. No surprise there. It seemed like they kept finding me.

Sleep came easily that night. Wisp, and probably the dog, would let me know if something or someone came close. Tomorrow I'd meet up with Jim and the rest, then I had a feeling things would get interesting. Of course, that was if I could get them to drop this hunting trip. Rich men and good sense didn't always go together. There were a few ideas bouncing around in my head about what to do next, but they would all depend on them.

The predawn light roused me from my bedroll like it always did, especially when sleeping in wild country. Laying there without moving for a few minutes just sensing the life around me. When I was sure nothing was out of place, my body started moving. The dog flinched away with a fearful look, like she expected to be kicked or something. A sharp whistle and she was back, waiting for whatever punishment that might come. When I scratched behind her ears, her whole body relaxed into my hand.

"Good girl." I praised softly. She came alive at those words, trying to climb into my lap. Her whole body was vibrating with happiness. "Been a while since you heard that huh?"

Laughing happily, I petted and scratched her for a few minutes. It was like whatever she had been through was fading away. Finally, she bounded off my lap and zoomed around the camp before leaping back into my lap. Her face had that happy dog smile with her tongue lolling half out.

"Can't remember how to spell it, but Mom always thanked Anya when something made her happy. She's an old Celtic goddess. If I remember the story right, she had some trials but managed to still spread joy."

In response, she bounded forward and gently nipped at my nose, making me jerk back in surprise. This led to a ferocious wrestling match between me and the quick little beast. Thankfully, it was only witnessed by Wisp and Shade, who both looked on in disapproval. I felt like they were judging me in some way, but I didn't care. It was one of the few truly childish moments I'd had in years and it lightened my heart.

When we were done and laying in a heap panting, I felt better than I had since the calf battle we had in a river. Seven hardened punchers fighting each other in the middle of a river all trying to save a calf. Max had offered the man who got the calf out five dollars. That was the start of it. Like then, a few minutes of childish play with no purpose or reason had helped ease the hardships. Looking back, I think Max knew we needed that break. It had been a long hot few days that put the herd constantly on the edge of a stampede. Everyone's temper was on edge, waiting for the next problem. It was another lesson, one I hadn't seen then, but now it was crystal clear. I looked at the panting dog next to me a smiled. She was going to be a good companion for me.

"Thanks, I needed that." She leaned forward and licked my face in response, then wandered over to the stream. "Yeah, I hear ya. Better get moving."

It didn't take long to pack up camp and load the panniers. Saddling the five horses took a bit longer with my arm still slowing me down. By the time it was done, my left arm wasn't happy with being pushed. It was still going to take time for it to heal fully. Hell, the wound was only a week old. Maybe my expectations were a bit high.

Saddling Shade took longer. He'd picked this morning to be difficult. I didn't want to reopen the stitches and was trying to move slow, this evidently annoyed him. Wisp stomped out of the blue, and I turned around to see her staring at Anya. The funny thing was she had to crane her neck back to see the dog, who looked completely satisfied. She was laying between the panniers. To both me and Wisps in shock, the clever dog leaned forward and licked Wisp's nose.

I froze, waiting for Wisp to kick off, but after a snort, she just turned back like this was all normal. Smiling, I went back to cinch the girth on Shade. It only took one more fight to finish tacking him up. Before I mounted up, both of them got half an apple. I'd picked up a few from a wild tree yesterday just for this reason. Shade took it as his due for putting up with me and Wisp like it was payment for tolerating the Anya. Laughing to myself about the quality and insanity of the animals that kept finding me, I stepped into the saddle. Soon I was following the scent of coffee on the morning breeze.

# CHAPTER 30

Wisp brayed softly, warning me something had changed. When I looked back, Anya had disappeared into the brush. Her calico grey coat making her invisible as she moved silently through the woods. Even knowing she was there, I couldn't see her after a second. She'd make up her own mind on how to act, all I could do was give her that freedom.

"Get whatever it was you needed to done?" Jim asked, crouched by the fire when I rode in. The others were still laying in bedrolls, awake but not motivated to move yet.

"Dropped off five bodies with the marshal there. He gave me an affidavit for the bounties." Turning to look closer, he realized I was trailing five horses and an extra mule.

"You took out all five?" Adams asked from where lay.

"Seemed like the thing to do after they shot me." That brought Jim to his feet and got the rest focused on me.

"Your shot?" Was the first thing out of JB's mouth.

"Got lucky, went through the meat by my neck, didn't hit anything vital. Wisp ran off when I fell, they took Shade and my guns and left me for dead. I followed her trail once I managed to get up. She found a small band of Cahuilla, they sewed me back together." It was the short version, but I hadn't had coffee yet. This was already more than I normally found acceptable.

"Who were they?" Gus seemed to have finally caught up with the rest. All of them were watching me as I loosened the cinch on Shade. I tied the rest off to their picket and loosened their cinches.

"The men sent by Nash to kill you four."

That landed like a boulder in still water. Ignoring their various statements of shock and disbelief, I finished with the animals and filled my coffee cup. It may have looked like I was being casual, but my eyes never left them.

"Gonna burn that bacon, Jim." The man stared at me in shock and the rest finally stopped their babbling to focus back on me.

"What?" Jim still hadn't looked down at the skillet.

"You're burning the bacon." Hiding my smile behind the coffee cup. Jim turned, noticing the bacon that was still cooking. With a quick curse, he wrapped the handle in a rag and pulled it off the fire.

"We might need more than that to believe the last of it." Adams glared at me and I turned my cold gaze on him before speaking.

"You calling me a liar?" The man's eyes followed my hand as it flipped the thong off my Colt. I watched him swallow and search for the right words.

"Not at all, that's not what he means JC." JB spoke fast, being the only one other than Jim to understand how serious that question was. Jim was staring at me. It was like he finally saw the man I'd become. "He, like us, just has a hard time picturing Nash doing that."

"Yes, that's it." Adams agreed, nodding rapidly. I didn't put the thong back on but did let the cold fade back a bit.

"He owes a gambler named Luke Short. This was his way of paying him off and getting away with something more in his pockets. They'd split the ransom and leave you to die out here or kill you outright. That's all according to the leader of the five."

"His wife and family." Adams almost whispered the realization. Then he acknowledged the rest. "I know he does owe that Short fellow several thousand dollars. He's been on a bad run with the cards lately."

"But this?" Gus seemed to be having the hardest time with it.

"Betraying our trust and killing us? For money? I'd have loaned him whatever he needed to pay off the man."

"That wouldn't have freed him." Adams admitted, stomping into his boots. "His wife is a horrid woman and she's turned his children into vile monsters. Not that I'm excusing his behavior, just explaining."

"You don't really think he'd go that far?" Gus still didn't believe it, but the truth was starting to dawn on him.

"A man who feels trapped is likely to do anything." JB said as he rose to his feet and stomped toward the fire. A soft growl from the brush made them all freeze. Evidently, JB had gotten too close to me.

"Anya." I said, snapping my fingers. The growl stopped immediately. Her body materialized out of the shadows and she came to stand beside me. "Found by a dog with them."

"Found by a dog?" Jim started laughing, just staring across the fire at me. "And of all things, an Australian cattle dog."

"Where?" JB had stopped to study the dog.

"They had her tied up when I found them." I answered while kneeling down to scratch behind her ears.

"Seems to have come through it alright." Jim smiled, holding out a piece of bacon toward her.

"Go ahead." It was like my words declared these men safe. She stepped around JB and took the bacon. When Jim reached to pet her, I watched carefully, but she didn't even flinch.

"Whip smart and good partners to have." JB said, kneeling down to pet her as well. "Know a few ranchers that use them. They must've robbed a ranch and taken her. I'd check with the sheriff in San Diego, make sure no one is looking for her."

"That was my plan. Someone trained her, but I have a feeling they're dead. Those five were bad men." I agreed before checking the biscuits, cooking over the fire. They were close to being done. "How do ya'll want to play this? Wasn't he supposed to be here with you?"

"Changed his mind at the last minute. Didn't feel up for it, was the story he gave us." Adams said stiffly.

"Figure we should head back. Seems like there's some business to settle." JB's anger was obvious.

"Much as I don't want to believe it, there really is no choice. I don't know if we can prove it with the men dead." Gus seemed to be studying the problem now.

"Won't be a problem. A U.S. Marshal took the statement from Frank Willis before he died." I chuckled, making the four look at me.

"You didn't mention there was a marshal with you?" Jim asked curiously.

"True." I laughed, then pulled my vest open, revealing my badge.

"That's not a deputy's badge." Adams gaped at the shining star.

"When did that happen?" Jim was seriously wondering what had happened to the young man he'd met in Dodge. I could see it in his eyes.

"Started in Albuquerque." I didn't really feel like explaining.

"That does change things. Nash and his conspirator can be arrested and formally charged." Gus finally relaxed. The law was going to handle things now.

"Albuquerque? Then you don't have jurisdiction here?" Adams asked curiously.

"Sort of nomad badge, Marshal Douglas sent me from New Mexico to Arizona to deal with a problem. Told me to check in for assignments as I traveled. My job is dealing with problems while the service catches up with the growing country."

"I had heard that some of the territories didn't have marshals assigned yet." Adams offered. "The Pinkertons have been getting a lot of work from some of the mining towns."

"So long as your authority is recognized, it shouldn't be a problem to arrest them." Gus brought the topic back to the present. Jim was studying me again. The man was going to want a private conversation at some point.

"They will. That's why I was thinking of going back first. If you'll stay here for a day, then follow me back. It'll give me time to catch them unaware long before they know things haven't worked out."

After laying out my plan and they all agreed. We had a few days to use before Nash would know something was off. It would let me have time to arrest him before he could flee. Luke was another matter. He wouldn't be taken to jail. If it wasn't handled carefully, he would kill more people trying to escape. I put nothing past him anymore. I had a few ideas, but truthfully, part of me knew it would come to a showdown. The feeling of betrayal still kept that cold fire burning in my chest, but it was banked with my responsibility to the badge I wore.

They agreed and JB said he'd buy the extra animals, which saved me another problem. It was impossible to come into any town or city trailing a string of empty saddles and go unnoticed. The man knew horses, and I trusted him to be able to handle the string. After we shook hands, he started pulling off saddles since they were staying here for the rest of the day.

Adams knew the city and its politics better than the others. He told me to use the marshal's office instead of the local law. Nash had contacts with the local sheriff and I had reasons of my own to doubt the town marshal's office. The US Marshals office was near the outskirts of town. The local deputy was Gerard North. Evidently, the North family were all lawmen. Their dad had been sheriff when this was a mining town.

JB offered his hand to the plan and gave me a letter for his ranch manager. It gave me permission to ask the punchers on his payroll for help. None were gun hands according to him. They were to a man just good punchers. I didn't think I'd use them, but took the letter just in case. Gus gave me a letter to his attorney in case that was needed. There wasn't anything else to be said. We shook hands agreeing to meet at the Star in three days.

Anya jumped back on Wisp when I stepped into the saddle, making the men smile at her antics. We were back on the trail to San Diego shortly after the sun fully rose into the sky. The next day went smoothly. After breakfast, the second day, I was waiting outside the marshal's office when he walked up.

"Morning." The man was maybe thirty, lean and just as solid as his brother. I could see the family resemblance between them. "Take a bit of coffee for me to be worth a damn, but what can I help ya with?"

"Bit of trouble, coffees always a good start though." I looped Shade's reins around the hitching rail and followed the man inside, Anya stayed on my heels. "First thing is about her, I reckon."

"The dog?" The man stirred the coals back to life in the small stove and set the pot on to boil.

"Yeah, heard about any ranches getting hit and losing a dog?" That brought him up short, and he took a good look at her.

"Might have at that. Names Gerard North, deputy U.S. Marshal." He stuck his hand out to shake mine.

"U.S. Marshal JC Stone." I said, shaking his hand. The man's face split in a grin and he chuckled to himself.

"Got a telegram from the boss the other day, mentioned you might show up. Something of a nomad marshal or some such. Anyway, got a flyer a few weeks back bout a small cattle ranch just this side of Arizona Territory. Rustlers hit'em and wiped out the family. The dog was only mentioned because the local law couldn't find it." He started searching through his desk, looking for the notice.

"Met your brother the other morning, dropped off five deadmen with him. Found the dog with them after they shot me."

"Good man, don't tell him I said that, though. It'll go to his head. Ahh! Here it is." He pulled out a piece of paper from a drawer. "Lupia Ranch out by El Cajón. Small place, lost forty some beefs and the whole family was found dead. Husband, wife and both young'uns. Remember a note cause it was odd. Family dog not found, one of the neighbors swears the dog wouldn't go anywhere willingly."

"They had her tied up. Here's the affidavit from your brother.

Can you send for the bounties?" After handing him the papers, I looked down at Anya. "Guess you're stuck with me."

She laid down beside the door, happy to wait for me to finish whatever this was. I laughed, tossing her a piece of jerky while Gerard finished making the coffee. He put a cup down near me before setting his down. Neither of us reached for the brew yet, both having learned how hot those cups would be.

"I'll get'em off today. They're mostly local, so it won't take more than a day to get the drafts. Any reason they shot you?"

"Now we get to why you find me at your door." I laughed while packing a pipe. "Mind?"

"Long as you don't mind my cigar." He chuckled, biting the end off and spitting it in the can.

After explaining what had happened and filling out a written report about it all, we started planning. He stuck his head out the door and called for a boy across the street. After handing him a nickel, the boy ran off to quietly make sure Nash was still at the Star. He came back twenty minutes later with good news. Not only was he still at the hotel, but his breakfast reservation wasn't for another thirty minutes. That meant we could catch him fairly quickly. When the boy mentioned the reservation was for two, my brows furrowed. The only person it could be was Luke, but I didn't want that to happen in a crowded dining room. Nash would be easy so long as you caught him unaware. Luke wouldn't be caught that way and he would fight.

"Don't want to deal with Short in a crowd." I said, thinking about the situation. "The man's fast from what I hear an won't go easy."

"Too late to separate them before breakfast, but neither of them knows me. I can see where they end up after breakfast." Gerard offered.

"If I had to bet, Luke will have a game waiting. The man approaches gambling like a job, always has. Nash, I don't know well enough to guess, not gambling if he owes Luke that much money."

"You said he's broke, right? Most likely back to his room."

"Works. Should be far enough out of town here. Mind if I sit here and drink your coffee?"

"Help yourself." He laughed, rising to his feet and pulling his hat on. After checking his guns, he walked toward the Star like it was just another day.

It was a bit more than an hour before he came back. We'd called it right, they'd had some disagreement about it, but Luke had loudly told Nash to wait in his room. Luke had then gone to a local saloon called The First Last Chance. Gerard had asked around and found he'd been playing there for the last week. The owner was probably paying him to lure in the rubes. Men would line up to try their luck against famous gamblers.

"Guard them." I told Anya, pointing at Shade and Wisp as we left the office. She whined once, then jumped to her perch on Wisps back. "Good girl."

Gerard filled me in as we walked to the Star. Nash needed to be arrested before word got around that I was back in town. The clerk didn't bat an eye when Gerard demanded the key. Evidently, he was well known in the area and if he asked, there was always a reason. We caught him sitting on a couch reading. The door being opened was the only warning Nash got.

"What do you mean by..." his voice cut off when Nash saw the badge on my vest.

"Don't think the men you're waiting for are going to make it." I grinned down at the man.

"You? A marshal? How..what do you mean?" I watched the man's eyes as they filled with panic. Finally, he landed on the reality of his situation. "I told Luke going after you was a fool's errand, but he wanted that damn horse."

We searched him after the cuffs were on. A new Remington was tucked into a well-made shoulder holster. It was the only weapon on the man. Gerard took it and turned to me.

"We run a risk of Short hearing about it if we march him out in cuffs. You said he wouldn't be taken alive if he got the chance?"

"He'll fight, even if he doesn't have a chance. He won't run, can't afford for word to get out."

Men like Luke couldn't do otherwise. It wasn't an option he had if he wanted to keep his name. I'd come to recognize him for what he was, a legend in his own mind. The man had read his own dime store novels and started believing them. There was no way his pride would let him face a noose or run. He might complain about his name, but the truth was plain to see. He liked his reputation, both as gambler and gunfighter.

"Can you take him? I ain't keen on having a marshal killed while I sit in a hotel room." Gerard wasn't happy about this, but accepted there wasn't really a choice.

"I can." The cold slowly started filling me, taking away the doubt and questions.

"If you can get him alive, will you?" The man was sharp. He knew there was bad blood between us.

"I'll do my job." I didn't mean for it to come out as icy as it did. Thankfully, he didn't take it wrong.

"Then you go deal with him. I'll wait thirty minutes before taking Nash to my office." Then he smiled at Nash, but it wasn't a friendly one. "To pass the time, maybe he'd like to give me a full accounting of events."

"Yes, yes I will. My plan didn't have anyone getting killed. That was all them." It was obvious the man would try to avoid facing the noose. He'd say anything to avoid that terrible fate.

"I'll met you back at the office." I spoke while moving my left shoulder around, unconsciously testing the motion. Then double checked my Colts, making sure nothing hindered my draw.

The saloon wasn't far and, as I wove through the crowd, my mind flashed back again to my first meeting with Luke. I should have known then, the man had been willing to kill me for Shade. It was only when Mike told him he'd lose that he backed off. Finding out who Jose was and that we both rode for the Bar C had shaken him further. Now it was just me, no ranch or amigo backing my play. The only things I had working for me were a badge and surprise.

The painted glass windows shimmered in the sun, soft beams reflecting off the dust that stuck to them. An old drunk slept in the alley, his face pockmarked and dirty. A lone woman hurriedly walked past the batwing doors like she was afraid of being sucked into them. Not an unrealistic fear at night, but during the day the real monsters normally slept.

The sun was behind me when I stepped in, hiding my identity. Moving to the left, waiting just long enough for my eyes to adjust before I scanned the place. It was mostly empty, a few drunks passed out at tables and one old man sweeping the floor. One poker table at the back had four strangers seated around it, Luke was the fifth. He wasn't paying attention to the doors. Something at the table kept his eyes focused there. A sizable pot had gathered in the center and only two men still held cards, Luke and an older man I didn't know.

The bartender started to speak before I put my finger to my mouth. He hesitated, wanting to speak, but then he met my gaze. Color drained from his face and he snapped his mouth closed. The man quickly found something that needed doing somewhere else and disappeared through a door at the end of the bar.

"Interfere, an you'll be a dead man." My eyes were locked on the man sitting further down. He worked, but I wasn't sure about his job. Sweat trickled down his forehead as he nodded. Every thing about him told me he wanted no part of whatever this was.

Finally, Luke turned to look at who came in. His eyes flashed as recognition filled them. Both of his hands stayed on top of the table, cards laying between them. It took a moment for the other players to notice that he wasn't moving. Slowly, silence fell as they recognized the pressure all men knew. Death had walked into the room and no one wanted to draw its attention. This feeling was something most men out here had known in some way before. This promise of violence that hung in the air that pushed them toward the walls. The space between us emptied with eerie silence that always hung over these moments. It was broken only by scrapping chairs and shuffling boot steps.

"Didn't know you were a marshal." Luke broke the silence first.

"Happened after I left Fort Worth. Did you figure on killing me back then?"

"Thought about it once I knew that damn scary mex wasn't travlin' with you." His eyes were green voids that held no emotion.

"Shame, you couldn't have to shot me in the back that way." The edges of my mouth curled up in amusement at the flinch when that hit home. "Course you've known that was the only way you could take me since San Antonio."

"Never did trust Mike after that. Still don't believe it." He sounded certain, but I could see a hint of fear in his eyes.

"Didn't trust it? You still hired someone else to do the job rather than face me." His hands hadn't moved. He'd stand up before making his play. "They're all dead, by the way. Mind not before Black Frank spilled the beans about the plan. Nash is already in a cell."

"An you came to arrest me?" His mouth quirked up into a smile at the idea.

"That's the idea."

"You know that ain't happening, don't you?"

"That's up to you. Give up and face a jury. You might beat the charge or face me and die. You're a good liar. Might be able to get out of it." I shifted slightly, then added casually. "Fooled me into thinking you were a friend. 'Preciate that lesson."

"You know that ain't happening. Especially not after you aired out my dirty secrets. My name won't be worth spit if you live to walk out of here."

"Won't be worth much if you kill me. These good folks already heard me and Nash won't hold his mouth. Already started talking. That man will say anything to avoid facing the long drop on a short rope. You'll be hunted no matter what.

Why not face it?"

"Face the hangman? No thanks, think I'll play it out here and now." Slowly he stood from the chair, his right hand dropped toward his pistol. The man wore a matched pair of black Schofields with pearl grips. Light danced off them when he eases back his jacket.

"Your choice, you call the dance."

The cold filled me now, highlighting every detail of the man who I'd once called friend. His eyes danced, taking me in. Time slowed and even that almost wasn't enough. His hands flashed and flame cut through the air toward me. The familiar feeling of steel bucking in my right hand was the only awareness I had of my movement. It had come a half second before flames shot toward me from his hand. The sharp twinge of pain from my shoulder when my left hand fanned the second shot matched his first shot exactly.

My first thought was he'd hit my shoulder again. That flashed through my mind as I watched the flame expanding toward me. Something stung the bottom of my left ear, like a horsefly biting me. Slowly, the flames receded, replaced with billowing smoke. My nostrils felt the sharp bite of it trailing up from my Colt. Luke's eyes widened, his mouth gaped like a fish. Another gout of fire singed the top of his pants, licking the top of his cloth covered thigh. Dying fingers pulling the trigger even as the strength fled his body. Then it tumbled from his hand and dropped to the floor with a thunk. Red slowly spreading across the front of his shirt, starting just two inches left of his third button.

"Guess Mike was right." They were the last words that escaped his lips in a wheeze.

# CHAPTER 31

His body seemed to die in stages. His ankles wobbled, then both knees banged into the rough cut floor boards. His weight shifted and his waist bent forward, leaving him posed like a man praying for just a moment. With one last exhale, his shoulders fell forward, pulling his head to the floor. With a dull knock, Luke Short's story ended there on the floor. Face down next to a spittoon that hadn't been cleaned in years.

Something ran down my neck, warm liquid slowly trailing down the side. When I looked past the white-faced bartender, the mirror showed me there was a red line drawn from front to back across my neck. It had been that close. The impact of my first round had jerked his shot up just enough to miss. My eyes trailed down from the thin line of blood, six inches at the most. That was the difference between this burn and my death. A bit down or in and that 44 would have left me dead on the floor.

My hands automatically reloaded my Colt before dropping it back in my holster. No one said a word. The stale air hung heavy in the saloon, filled with silence and smoke. Footsteps sounded outside, and I turned to face to door. A man wearing a policeman's badge stepped in and froze when he saw my star.

"Marshal?"

"Tried to apprehend a suspect. He decided not to go peaceably." I didn't know the man or even his boss, but didn't feel like dealing with it. "North knows I'm here. He's expecting me at the office. Could you fetch the undertaker and ask your boss to meet us there?"

"Yes, sir."

The man really couldn't do anything else. My badge meant I could fire his boss and he knew it. The threat was made that much more real because he knew the crooked things his boss did. All of that added up to him just going along with my orders and hoping things would change.

I went over to Luke and took his pistol belt, key to his hotel room, and his wallet. It took another minute to retrieve his money belt. His horse would be at the Star, along with the rest of his belongings. The last thing I took off his body was the pinky ring he always wore. A small black star sapphire danced in the gold setting. There were nine double eagles in front of his seat at the table. I picked those up as well before turning to the bartender.

"You know his name?"

"Yes Marshal, Luke Short." I flipped him one of the double eagles.

"That'll cover burying him right with a decent headstone. Make sure it happens or I'll be back."

"Yes, sir." The man was so pale I could almost see through him. The very last thing he wanted was me coming back here.

I took a clean bar towel and left without looking back. Walking back toward the marshal's office, I felt hollow. Part of me kept playing through my interactions with Luke over the years. Then I'd examine the way I felt. There was no remorse, no sorrow for his death. There were just my regrets for trusting the man and the lessons I'd learned from it. Hindsight, being what it was, I could spot the looks. The way his eyes tracked Shade every time he saw him. I should've seen it, should have known the man wasn't going to be denied. Behavior like those wouldn't go unnoticed in the future, never again.

Anya jumped off Wisp to follow me inside the office. Nash was pacing in a cell at the back of the room while Gerard was reading over a statement. He looked up when I came in, then leaned over to get a look at my neck.

"Bad?" He finally asked.

"Naw, just burns like hell."

Hanging Luke's belt on a peg, I dropped the money belt on the desk and reached for a cup. After filling it with coffee, I fell into the chair and tossed the rag into the trash. There wasn't much blood on the white material. It had been just bad enough to ruin yet another shirt. Smythe was right, I was hell on clothes.

"Guessing it went 'bout how ya thought." He asked, rocking back in his chair.

"Yeah, city marshal ought to be along soon. Might as well only tell it once."

"He ain't gonna like it. Man's awful funny about what he sees as his territory."

"So?" I shrugged, unconcerned.

"I gotta work with him, ya know?" Gerard chuckled softly. I knew better, and so did he. We only had to play nice when we wanted to. A U.S. Marshal or deputy could easily pull rank if they want to, most just don't out of politeness. Working with the locals was always better than having an adversarial relationship after all.

Heavy stomping steps came up the boardwalk outside. Gerard hung his head and pinched the bridge of his nose. The door banged open, and a man stormed in. He was big, sadly what was probably once muscle had started shifting from his chest to his belly. The heavy breathing was another give away, this man was going to seed.

"What the hell do you think...." A soft growl echoed from my right and Anya made her presence felt. Sadly, the man had his hackles up. "Get that mutt under control or I'll shot it."

"You'll what?" To the man in front of me, it seemed like I'd just appeared there. The cold flowed through me. Surprise filled his eyes, and he took an automatic step back. I didn't give him the space, stepping with him. "You come in here full of bluster an think you can order me around?"

"Well..." I cut him off again.

"Then you threaten my dog? The man I killed today hired someone else to shoot me in the back for my horse. A man,

I might add, who was collecting bounties while being on a dodger himself." I knew this man had nothing to do with all the rest, but that ought to put him on edge.

"Wait, hold on Marshal." His whole demeanor changed, but not when expected. It changed when I spoke about being shot. "That man hired someone else to kill you?"

"Yeah, sorry if I'm a bit on edge." I stepped back, giving him some room.

"Then he got what he deserved. First for not stomping his own snakes and second for hiring the assassination of a U.S. Marshal. I can't abide with either act." There was real anger in the man's voice. "Having been shot in the back, I have strong opinions on the matter."

"Been a long week." I reeled my temper back in. "Sorry for the abruptness. Please join us. I was actually waiting for you to arrive before telling the story. No sense telling the same thing twice."

"Coffees mostly fresh, Terry." Gerard spoke for the first time.

"Anya." She looked at me and I waved outside. She shot out the door. A second later, I heard a gentle nicker and knew she was with the others.

"Thanks Gerard." He stuck out a meaty hand to me. "Names Terry Waters."

"JC Stone." Taking his hand and returning the firm grip. "Gerard, is there a doc around? Need to have them check this and that patched up bullet hole at some point."

"Your neck? I can clean that up."

"No, the hole in my shoulder." I laughed.

"When did ya get shot? I never asked." Gerard asked, while dragging another chair over for Terry.

"What day is it? Guess maybe a week, close to that anyway." I looked up when silence suddenly filled the room. Both men were staring at me.

"Let me see if I get this right." Gerard held up his hand to cut off Terry's question. "You got shot around a week ago, shot off your horse. Hunted down the men who shot you, killed all five of them. Then you rode back here and had a gunfight with a known man?"

"Think it might be a little over a week." It was all I said to the two stunned lawmen. "Cahuilla woman stitched it up for me."

"Wait, where did this happen?" Terry finally managed to get something out before Gerard.

"Santa Rosa range. The other men involved should be back in town tomorrow."

My response made Terry open his mouth, but Gerard took charge again. He filled him in on the story and let me just relax for a minute. Once he'd finished catching Terry up, I told them both about what happened at the saloon. Both of them just shook their heads. Neither could believe it.

"Son, I don't know if you realize how remarkable that is. Never mind the rest, just that you uncovered a kidnapping plot, foiled it and saved four men. Not just any four men either, but all of them have dined with Grant. These are not casual men." Terry sat back, amazed once he'd heard it all.

"Look at him." Gerard smiled, nodding toward me. "He don't get it. Has no idea what he's done."

"Far as I'm concerned, an unnamed marshal did it with a lot of help from you two." I shrugged, then instantly regretted it when the pain hit me. It must have showed on my face because Gerard suddenly changed his plan.

"Doc's two blocks on the right. Go get checked out. Just write out an accurate report on everything tonite so I can send it with mine tomorrow."

"I just appreciate hearing it." Terry chuckled good-naturedly. "Ain't often I get stories like this."

"How bout I let you know when they get back tomorrow? You can join us at the Star and get their statements." I offered both men, then stood and turned to Terry. "Sorry again about the rocky start. Glad to have met you."

"Pleasures mine an don't worry about it. Partially caused by my attitude about things happening on my porch." Terry smiled. "Gerard can let me know when to be at the Star."

"That'll be fine. Ain't planning on going anywhere. If something comes up an I do need to, you can take their statements and leave them here. Man named Daughtry watches the jail when I have to leave town." Gerald agreed before I made it to the door.

"Well do, I'll be at the Star if y'all need me. That is, after seeing the doc."

Rolling up Luke's gun belt, I put it and his money belt in one of the panniers before untying Shade. Anya was already perched in her spot on Wisp. Stepping into the saddle, I rode the short distance to the doctors, mostly just to keep my animals close. To my complete surprise, the doc complimented the work. Said who ever did it managed to do a fair job and kept it clean. My neck got cleaned up, and he told me to come back in a week to get the stitches out.

The Star told me Luke's suite was paid for a month. When I said he was dead, the clerk had to get the manager before we could work something out. In the end I'd keep the room for two weeks if need be. There was more debate about Anya, but they had to give that up when a wealthy older lady walked by with her dog. Luke had one of the bigger suites, so keeping it made my life a bit more comfortable. He must have come in by train because there was no horse in the livery under his name. The bell boy brought up my saddle bags and panniers not long after I got to the room. He promised to bring my dinner up after taking my order before leaving.

He was back with it thirty minutes later. Two thick pork chops, baked potato, fresh green beans and carrots with a basket of rolls. There was also a small pot of coffee. The last thing on the tray was a nice big slice of apple pie, steam still trailing off the crust. Besides my dinner, there was a mostly raw steak for Anya. Using the basin from one of the bedrooms, I left water for her on the balcony. It probably wouldn't win me any friends on the staff, but it worked.

After finishing the food, I looked around at the suite. It was huge, far more than I'd have ever asked for. Two bedrooms, a living room, a large balcony and my new favorite room. The magical indoor plumbing, complete with tub and toilet. Anya wasn't a fan when I insisted on giving her a bath, but she lived.

After several tubs of water, she was a full two shades lighter in color than I'd thought. She didn't fight, just looked annoyed, then zoomed around the room, trying to dry off. It did mean some of the blankets on the bed were going to be a bit damp later, but I had another one to sleep in. I left the balcony door open for her once I finished laughing at her antics.

Finally, I climbed into a fresh tub of water and just soaked for a while. Finally washing off the last of the blood that had dried on my chest and neck. It took as many tubs for me as it did for the dog to get truly clean. The wound in my neck burned a little from the soap, but it was worth it to avoid infection. My shoulder voiced some strong opinions about the process, but neither were too bad. I set my clothes out for the laundry service and took my last clean set out of the panniers.

I had every intention of looking through Luke's stuff and counting the money, but that could all be done tomorrow. Just sitting on the balcony smoking a pipe sounded perfect for tonite. My hand idly scratched Anya as the sun slowly dipped below the horizon. The show of color dancing across the waves of the harbor was mesmerizing. Finally, I just relaxed, letting the darkness engulf me. Long after dark, I made my way into the comfortable bed. The last thing I remembered was Anya jumping up at my feet and laying down.

The faint predawn light found me doing what little I could of my routine. My shoulder was informing that it had been pushed too far and I needed to let it heal. I made my own coffee on the small stove in the room and sat on the balcony with Anya by my side. My eyes scanned around, watching another place come to life around me. Like always, there was a barrier that separated me from the life waking up around me.

Years ago, I'd accepted this feeling. I was a guest and not part of this process for now. At first I worried that something was wrong with me, that I couldn't connect to the world around me. The last three years had erased that fear. Now my understanding of the world had grown. It was nothing more than I hadn't found my place yet. It was out there somewhere. Part of me knew it was north. Well, technically northeast, I'd felt it as soon as Jacob said Montana, but that might not be the case. I'd know it when I found it though.

For some reason, this morning a longing to be there found me in the silence. Maybe it was the close call yesterday or last week. Maybe it was this feeling that something was that missing. Watching the dazzling light of dawn slowly creep over the roof and dance on the water helped push those feelings away. I'd had a place on the Bar C, not mine but the men around me filled in the gaps. Now I'd traveled across three states and that feeling was gone. I was truly the nomad my badge proclaimed me.

It didn't bother me like it might have. There was no melancholy, no sadness that came from the understanding. This was who and what I was. That truth settled on my shoulders like a mantle. It fit perfectly for now and thinking about it in the future served no purpose. There was no denying its comfort right here, right now. The light fully cleared the Star, cascading across the buildings, still leaving me in shadow. That image suited my thoughts. I'd move in shadows doing what I could to help until she called me to my home.

This wasn't some crazy religious zeal, the land didn't require worship. What's more, she had no use for it. There was no part of her that cared one way or the other about me. I was a piece of something bigger and no piece was irreplaceable. If one died, it was easily replaced by another. Everything I wanted was there for me, but nothing would be given. I'd have to earn every inch, pay for it like everyone else. Blood, sweat and tears were the only currency she accepted.

That was exactly the way I wanted it, nothing given but the ability to earn everything. People never valued what they were given, only what they earned. I'd seen it when I was young in the pampered children who broke or threw away precious things because they held no real value to them. Meanwhile, the street urchins who scrabbled and bleed for every scrape cherished all they had. Cared for it and worked to maintain it.

My mind flashed back over two scenes. I was sitting in a park watching some kids play under their nanny's watchful gaze. A young boy had a puppy on a leash, playing on the green grassy patch he'd claimed. He was yelling at it, trying to make it play fetch. Even at my young age, I knew the dog was too young to understand. It was only a few months old and had no bond with the boy yet. In frustration, the boy had dropped the leash and started beating the dog with a stick.

It cringed back at first, then jumped forward and nipped the kid's hand. He cried out in a pain, the puppy wisely picked that moment to run. In the blink of an eye, it disappeared into the bushes around the play area. The nanny, uncaring about the dog, scooped the boy up. After carefully checking the boy over, she set him down, assuring him everything was fine. The puppy was completely forgotten by both. The boy walked over to play with the other kids in a sandbox and never looked back.

The next memory was a friend who'd wound up in jail. Karl was a bit older than me. His parents had immigrated from Germany and they lived in the slums like most of the others. Karl adopted a cat, no matter what the cat thought about it. He'd pick it up and no matter how badly it scratched or bit him, he wouldn't let it go. Did everything he could to take care of the evil beast. Even giving it his own food, despite the fact that he went hungry.

Karl lost part of a finger, saving the thing from one of the dogs that roamed the neighborhood. He'd jumped in between the two and the dog bit it off. Waving the bloody stump and howling like a madman, he'd chased the dog off. When he came back to soothe the pissed off feline, the cat finally accepted him. They were inseparable after that. The damn thing even attacked when older boys went after Karl. The cops only got him to confess about a robbery by promising to let him take the beast with him to jail.

He paid a heavy price for that friendship and valued it because of that price. Even then, I recognized that truth. The kid in the park? His family probably just bought him another puppy. He'd never worried about the puppy that ran off, probably didn't remember it after that moment. He didn't care because it hadn't cost him anything. Karl had to earn that cat in every sense of the word. That was why it meant so much to him.

Realizing I was puffing on an empty pipe got me moving. Sitting here skylarking wasn't going to get things done. The city was fully awake now. Noises from the street below echoed off the buildings when I unfolded from the chair. Anya jumped up when I moved and looked at me expectantly. Maybe I wasn't as alone as I thought. Maybe I understood Karl a bit better now. Smiling at the wagging tail, I reached down to scratch her. This, of course, made the tail pick up speed and her entire back half waved back and forth.

"Come on, let's get some breakfast." I laughed at the smiling dog.

We walked out of the hotel to a cafe I'd noticed with a few tables outside. The small porch that hung off the side of the building looked empty enough. The sign out front read Becky's Bakery.

# CHAPTER 32

"Morning." A friendly young girl, maybe fifteen or so greeted me.

"Mind if me and the dog sit outside?" This got a high-pitched squeal in response and Anya tried to back out the door. Sadly, there was no escaping the enthusiastic girl coming for her.

"She's so cute. What's her name? What is she? Do you know the breed...?" The constant string of questions overwhelmed me as much as her attention did Anya. She was kneeling in front of the accosted hound, scratching behind her ears.

"Mary Elizabeth!" The sharp voice came from the back and the girl froze in place mid-question. "Let the poor dog and the gentleman sit down and breath."

"Yes, momma." She never took her eyes off the dog, but spoke to me. "Yes, you and she are welcome to sit outside. Please follow me."

"Her names Anya." I smiled, finally answering one of her questions before following her out the door to the porch.

"She's so cute! What can I get you? Coffee, I know, but I mean to eat."

"Is there a breakfast, eggs and such?" There wasn't a menu I could see.

"Oh! Sorry. Two eggs, ham steak, fried potatoes and biscuits is the special." She looked up absently, thinking for a minute before adding. "It's the special every day, I'm not sure why. Maybe that's all momma has. Either way, it's two bits."

"I'll take two, one for me, one for her." I motioned toward Anya. "Just set both on the table. Don't think she needs the potatoes."

"I'll just have momma put the rest in a bowl for her. What about the biscuits?"

"Give her one. She likes them but probably doesn't need many." I looked down at the dog trying to hide under my chair and laughed.

"Did I scare her?" The girl hadn't looked away from the dog while we talked.

"Might have been just a bit much for her. Just take it a bit slower. She likes the attention but maybe ease back on the ferocity."

"Momma says I'm too excited sometimes." She said with a shrug. "I'll go get your food and be right back with the coffee an some water for her."

Smiling to myself, I watched the girl flounce back into the small bakery. Maybe I'd overestimated her age. She was tall but maybe closer to thirteen than fifteen. She'd made me smile and something told me I'd be eating here just because of that. If the food was good, that'd be a nice bonus. It was nearby, had a porch and friendly people who didn't mind Anya.

She brought a small pot of coffee back while balancing a bowl full of water in her other hand. I had to admire the dexterity. Not a single drop of coffee or water hit the ground. This wasn't the first time she'd done this trick, but it still impressed me.

"Food will be a minute, I'll bring it out, an momma said no problem about the bowl." She scratched Anya once while the dog lapped up the water before walking back inside. I laughed, the girl had still not looked at me once. She only had eyes for Anya.

"Think you've got a fan." I laughed, scratching the top of her head before pouring myself a cup of coffee.

"She loves anything with fur." The light voice surprised me. It came through a window at the back of the store. I blushed at being caught talking to my dog.

"Isn't that fairly normal, ma'am?" I asked, trying to hide my red face behind a coffee cup.

"Might be. Been so long since I was that young, think I forgot the rules." Her laughter tinkled out like wind chimes in a summer breeze. "Don't think you're as far from that age as me."

"Feels longer than the years." I admitted, thinking about how distant my childhood felt.

The head that peered out from the window was in her late thirties. A warm round face with a smile that held all the reassurance of mothers across the country. She studied me wordlessly for just enough time to make the silence uncomfortable.

"Can see that on you. You've not had a bad life, but look like someone whose made the hard choices." She said astutely. "Course ya need a haircut and a shave, so it's hard to say for certain."

"I'll work on the shave, ma'am, but the hair stays." I smiled at her.

"Suits you, I admit. Food'll be out in a minute. Names Becky, welcome to my cafe." She ducked back in the window and I heard dishes clattering as the woman worked.

Another home away from home, that feeling a place like this lent folks was priceless. It was a pleasant surprise to find one here in this big city. The door opened and again the young girl bounced toward us. This time, she held a bowl full of food and a plate that matched.

"Here ya go." She spoke to Anya, feeding her first, of course. She looked confused when the dog refused to start eating. Anya looked at me and didn't move until I gave her a slight nod, then she dove into her breakfast. Only then was my plate but down. "Be back with the biscuits."

I nodded, pulling the plate toward me. Reaching for the salt and pepper to season my eggs, I paused. There was a small bowl on the plate full of a red liquid, one I recognized. It was a chile-based hot sauce I'd grown to love in Texas. Ignoring the salt and pepper in favor of liberally pouring the hot sauce over my eggs and potatoes. I'd be back here for breakfast every morning just because of this sauce. There was no question about it.

While I ate, that question rang out in my head. How long was I staying? I had two weeks at the Star and needed my shoulder to heal. Two weeks wouldn't have it fully healed, but it would be close. Staying that long should be easy. Especially since I wasn't running on a time table of any kind. Two weeks, then I'd head north to Los Angels. It'd give me enough time to get some much delayed letters off to my mom and maybe recieve one.

The food was done and things needed to be sorted out back in the room. I still had to go through Luke's things, figure out the money belt, pick up the drafts from Gerard, then finally make a deposit. Maybe some shopping after that. Some new shirts that weren't blood stained to start, maybe I should move that up the list. Considering the shirt I was wearing was the only one with no bloodstains.

I passed the girl on my way out and handed her a dollar fifty, enough to cover both meals and her tip. She never bothered looking at it. Her smiling eyes were still locked on Anya. When she knelt down and gave her a small piece of ham, I was certain they'd be friends for life. Thankfully, Anya fell in beside me without having to be called.

We walked back to the hotel. The clerk pretended not to notice when we passed him. He was the same one who'd tried to deny me yesterday. Up in the room, I laid his pistols on the table along with mine. I'd be cleaning them all later, honestly I felt guilty for not doing it last night, but my body needed sleep. Sorting through his clothes didn't yield much. Luke was shorter and liked flashier clothes than me. I still emptied his trunk, making sure to search it throughly.

When I hit the bottom, one knock told me there was a false bottom. It took me a little while to find the latch but then it only took a quick twist. It popped open easily. It wasn't full of diamonds and gold, just a custom padded compartment designed to hold his guns. The shoulder holster was decent, but there wasn't anything that I cared about in it. Packing the clothes back into it took a few minutes, then I pushed it into the corner. After adding the clothes from the armoire and dresser, it was packed tightly.

The money belt wasn't a grand treasure trove. Another three hundred and sixty dollars to deposit wasn't unwelcome, I was surprised it was so little though. That just left cleaning the guns. I did admire the craftsmanship in his and smiled when I spotted the intricately carved H on each butt. He must have had these done by Henk before coming to Fort Worth. I knew he didn't have them teh first year we met.

They were too flashy for me, blued so heavily they looked almost black, contrasting with the pearl grips. Still, I'd keep them for a while. Maybe if I changed the grips to wood they wouldn't bother me as much. I'd debated the new model Remingtons several times. They had some advantages over my Colts. Primarily, they were easier to load, but they weighed a bit more. That wasn't something I could just ignore, it would slow my draw. After oiling them heavily, I rolled them in their holsters then wrapped them in a piece of tarpaulin before setting them beside my panniers. This pair was chambered in the 44-40 I preferred so given a chance, I'd prcatice with them then decide.

The familiar act of cleaning my guns kept my hands busy while I planned out the day. I'd write a letter to Jacob and Mother after this. Mostly to let him know to keep investing the money in my account. Mom, I'd tell her edited versions of my adventures, trying to skip over the danger when possible. She already knew I was going to Los Angeles. There was probably a letter waiting for me there. Possibly two, since I told her not to try and reach me back in New Mexico Territory. Western Union's telegraph was faster but expensive when priced per word. I still preferred writing letters through Wells Fargo. It was one stop shopping since they handled my banking.

After that I'd go to a general store, buy some new clothes a few things for the room. That was all I really needed for now. Maybe there would be a simple set of bowls for Anya. With Wisp I could carry them, if we ever set out with just my saddlebags she might have to rough it. I'd have to restock on supplies. Most of mine had been left with the Cahuilla. Some I'd replaced from the outlaws but I only trusted them so far. That meant replacing my camp gear, I could only hope they had a decent selection.

Looking up after reloading and holstering my pistols, I smiled at Anya. She was on the balcony near the rail. It was the only place still not draped in shadows. Her body was stretched out in the warm sun, asleep. Her back feet twitched every once in a while in some puppy dream. She hadn't been with me long, but I hoped she'd stick around. One short whistle as I rose from the chair and she jumped up. It was time to be about the business of the day.

"Sorry girl, there'll be time for naps later." I apologized, walking out the door.

I actually managed to get everything done before lunch. If Jim and the others weren't back, I planned on exploring the city later this afternoon. That, of course, meant there was a message waiting for me. A different clerk flagged me down when I walked back into the lobby. "Mr. Stone, I have a message for you from Mr. Standom."

JC
*Met in the Pelicans Roost, when you're back. We are having lunch there.*
Jim

"Excuse me, where's the Pelicans Roost?" The man looked up from his work, smiling.

"Third floor sir, I believe it's directly across from your room."

"Thanks again." I nodded and walked up the stairs.

He had been right. I just never noticed the names. My suite was called Harbors Rest, directly across the hall was the Pelicans Roost. I could hear the men inside talking loudly. It was some discussion about trying another hunting trip. That just made me shake my head, there was no way I'd get roped into that mess. Anya whined and scratched at our door, making me pause before knocking.

"Prefer to avoid them?" I laughed, unlocking my door. After I opened the balcony door, I took a few minutes to refill the basin with water for her and left some jerky beside it. "Be good. I'll be back later. Maybe we'll go see the city before dark."

She wagged her tail with a chunk of jerky hanging out of her mouth. There was an odd yip that came out around it and she turned for the balcony. I closed the door behind me and stepped across to knock on the other door. The voices quieted, then Jim's voice carried through the door.

"Yes?"

"It's me Jim." The door opened before I finished speaking. Jim was smiling and I could see an arrayed around a table full of food. The other three sat around it looking at the door.

"Come in! Good to see you JC." Jim stepped back, letting me walk in.

"Gentlemen." I nodded to the table. "Glad everyone made it back."

"Easy ride back. Please join us. Oh, and before I forget." He reached into his wallet and took out a five hundred in gold certificates for the horses. "As agreed, five hundred dollars."

"Thanks." I said, tucking them into my wallet, forgot about those. I'd be stopping by the bank again tomorrow. After taking the vacant seat at the table, I grabbed a plate. Jim got credit for making sure my chair didn't face the door or balcony. "Any trouble on the way back?"

"None." Adams said. "What about Nash?"

"Locked up and already signed a confession. Deputy Gerard is holding him at the marshal's office. They'll probably transfer him to the city jail today or tomorrow. His crimes were committed in the state, so they'll be the ones charging him. Since he confessed, there won't be a trial to worry about."

"That's the biggest relief of it all. The last thing any of us wants is a public trial." Gus poured some coffee for me as he spoke. "It doesn't seem to matter what it is but a trial always comes with a financial loss."

"After '73, the last thing my bosses want is another scandal." Adams looked more relieved than the others.

It made sense when I thought about it. JB was a rancher, it wouldn't affect him at all. Gus owned his company and folks wouldn't stop buying beef, no matter what. Adams, though, he worked for the railroad. After the market crash in 1873, they were all still walking on pins and needles.

I knew from Jacob's last letter that the same crash just made him buy more stock cheaply. He'd switched our stock to the Union Pacific almost as soon as we had it. I didn't know why, but in '74 he'd split it between the Union Pacific and the Central Pacific. It never hurt to play both sides and as far as I knew, it was paying off.

All this was going through my mind while I stabbed a slice of roast from the plate. A small smile split my face, wondering what they would all think if they had any idea what my net worth was. In truth, I didn't really know myself. The vast majority of my money went into my account and Jacob invested it. We had some in the railroads, but more was spread through real estate and several other businesses. I was pretty sure some of it was in Swift's company. Jacob had mentioned signing our vote over to Gus.

They were all talking about the excitement and planning another hunt. This time, they'd do it on JB's range and his hands would help keep them safe. None of that was my problem. I'd done this to help Jim out, nothing more. My part was done except for the story telling.

"So it was all about money?" Jim asked.

"And a horse. I seem to attract horse trouble." I laughed think about Danu and the trouble that had come with her.

"A horse?" JB asked. The rancher in him was curious.

"Luke Short tried to buy my horse three years ago. It stuck in his craw when I turned him down. He's the one who hired them to kill me."

"He did all that because of a grudge from three years ago?

What's the story with this horse?" JB was the only one at the table who knew horses, so of course this part caught his attention.

"He's a Nokota Blue Stallion, second best horse I've ever seen." I said, with no small amount of pride.

"That's a fine animal and hard to find." JB whistled then asked the obvious follow up. "Second best?"

"Danu, I heard that story." Jim stepped in.

He told the story for me but I had to correct the bounty part. Jim thought I had taken the money. When I explained the deal, each man's opinion of me went up a few notches. JB knew the Circle T reputation and was doubly impressed.

"You do have a history of problems with your horses, but seems like you know horse flesh." JB laughed after he'd heard it all. "Likely to become a good problem to have if it doesn't kill you."

"Probably going to be buying horses from you in a decade." Adams was studying me carefully now.

"Reach out when you're ready to sell cattle. I'll get you a fair price." Jim smiled. He'd made the same offer every time we met.

"Better than market." Gus added.

"I know, already promised you'd be my buyer." It was a long-standing agreement between us.

"If there's shipping involved and I'm still with the railroad, I'll help you out." Adams said seriously. "The horses from Louisana too."

"That I might really need when the time comes."

The conversation was pleasant and the four let the weight lift from their shoulders. These men weren't used to being under fire. Power and wealth normally came with a sense of security that had been shaken by these events. One of their own betraying them wasn't something they'd ever considered. In that we all shared in the confusion. I hadn't seen it coming either. Maybe everyone needed a reminder about that once in a while.

Finally, I made some excuse and got up. They'd be at the hotel overnight then Gus and Jim were headed back to Chicago. JB would be back at his ranch and Adam's back on the train the next day. The man evidently lived in a deluxe car of some sort. Most of his work was as a problem solver for the company so he traveled constantly. The talk of a hunting trip had changed to arranging it for the following spring. Game and the weather would be better, it also gave JB time to get the security plan ready. Before I left Gus stopped me.

"This is for you." He gave me a business card with his signature on the back. "Jim mentioned you're headed to Los Angeles when you leave. This card will let you use my home there. It's fully staffed and secured by armed guards. I also have one in Denver and another in New York. Telegram me anytime and if they're not in use, you're welcome to them. The one in Los Angeles will be vacant until May, so stay as long as you like."

"Thanks Gus, I appreciate it." I shook the man's hand after putting the card in my wallet. "Think I'll take you up on it as long as you don't mind Anya being with me."

"The dog?" His face split into a grin before he responded. "This is my first trip without my hounds. They are always welcome in my homes. Besides, Jim told me you wouldn't take money but thought you'd welcome friendship."

"He wasn't wrong. I look forward to meeting you and your hands sometime." That told me a lot about the man. Anyone who didn't like animals always made me leery.

# CHAPTER 33

I spent the next two weeks healing my shoulder and exploring the city. Breakfast was always at the same small cafe. It was never busy, but there were always people there. The food was good, but I liked it for the feeling of home it gave me every day. It took the edge off of being stuck in the city, not that I stayed in the town constantly. Every other day I was on either Shade or Wisp exploring the land around the area. It was a beautiful part of the country, diverse and full of life. On one ride, I ran into a group of men studying a particular group of trees. It turned out they were part of the San Diego Society of Natural History. It was a new organization founded in 1874, dedicated to studying and preserving what they could.

Over coffee I made at a small fire, one of them showed me some drawings. On one page were some of the paintings I recognized. After retrieving my notebook, we compared notes. He copied a few of mine and I copied some of his. That night I made it back well after dark, but I had an invitation to attend one of their meetings the following evening. There was still a bit of the scholar buried inside me. It was in full force the next evening and I truly enjoyed myself. These men reflected the part of me that studied those paintings. We shared a curiosity that drove each of us in our own way to discover and understand the world around us. When I walked in with spurs and guns, they gave me some odd looks. After Charles Coleman introduced me, the raised eyebrows eased back down to their normal positions.

I'd brought my notebook which got a lot of interest.

Especially once they realized how many places I'd found and how much land had been covered. Some of them had traveled, but by train or boat. Riding overland like I had wasn't something most people did. There were several offers to buy it and some surprised looks when I turned them down. They all turned to smiles when I agreed to leave it with Charles so he could copy it at no cost.

They were thrilled when I agreed to send copies of future notebooks back as I filled them. This caused a new discussion about offering bounties to punchers for information. Like many before them, the elite that had the luxury to spend evenings in conversations like this they hadn't ever considered the interest many punchers had in the world around them. When I laughed and started telling them about the reading habits of the men, I knew it drastically changed their perspective.

The evening was a reminder of gentler times in my life. Chatting about things that might or had been here before us. There was no danger here, just men who shared an interest in something and happily educated one another on it. They were entertained by my stories of adventure but truly showed interest in my observations of the changing land. They wanted to preserve some parts, knowing that the growing population would alter the natural world. Many of them feared the loss of undiscovered animals and plants. They also had very strong opinions on how the buffalo were being hunted.

Late that night, I was sitting on my balcony thinking about the difference between the two worlds. There was so much shared between the two groups, but they'd never know it. Punchers and the other men who worked with the land considered it precious and hated the changes they saw. Fences were coming, men traveling west brought stories of ranges being blocked by a new type of wire. One meant to stop cattle from crossing it. Most laughed it off, the idea of the range being fenced off in to sections didn't seem possible. Others, like myself, knew it was coming. Resources were limited and men were greedy. Already the drives were changing, some because of the convenience of the railroads. Still others because ranchers whose land they once crossed now collected tolls or used the threat of violence to stop the herds from crossing.

It was hard to believe, but the writing was on the wall, land wasn't infinite. Soon more families move to the pockets of civilization, transforming towns to cities. Farmers would need more land to support them, as would ranchers. Range wars were starting already, homesteaders were declared squatters by some unseen court. Then armed men brought violence to them, forcing them to move on. All so some man who never set foot on the place could make money from it. The promised land given to the tribes was shrinking. Gold, silver, coal were all things you needed to build a country. Every one of them existed in the land and when we found them, the race began. Men would flood to an area chasing one precious metal or another. Some stayed when the mine played out and towns grew from them.

Gold and silver boom towns rose and fell with the depth of the strike. Mountains were stripped bare to harvest the coal. That dark gold heated homes, built communities and fueled the ever-expanding railroads. They, more than anything, fed the advance of civilization across the country. Those great iron horses spewing their smoke across the plains. Always with people on them hoping to find their future in the amazing land they could see rolling past them.

As much as I respected the growth of this country, I mourned the loss that would come with it. The great herds of buffalo on the open plains flashed through my mind. I tried to picture what it would look like without those oceans of brown. It seemed impossible that they might become insignificant in numbers. One herd had passed by that was so large i couldn't see anything but an ocean of fur and horns. I'd seen the piles of bones left behind when the pickers brought them in by the wagon full. Skulls stacked taller than a two story building proudly declared how many we had killed. The amount of slaughter committed every day by hiders put the lie to that impossibility. No population could survive that level of death.

Still, the idea that we could kill so many just seemed beyond reason. I remembered looking down on them. That sea of brown washing across the plains, their bodies moving like waves. There was no way we'd kill all of them, not when one herd numbered in the tens of thousands. Then I remembered that you couldn't find one back east anymore. Something that had once been a stable part of the tribe's diet was gone from the area. I shook off the disturbing ideas and tapped my pipe out in the ash tray. Swallowing the last bit of lukewarm warm coffee, I stood. A need to move pushed me to walk for another hour, just trying to shake off the idea of that much death.

The next day, I went by the docs to have my stitches taken out. He was surprised at how fast the wound had healed, pointing out how lucky I'd been. Using his finger, he traced up a half inch closer to my neck.

"If it had managed to rupture the vein here, you'd a been dead before you hit the ground." The thought sent a chill down my spine. Once again chance had saved my life.

"Wasn't my choice, Doc."

"Very rarely is, young man. Sad truth of it is, most of the bullet wounds I see don't come from the front." He looked up, thinking for a moment before adding. "It's better now than when it was a boom town shipping gold. Local law does what it can. There is still some death but mostly in certain areas of town. Stay out of those an it decreases your odds of dying from lead poisoning."

"Been here that long?" I studied the man. He didn't look that old. The boom around here had been before the war.

"Not as a doc, ain't that old. Back then, I was just a scamp running around like the rest. Stealing, robbing, doing whatever I needed to survive. Local saw bones is who taught me doctoring, went to school later. Still don't know why he did." The man scratched his beard, thinking back over the years. "I was just another orphan, but the man took an interest and I owe him for it. God rest his drunk'n soul."

"Must have been crazy round here back then." He had my curiosity going, and I wanted to hear how this place had changed.

"You ever been to a real boom town? It's like a multi-headed monster fighting over which head gets to eat its own tail. That metal does something to folks."

"Ain't had the pleasure."

"No pleasure in it. If ya get near one, turn around and run." He said it with such surety I believed him. "Even the towns near it. Just leave the territory, mark my words. It ain't a precious metal, pure poison meant to drive men mad."

"Got no interest in it." I assured him. "What do I owe you?"

"Two dollars didn't have to do much."

For the next five days, I managed my full routine in the mornings, doing my best not to push my wound too far. At first it was stiff and I had to work it slowly, but by the end of the week my range of motion had returned. It still felt tight and wasn't fully healed, but it was close enough. I had two days left on my free stay. After breakfast, I stopped to check for mail and got two letters from New York. Jacob was glad I kept putting money in the account and told me the investments were doing well. He talked about his wife and daughters, told me to be careful and wished me well.

Mother's letter was longer, but said much the same. She was doing well, retired into a small house Jacob had bought for her. He also kept a lady on staff for her and made sure she wanted for nothing. Having rediscovered her love for reading, she spent most of her time with the books she so loved. She was also helping out with a couple of organizations that were trying to aid the poor. Teaching some of the young how to read and do their figures. She ended with love and told me to be safe as usual.

The last day I arranged for supplies at the general store food, ammunition and the like. I bought a replacement grill, two bowls for Anya, and a new dutch oven. Thankfully, they also had a skillet and decent coffee pot so I didn't have to use the ones i found. It would all be ready at first light the following day. That night I cleaned my guns, including the Sharps and Greener. Finally getting my saddle bags packed and ready to go.

When I found Luke's ring tucked into the pocket of my vest, I paused. It wasn't my style, but at the same time I wanted to keep it as a reminder. Tucking it into my wallet for now, it would stay there until I figured out what to do with it. I could be sold later or the reason for keeping it would show up. Maybe I wasn't ready to get rid of it because it reminded me about trusting people too quickly. That night, sitting on my balcony, I watched the sunset again. Anya's tail thumping as I scratched her head absently had become a familiar sound. The shadows seemed to grow before my eyes, slowly eating the city as night fell. Small lights flickered in the darkness while the last rays of the sun danced on the water in a cascade of color.

Somewhere far off, I could hear the tinny piano of a saloon mixing with the hum of the city. Another night, draping the city in shadows, welcoming the predators to the streets. Men would die, some would wake up on ships after being shanghaied, still others would be counting their coins. The cycle continued as the night darkened. It had been nice to relax for a few weeks, but I was ready to be out in open country again. Maybe finally find my way to Los Angeles without anymore delays. After that I still wasn't sure. Winter was coming and continuing north might need to wait for a few months. Maybe head for San Francisco and spend the winter there. In the spring, I'd head to Washington Territory, just to see what all the talk was about.

All of that was dependent on one thing. If the marshals didn't reach out to me for some job that needed doing. A part of me was depending on that in a weird way. I could go and get a job working cattle, but right now I was happy drifting and their jobs could gave me a direction. Two years of freedom, then I'd be back to working cattle. Maybe a couple of years in Colorado, then the same in Montana. It would round out my education and give me contacts in the area.

That was my plan anyway. I had quickly learned that it was best to keep those pretty flexible. It suited me perfectly for now. The only thing set in stone was finding work in Montana by 1880. Hopefully in the area of my land, it would give me contacts and experience in that terrain. One thing for certain was that every place had a different cycle to follow and the best way to learn it was by doing. Learn to read the land, weather, cattle and anything else that might warn you about trouble before it got to you.

None of that was important right now, not the ranch or the plans I was trying to make. Tomorrow morning, I was heading back into open country. My focus needed to be on that. Skylarking about the future wouldn't end well for me. Not traveling alone through wild country. It would take three days to make Los Angeles, if I didn't get waylaid or wander off in my own direction. That seemed to keep happening to me. Honestly, I had no complaints about it. If something caught my attention, there was nothing to stop me from exploring it. Wasn't that the point of drifting?

The first light of dawn was chasing shadows across the city when I left the livery. Anya trotted alongside side sniffing here and there as we moved. Once we left the city limits, she started ranging out further. Chasing the odd rabbit or other critter. At one point, it looked like she was herding some deer. Slowly the land changed, cultivated ground gradually mixing with wild country. Access roads started spreading out, slowly growing fewer and fewer. Long before I stopped for breakfast, there were easily a few miles between them.

There were still a few ranches around, but this was a good spot to stop that didn't cross any markers I could see. It was near a small stream with a bit of graze nearby. After loosening the cinches, I started a small fire to make some coffee. With a grin, I added a little chicory to the grounds, a luxury I'd picked up before leaving town. The biscuits and bacon were wrapped in paper. Thankfully, they'd survived the saddlebags well enough. More than once there'd been little more crumbs when I unwrapped the paper.

Anya came in from the brush and sat expectantly across from me. I laughed at her greedy smile before tossing a small piece of bacon to her. The blood drying on her muzzle said she'd already had her breakfast. That didn't seem to matter when it came to my bacon. She still wanted her portion. Snapping the piece I tossed out of the air she watched me with hopeful eyes. Any piece that escaped my grasp would be snapped up long before it hit the ground.

Shade and Wisp grazed happily where I'd left them. Nether of them interested the contest of wills between me and the dog. This was me at peace, away from the noise of a city surrounded by my animals. Crouched beside a fire sipping the bitter brew of life, everything about me was tuned into my surroundings. The heat of the day was still a few hours away and this time of year, the crisp air carried a chill. Smiling, I looked around. This was why I left New York.

This was, of course, when the rumbling noise of a wagon broke my reverie. It was coming from San Diego, probably heading to a ranch or maybe even Los Angels. Either way, it was no business of mine, so long as they passed me by, there was no reason to pay attention. I stayed back in the small grove, out of sight, but did flip the thong off my colt and check my Winchester. It wasn't that I expected trouble, but it was always better to be prepared. Five minutes later, it moved past me leaving a trail of dust hanging in the air. They hadn't been moving fast, but in the dry climate the dust could left in its wake was impressive.

Not long after, I was putting out the fire and tightening the cinches on both animals. This time, evidently satisfied with her breakfast, Anya jumped on to Wisp's back. Situated on her perch, she looked at me expectantly. Smiling, I stepped into the saddle and we set off back down the road heading north. The rest of the day was pleasant and dry. The wind was a bit much, but I'd been warned about that.

More than once, an old timer had told me it would get bad enough some days to blow over beefs. I wasn't sure about that particular story, but the way it felt they might have been telling the truth. He'd called them the Devil Winds, hot, dry and gusting strong enough to stagger a man on horseback. To me, after driving herds across Texas in July, it wasn't too bad. For most people, they'd be uncomfortable for sure. Anya crouched tight on Wisps back and the rest of us trudged on, ignoring the wind as best we could.

# CHAPTER 34

The second day well before sunset, I found a nice cold spring against the wall of a canyon. It broke the wind and was obviously a regularly used as a camp. There was even a ring of stones already there with scorched earth inside them. I decided not to hope for better and made camp early. There was enough scrub around that I might take some fresh meat for dinner. After stripping off Wisp and Shades tack, I left them on some good graze after stringing my bow. Switching to moccasins, I slipped into the brush. Anya seemed to know what I was doing and stayed to guard the camp.

Slipping from cover to cover, my eyes were constantly scanning the area for sign. There was a rabbit and a few others, but nothing big enough to make it worth hunting. Finally, a few tracks cut into the sand in a soft spot. They looked like deer sign. Slowly, I followed them and eventually found a small herd of black-tailed deer that looked relaxed enough. Creeping closer, I notched an arrow and got ready to line up a shot. Just as I drew back to release, something caught my attention to my left. It was too late to change my mind if I wanted to take a deer. The arrow flew true and punched into the buck just behind the front shoulder. It took a quick leap and fell spasming to the ground.

Another deer fell on the other side of the small herd almost at the same time. The rest broke and disappeared into the brush. Three young braves stood up, eyeing me with suspicion. Two had arrows notched and ready to draw. The third must have been the one who shot the deer. I let my bow hang to my side and used my other hand to sign peace. The older of the three signed it back before he spoke in a dialect I didn't recognize. When it became obvious that I didn't understand, he smiled and spoke in English.

"Nice shot, white man." His voice was filled with humor.

"Same could be said of you." I grinned back.

"Why are you hunting on Tongva land?" The smile was still there, but a hint of anger was concealed under it.

"I didn't know I was, but meant no disrespect. If you need the meat, take my kill." That surprised him, but he recovered quickly.

"That bow, it is Shoshone. Where did you get it?"

"Traded for it."

"We don't need your meat, just what we have." It wasn't just his pride, I could tell that much from his tone.

"Then we should take care of our kills." I reached for the piece of rope hanging from my belt.

"Agreed." The two beside him dropped their bows and they walked toward their buck.

After dragging mine over to a tree, I gutted mine and started working on the skin. This time I did remember to take off my shirt so it didn't get covered in blood and viscera. Harvesting the buck didn't take long, signing peace to the other party I left the area. The small make shift smoker I'd built would be big enough for this but it meant I'd be camping here at least a day.

None of the Tongva came to visit, but I knew they were watching me. I'd spotted them a few times but never let them know. Once the meat was all smoked, I packed most of it in a pannier and some in my saddlebags. It was more than I would need, but it should be safe to eat for a while. That night I cooked the last steak I hadn't smoked. Anya shared it with me, and the next morning we were back on the road before the sun fully rose.

Los Angels grew larger throughout the next day as I got closer. Lush land changed to farms and lowing cattle. Dairy farms mixed with the rest here, showing the stability of the area. I smiled, watching an older man drive them toward a barn for milking. The traffic increased the closer I got to the city, more carts and wagons than single riders. Most of those were vaqueros decked out in their finery, silver glinting in the sun. A few expensive carriages started to appear the closer I got. So finely designed that the lacquer was almost blinding when the sun reflected off them. Just watching the travelers, you could see the wealth this city held.

Some greeted me, while others ignored my presence. A few of the vaqueros just nodded in acknowledgement. Just as I was entering the outskirts of the city, I noticed a puncher drifting down the road. A quick tip of my hat caught his attention, letting me drift over to him. We studied each other for a second before I broke the silence.

"JC, just drifting, but I was working in Texas the last few years."

"Web, been on the drift a few months. Headed to Colorado when the weather breaks, got a small spread out there. This year I can finally get it up and going."

"Decent hotel around?"

"End or beginning?" He asked, but I knew what he meant. Did I want to spend end of the drive money or beginning money? Basically, it was a polite war of asking how much money I wanted to spend.

"Bout the middle, more toward the end." I smiled, recognizing the short speech many punchers shared.

"I'd say either the Royal or the Bunkhouse. Don't let the name fool you. That last one is my preferred place, good beds and chow. The names just a moniker the owner hung on it. He was a puncher until a bronc busted his leg. Took his money an opened the place with cookie he knew."

"Sounds like the place for me." It did sound about perfect, especially if the cook was good.

"Three streets down and hang a left. It's about 6 blocks from there. They got a good stable out back, so ya won't need a livery."

"Buy you a drink in thanks?" I asked, knowing it was likely to be turned down.

"Leaving town before it's too late." He grinned. "Got a pard with a place a few days down the trail, going to winter with him and then go start my place."

"Best of luck." We shook hands and parted company without another word.

I found the Bunkhouse exactly where he said and found it to be exactly as described. The man working the desk was older, but you could still see the hardness of trail life on him. I noticed his hands when he spun the book for me to sign, gnarled with scars across the knuckles. He'd worked hard and been in some brawls.

"Where out of?" He asked causally.

"Drifted this way from Texas, was working the Bar C for a few years."

"Know the brand, good men. Worked for King on a few of his drives so we likely tramped some of the same ground. Names Robert, but folks just call my Bucket. No, I aint tell'n that story standing here. It'll cost ya a drink just to get me started." His grin was infectious. I recognized the type easily, he reminded me of Chet.

"Might have to pay that toll if the opportunity comes along. Names JC, pleasure to meet you and find a place like this."

"Aint the first one ta say that. Boss does his best to make it feel right. Just keep the gun play outside." His voice got serious with the last. "Cookie puts out a good spread but ain't got no patience for foolishness an if I recollect, you'll understand how he is. Smythe still running the chuck?"

"He is and his sun shining personality ain't changed." We shared a laugh at that. Both of us obviously knew the man.

"Rusty's bout the same. Got this damn spoon he'll knock ya out with."

"Noted. Be sure to mind my manners 'round him."

"Rooms on the second floor. Just turn left at the top. Got

a shared balcony, but the other room is empty right now. Livery's out back but aint no one tending your animals. We pay a kid to muck them out but the rest is on you. Everything ya need is there." This wasn't a surprise. Most punchers trusted livery men but always checked on their animals. "Tack's safe, same as the rest, but wouldn't be surprised if a bit of chow drifted off. Call it a fee for the kid mucking the stalls, it won't be much an never anything but food. Kid feeds his whole family most of the time."

"Seems fair enough. Might just give him some smoked venison I took on the trail."

"Do that an he won't touch anything for a while. Kids a bit a sneak, but we're working on him. Rusty keeps draggin' him into the kitchen. Swears the boy'll be a cook when he's done with him."

"Aint doing me any good." I said, taking the preferred keys and turning to see to my animals. Then I thought of a question. "What's the kid's name?"

"Just call him Buster. He'll answer to it."

I tipped my hat and stepped into the light of day. Taking Shade's reins, I lead them around back to the livery. Anya jumped down and started sniffing around. She disappeared into the shadows chasing rats, probably. I started stripping off the tack and looking around for the kid. He showed up after I'd put my saddle up, but was just reaching for the panniers.

"Last two stalls are clean, mister."

"Buster I'm guessing?" The kid had flaming red hair, looked to be about ten years old. I recognized the look in his eyes. It had been common in the kids I knew as a child. Hunger and determination filled his gaze. The piercing blue eyes wouldn't miss a trick. The streets had taught him some hard lessons over the course of his short life.

"Yup." His voice wasn't friendly. It was more neutral than anything else.

"Got some smoked venison in here, 'bout twenty pounds of it. You might as well take it cause I won't use it before it turns."

"Seriously?" That caught the kid off guard. I watched the suspicion fill his gaze. "What do you want for it?"

"Help me take care of these beasts. Maybe some hints about the city."

"That's it?" Trust wasn't high on his list of traits.

"Don't waste the meat. That's mostly why you're getting it. Can't stand to see it thrown out, disrespects the animal who died for it." It was an honest answer. I did hate to see meat go to waste. The questionable part was the meat going bad. I'd smoked it right and it would stay good for weeks.

"Fair trade." Buster said and reached to help me with the panniers. I took out the meat and set it aside for him, the rest I'd take to my room.

He not only helped me see to the animals, but then helped me get everything to my room. I was surprised when Wisp didn't mind him, but was thankful for it. Anya was more than happy to let him pet her. Maybe that was why Wisp hadn't minded him. Those two seemed to be partnering up in some way I couldn't understand. Shade acted like everything fit into his domain and was perfectly acceptable, even cowing a young stallion as he passed his stall. He was becoming the stallion I knew he would. Hopefully he'd still be as strong when I let him out to stud his own herd.

The room was decent, two rooms, like most of the cattlemen's hotels I'd stayed in. It didn't have private water closets, but there was a shared one at the end of the hall with baths out back. The main room had a small stove with enough wood, a desk, couch and chair with enough tables to be useful. The balcony had two chairs with enough room for my routine. The last room was a comfortable bed, dresser and end tables with a lamp. It was almost a copy of the cattlemen's rooms in Dodge.

Anya ignored me and flopped down on the balcony. I left her some water and grabbed some clean clothes before heading to find a bath. Out back I found more than just a bathhouse. It was a complete barber shop. After the normal argument

369

about my hair, I managed to get shaved after my bath. That conversation reaffirmed my belief that all barbers made a pledge of some sort about cutting long hair. I left all my dirty clothes with the laundry service. It was in the back of the barbers.

I heard it before anything else. A deep growl paired with a high pitch whine. Opening the door, my eyes found a thin rough looking man with his back to a wall. He was gripping a knife so tightly it might break in his right hand staring at Anya. She was crouched in front of him, blood dripping from her muzzle. The low growl coming from her was what kept the man trapped against the wall. I worried about the blood for a second until spotting the gash on the man's arm.

"Guessing you're not here to clean the room." My Colt was already in my hand.

"Call that mutt off or I'll kill it!" The terror in his voice told me even he didn't believe that lie.

"I could just watch the show. I'd put my money on her." He didn't like my response.

The man was quick. Pushing off the wall, he launched himself toward the balcony door. Sadly, he wasn't as fast as Anya. She grabbed his ankle tripping him, his body hit the floor with a loud bang. Struggling to breathe he tried to stab down at her, but I was fast enough to grab his wrist. I gave it a sharp twist, the bones under my hand ground together, then snapped. The knife fell to the floor and he screamed. Whether it was from the dog savaging his ankle or the broken wrist was anyones guess.

"That wasn't the smartest move." I stood over the man and snapped my fingers. Anya let go of his ankle but didn't stop growling.

My door was still open and I could hear boots coming toward us. Unsure of the situation, I stepped to the side and put my back to a wall. Bucket was the first one to step into the doorway. His eyes scanned the room in an instant and he accurately assessed what was going on. A grimace crossed his face when he spotted the man bleeding on the floor.

"Mitch, ya been warned 'bout thieving here." Bucket looked fit to kill as he spoke. A big man wearing an apron filled the space behind Bucket. Rusty, if I didn't miss my guess.

"I'll fetch the police. Let them deal with this skunk." Rusty had a deep voice, but looked at me while he spoke. I knew what he was asking. Was I worried about the police?

"Works for me, rather not hang him from the balcony." Rusty nodded, understanding my meaning.

"Buster, go find Potts. He should be on his patrol this time of day." Rusty spoke over his shoulder. The kid must have come up to see what all the noise was about.

"Yes sir." I heard him race off down the stairs.

"He aint going no where from the looks of it JC, reckon you can holster that shootin' iron." Bucket spoke to me, but his eyes never left the man cradling his wrist on the floor. "He's been caught trying to break into the stables once afore. Got off with a warning that time. Now he'll be the law's problem."

The Colt slid into my holster and I set his knife down on the table near me. With a sharp whistle, Anya immediately trotted to my side and laid down at my feet. For a few minutes, the only noise in the room was the groaning Mitch, and no one was interested in his pleading. Finally, after what seemed like an eternity, heavy footsteps echoed down the hall. Bucket stepped inside and to the left, making room for a big man wearing a uniform of some kind, stepped into the doorway.

"Rusty, what's the story here?"

"Mitch tried stealing from that fella an it didn't go well." The cook summed up everything in the most direct manner.

"That true mister?" Potts, I am guessing, turned his heavy gaze on me.

"Can't think of another reason he had to be in my room while I was out. Didn't know that Anya was here. Reckon that's the only reason he hadn't left yet. Ain't checked to see if he stole anything yet."

"Damn dog bit me for I got a chance to take anything." Mitch had finally collected himself enough to speak. "That bastard broke my wrist."

"Looking at him I'd say that was a lucky break for you, aint sure why he didn't just kill you and save me the trouble." Potts grumbled, look'n at the man with pitiless eyes.

"Bucket warned me about gunplay on the premises, said it offended the cook. Last thing any puncher wants is a cookie who ya pissed off." My explanation made more than one of them smile knowingly.

"True enough, Rusty don't like folks who put holes in the place." Potts chuckled as he spoke, then turned back to Mitch. "Get up, an if you have anything on you drop I now. If I find it at the jail, things will just go hard for you."

"Got a few things in my right pocket. Can't fetch them out with this busted wrist." He protested, but the outcome probably wasn't what he hoped for.

Potts stepped forward and took out a barlow. With a quick slash the top of the pocket was slashed open and a few trinkets fell out of his pocket. None of it was mine, and I shook my head when Potts turned to ask. He scooped up the items without another word and grabbed Mitch by the shoulder.

"Come on, if ya act right I won't put ya in cuffs an we'll stop by the docs. Give me any trouble an you can guess the alternative." He started leading the man out of the room. He glanced at me before leaving to ask a question. "Mind coming by in a while to write a report?"

"No problem long as I can find it, just got into town." I admitted with a grin.

"Bucket can tell ya where to find me. Makes the trial easier if we have a statement." With that, the man walked away leading his prisoner without another word.

"Ya want a different room?" Bucket asked, but I shook my head.

"There ain't much blood, not enough to worry about anyway. Wouldn't mind some rags, ain't got much more than bandages since I dropped things off to be cleaned."

"Preciate you not shooting, tired of patching holes." Rusty said and without another word turned and stomped back down stairs.

"He ain't much on words." Bucket laughed. "Let me get them rags for ya. Reckon ya can take an extra night for the trouble."

He was back shortly and in no time, I had the mess cleaned up. The door was closed, leaving me an Anya alone again with another blade. This one was a cheap piece of trash, honestly I didn't know what to do with it. If it cleaned up well enough, maybe it would be something Buster might find a use for. It wasn't the most welcome I'd felt in a new place, but reaffirmed my faith in Anya. If she was here, I didn't have to worry about anyone breaking in.

An hour so later I walked down stairs to eat dinner. It was as advertised. Both delicious and plentiful. The coffee was made the right way, with just enough chicory for flavor. This was the right place for me while I was here, unless I wanted to stay at Swift's house. That was something I'd explore tomorrow. It might be nice to stay at a fancy house with servants for a bit. Besides, it was free and despite the amenities on offer here, it still cost money. True, it wasn't something I couldn't afford, but that didn't mean I wanted to spend the money.

Right now, I felt like having a beer. Bucket recommended a saloon a few blocks away. It was called The Bucking Bull. He said it would feel about right to me. Punchers and vaqueros were most of its clientele. Wandering down that way gave me a chance to see some of the place. I passed a few shops that were still open, but nothing that caught my attention. Just as I walked across a side street, three men stepped out of the shadows across from another hotel. The sign out front read The Royal. It was the other one Web had recommended.

The three weren't paying me any attention, all of them were focused on the door across the street from them. Not being sure what was going on, my hand dropped down casually flipping the thong off my Colt. They already had their hands filled with iron. Whatever they were up to, it would involve gun play. I wasn't sure about getting involved until the door to the hotel opened. I couldn't exactly see who it was, but one of them was female. That was enough to make the choice for me.

"Look out!" My shout started the ball rolling.

The man swept her behind him and his right hand came up filled with a gun and spitting flame. One of the three dropped before getting off a shot, but the other two fired. My first shot dropped one of them, the other fired again at the man on the steps. I heard a scream, but it barely registered over the sound of my Colt firing again. The last man spun, falling to the ground. His last act sent another round sparking off the cobblestone.

I didn't leave the shadow immediately. First, my eyes scanned the street for any other attackers. While that happened, my hands worked to eject the spent cartridges and replace them. Then it snaked my badge out and pinned it on my vest. It would make dealing with the after math easier. I could already hear people coming, but first my eyes fell on the two near the door of the hotel. She was laying across the fallen body, sobbing and calling his name.

"Elias! Don't die, please don't die." The name didn't register until I stepped into the light around them. It was Elias, the same man who had worked that last drive. Then she looked up at me. It couldn't be. That made no sense at all, but there was no denying what my eyes saw.

"Jesse?" The shock in my voice must have jarred her, or being recognized did it. Her face turned up to look at me so fast I thought it might break her neck. My brain froze when our eyes met. She was stunning, the kind of beauty that stole your breath. It all made so much more sense now, the strange habits, even that feminine gasp.

"JC? Is that really you?"

# THE END.

Made in the USA
Monee, IL
24 May 2025